DANGEROUS BETRAYALS

SUSAN HUNTER

Copyright © 2025 by Susan Hunter.

All rights reserved.

No part of this book may be reproduced in any form or by any electronic or mechanical means, including information storage and retrieval systems, without written permission from the author, except for the use of brief quotations in a book review.

Severn River Publishing
www.SevernRiverBooks.com

This is a work of fiction. Names, characters, businesses, places, events and incidents are either the products of the author's imagination or used in a fictitious manner. Any resemblance to actual persons, living or dead, or actual events is purely coincidental.

ISBN: 978-1-64875-626-9 (Paperback)

ALSO BY SUSAN HUNTER

Leah Nash Mysteries

Dangerous Habits

Dangerous Mistakes

Dangerous Places

Dangerous Secrets

Dangerous Flaws

Dangerous Ground

Dangerous Pursuits

Dangerous Waters

Dangerous Deception

Dangerous Choices

Dangerous Games

Dangerous Betrayals

To find out more about Susan Hunter and her books, visit severnriverbooks.com

For Gary
Blessed is he who plants trees under whose shade he will never sit.

PROLOGUE

Galen, Wisconsin, Trenton County Circuit Court

Hannah Vining, wearing a simple black dress, sits tall and straight at the defendant's table in the small county courtroom. Her curly red hair is severely pulled into a bun at the nape of her neck. Her wide-set green eyes stare straight ahead. The only visible signs of her fear are her tightly clasped hands, and the right thumb that repeatedly rubs up and down on the left one. Hannah's expression is neutral. But her mind is racing as she waits for the jury to file in.

How can this be happening? It doesn't feel real—her, sitting in front of a judge's bench, waiting to hear if twelve strangers are going to find her guilty of murder. It's the stuff of a television movie. But this isn't fiction. This is horribly, irrevocably, unbelievably real.

If only Matthew had never walked into her shop. If only they hadn't run into each other a few weeks later, when her husband and his wife were out of town. If only she hadn't given in to her emotions. Such a stupid, stupid thing to do. But the feeling that had swept through her when Matthew had shown back up in her life had overridden everything else—for a time. She understands why the jury may decide that she is Matthew's killer. The evidence is damning. She didn't do it, but that doesn't seem to matter.

If she's found guilty, what will happen to Olivia? Her fourteen-year-old daughter is so vulnerable, so emotionally fragile. How will she cope? Her husband Joel is wrapped up in his own pain and anger at Hannah's betrayal. How will he provide the support that their daughter will need?

The jury is entering now. No one looks at her. She read somewhere that it's a bad sign when they don't. Hannah's heart is racing, and she tries to steady her breathing. She unclasps her hands and grips the edge of the table, hard. Her lawyer, sensing her rising anxiety, touches her arm in a gesture of support, but it offers no comfort to Hannah. The tension in the courtroom is oppressive, bearing down on everyone as the judge speaks.

"Madam foreperson, has the jury reached a unanimous verdict?"

"We have, your honor."

Hannah's breath catches in her throat as a cold sweat breaks out on her forehead. The room and everyone in it fades away. For a moment, the pounding of her own heart and the rustling of paper in the foreperson's hand are the only sounds she can hear.

Then the judge's voice breaks through her panic.

"The defendant will rise to hear the verdict."

As she stands, Hannah's knees buckle, and her attorney reaches out to steady her.

"Madam foreperson, please read the verdict," the judge says.

The woman clears her throat, then says, "In the case of the State of Wisconsin versus Hannah Vining, on the charge of first-degree intentional homicide, we the jury find the defendant . . . guilty."

The words hit Hannah like a physical blow. The air rushes out of her lungs. She sways for a second but regains her composure.

"Members of the jury, I ask each one of you individually, is this your verdict? If it is, say yes. If it is not, say no," the judge says, his voice solemn and his gaze steady.

As each successive juror responds yes, Hannah feels the room begin to spin. She collapses into her chair. Her lawyer is saying something to her as the judge thanks and dismisses the jury. He sets the sentencing date, but Hannah can't focus.

As she's led away, the weight of the guilt she feels for the betrayal of her husband, her daughter, of their family presses down on her. Now she's trapped herself in a prison built of the secrets she kept and the lies she told. She was the architect of her own unbearable future.

1

Eight months later, Himmel, Wisconsin

"I know who I'm going to kill, but it has to look accidental or natural. I'm wrestling with how to do it," I said.

"A fall down the stairs or off a ladder is reliable. Have you thought about an 'accident' with a gun?"

"I'm looking for something with a little more flair. I've got an idea, but I'm just not sure."

"Poison?"

"Maybe, but not exactly."

"Now you've got me hooked. How do you poison someone, but not exactly?"

Wait a sec. Maybe I should explain that this wasn't a conversation between two sociopaths, it's a discussion between two mystery writers, of which I am one. Although given the number of characters we've killed between us, maybe we *are* somewhere on the psychopathy scale.

My name is Leah Nash. I'm a journalist as well as an author. I also co-own a struggling weekly newspaper in the small town of Himmel, Wisconsin. At that moment, I was sitting in my apartment, bouncing ideas off the mystery writer Nora Fielding. She'd moved to the area recently and had become something of a mentor to me.

"I've been thinking about using *naegleria fowleri*," I said.

"Neg-a-whatsis? It sounds like a disease neglected chickens get," Nora said.

"It's nuh-GLEE-ree-uh FOW-luh-ree," I said, slowing down the complicated pronunciation. "More commonly known as the brain-eating amoeba. It's almost always fatal, it progresses very rapidly, and it's easily confused with meningitis because the symptoms are very similar."

"Ah, I see where you're going. You want your murderer to kill someone using this amoeba, but get away with it because it's assumed to be meningitis—until your detective comes along, right?"

"Basically, yes. But I need to do some in-depth research to see if it's plausible as a murder method. I'm also thinking of setting the murder in the past—in the 1980s—because vaccines against meningitis weren't widely used then. But the murder in the past will tie into a present-day murder case that my detective Jo Burke is investigating. What do you think?"

Nora was quiet for a minute as she tapped her index finger lightly on her upper lip.

Finally, she nodded and said, "I like it. I've never come across a mystery—and I've read thousands—that used a brain-eating amoeba as a murder weapon. And I like the idea that an undetected crime from the past will tie in with one that your detective is investigating in the present. I always enjoy a dual timeline story. But why are you working on your third novel when you haven't finished your second one yet?"

"I'm in the hurry up and wait phase. My editor at Clifford & Warren Publishing has my draft, so there's nothing really for me to do until I get her edits back. Usually I fritter away this particular downtime, because it's hard for me to start thinking about the next book when I'm still working on the current one. But then that means I'm in full panic mode when the current book is done, because I've dawdled my time away and don't have a plot ready to start the next one. Then it's a mad scramble to come up with something."

"I understand totally. I'm not a natural long-term planner either. I've found over the years, though, that life is easier when I have at least a rough idea of the next book while the current one is still in process."

"The hardest part about writing fiction for me is thinking up the plot. When I was a reporter and then later writing true crime books, I thought fiction writers had it pretty easy. That they could just make stuff up, no fact checking, no interviews, just all pretend."

"And now you know better?" Nora asked.

I nodded.

"Oh, yeah, I do. Fiction—mystery fiction anyway—is way harder. At least for me. When I write true crime, there are challenges, sure. You have to interview tons of people, verify what they say, get multiple points of view on the crime, dig up witnesses, police don't want to talk to you, on-the-record sources change their minds. But none of that is as hard as having to make everything up out of nothing. For mystery fiction, you have to create characters, motivations, and locations. Who gets killed? How and why? How will your detective find the solution? You have to provide clues for the reader, but they can't be too obvious, or they'll figure out the answer too soon. But the clues can't be so hidden that no one can see them, because that's not fair. Plus you still have to do tons of research and no matter how hard you, your editors, and your advance readers try, there's always something you get wrong or miss."

"Put that to music and you've got the mystery writer's lament," Nora said.

"I've accepted that I'll never be good at detailed outlining. But I'm trying to do better at getting all the research I need done ahead of time and making sure I have the key points I need to hit in each act identified. I think it will make writing less stressful."

She laughed and shook her head, making her gray curls dance.

"Leah, in my experience—and after 40 years in the business, I have a lot of it—nothing makes writing less stressful. The only author I ever met who claimed to never stress over writing was Robert Parker. In his prime he could turn out five or six books a year. I asked him once how he could be so insanely productive. He said he just sat down at his typewriter and the ideas came. And he saved time because he only wrote one draft and never went back to edit. He was a very nice man, but I could have punched him right then."

"Whoa! It would be absolutely amazing to just sit in front of my computer and have the words flow. The only thing that happens when I try is a stare down between me and a blank computer screen. I need to have some idea where I'm going before I start. But you do think this *naegleria fowleri* idea as a murder method is feasible?"

"More than that. It's a killer method—pun totally intended. The uniqueness will make it harder for the reader to guess what you're up to. But a word of caution," she said.

"What's that?"

"Be careful who you share your idea with. I had a long discussion once about the next mystery I planned to write with another author over drinks in a hotel bar. He was very encouraging, and I was very talkative, thanks to the martinis he plied me with. He kept telling me that he really loved the concept. I didn't realize how much until nine months later when I was ready to start writing my new mystery. That's when his book came out. With my plot."

"You're kidding! He stole your idea? Who was it?"

"He did indeed. Became a best seller, too. Critics were wild about the—and I quote— 'cleverly crafted plot with that rarest of all things, a truly surprising ending.'"

"The fact that you memorized that line tells me you're still pretty mad about it. I would be, too. Who was it?"

"I'm not going to name the author. I never have. He knows what he did and so do I. I'll let karma do its work," Nora said.

"I think you should write a book about an author who steals another author's idea and winds up dead."

"Don't think I haven't considered it. But I'm at the stage in life where I don't want to waste any of the time I have left on petty revenge."

"Personally, I've found a lot of satisfaction in petty revenge, but you do you," I said.

She laughed. "Thank you, I will. But I have one more piece of unsolicited advice for you. You need to be sure that 'planning' isn't just a way to avoid the hard work of writing."

My first instinct was to deny that I ever did such a thing. My second was to consider what she'd said in relation to the way I typically write a book.

"I do amass a lot of notes and character sketches and background research before I get off the launch pad and start writing. And I suppose sometimes it could be more about fear of taking the leap and actually typing 'Chapter One' than it is about laying down a roadmap for the story," I admitted.

"All I'm saying is that after a certain amount of thinking and talking and researching, it's time to start writing."

"Noted. Now, tell me what's going on with your next book."

"That won't be a long conversation. But it would go better with a second cup of coffee."

As I got up to make coffee, Nora stood and stretched with a slight groan.

"You okay?" I asked.

She grimaced.

"I'm fine. I'm just at the age where after sitting for a while, when I stand my knees like to remind me that they're here. Speaking of here, you've got a very lovely place, Leah. The window seat is charming. I'd probably spend all of my time sitting there watching the world go by on the street below, if I lived here."

"My secret is out. I do more of that than I should, but it's very nice to sit there with a cup of tea, my cat on my lap, and me doing absolutely nothing. Hmm. Maybe that's why it takes me so long to write a book," I said, and grinned as I handed her the coffee she'd requested.

"Now, tell me what's up with your new book," I said.

"Nothing, I'm sorry to say. I've had writer's block before, but this is the longest bout ever. I just can't find the right story to tell. To borrow a baseball term, I think I've got the writer's version of the yips. I know how to write, I'm a good plotter, I understand what makes a good twist, a worthy villain, how to raise the stakes—all the things that go into writing a solid mystery. But for some reason I can't pull a story together this time. I'm starting to think that my brain is trying to tell me it's time to retire. And there's some appeal to that. I've been writing one or two books a year for a long time. Maybe this should be the end.

"But if this is my last book, I want it to be really good. A tight plot, a strong motive, fully fleshed out characters, plenty of twists and tension, and a really big ending—the whole nine yards. If I'm going out, I want to go out with a bang not a whimper. And I think the book that came out last spring is more in the whimper category. I want to write at least one more to finish strong."

"That's crazy. Most writers would be thrilled to turn out a book like your last one. *Down into Darkness* is a great read. And don't talk about retiring around my mother. She'll go into deep mourning if she thinks there won't be a new Nora Fielding book every spring."

"That's sweet of you to say. And truthfully, I'm not sure what I'd do if I retire. I'm not creative at all—no latent artistic skills and I'm all thumbs when it comes to crafts. I'm not sporty either. I tried pickle ball once, but those people are way too competitive for someone like me, who only passed gym class because of the written exams."

"I'm sorry you're stuck right now, Nora. But I'm sure you'll find your way through. Sixty-seven is way too young for you to retire. P.D. James was still writing in her 90s. Elmore Leonard's last book came out when he was 87. Agatha Christie wrote into her 80s."

"You had me until Agatha Christie. I adore the Queen of Crime, but the books she wrote toward the end were, well, not good. I'm not comparing myself to Dame Agatha, but I don't want people saying 'Poor Nora Fielding. She's lost the plot—literally.' I haven't decided yet that the book I'm writing now—or trying to—will be my last. But in case it is, I want it to be among my best."

"I refuse to believe it will be your last, and I'm absolutely sure you're going to pull the rabbit out of the hat."

"Thank you, Leah. It's been fun for me this morning to toss possibilities around with you, someone just starting out full-to-the-brim with ideas—and talent. It's been a little sad, too, because I know I've lost some of that."

She smiled ruefully.

"Sorry for getting all old-lady maudlin on you. I'll be fine," she said, gathering her phone and purse to leave. "And whether I decide to retire or not, I know I have one project to work on that intrigues me very much. I'm so glad you asked me to serve on the board for the new nonprofit version of the *Himmel Times*. The whole process of setting things up has been fascinating. I'm really looking forward to being involved when the project actually launches. Thanks for putting something new and engaging into my life."

"All thanks go to you, Nora. Frankly, we went after you for the name recognition and your connections, which have been very helpful. But your ideas on ways the local paper can serve the county have been great."

"I'm glad. I find the whole idea of nonprofit news very stimulating. Now, I'll leave you to get on with your brain-eating amoeba plot. Keep me posted!"

"Will do."

2

After Nora's pep talk, I went to my office, shooed my cat Sam off my closed laptop, a favorite resting spot for him, and sat down with best intentions to get my focus on. But then a notification popped up on my computer screen. I had a new email that had been sent to the author account I use for corresponding with readers. So, of course, I abandoned the hard thing I should be doing for the easy thing I knew I'd enjoy. I've found my readers to be smart, funny, quirky, kind, and interesting. And they're from all over. The email that caught my eye was from Australia. When I went to the file and clicked on it, the subject line puzzled and intrigued me. It said simply: Please Help.

Dear Leah,

You don't know me, and I know this is presumptuous to ask, but I really don't have anywhere else to turn. I just finished reading your first true crime book. The way you didn't give up, you just kept digging even when no one else thought you were right about your sister's death—it was amazing. Then when I looked you up and found out where you live I had to reach out and ask—no, beg—you to help me.

I paused for a minute, thinking about my youngest sister Lacey. I'd written my first book, *Unholy Alliances*, after finding out the truth about why she'd died. I read on.

My name is Marguerite Pierce. I'm a psychologist living in Australia, but I was born and raised in Galen, Wisconsin, just 20 miles north of Himmel. That's where my sister Hannah Vining was tried and convicted last spring for the murder of Matthew Ferguson. I don't know how much you know about the case but living so close you've probably at least heard about it.

She was right. I had, but I didn't know any more about it than she had just described. At the *Times* we have all we can manage covering Grantland County. We don't go beyond the county line into Trenton County where Galen is located, unless there's a strong local connection. I read on.

I think she was convicted more for having an affair with a married man whose wife had cancer, than she was for the actual crime—which I'm telling you she didn't do. If you knew my sister Hannah, you'd understand. She's kind and caring, a wonderful mother. She's been a good wife to her husband Joel, too. Before Matthew came back into her life, she and Joel and their daughter Olivia were very happy.

That seemed a bit unlikely to me, given the whole extramarital affair thing.

Hannah is my older sister. She's always looked out for me. I'm devastated that when she needed me most, I couldn't help her. When she was arrested last year, I was in the first trimester of a high-risk pregnancy. I'd already had three miscarriages. My doctor said I'd be in danger of another because of the physical and emotional stress if I flew over for the trial.

Hannah kept telling me that she was fine, that I didn't need to be with her. But I knew then, and I know now that I should have been there. She didn't have anyone. Our parents are both gone and we don't have any other close relatives. Hannah had to face everything alone. It just about killed me to abandon her like that. I was a basket case—which led to me having our baby girl two months early. As Hannah was being sentenced to life in prison, my husband and I were in the Neonatal Intensive Care Unit while our daughter Alice fought for her life. She was there for two months. She just came home a month ago.

I know from your book that you believe in fighting for justice. My sister's conviction is a massive injustice. Please say you'll help. I'm so worried about Hannah. She's in a very dark place.

I have a weakness for lost causes and for people who have no one to fight for them. But I have to believe that what I'm fighting for is grounded in an actual injustice. I stopped reading the email then and did some online research into the Matthew Ferguson murder.

- Hannah Vining and Matthew Ferguson had been an item in high school in Galen.
- Hannah had moved away in their senior year, and they lost touch. He married, she married, they both had families.
- Twenty-something years later Hannah, her husband Joel, and their daughter Olivia moved back to Galen.
- Hannah, an herbalist, opened Moon Rise Compounding Apothecary in Galen, a town of 35,000 people.
- She and Matthew reconnected when he stopped by chance at her shop.
- A few months later they began an affair.
- Matthew's wife Ellen, a cancer survivor, had testified at Hannah's trial that he had confessed the affair, asked her forgiveness, and said he wanted to stay with her.
- Ellen also testified that Matthew had said that Hannah was very angry when he broke things off with her.
- Matthew was killed with aconite, a deadly herb used carefully and rarely by well-trained herbalists like Hannah.
- The police had found a text from Hannah to Matthew, sent shortly after the affair ended, that seemed to indicate Hannah would be seeking revenge.
- The prosecution had argued that Hannah had access to Matthew's cabin, where he died, and could easily have substituted aconite-laced tea for the regular special brew that he used.

The facts seemed plain to me. Hannah had the motive, revenge; the means, aconite; the opportunity, access to Matthew's cabin. There didn't seem to be anything except Marguerite's faith in her sister to base an alternate theory of the crime on. Apparently Hannah's attorney hadn't found one, anyway. All that she'd offered was Hannah's denial that she did it. She didn't have Hannah take the stand either, which, fairly or not, always makes a defendant seem like they're covering up their guilt.

I understood Marguerite's desperation. So, I turned her down as gently as I could, citing the writing deadlines I had and the complicated process of converting the newspaper to a nonprofit publication that my business partner and I were in the middle of.

It was the sensible thing to do. But I didn't feel good about it.

3

I'd spent so much time reading Marguerite's letter and googling her sister's trial that I didn't have time for the deep dive into *naegleria fowleri* that I'd planned. I had to hop in the shower, or I'd be late for dinner with my significant other David Cooper. Coop is the county sheriff, my life-long best friend, and my recent partner in romance.

As I dried my hair, my thoughts turned to the paper—it's never far from my mind, especially now. Before his death I'd persuaded my friend Miller Caldwell to join forces with me to save the only paper in the county. After he died, his daughter Charlotte had taken his place in our partnership. She and I had spent the better part of the past year attempting to move the *Himmel Times Weekly* from struggling to solvent by transitioning to a nonprofit newspaper model. Nonprofit media get their funding primarily from partners, sponsors, major donors and members (basically subscribers). The plan was to free us from dependency on advertising which was on a steep downward trajectory.

We had a board in place, our paperwork was mostly done, and we'd even hired a director to run the organization.

Our goal was to formally transition to the new status by the end of the year. And then we hit a snag. The person we hired, an old friend of mine, had recently resigned. Connor had been a good hire. He got along well with the board and the staff. Even with our editor Maggie who I love dearly, but who can be a bit of a curmudgeon. But Connor's heart was in reporting, not in management. When he got a call from an editor friend of his at the *Philadelphia Inquirer*, he couldn't say no. I didn't blame him. But it meant we had to open the hunt to fill the director job all over again.

Almost as though she'd been telepathically reading my thoughts, Charlotte called as I was pulling my hair up into a clip.

"Have you got a minute?"

"Just about that. I'm running late for dinner at Coop's. But I'll put you on speaker while I get dressed. What's up?"

"Well, maybe it should wait until tomorrow. What I have to tell you isn't going to put you in a happy mood for dinner."

"With an opening like that, you have to tell me. What's going on?"

"You know how we've been talking about a replacement for Connor?"

"Yeah, do you have someone in mind?"

"I don't. But Marilyn Karr does."

I groaned.

"No. Whoever she wants, it's a hard no. Who is it? Hitler's great-grandson?"

"No, she's pushing for her son, Spencer."

"Did I hear you right? Marilyn wants to install Spencer as the executive director for the *Himmel Times News*?"

We'd decided to keep the name *Himmel Times* but drop the "weekly" part. It wasn't really accurate anymore—we do so many updates online between print publications that we function more like a daily than a weekly. But keeping it the *Himmel Times* would keep its new incarnation familiar to our readers.

"I think you know you heard me right, Leah. I didn't talk to her directly. She left me a voicemail—a long voicemail. She talked about Spencer's experience in digital media, how he took *Go News* from a start-up to a successful business, how he had lots of background in marketing, too. She even made a little joke about nepotism. Then she invited me to lunch tomorrow to discuss the idea in more detail. I haven't called her back yet."

I can't say that I was truly shocked by what Charlotte had said. Horrified is more like it. Marilyn Karr and I go back a long way. She's the ex-wife of my mother's significant other Paul Karr. She had convinced herself that my mom was some kind of femme fatale who stole her husband and ruined her marriage—even though the Karrs had been divorced for five years before Paul and my mother got together. As a result, she hates my mother and, by extension, me.

Marilyn's done a number of mean-spirited things to both of us over the years. But she kicked it into high gear in my direction when Spencer bought *Go News,* an online publication that tried to take down the *Himmel Times*. It might have succeeded, too. But then Spencer's cocaine habit put him in the middle of a drug deal that went very wrong. He almost landed in prison but saved himself by turning on his partners. Instead, he went for an extended stay in rehab. In Marilyn's mind, somehow that was my fault.

"Is that even legal? I mean having the executive director and a member of the board be related?"

"There's no law against it. And our bylaws don't forbid it either," Charlotte said.

"Okay, well, let's kick Marilyn off the board."

"We'd need to have cause, like breach of fiduciary duty, or chronic absenteeism, or inability to fulfill the functions of a board member. At this stage she hasn't given us any reason to remove her from the board. Worry about what she *might* do isn't sufficient. I'm sorry, Leah. I agree with you that it would be a very bad idea to have Spencer as director. But when I was lobbying to put Marilyn on the board, I had no idea that the money and influence Marilyn could bring to help us might also bring us Spencer. Who could ruin us."

"Don't beat yourself up, Charlotte. I knew what she was like, and I still said yes. I'm not immune to Greeks—or board members—bearing gifts either, I guess. I should have listened to my gut though. But her dream for Spencer isn't a done deal. After all, the board can't hire someone who hasn't even applied, let alone been interviewed. Spencer isn't even a real candidate for the job yet."

"That's true," Charlotte said. "I am kind of jumping the gun here. It's just that I want this nonprofit news idea to work. The thought of Spencer as the director makes me very concerned that it won't. And we've both put so much into it already."

"Okay, let's think this through. First of all, we don't know how Spencer feels about this. He's in some halfway house program now that he's out of the rehab center. If I were him, with everything that came to light last year, Himmel is the last place I'd want to come to. I can see why Marilyn wants him here, she's his mother after all, but that doesn't mean *he* wants to be here. I say we monitor the situation and only start to panic if we get Spencer's application and Marilyn starts lobbying the other board members. I'm pretty sure Nora would be able to see through him in an interview situation. You and I know what he's like, so he wouldn't get our vote, and we only need one more board member to agree with us. We picked really smart, really ethical people for the board. I'm sure if the need arises, we'll be able to get at least one more vote against hiring Spencer."

"All right. I feel a little better now. I'll have lunch with Marilyn. I'll listen, but I'll be noncommittal. If Spencer does put in an application, we'll deal with it then. But I still wish I hadn't pushed to have Marilyn on the board."

"Hey, let it go. Look at it this way, if Spencer does apply and he doesn't get the job—and we will fight to the death to make sure that doesn't happen—maybe Marilyn will quit the board in a snit and we'll be free of both of them. Listen, Charlotte, I've really got to run. I'll talk to you soon."

4

I'd managed to get dressed while Charlotte and I had been processing the Spencer development, but I still had to feed Sam before I left.

He was waiting by his empty food dish in the kitchen when I walked in and the look he gave me made it clear he wasn't pleased.

"I'm sorry," I said. "But it's only ten minutes past your usual supper time and I had a lot to talk about with Charlotte. Will you forgive me if I give you a can of Salmon Delite tonight?"

He didn't give me a yes or no, but he purred while I spooned the smelly stuff into his dish. I took that as a sign that I was absolved for my sin of delaying his mealtime. As he ate, I grabbed the potato salad made by my mother and the cookies made by Clara Schimelman at the Elite Café, which were my contributions to dinner. Maybe I'm not a great cook or baker—okay, so there's really no *maybe* about it. I'm not. But I do have connections with people who are, so the end result is kind of the same, right?

"I'm leaving now, Sam. I'll be back around ten, probably. Charlotte gave me some not great news. I'm going to Coop's now and I know he'll do his best to soothe my troubled mind, but I'm putting you on alert that I may require a lap cat to complete the process when I get home."

In addition to his charms as a boyfriend, his skills as a sheriff, and his excellence as a cook, Coop is a very good listener. But Sam has the edge because he never interrupts or offers unwelcome advice, which Coop sometimes does. We've been best friends for more than twenty years, ever since sixth grade when his family moved to Himmel just as mine was falling apart. In all those years, he's never let me down, and he's always had my back. Not that long ago we finally figured out that we were actually more than friends, though apparently the people around us had known it for quite a while.

"Okay, I really have to go. See you later!"

As I was leaving, Sam jumped up on the window seat, his favorite perch in the apartment—mine, too—and curled up to wait for my return.

As I drove through town toward Coop's house, I looked around at the business district, which had suffered severely after a succession of factory closings and big box store openings. It was much different now than it had been when I first came back to my hometown after years away. Then I had been shocked to see that Himmel looked like the real-life version of a Bruce Springsteen song—one about textile mills closing and vacant storefronts downtown, where no one comes anymore. That sad version of home was slowly improving, largely due to Charlotte's late father, Miller Caldwell.

Miller was a tireless advocate for revitalizing the town. He had bought, renovated, and repurposed a number of old buildings. One of them is the former department store, built in 1910, where the *Times* and I both live. The paper is on the ground floor, my apartment is on the third. I love the exposed brick walls, hardwood floors, and three, tall arched windows in the front. The gas fireplace is perfect on rainy fall nights and wintry afternoons, and best of all is the window seat Miller had installed. Sam and I spend considerable time there, looking outside at the traffic and the people moving by below us. Across the street is another product of Miller's vision, the Wide Awake and Woke Coffee shop with a yoga studio above it. It's been a good draw to bring people to Main Street, and that's helped perk up the businesses that have managed to hang on during the lean years, like the book store and the cat boutique.

I don't want to make it sound like we've achieved a total return to the vibrant downtown of yesteryear. Anyone interested in restoring Himmel to its glory days has a steep hill to climb, but Miller—a member of one of the families that originally founded the town—had started the upward journey for the community. Charlotte is committed to carrying on her father's legacy. And thank goodness for that, or the *Times* wouldn't have lasted as long as it has.

As I neared the corner to turn toward Coop's street, I spotted Dale Darmody, a recently retired cop from the Himmel Police Department, walking around the outside of an empty building that had once housed a chocolate shop. The store had been vacant for years. Even though I was running late, I couldn't resist pulling over to the curb, rolling down the window, and calling out to Darmody.

"Hey, what's going on? Why are you prowling around in front of the old candy shop?"

He turned and a smile spread across his chubby face as he walked toward me. He leaned into the passenger side window to answer me.

"Leah, I haven't seen you in a while. You didn't hear? I'm startin' a new career."

"A new career? You just retired. I thought you'd be tying flies for fishing or visiting your grandkids in Eau Claire. These are supposed to be your kick back and relax years, Darmody."

Darmody had been a cop when I was a kid, maybe even as far back as when my dad was a kid. He never made it past patrol officer, but boy did he love his job. What he lacked in smarts or finesse, and to be honest that was quite a lot, he made up for in loyalty to his department and his town. Most cops in town are retired by their late fifties, but Darmody had hung on until he hit the mandatory retirement age, and he had no choice but to go.

"I just got my private investigator license. I hadda take the exam a coupla times—those questions are really tough! But now I got it and I'll be open for business next week."

I was speechless. Darmody was no Sam Spade. He wasn't even Scooby Doo, to be brutally honest.

"What does Angela think about this?"

"It's her idea. She says I need something to keep me busy, and she does too, so we're gonna work together. Angela's gonna be my secretary. Kinda like Perry Mason and Della Street, except we're married, and I'm not a lawyer."

"Oh, I see."

I tried to keep the astonishment out of my voice.

"You know there's a private investigator in Omico, too. Do you think there's enough business in Grantland County for two private eye agencies?" I asked.

"Sure. Me and Angela got a business plan and everything. I figure we'll mostly do divorce work, surveillance stuff, maybe some skip tracing—Angela's real good on the computer, and we're gonna look for lost pets, too. Angela says every business has to have a specialty. Besides, it's not like we're tryin' to get rich. I got a good pension, and Ange has a nice IRA. So the detective business is kind of our hobby. But we're serious about it. Want to know the name of our agency? It's D&D Investigations. You know, because we're Darmody and Darmody," he said, not waiting for me to answer.

"Very direct and to the point."

"Yeah, that's what Angela said. We're workin' on a slogan now. I like "Discreet, Dependable, Darmody." What do you think?"

"It's easy to remember. And your office is in a good location."

The narrow, one-story building that would soon be D&D Investigations was sandwiched between an old office building that now serves as a church and another vacant storefront. But Darmody's new venture was on the same street as the Himmel Police Department, so he'd at least get some daily traffic passing by to give his office visibility.

"Hey, you wanna come in and have a look-see?"

"I would but I'm running late for dinner at Coop's. I'll come by for your grand opening though," I said.

"Great! It's gonna be Monday the week after next. We signed the lease last month and we got most of the work done on settin' up things in the office."

He stepped away from the car and rapped on the hood by way of goodbye. But as I moved the car out of park, he leaned back in.

"I just thought of somethin'. Maybe we can work together sometime. You know, like I could give you some background stuff on private eyes for your books. Or if you're investigatin' something and you need some help, you can call me. I mean because now I'll be able to really help, like I couldn't so much before on account of conflict of interest with me bein' a professional law enforcement guy. What do you think?"

"Good to know, Darmody. But I don't have any investigations on tap at the moment. My goal right now is to finish the book I'm writing and get the paper's nonprofit status sorted out. Thanks for the offer, though. I'll keep it in mind if anything comes up."

He smiled happily and waved as I drove off.

5

When I got to Coop's I followed the tantalizing smell of hamburgers on the grill to the backyard.

"Hey, you. I was beginning to wonder if you were going to make it," Coop said as he flipped the burgers and looked up at me with a smile and a warm expression in his dark gray eyes. Coop doesn't say a lot of romance-type things, but he doesn't need to when he looks at me that way.

"I'm sorry I'm a little late, but I come bearing my mom's potato salad and some chocolate chip cookies from the Elite Café. So I'm assuming I'll be forgiven. I was working with Nora on some plot ideas for my next book this afternoon and the conversation ran a little long. And after that Charlotte called. Then on my way over I saw Darmody. So, if you cut all those things out, I'm actually here early. Did you know Darmody's going into business as a private investigator?"

"I heard the rumor. So it's a real thing?"

"The real-est. He and Angela are going to team up to become the Perry Mason and Della Street of Himmel."

"I imagine that will make Owen happy."

Owen Fike is the Himmel Police Department captain. He and Coop are pretty good friends, but Owen and I have what I'll call an "uneasy" relationship. I don't dislike him, but he's got no use for journalists. We've butted heads a few times but haven't come to blows—yet.

"You mean because if Darmody is busy trying to be a private detective, he won't be hanging around the police station so much?"

"Exactly. I hear he's gone into the cop shop every day since he retired. I can see why Owen's not crazy about that. Maybe this private eye stuff will keep him busy."

"Yeah, but, Coop, come on. You know he's not going to be good at it."

"No, I don't know that. He's not a quick thinker, that's true. But it's not that hard to do surveillance or background checks. He's not likely to get any jobs more complicated than that. And he won't have to do the piles of paperwork you have to do when you're a cop."

"He's going to take lost pet cases, too. So there's that."

"There you go, that's right in his lane. I hope his new business works out for him. He just wants to do something that makes him feel like he still matters. You can't fault him for that."

I put the cookies and the potato salad I was carrying on the picnic table and walked over and kissed him.

"That was nice, but what was it for?" he asked.

"Because *you're* nice. And you're exactly right. I want to be like you when I grow up."

Just then I felt a spattering of rain from the clouds that had been gathering. It quickly became a deluge.

"Come on, I've got the potato salad and cookies, you grab the burgers and let's make a run for it," he said.

"Is Miguel coming or no?" I asked as we dashed into the kitchen. Just as I uttered the question, there was a quick knock on the front door, and we heard Miguel call out as it opened.

"Hello, I'm here! Are you inside or—there you are!" he said, bursting through the kitchen door, carrying his contributions to the dinner. He put his Aunt Lydia's homemade salsa on the counter and kept up a running stream of conversation as he got a bowl from the cupboard and filled it with chips.

"Coop, those jeans are fire. *Chica*, where have you been? I've hardly seen you," Miguel said as he turned and gave me a hug.

Miguel Santos is the senior reporter at the *Times*. It's true that we only have two full-time reporters, Miguel and Troy Patterson, so "senior reporter" might seem a bit grandiose. But we don't have the budget to show our appreciation in dollars, so we tend to compensate with titles.

"These jeans are the same brand and kind that I've been wearing for fifteen years. In fact this pair is almost ten years old," Coop said, amused by Miguel's fashion assessment.

"Ah, yes, but you have the classic style. The man's man with the no-nonsense look. You are never out of fashion if you are true to yourself," he said with a grin.

"Well, what about me? I'm true to myself."

"You? No. You just buy whatever is on sale so you can get out of the store. Sometimes it works, most times . . ." He paused to shake his head. "You have no sense of style."

I turned to Coop. "Are you going to let Miguel trash your woman's fashion sense?"

He shrugged. "I'm not stepping in between you and your fashion advisor. Except to say you always look good to me."

"Nice save, and thank you," I said.

"Miguel, we can't all be fashionistas like you. Besides, you have more to work with than I do."

It's true, he does. Miguel is tall, with great hair, a wide white smile, dark brown eyes,, and eyelashes to die for. I have fairly good eyelashes myself, but the rest of me is pretty basic. Reddish brown hair, hazel eyes, and a smattering of freckles that fade in the winter and pop out every summer.

"You do not work it at all," Miguel said, sadly.

"Okay, enough fashion talk for the evening—for the year, as far as I'm concerned," Coop said. "What can I get everyone to drink?"

Once we were seated at the table with our plates piled high and our beverage of choice—Leinenkugel for Coop, iced tea for me and Miguel—we caught up on what we were each doing.

"Coop, how is your new house coming?" Miguel asked, before taking a giant bite of one of Coop's master-chef-level grilled burgers.

"Pretty good. We've got it framed in, and we'll be starting on the exterior walls next. We need to get them done, install the windows and doors and get the roof on before the end of fall. Then we can work inside and finish it up over the winter."

Coop had wanted a piece of land in the country for a long time. He hadn't been able to find anything that was both in his price range and had what he was looking for—some acreage with woods, a stream or a pond, a house that could be remodeled and a barn or other large outbuilding. I'd been secretly happy that there hadn't been anything on the market that met his needs. I like having him just a few blocks away.

Then last winter his Uncle David (Coop is his namesake), died. He was a widower with no kids, and he left his place in the country to Coop. It's twenty acres of mostly wooded property with a nice eight-acre pond for Coop to fish, a big barn, but no house. That had burned to the ground years ago, and rather than rebuild, his uncle had moved into a condo in town. Coop and his dad Dan, a mostly retired carpenter, had spent the spring doing some remodeling on the barn. Coop had set up his wood shop there —he's a pretty good carpenter himself, and they were using the barn to store lumber and other building supplies they needed while they built Coop's house.

"But you have been working so hard," Miguel said. "Why does it take so long?"

"It's mostly just me and my dad doing the work, and some friends now and then. I don't really mind if it takes a while. I like the work and the time with my dad."

And I liked that it sounded like he wouldn't be moving out of town for months yet.

"Now you, *chica*. I want to hear about you. I have hardly seen you this week. You haven't come into the newsroom once since Tuesday. What has been keeping you so busy?"

"That's only two days ago, Miguel. I've been working on the plot for my next book while I'm waiting for my editor to get back to me on the draft I turned in for my second one. In fact, I spent the afternoon consulting with Nora Fielding about it."

"Oh, I love her. She is going to be on my podcast next week. You should come on with her."

Miguel had started writing an advice column in the *Times*, called *Ask Miguel*, a while ago. He dispenses opinions and advice on fashion, family, friendship, romance, music, food—pretty much anything anyone wants to ask about. It got so popular locally that we decided to try a podcast of the same name. He features interviews with local politicians, educators, business leaders, farmers, and the occasional well-known celebrity who happens into the area. And he's always happy to respond to listener requests for advice on all kinds of topics.

It's a funny, engaging, and smart show. My secret fear is that his podcast will gain such a large audience that some podcast network will make him an offer that takes him away from the *Times*. I've never said that out loud though, because that might make it come true, and also because it makes me sound incredibly selfish. Which I guess I am about losing Miguel.

"I did your podcast last spring, remember? And I promised my agent that I'll do it again when the next book comes out. But that's enough for me. You know who you should have on? Darmody. He'd love it."

"He and Angela are already booked for next week to talk about their detective agency. I will still keep asking you, though. But why are you working on a plot for your third book when you haven't finished your second one yet?"

"I'm starting a new way of life. I'm committing to developing the plot for my next book every time I reach the end of the first draft stage of my current book. So I don't feel like I'm always running behind."

"Is that going to be like your new way of life commitment to go to the gym every day? Or is it closer to your new way of life pledge to eat healthy?"

Coop cocked an eyebrow at my plate heaped high with potato salad, chips and salsa, hamburger and coleslaw.

"That is not the way to encourage me in my quest for a healthy lifestyle. In fact, the mockery is probably going to force me to eat two of the cookies I brought instead of one. Come on, I'm serious this time. I'm committed to finding a better method for writing."

"But Coop and I, we are just very interested in your latest new way," Miguel said.

"I can't believe you're ganging up on me with Coop, Miguel."

"We are not ganging up on you. But you have started a lot of new ways of life since I've known you. I think at the beginning of summer it was—"

A soft chime from my phone caused me to pull it out and check the banner on the screen.

"Oh, boy. I really hoped I wouldn't get this email," I said.

6

"Why? What is it?" Miguel asked

I opened the email and gave it a quick read. It was shorter, but just as fervent as the first one Marguerite Pierce had sent me.

"*Please, Leah. I know you're busy, but this is a matter of life and death, literally. You said in your email that you read the news coverage, but that's only part of the story. Please think about it again. Don't close the door on me. Here's my phone number, call me anytime. Don't worry about the time difference. I'm up with the baby at all hours anyway. Please!*"

I explained Marguerite's request in brief.

"But that sounds like Erin Harper's case, and you helped her," Miguel said.

"That's because Gabe was her attorney, and he asked me to."

Gabe Hoffman had been Miller Caldwell's law partner. He and I had a brief romantic relationship with a painful ending for both of us. But now we're each with partners we're better suited to. Luckily we've been able to stay good friends.

"Also, I knew Erin personally and I believed her when she told me she didn't commit murder."

"But her sister knows Hannah and she is telling you that she believes her," Miguel said.

"True, but I wouldn't expect anything less from the sister who loves her. And I'm busier than I've ever been just now. I have to finish up my current book, get something organized for the next one, and make sure that the *Times* transition to a nonprofit is successful. And that's looking like it could take a lot of attention at this point."

"Do you know anything about the case, Coop?" Miguel asked, not ready to give up. I may be drawn to underdogs and long shots, but I can say no sometimes. Miguel, who has a very tender heart, has a harder time.

Coop shook his head. "I didn't really follow it. I've got enough on my hands here in my own county."

"Miguel, I did a pretty deep dive online for background on Hannah's situation before I answered Marguerite. The case against her was very strong, and the defense theory of the crime was nonexistent. Her attorney put on a couple of character witnesses, but not much else. And the murder weapon—aconite—points right at Hannah Vining."

"Wait, what is aconite?"

"It's a flower. A lot of people grow it in their gardens, and it grows wild, too. But it's a powerful poison. If you ingest it, chances are very good you'll die. Even if you just handle it without gloves and it gets absorbed through the skin, you could die. It's that toxic," I said.

"Why would anyone grow poison in their garden?" Miguel asked, horrified.

"Because it's a pretty flower, and gardeners know how to handle it safely. It's used in herbal medicine too, especially in Eastern European countries and in China," I said.

"How do you know so much about it?" Miguel asked.

"Because aconite was the murder method in the first case Leah ever solved. When she was eleven years old. You can read all about it in *Life on the Street*, the neighborhood newsletter she published when we were kids. I think I've got some copies tucked away somewhere," Coop said.

"What? What is this? How did I not know you were a middle school murder hunter? That's amazing!" Miguel said.

"It was just kid stuff. And it was a long time ago. I didn't really solve it, I kind of stumbled onto the answer," I said. "Coop was part of it, too."

"I told her to leave it alone. She wouldn't listen. So, I saved her. Just like always," Coop said.

I knew he was teasing, trying to get a rise out of me. But it worked anyway.

"Hey, you did *not* save me. You just showed up before I had finished saving myself. Anyway, we're talking about Marguerite Pierce and her sister Hannah, not something from a million years ago."

"Oh, but I must read your newspaper story you wrote about it. Coop, you will find it for me, yes?"

"Happy to, Miguel."

"Okay, whatever," I said. "But back to the subject at hand, Hannah Vining's murder conviction. To sum up, the jury believed the case against Hannah, and I have to say, I do, too. I guess I'm going to have to answer Marguerite with a firmer no this time."

I used getting up to get more chips and salsa as a chance to reset the conversation away from Marguerite and her request. As I sat back down I said, "Miguel you were just saying something when we got diverted by the email. What was it?"

"We were talking about your very many new ways of life. I was just going to ask how you are doing with the new way of life you started this summer—the one about not checking email after 5:00 p.m. How is that going?"

"You guys think that's funny, but it's not," I said.

"Yes, it is," Coop said, not bothering to hide the laughter in his eyes.

"Okay, I'll stipulate it's a little funny. But can we move on, please?"

Miguel took pity on me.

"Yes, we can. So, did Nora like your idea for your next book after this one?"

"She did. Plus she gave me some advice," I said, as I dipped a chip in salsa. "Mmm. Tell Lydia this is her best salsa ever, Miguel."

"I will, but what is the advice Nora gave you?"

"Loose lips sink ships—or the author's variation of it anyway."

"What does that mean?"

"It means that apparently writing can be a treacherous business."

I gave them the story of Nora's "friend" who took the plot she shared with him and beat her to the punch by writing a book using it before she could.

"That is terrible! You should listen to Nora. Who was the author who stole her idea?"

"She wouldn't say. She told me she'd let karma settle the score."

"Ah, but I have ways of making her talk. I will ask her out for coffee, and I'll see what I can find out."

"I can testify to your ways, Miguel," I said.

"But then tell us about *your* plot. What did Nora say about it? And what even is it? You haven't told us anything."

"That's because I don't want you to steal it."

"No, don't tease. Tell us, we want to know."

"I'm going to drop back on this one, Miguel," Coop said. "I don't want to know what the story is about. I like reading Leah's fiction books when I don't know what's going to happen."

"I don't want to know everything. Just a little bit, no spoilers," Miguel said in a wheedling voice. "Come on, tell your Miguel."

"I'll tell you this much. It involves a biohazard, and a crime in the past that ties into one in the present. How, I have no idea yet. And I may end up ditching the whole plot line if the research shows that what I have in mind couldn't happen in real life."

"What kind of biohazard?"

"*Naegleria fowleri*. It's what news stories, especially tabloid news stories, call the brain-eating amoeba. But I'm not far enough along in plotting to know if I'll be able to make things work out."

"But how will you—"

"Sorry, that's all you get for now, Miguel."

"But later, when Coop is not around for the spoilers? Then you'll tell me all, right?"

"You're incorrigible. But probably right. You *are* an excellent sounding board. Now, it's your turn. What's going on in your life right now?"

"I just found out today that I am going to be homeless."

"What do you mean? Why?"

"You know I sold my house, and I have to move by the end of next month. I was supposed to sign the papers for my new house, but the people selling backed out. So now, I have no place to go! I am looking now for a rental, but the rent is higher than my house payment was!"

"I've got an idea," Coop said. "Leah, if you moved in with me, Miguel could rent your place."

Miguel's face lit up.

"Oh, that would be so amazing. I love your apartment *chica*! I have so many ideas to decorate, and I could—"

"Hold it, hold it. No fair, Coop, trying to get Miguel on your side by dangling my apartment in front of him. And Miguel, I love my apartment. The window seat view is amazing, the kitchen is fantastic—"

"Yes, but you hardly ever cook. And also you could retain visiting rights. I would welcome you to my loft apartment any time."

"Let me shut that idea down right now. I am not giving up my apartment, not even for you Miguel. If you need to, you can camp out on my sofa. But with your connections, I doubt it will take you long to find something, so don't worry."

"I never worry. Even if you will not give up your apartment for me, something will turn up," he said. I don't share the character trait, but I love Miguel's ever-present optimism.

"You know, if you put out on your podcast that you're looking for a place, I'll bet your listeners would be able to help you out," Coop said.

"Yes, that is a good idea, and—" Miguel's phone pinged, and he stopped mid-sentence to look at the screen. "Oh, I have to go! Della Toomey and I are going to classic film night at Himmel Tech. They are showing *Singing in the Rain* tonight. It's her favorite movie."

"Della Toomey? Is she your friend who lives in Delving and used to be a Rockette?" I asked.

"That's her. She doesn't drive at night anymore and she really wanted to go. She met Gene Kelly at the movie premiere in 1950 at Radio City Music Hall."

"Miguel, you are a very nice person."

"No, I like that movie, too. It's very funny. And Della, she's very funny too. I love older ladies."

He jumped up and took his dishes to the sink.

"Take some cookies with you for the road," I said, getting some out of the bag and handing them to him. "Have fun and don't let Della keep you out too late."

"I won't. Thank you for dinner, Coop. It was fabulous."

Turning to me he said, "We will talk more later about you giving up your apartment for me. I know you will love the idea in time."

I reached up and rubbed his head to tousle his perfect hair.

"No! Why do you always mess with the hair?"

"Because it's the only time I ever see you ruffled—physically or emotionally."

"No wonder you like the buzz cut, Coop, with this one around," he grumbled. But he smiled as he restored his hairstyle with a few practiced moves of his fingers.

"I will see you both soon."

7

It was still raining when Coop and I finished cleaning up the kitchen, but it was muggy and a little stuffy inside. Coop doesn't have central air. Rather than stay in the house, we got a couple of lawn chairs out and settled in for some old-fashioned garage sitting. I don't know if it's common practice in other places, but in the Upper Midwest, turning your garage into a semi-outdoor space is pretty mainstream. You just raise the garage door, set your chairs up so you're toward the front, but in the shade (or out of the rain) and watch the world and your neighbors go by while you relax and chat.

Coop had another Leinenkugel, and I had a shot of Jameson over ice as our after-dinner drinks. For a long time we sat in companionable silence, listening to the rain hitting the roof, watching the cars throwing up water as they ran through puddles on the street, and waving at umbrella-carrying people walking their dogs. It was very pleasant.

After a while Coop said, "Do you have time tomorrow to take a ride with me to see the property? You haven't been out since Dad and I really got going on it."

"Yes, sure. I'd like to see what's been keeping you busy so many nights and weekends."

"Great. Does noon work?"

"Perfectly. I promised Jennifer that I'd watch the twins in the morning while she and Ross go birthday shopping for the boys. It still seems kind of weird that they're together, doesn't it?"

Charlie Ross is a detective sergeant in the Grantland County Sheriff's office. Jennifer Pilarski, my friend since kindergarten, works as Coop's administrative assistant. She's also going to college to finish the degree she gave up to put her ex-husband through school.

"They seem happy with each other. Why do you think it's weird?"

"They're just so different. Jen is warm, easy-going, upbeat. Ross is so, well, so Ross. He's kind of crabby, he's a pessimist, and there's nothing easy-going about him."

"Maybe that's why they're together. They complement each other. Don't be so hard on Charlie. He can be a fun guy."

"Hey, I'm not down on Ross. Actually I'm a little worried about him. I think he might be more serious than Jen is. I don't want him to get hurt again. Not after what happened with his last serious relationship."

"How do you know how Charlie feels? I can't see him turning to you for romantic advice. Or to anybody."

"He hasn't *said* anything to me. But it's kind of obvious isn't it? You can hardly have a conversation with him without Jennifer's name coming up. I'm not sure Jennifer feels the same way. Whenever I ask her how it's going, she just smiles and says 'fine.'"

"Could it be that—now I know this is kind of an out-there idea, so hear me out. Could it be that's because it *is* going fine?"

"Oh, stop it. You know it's not like her to be so reserved. Jen is an over-sharer, but not this time. If she had strong feelings for him, I think she'd talk about it."

"Leah, this really isn't any of our business. Charlie's a big boy and he'll take care of himself. I think we have to leave it at that. Or you can put Miguel on the case. He claims credit for bringing them together. So if anyone should be monitoring the situation, and for the record I don't think anyone should, Miguel would be the one to do it."

"I guess you're right. But I'm still a little worried for Ross."

"Understood."

We lapsed into silence for a few minutes before I launched into the worry that was troubling me even more than Jen and Ross's relationship.

"Coop, there's something else I'd like to talk about."

"That sounds serious."

"It could be. It's about Marilyn Karr. She's up to her usual machinations. She's angling to get Spencer the executive director job at the new and improved nonprofit *Himmel Times News*."

It was very gratifying to see the same stunned expression on Coop's face that I'm sure I had on mine when Charlotte dropped that particular bomb.

"You're kidding. No, of course you're not. But that's a lot of audacity even for Marilyn."

"Agreed. I knew she'd do something to make me regret that she's on the board, but I didn't see this coming. Spencer is a horrible human being, and he wasn't a good journalist even before he went off the deep end with drugs. I don't want to infect the new *Himmel Times* with the old Spencer."

"But a majority on the board would have to get behind Spencer, right?"

"Yes, and I'm trying to keep calm about it by repeating that to myself. But I don't know all the board members well, so I'm not positive I can count on that. I downplayed my worries when I talked to Charlotte, but Marilyn can be very persuasive. I shouldn't have gone along with Charlotte when she first brought up Marilyn for the board. I knew it was fraught with peril. But I was bewitched by the money and contacts she could bring. And to be fair, she's come through on that."

"Look, you guys vetted your board pretty carefully. I think you should trust that if Spencer actually applies, they'll see through him. In the meantime, just wait and see how things play out. It may be much ado about nothing."

"I know, I know. But wait-and-see isn't really my default setting."

"That I know very well."

8

When there was a knock on my door the next morning while I was putting my shoes on, I knew it was my mother before she even called "Good morning!" That's because the tantalizing aroma of apples and cinnamon reached me as soon as she opened the door.

"Hi, Mom. You must have gotten up super early to be on the move with apple bread at 8:00 a.m."

"Not that early. I did the prep work last night, so I just had to throw it together when I got up this morning. Let's have a piece right now with some coffee."

"You don't have to ask me twice."

My mother is in her early sixties, but she looks younger. She's very pretty and has a lovely alto voice that she often puts to use in Himmel Community Players musicals. Her eyes are a deep blue with nice thick eyelashes.

As I made the coffee and got down plates for the apple bread, I said, "I thought you and Paul were going to dinner in Madison last night and then to a play. How did you have time to do the apple bread?"

"We didn't go to the play. In fact we didn't go to dinner, either."

Something in her voice made me turn around to look at her.

"Why not? Mom, is something wrong? Is Paul ill, or—"

"No, nothing like that. Let's sit down and have our coffee and I'll tell you."

"It's something I need to sit down for? Just tell me," I said as a ripple of fear went through me.

"Mom, is it you? Are you sick?"

"Leah, no. It's nothing to do with anyone's health."

She carried the cups to the kitchen bar. I brought the apple bread, pulled up a bar stool and joined her.

"All right, now what's going on?"

"Paul and I are taking a break. It was a mutual decision."

"What? You and Paul are breaking up?"

I couldn't imagine that Paul had initiated this shocking turn of events. They'd been together for years. Paul has always wanted to marry Mom, but she's always refused. She says that she needs to have her own space as much as she loves Paul. It had seemed to work for them. Until now.

"I didn't say we were breaking up. I said we were taking a break. It was mutual, Leah."

"I don't believe that. Paul adores you. He asks you to marry him at least every six months. He would never want to take a break from you. What happened?"

"Nothing 'happened,' Leah. All right maybe it wasn't exactly a mutual decision. But I just feel in my heart that I need to step away for a while. Paul reacted the same way you did, and I feel terrible that I upset him. I didn't articulate it to him any better than I'm explaining it to you. I just need to figure some things out. I wanted you to know about me and Paul, but I don't want to talk about it right now, okay?"

"Yeah, okay, I guess."

"Now, what's going on with you?"

I told her about Marilyn Karr's latest ploy to destroy my life, and she was concerned but reassuring.

"I know it's upsetting to you. It is to me, too. But lots of times the worries we have never come to fruition. There's no point in stewing about it ahead of time. Now, how's the plotting for your next book coming?"

I filled her in on the storyline, despite Nora's advice to keep it to myself. I was pretty sure my mother wouldn't use it to start writing her own book.

And then I told her about Marguerite's original email on behalf of her sister.

"It was hard to say no. She hit me where it hurts the most—a sister in trouble story."

"I know, hon. But I think it's a sign of maturity that you realize sometimes you can't fix things. This looks like one of those times to me."

"It is, but she emailed me back after I turned her down. So now I have to tell her no again."

Before I left the next morning to babysit for Jennifer's boys, I sat down to answer Marguerite's second email.

Dear Marguerite,

I understand how much you love your sister and want to save her—probably better than most people would. But I'm not the person to help you with that. I'll be blunt. I don't see much daylight between the facts of the case and the guilty verdict that the jury reached. Even if there is something new to discover, it would take more time and energy than I have at the moment. I suggest you hire a private investigator whose sole job is digging up information. They'll have more resources to help you than I do. And I have to focus on my writing and the newspaper I'm trying to save. I wish you the best possible outcome, I mean that. But I can't help you.

Sincerely,

Leah Nash

It was pretty cold-hearted, but I didn't want to give her room for false hope. Still, I hesitated before hitting the send button. And I felt guilty when I did.

9

As soon as I walked through the door at Jennifer's, her boys Nathan and Ethan burst out of the kitchen and ran up to me, talking over each other.

"Leah! Look what Uncle Charlie gave us!"

"We're deputies now!"

"No, we're junior deputies!"

"No, stupid head, Uncle Charlie said—"

"Mom, Nathan called me a stupid head!" Ethan yelled loudly to Jennifer, who was still upstairs.

"Hey, hey guys. No name calling. Or I'm going to have to arrest you. I'm a junior deputy, too," I said.

They giggled and I said, "No, I'm serious."

I reached in my purse and pulled out an official Grantland County Sheriff's Office junior deputy badge, which Ross had given me once as a joke.

"But you're old. Did Uncle Charlie give this to you when you were little?" Nathan asked.

"All right, all right boys. Give Leah a chance to breathe before you tackle her," Jennifer said as she walked down the front stairs and into the living room. "Go on and get dressed and make your beds. And maybe Leah will take you to play on the new swings at the park."

"Will you? Will you, Leah?"

"I will, as long as you do what your mom says."

They both took off at a run as Jennifer said, "Charlie just texted he's on his way. Will you think I'm rude if I run upstairs and finish drying my hair?"

"Yes. In fact, if I have to get my own coffee it will probably mean the end of our friendship. No! Go, dry your hair. I know my way around your kitchen as well as I do my own."

After Jen went back upstairs, I decided it was just as well she didn't have time. I'd been about to ignore Coop's good advice and talk to her about Ross, when I knew I shouldn't.

Just as I sat down at the kitchen table with a cup of coffee, Ross walked in the back door.

"Hey, you're not Jen."

"Nice to see you too, Ross. Jen's upstairs, she's—"

"No she's not," Jen said walking into the kitchen. "All done. Hi, Charlie. Ready for a shopping extravaganza?"

"You know me, I was born ready," Ross said, smiling and looking at her in exactly the way I'd told Coop that he did. He turned back to me for a second.

"Thanks for taking care of the boys for us, Nash."

"You're welcome, Ross. I'd rather be here than shopping any day."

I'd caught his use of the proprietary "us" and looked at Jen to see if she'd noticed, but she was digging in her purse. "Shoot, I must have left my list upstairs," she said and left the kitchen.

Ross went to the foot of the back stairs and shouted, "Hey, where are my junior deputies?"

In answer, the boys came clattering down and launched themselves at Ross. He had squatted in a catcher's stance, the better to grab them and tickle them into fits of giggles as he caught them.

"Leah said she's a junior deputy too, Uncle Charlie. Is she really?" Ethan asked.

"She was," Ross said. "But lean in closer. I'll tell you a secret," he said, as he continued in a stage whisper. "I had to fire her, because she wasn't very good at the job. I let her keep the badge anyway. Do you know why?"

"Because you didn't want to hurt her feelings," said Ethan, the more tender-hearted of the two.

"Exactly right. We should be nice to people who aren't as smart as we are. It's not their fault," Ross said, looking over Ethan's head and grinning at me.

I rolled my eyes at him.

As Ross stood up with a slightly muffled groan from a position his middle-aged body wasn't used to, both of the boys came over and hugged me.

"You should keep trying, Leah. Maybe you can still be a deputy. You should never give up. That's what our teacher says. Maybe if you take us to the park today, we can help you practice being a junior deputy."

"Why thank you, Ethan."

"Or if you just can't learn, that's okay. Hey, maybe you might be good at something else."

"I appreciate that, Nathan."

They glanced at each other, and then smiled kindly at me, secure in the knowledge that they themselves were very good junior deputies.

Ross was laughing but trying to conceal it from the boys by coughing. I discreetly gave him a salute with one finger, which only made him laugh harder.

10

"So, how was your morning with Jen's boys?" Coop asked as I got into his SUV for the ride to his property.

"Good. I took them to the park. I thought I'd spend most of the time pushing them on the new swings. But no, we had to play deputy for two hours. I was the bad guy. I got chased to the top of the slide, under the bandstand, around the track, and behind the stone wall at the back. I'm exhausted. Twins are not for the faint of heart, mind, or body."

"It sounds like fun. Next time you babysit, I'll see if I can join you."

"They would really love that. They're impressed that Ross is a detective, but you're the big boss—the sheriff."

"So, did you do it?"

"Do what?" I asked with studied innocence.

"Poke into Jennifer's private life and ask about her and Ross?"

"No. I did not. I was going to, but she was too busy getting ready. But you should have seen Ross. He's in love. Coop, I know I'm right."

"You usually are," he said as we made the turn and began bumping down the rutted gravel road that leads to Coop's property. "And if you're correct," he continued, "Have you considered the possibility that Ross already knows that Jen doesn't feel the same way he does? And that if all Jen is offering is friendship, that's enough for him, at least for now? I made do with it for a long time, waiting for you to come around. Slow and steady wins the race, and sometimes the girl."

He took his hand off the steering wheel and reached over to squeeze mine.

"Ross is different than you. He acts tough, but he's very vulnerable. I'm just worried about him. And do NOT tell him I said that, please."

"Hey, I'm staying totally away from the whole thing. No worries there."

Just then we hit a large pothole that sent us both bouncing in our seats.

"Is this part of a plan to keep people away from your fortress of solitude? You can't afford a moat so you're just randomly strewing the path with craters?"

Before he could answer we hit a stretch of washboard road so bad neither of us could talk without stuttering as the SUV drove over it.

"Tell me again about peaceful country living. Driving that was like bouncing around in a popcorn popper. This road needs regrading, bad."

"I talked to Dwight Hightower about it. He says the county knows there are issues with all the roads, but they don't have money to do the regular repairs and maintenance they need. So they're 'triaging' and doing the worst ones."

"Huh. If this road isn't the worst, I'd hate to see what is. I think I just got a story idea to share with Maggie." We had hit another patch of washboard road, so that whole sentence came out like I had the hiccups.

"Geez, are we there yet? I don't remember it being this far out the last time I came."

"Just another quarter of a mile," he said. "So what did your mom say about Marilyn's idea for the new director at the *Himmel Times News*?"

"She thinks I should wait and see what actually happens, not spend time worrying about something that may never come. I know she's right. I know you're right. And it's what I plan to do—but it won't be easy. Oh, I can't believe I forgot to tell you this. Paul and Mom are breaking up. Well, Mom says they're taking a break, but I'm not sure that's all it is."

"Even if it is, that's a lot. Why?"

"I'm wondering if Mom might be thinking that things with Paul have just run their course. She's seemed kind of, I don't know, restless I guess, lately."

"I see. Are you going to add them to your list of couples who need your guidance, like Jennifer and Ross? Maybe you should partner with Miguel. He arranges the matches, and you do the maintenance?"

I turned to punch him lightly on the arm, but we hit our biggest pothole yet as he turned onto his property. I wound up hitting myself in the chin.

"Ouch!" I said, rubbing my jaw. "Did you do that on purpose?"

"I did not. Though I think it would have been justified given that right hook you were about to throw me."

"That wasn't a right hook. It was a light love tap, reminding you that teasing has a limit and you're close to exceeding it."

"Ah, I see. Noted."

The two-track road leading to the clearing where the barn stood, and where Coop's house was being built, was in better shape than the main road had been. On either side were stately pines mixed in with maple, oak, and birch trees. And then the clearing where Coop's house was under construction and where his barn stood came into view.

As we got out of the SUV and slammed our doors shut, Coop said, "Wait a second. Listen. Close your eyes."

I stopped and obeyed.

"I don't hear anything but birds."

"I know. Isn't it great?"

"It is. I just wish it was closer to town," I said, as a blue heron flew over our heads and swooped down to rest on a fallen tree.

"Then it wouldn't be this peaceful."

"True. Oh, I really like where you sited your house," I said, as my eyes lit on the skeletal structure that would soon be his home.

"Yeah, the master bedroom and the living room will face the pond. I want to see it first thing when I wake up. And on a snowy afternoon when I'm reading by the fire in the living room, I want to look out the big picture window and watch the wildlife out there. Come on, I'll take you through it."

We walked through what would soon be walls and Coop gave me a tour.

"The living room and kitchen kind of flow in together here," he said pointing. "There isn't really a dining room, but the kitchen is pretty big and there's space for a table and chairs. For me a dining room is kind of wasted space."

"But what about all those formal dinners you like to host? Himmel society won't be the same without them. Plus I won't have any place to wear my closet full of evening gowns."

"I'll host my dinners the way I always do, standing over a hot stove or a barbecue grill while you watch me work."

"Those would be fighting words if they weren't true. Ok, so what's at the other end of the house?"

"Two small bedrooms and a bathroom/laundry room combined. I'll use one bedroom as an office—no more doing all my paperwork on the kitchen table. The other will be a guest room. The kitchen and living room take up the most footage, but overall the house is a pretty compact space. I expect to spend a lot of my time outside or in my wood shop."

"Is that why your barn is way bigger and taller than your house?"

"Well, that's the way Uncle Dave built it, but I'm glad he did. I'm going to need all that room. Once the construction stuff is out of there, I'll be storing my SUV, a snowmobile, and a tractor for mowing and plowing in there. My wood shop is already in the back end."

"What are you going to do with the loft in the barn?"

"I'll use it for storage for a while, I guess. Maybe I'll give up sheriff-ing and go all in on furniture making. That could be my showroom."

"As if you'd ever give up police work. Do you think you'll be able to get the exterior of the house done before winter sets in?"

"Yeah, I've got a lot of vacation time to burn. Things are holding pretty steady now, so I'm going to take a couple of weeks. Dad's bringing his fifth wheel down. We'll stay out here in that, and we can knock out a lot of work. He's got some friends willing to help and I've got a few, too. We'll be ready to go way before winter. You're welcome to come out and lend a hand, too," he said with a teasing smile.

"You think that's a joke, but before I met you my dad used to flip houses. My sister Annie and I used to help. So don't sound so patronizing. I know my way around a building site."

"Really? You were what, eight or nine years old? That's a little young for a carpenter's apprentice."

"Ten. I was a very mature ten-year-old. And I was trusted with the most critical element of a building project—running to JT's Party store to get snacks."

"I see. Well, since there isn't a party store nearby, I don't think I can put your particular skills to work on the house."

"Okay, but don't say I didn't offer. Come on, let's get a couple of chairs and take them down to the edge of the pond."

We took off our socks and shoes and dangled our feet in the water as we each shared iced tea from the thermos Coop had brought. The day was warm, but a light breeze rippled the surface of the water. While we sat looking out, an eagle swooped down and plucked a fish from the pond.

"Whoa! Did you see that?" I asked.

"I did. He lives around here somewhere. I see him most every time I'm out here."

"That's amazing. It feels like a different world. You can't even hear any traffic. Won't you get lonely?"

"Maybe sometimes. But I wouldn't if you moved in with me. I know we joked about it last night, but I think you'd really love it out here. It's not really that far away from town. From the barn loft, you can see all the way to Himmel. In fact you can see for miles all around. Imagine what the woods will look like in all the different seasons. Plus, Miguel wouldn't be homeless. He could rent your apartment."

"Coop, you know why I can't."

My chest had tightened a little, the way it always does when we discuss the subject.

"Don't you mean won't?"

"Won't or can't, the end result is the same. Maybe want is the right word. I love you, but I don't want to live with you. I don't want to give up my independence. I don't want to lose my sense of self, I guess."

"I don't understand how moving in with me would make you feel like you're losing your independence. We already spend half our lives at each other's places. What would be so different?"

"This is your place, your dream, and I'm glad you're achieving it. But I like having my own place, my own space. It's got nothing to do with how I feel about you. Maybe I'll change my mind at some point. But I don't want to rush into it."

"Leah, we've known each other for more than twenty years. I don't think we'd be rushing it."

I didn't say anything.

"Sorry. I didn't mean to ruin the moment. It just makes me happy to have you here and it popped out again."

"You didn't ruin it. But I feel how I feel. Can we just be happy with the way we are now? Are you unhappy?"

"No, I'm not. I just think we'd be even happier if we were living together. But I won't ask again. For now."

"Believe me, if I change my mind, you won't have to ask. I'll tell you straight out. Okay?"

"Okay."

"Now, how about a walk around your kingdom before we go? You can show me the place where you want to put your deer blind."

11

Coop dropped me off at home after our wilderness adventure and I hurried upstairs to do a little work on a presentation I had the next day. During the summer and early fall, the Himmel Parks Department hosts a series of events on Sunday afternoons at Founders Park. The programs are an eclectic mix, and thus far had included the high school jazz band, a talk on local history, a classical music quartet, and scenes from popular plays put on by the Himmel Community Players. The program for the next day was local author readings. Both Nora Fielding and I had been invited to read from our books. I needed to find a segment that fit the time frame and would be—I hoped—interesting to the audience.

After an hour or so of trying to make up my mind, I was ready for a Diet Coke. I knew there wasn't one in the fridge so I ran downstairs to grab a can from the pop machine in the office.

As I approached the newsroom I heard the sound of furniture scraping across the floor. When I poked my head in, I saw our receptionist Courtnee Fensterman. It's quite difficult to get Courtnee to put in a full day's work during her regular Monday to Friday schedule. The sight of her in the office on a Saturday was unprecedented.

"What are you doing?" I asked.

She jumped and, with a thud, dropped the corner of the desk she'd been tugging across the floor.

"Leah! You scared me! You shouldn't be sneaking up and spying on people!"

"You may recall, Courtnee, that I live in this building, and I'm also the co-owner of this newspaper. I'm not spying. I came down for a Coke. Why are you rearranging the newsroom furniture?"

"I saw Marilyn Karr when I was getting my nails done this morning. She told me that Spencer is going to be the new executive director for the *Times*. I was just trying to see where my desk should go."

"It won't go anywhere in the newsroom, Courtnee, because you're a receptionist. You receive people. You have to do that at the reception desk in the front of the office."

"Well yes, I know that I'm a receptionist *now*," she said, accompanying her words with a slight roll of her eyes. "But Spencer will need an administrative assistant, and I've been here long enough to get a promotion. Way long enough. I know Spencer will get Maggie's office, because he'll be her boss. She can move into that little one we use for storage. I'll need to be right outside Spencer's office, so I'm seeing where I want my desk to go."

Courtnee is in her early twenties and quite pretty, with long blond hair and big blue eyes. She is blessed with supreme, though unwarranted, confidence in her own abilities.

"Okay, first of all, Spencer hasn't even applied for the job. The board hasn't vetted any of the candidates yet, so Marilyn is getting ahead of herself."

And she was doing it purposefully, I thought, in order to start the rumor moving through the community, to make Spencer's candidacy seem inevitable. And she had chosen her messenger well. Courtnee is not a good receptionist, but she's highly skilled at spreading gossip.

"Second, we haven't decided yet what type of support the new executive director will need. Connor didn't have any direct support while he was in the position."

"I know. I had to help him besides doing everything else around here. But that means I have the experience, so that makes me the best qualified, so I should get the job. Marilyn said that she thought I would be an interesting choice for Spencer's assistant."

"If and when we create the position of administrative assistant, you can apply for it like anyone else who is interested in the job. And that is not Marilyn's call," I said, noting that Marilyn's choice of the word "interesting," which was hardly an endorsement of her candidacy for the non-existent position, had flown right over Courtnee's oblivious head.

"But right now, you are the receptionist. Which means there is no place for you in the newsroom. So stop moving furniture and go home and enjoy your Saturday."

"That isn't fair. Why should I have to apply when I'm already working here?"

I wanted to say that if I had my way, she wouldn't be working at the *Times,* but I restrained myself. Until we were able to pay a decent salary, Courtnee was, sadly, the biggest bang we could get for our buck.

"Courtnee, that's it. End of discussion. And don't be talking about it to the rest of the staff when you don't have the facts. I'll see you Monday."

There was a pout on her carefully made-up face, and her blue eyes were full of mutiny.

"Maybe I won't come in Monday. Maybe I'll be looking for another job."

"Oh? Are you thinking you'd like to go back to being a secretary at Himmel Technical College? As I recall that job didn't end well."

She glared at me but contented herself with saying, "Fine. I'm leaving. And maybe you'll see me Monday, and maybe you won't."

I gave myself a lot of credit for not calling, "I can only hope," after her as she stomped out of the office.

12

"So, what do you think?"

Coop had come over for one of our Saturday night binge watches. This time it was going to be *Mare of Easttown*, a profane, but very good series about a cop in a rundown town. I knew Coop would enjoy it. But first I wanted his thoughts on what I should do for the Sunday in the Park author program the next day.

"You haven't decided that yet? Nothing like leaving it to the last minute."

"It's not the last minute. It's almost twenty-four hours away. Besides it's not like I have to write a speech and I waited until now. I just have to read something that I've already written. I can't decide if I should do the prologue, or the first chapter of *Blood Moon Rising*. The prologue fits the time limit I've got, but I like the opening of the first chapter. It gives a good sense of who my lead character is."

"Why are you worried about it? You've done lots of readings."

"I know, but not on the same stage with Nora Fielding! I wish I wasn't going first. No one will listen to my reading, because everyone will be impatient to hear Nora."

"That's true. She's the big draw. The crowd might boo you right off the stage," he said.

"Oh, very nice. I'm looking for support and you diss me? Give me back that popcorn I just made for you."

"No, not the popcorn!" he said, clutching his bowl to his chest. "I misspoke. Of course everyone will want to hear you. You're Himmel's Agatha Christie, that's what Mrs. Schimelman told me when I stopped at the Elite yesterday. And I said to her, 'Mrs. Schimelman,' I said, 'Leah is better than Agatha Christie. In fact, she is probably the greatest mystery writer of all time. In fact—'"

"Okay, okay. Enough. So which should it be? Exciting prologue or get-to-know Jo Burke first chapter?"

"Go with the prologue. It's got a good hook and a nice tie-in to the middle of the book. You'll probably convert everyone there into Jo Burke fans. Seriously, I'm really proud of you, Leah, and the great job you've done with everything on your plate—the books, the paper, raising our son, Miguel."

I laughed and said, "Thank you. That's a very nice thing to say. I'm very proud of all you've done too. Everyone should have a Coop in their lives. I'm glad you're in mine."

He put the popcorn bowl down to lean over and kiss me, and after a while, we decided to binge watch *Mare of Easttown* on another night.

The next day was perfect weather for an outdoor event, sunny and warm.

Nora did a reading from one of her most popular books. As expected, everyone loved it and peppered her with so many questions that Marty Angstrom, the emcee for the event, had to remind the audience that there was another author on the program (that would be me).

When I finished reading the prologue of my first book, there weren't as many questions as there had been for Nora, but there were enough that I felt I'd made a decent showing.

"Leah, when is your next book coming out?"

"January."

"What's it about?"

"A body is found in the wall of an old house when new owners are doing major renovations. DNA reveals it to be the wife of the former homeowner. The issue is the wife—or someone who seemed to be the wife—was buried in the family plot fifteen years earlier. So why is her body hidden in the wall, and who is buried in the cemetery?"

There was a satisfying round of ohhhs in response to the summary.

"What's the name of the book?"

"*If Walls Could Talk*," I said.

"Hey, Leah! What about the one after that? When's that coming out?"

I laughed.

"Now you sound like my publisher. It won't hit until about a year from now, but I actually have an idea for the plot already. Which is unusual for me."

"What's that one about?"

"It's way too early to say. I need to find a microbiologist to spend some quality time with, so I can decide if the murder weapon I want to use is possible in real life."

"Oh, come on, can't you tell us more than that?"

"No, I really can't, mostly because I don't know much more than that yet."

Marty Angstrom took over at that point.

"Okay, everyone. Thanks for coming this afternoon. And thank you, Nora and Leah, it's been a real good program. How about a big Himmel hand for the ladies?"

As the applause died down, Marty said, "Don't forget we got some refreshments over on the picnic tables, there. And Leah and Nora are sticking around for a while, so you can do a little one to one chatting with them."

As I walked off the bandstand, Peter Sullivan, one of the board members for the *Times,* walked toward me.

"Peter, hi! Thanks for coming."

"You're very welcome. I'm on the Himmel Parks and Recreation board, so I try to come to all the events the department puts on. But I had an added incentive this time, the opportunity to support two of my fellow board members, you and Norah," he said.

Peter's voice is deep and rich and sort of wraps around you when he's speaking. He's in his early seventies, with a lean and fit build. His gray hair and well-trimmed beard give him a very distinguished look, but he has a nice smile that makes him very approachable.

"Well, I'm glad you made it."

"You both did a marvelous job. I've read your first book, Leah. I'm looking forward to your second, and I'm here to offer my services for your third," he said.

That took me by surprise. I wasn't sure what to say. Sometimes people volunteer to be early readers, to give feedback on a plot in progress. I haven't ever taken advantage of an offer though, because my works in progress are always such a hot mess. Feedback before I go through that really ugly first version isn't much help, because so much of what anyone might read at that point is going to get thrown out anyway. But I didn't want to offend Peter. I didn't know him very well, and I might need his support if Spencer became a serious candidate for the director job at the *Times* nonprofit.

"Oh, wow, that's very nice of you. But I'm really just starting to think about the third one. I won't be doing any writing on it for quite a while. And after I find a microbiologist to answer some questions, I might have to throw out the whole plot idea anyway."

"But that's exactly where I can help. My doctorate is in microbiology. Before I worked at Kelmar Pharmaceuticals, I was a professor at Buckner College in Alabama."

"You're kidding! I had the impression you were a lifer at Kelmar. I had no idea you were ever a professor."

"It was only for a few years some forty-odd years ago. I enjoyed working with students, but academia wasn't for me. I started at Kelmar in direct research. When I became Director of Microbiology I got away from the hands-on aspect of being a microbiologist. But I still keep up with the field. So if my qualifications fit your needs, I think it would be great fun to serve as a consultant for your book."

"Do you know much about *naegleria fowleri*?"

"A fair amount. I collaborated on a paper when I was at Buckner. And I've kept up with the research. It's a fascinating amoeba. Am I right in assuming that it's going to be your murder weapon?

"If I can make it work, yes."

"I'm at your disposal if you like."

Sometimes good luck does just drop in your lap.

"Thank you so much, Peter! I'll definitely take you up on that," I said.

"Marvelous. Now, this isn't a *quid pro quo*—I still want to serve as your *naegleria* resource—but if you have the time, I'd appreciate a little help in return."

"Sure. What can I do for you?"

"I'd like to get your thoughts on a manuscript of mine."

And sometimes, good luck comes with a price tag.

I hate it when people ask me to look at something they've written. If it's good, no problem. But if it isn't—and lots of times it's not—it's really hard to deliver an honest assessment. For most of us, writing a book is really hard. No matter how it comes out—good, bad, or mediocre—the person who wrote it put their whole self into it. I've had too many soul-crushing rejections myself to want to deliver a negative review to anyone else.

"Mmm. Well, I don't have any kind of scientific background, so I might not be—"

"No, no it's not a nonfiction book. It's a historical mystery set during the Peshtigo fire here in Wisconsin in 1871. I'm not quite finished with my manuscript yet, but I'd take it as a great kindness if you'd take a look at it when I am."

He was being so nice, I felt guilty for my reluctance to read his story. Especially when he'd volunteered to help me with mine.

"If you can wait until I wrap up the revisions and edits for my second book, which should be in the next six weeks or so, then yes. I can read your manuscript."

"Wonderful! Thank you. Now, how soon would you like to consult on your newest book?"

"Whatever fits into your schedule, but the sooner the better. If *naegleria fowleri* won't work as the murder weapon, I'll have to come up with something else pretty fast."

"How about a first meeting tomorrow for coffee?"

"Works for me. 8:30 at the Elite?"

"I look forward to it."

13

The next morning when I walked into the Elite Cafe, the owner, Clara Schimelman greeted me.

"Leah, your friend Peter, he is already here. I sit him at the back table. He only wants coffee. No carbs, he says. I tell him, you're a good-looking man, but too skinny. But you, you want a chai and an apple walnut muffin, yah?"

"Yes, please. It's scary how well you know me, Mrs. Schimelman. That muffin smell is driving me mad."

"You sit, I bring to your table."

I'd picked what is usually a good meet-up time at the Elite, when early morning coffee goers have left, and mid-morning coffee breakers haven't yet arrived so it's pretty quiet and easy to talk. The squeaks as I walked across the slightly tilted wooden floor alerted Peter to my approach. He looked up from his phone and smiled.

"Good morning. I've done a little refresher reading on *naegleria fowleri* so I'm ready to answer all your questions. The coffee here is very good. Aren't you having any?" he asked, noticing my empty hands as I sat down.

"Hi, Peter. I'm having a chai instead. And a muffin. I can't believe Mrs. Schimelman let you get away with just coffee."

"I'm cutting down on carbs and sugars."

"Yeah, me, too. Soon. Very soon."

"Well, the low carb life is my wife's idea. But I promised I'd give it a good try. So, what would you like to know about *naegleria?*"

"I'm not sure yet, actually. How about if I give you a big picture rundown on the plot, so you know how and why I want to use *naegleria* in the story. Though first I need to ask you to keep the plot to yourself for now. I heard a cautionary tale from another writer, and it's made me a little wary."

I shared Nora's story of plot theft.

"I hope you don't think that I—" he began, sounding a little annoyed with me, which I definitely didn't want.

"Oh, no, it's not that. I've just become a little paranoid after talking to Nora. Once I figure the story out enough to give a reasonably detailed summary to my publisher, they'll get a description out to promote presales, and you can shout the plot summary out to the world. Actually at that point I hope you do. It will help with preorders," I said with a grin.

"Then I'll certainly share the story—sans spoilers—far and wide once you give me the word."

"Great! Okay, so my killer is a man who is having an affair. He wants to be rid of his wife, but it's her money that's putting him through graduate school. If he divorces her, the money dries up. But if he kills her, he can collect on the insurance policy she has. He's been thinking about the murder for a while, trying to figure out how to commit it without getting caught. If her death appears suspicious, he knows he'll be the prime suspect. Then an outbreak of bacterial meningitis hits the campus in the rural area where they live. And the killer suddenly sees an opportunity."

"Ah, I see. The symptoms caused by *naegleri*a are very similar to the symptoms of meningitis. So you're thinking that your killer will use the meningitis outbreak as cover for killing his wife, is that right?"

"Exactly."

"That's a very intriguing premise. The disease caused by the amoeba, primary amoebic meningoencephalitis, is commonly known as PAM. There's no effective treatment for it. It's fatal 99% of the time. But the occurrence of PAM is quite rare. Most often the *naegleria* is picked up from swimming in a pool or lake in a warm climate. There have been a few occurrences from water parks as well because of water improperly treated. But how is your killer going to put his wife in contact with it?"

"Right now I'm thinking that he's a lab assistant at the local college. He's working for two professors doing research on *naegleria* for an academic paper. That would give him access to the amoeba. Plus, he'll know lab protocols and be able to conceal his theft. Is that even possible? I mean that he'd be able to get the *naegleria* out of the lab without getting caught?"

"Oh yes, definitely if he worked in the lab. But how are you going to get the *naegleria* into the wife? The only way the amoeba causes PAM is by getting into the nasal passages. It uses them as a highway to the brain, as it were, where it then proceeds to destroy it."

"I'm going to have his wife be someone who regularly uses a neti pot. That's one of the little teapot-looking things with a long straight spout. You fill it with distilled salt water, tilt your head sideways, and let the water run through one side of your nose and out the other. People use it to help rinse out allergens or to clear out the nose during a cold. My killer can put the amoeba in the distilled water his wife uses for her neti pot."

"That's good. Very good. But I do see a possible problem."

"Share, please."

"It's true that symptoms of meningitis and PAM are very similar. But an autopsy of the victim would show the real cause of death was *naegleria* not meningitis."

"Yes, it would. But that's where the meningitis outbreak will help. My rural hospital and its staff will be overrun with meningitis cases. People are dying, others are critically ill. When my killer brings his wife to the ER with symptoms that mimic meningitis, she dies shortly after admission, apparently from the same illness that has killed a dozen other people. The coroner decides there's no need for an autopsy when the cause of death is so obvious, and the medical community resources are stretched to the max. I checked with the local medical examiner, and she said the scenario was possible in the middle of an outbreak."

"Ah. I see I'm not the only expert witness you're turning to. And here I thought I was getting the exclusive inside story on the new Jo Burke mystery."

"Oh, but you are," I said. "Connie Crowley, she's the medical examiner, would only answer my question on condition that it wasn't a spoiler for the plot. She doesn't want to know what the book's about, so I just asked her to give me some instances when an autopsy wouldn't be done. You're my one and only for this book, Peter."

At that moment Mrs. Schimelman arrived with my chai and muffin, and a few words of advice for Peter.

"You sure you don't want apple walnut muffin? They are extra good today."

He shook his head sadly. "I promised Adele I'd stick with the low carb plan for a week. I really can't."

"I like a man who keeps his promise. Okay, I leave you alone. But you bring your wife next time, I have a talk with her. A man needs a little sugar in his life, right?"

"You're a temptress, Mrs. Schimelman," he said.

She pulled the ever-present white tea towel off her ample shoulders and flicked it at him lightly.

"You don't know the half of it," she said and walked away shaking with laughter.

"She's quite a character," he said.

"You don't know the half of it," I said, mimicking Mrs. Schimelman's German accent.

We both grinned.

His watch dinged and he paused to look at it.

"Oh, I'm sorry to cut this short, Leah. But speaking of Adele, that's a text from her. She can't find her glasses, so she can't find her keys, so I need to go home and rescue her. Do you have a homework assignment for me? Are there some specific things you'd like to know?"

"Yes. I've got a list on my phone—where does a lab get *naegleria* to use in research, how would you have to transport it, how long does it stay alive, is it dangerous to handle, and lots of other things. They won't all actually turn up in the book, but I like to have as much background as I can get. You never know what might inspire a good clue or twist. Can I text the list to you, and then we'll meet up again when you've had a chance to look it over?"

"Of course. Are you free to meet next Monday? I've got some things in the hopper this week, and that will give me enough time to finish them up and also get some answers for you."

"Sure, that's fine."

"I'll call you to set a time," he said.

14

Talking with Peter had gotten me excited about the *naegleria* plot and I spent most of Monday and Tuesday refining my ideas and doing some preliminary character sketches. On Tuesday evening I called Nora Fielding.

"Hello, Leah. Have you recovered from our moment in the spotlight on Sunday? I always have to work myself up for appearances like that."

"You mean you get nervous? You must have done readings a thousand times," I said, surprised.

"Not nervous, really. But as a member of introvert nation, I'd always rather be home in my pajamas."

"But you seemed to really enjoy the event."

"Oh, I did. I should have added that I'm also a situational extrovert. When called upon I unpack my outgoing personality for the evening, but unlike Cinderella, I'm always ready to leave the ball before midnight."

I laughed.

"Well, no one would have known that."

"Years of practice, my dear. But what's on your mind?"

"First, I met with Peter Sullivan on Sunday. Did you know he used to be a microbiologist? He's now my resident expert on all things *naegleria fowleri*. Do you have a minute to give me your reaction to what I've come up with so far?"

"I have more than a minute, and I'm all ears."

I repeated the loose plot line I'd shared with Peter.

"I love the neti pot angle. But how does the killer get the *naegleria fowleri*? I assume he can't just order it up from the Brain Killing Amoeba Store."

"That's the great thing about Peter. He not only knows about the amoeba, but he also knows how lab protocols work, and he'll be able to help me figure out how my killer/lab assistant gets the amoeba out of the lab without pointing suspicion at himself. I'm feeling pretty good about book three already."

"So you should. I think you've got a really good idea to work with."

"Thanks, Nora! Validation from you means a lot to me."

"I cannot believe you didn't tell me," Miguel said without preamble.

I had just joined him for a Wednesday morning chai latte at Woke, the coffee shop across the street from the *Times*. Although its full name is Wide Awake and Woke Coffee Shop, most people just call it Woke, or the Woke. The coffee is so good, the staff is so friendly, and the atmosphere is so laid back that it draws an eclectic crowd, whether they're personally "woke" or not.

"Didn't tell you what? What are you talking about?"

"I had to find out from Courtnee that your mother and Paul Karr broke up! I am shocked."

"Are you shocked that they broke up—which by the way, they didn't. Mom insists they're on a break—or that I didn't tell you about it?"

"Both. But why? What has happened?"

After I gave him my mother's explanation, Miguel said, "Ah, of course. Carol, she has an adventuring spirit. Paul, he is a good man, but he does not. Maybe she is worried that when he retires, he will do like some men do: the morning coffee with the boys, the weather channel afternoons, the evening TV sports. Carol, she needs more. But Paul, he loves her very much. I will monitor the situation and see if they need my help. If so, I will be there. Very subtly, of course. Now, what is happening with your book plotting?"

"I've been talking to Peter Sullivan, and he's going to help me work out the details of the murder."

As I said that, my words fell into one of those weird lulls in conversation that happen sometimes. One second everyone is talking, the next no one is. Except me, this time. The woman seated at the next table turned to stare.

"I'm talking about the plot for a book," I felt compelled to say. "Not an actual murder."

She nodded but I wasn't sure I had convinced her.

By then the conversational buzz had returned to full volume, but I still leaned in closer to Miguel for the rest of what I had to say.

"Nora has been really helpful, too. It feels strange, but good, that I can call up a famous writer and have her talk to me like I'm a real author, too."

Miguel shook his head.

"You have the imposter syndrome, *chica*. You *are* a 'real author.' Maybe not so famous as Nora, but you are just as good. Own your excellence!"

I smiled at his totally biased opinion.

"Thanks for your faith in me. But you do know what I mean, don't you? Nora is so good, it's pretty intimidating. I'm afraid that I won't measure up to her standards."

"No. It is your own standards you don't measure up to because you are too hard on yourself. You are a good storyteller. After you've been writing mysteries as long as Nora has, you'll be the author that some new writer is afraid of," he said.

"Maybe so. But that day is a long way off."

I was ready to leave but then I realized I hadn't told Miguel about Spencer. I was a little surprised that Courtnee hadn't served up that information along with the news about my mother and Paul. But it wouldn't be long before she did. I wanted Miguel to have the facts to counteract her speculation. When I finished his face registered alarm.

"Don't look so worried," I said.

"But Spencer, he can turn on the charm and fool people."

"He hasn't put an application in. And there's a good chance it's Marilyn's dream, not his. But even if he does and he gets an interview, there are too many smart people on the board to be taken in by him. Unless he found Jesus in rehab—this time he went to a Catholic-affiliated center, not a secular one—he'll come across like the jackass he is, clean and sober or not. I'm not worried." I was, a little, but no need to burden Miguel with my paranoia.

"That is true," he said. "Then I will not worry either. It puts lines in the face."

"And your face is way too handsome for that. Listen, I got my first round of edits on my current book from my editor. I need to look them over and get the revisions back to her. So, I'll see you later."

15

And I did fully intend to get right on the revisions from my editor. But the gray morning skies had let loose with the rain they'd been holding. I dashed across the street as fast as I could, but I still got wet enough to leave a trail of puddles on my front stairs as I ran up to my apartment.

I stripped off my soggy shoes and damp jeans and put on sweats and slippers. When I walked into the living room it felt cold, so I switched on the fireplace. Then I turned on my favorite rainy-day playlist, snuggled into the corner window seat spot with Sam, my laptop, and a blanket, and took a minute to watch the rain come down before starting work.

I woke up with a start as Sam jumped off my lap. A glance at my watch told me that I'd been in la-la-land for over an hour. I yawned and tried to shake off the coma-like sleep I'd fallen into. I opened my laptop, thinking that before I dove into edits that would require focused attention, I'd check out my book email account. That only requires interest and a polite response.

I don't get a ton of email from readers, but I usually get some every day or so. When a reader takes the time to write to me, I like to answer as soon as I can. Maybe that would be different if I received hundreds of emails a day, but for now answering them within a day or so is very do-able.

The first email, as happens sometimes, turned out to be a rather harsh critique of my first attempt at fiction, *Blood Moon Rising*. The reader found the plot boring, the character development nonexistent, and suggested that I should seek an immediate career change, possibly something in fast food. He didn't sign his name, and his email identified him only as FisherKing97. On the plus side, he'd taken the one-to-one approach to criticism, rather than posting it online for all the world to see, like most harsh critics do.

I resisted the urge to defend myself and my characters. There's no point. Every book isn't for everybody. I thanked FisherKing97 for his frank assessment of my work and suggested that he might want to hop off the Jo Burke train, because it wasn't likely that the series would meet his needs—or standards.

The next email couldn't have been more different. I read it out loud to Sam.

"Dear Leah,

I hope this letter finds you well. My name is Sharla, and I am one of your biggest fans.

From the moment I picked up Blood Moon Rising, I was utterly captivated. Your ability to weave an intricate plot with such vivid, lifelike characters is nothing short of magical. I feel such a connection to your characters, it's like they're actually friends of mine, making the nights a little less lonely for me.

I'm counting down the days until your next book comes out and I can dive back into Jo's world. You have touched my life in ways that words cannot fully express. Please continue to write, to create, to inspire. I will be here, ready to devour every word you pen.

With ardent admiration,

Sharla

"So, take that FisherKing97," I said. "What do you think, Sam? Are you impressed?"

In answer he jumped down and walked toward the kitchen, turning once to indicate I should follow. When I did not immediately leap up, he meowed loudly and moved to stand in front of his empty food dish.

"I see that it's true, Sam. Just like a prophet, a writer is not without honor save in her own country and in her own house."

His response was to meow loudly until I filled his dish.

After lunch I moved to the desk in my office to avoid the siren song of the window seat. When I finished with the edits I decided to take a break and stretch my legs by going downstairs to the *Times* office to see if anything was happening. As I walked through the reception area, Courtnee was on the office phone instead of her cell phone, an unusual but gratifying sight. She appeared to be so immersed in her customer service duties that she didn't notice me when I walked by. I suspected her real reason for ignoring me was that she was punishing me for crushing her career dreams on Saturday. I found the blow easy to withstand.

Troy Patterson, our other full-time reporter, was the only one in the newsroom.

"Hey, Troy what's happening?"

"Hi, Leah. The Rotary Club president is mad at us because I told them we don't have anyone to cover their lunch speaker tomorrow. I can't because I've got an interview at noon, and Miguel is shooting photos at the high school. Maggie has a dentist appointment, and none of the stringers are available. Roger yelled at me for a long time."

Troy is not long out of college. With his sandy-colored, side-parted hair, wire-rimmed glasses and slender frame, he still looks like the captain of the high school chess club.

"Well, Roger's an excitable boy. I suppose I could go cover it. Who's the speaker and what's the topic?"

"It's Roger. He's talking about funeral planning."

"On second thought, I think I'm busy, too. In fact, I'm heading upstairs right now to do some more work. I wouldn't worry too much about Roger, Troy. We can't cover everything with the staff we have. And he'll get over it. I'll see you later."

"Oh, also, some lady came in to see you this morning when you were at Woke. She didn't want to wait, so I asked for her name and number so you could call her back, but she said she'd come by later."

"That's kind of odd. What did she look like?"

"Tall, with long, really shiny dark hair. About forty, I'd say. She was pretty," he added.

"Doesn't sound familiar. Okay, well, carry on, Troy. I'll catch you later."

Back upstairs with my edits completed, I moved on to working on ideas for book three. I grabbed a yellow legal pad and a pencil, my favorite thinking tools, and returned to my window seat corner. Sam soon joined me, nestling himself against me. Rain began to pelt the windows again. I looked down at the street and saw people scurrying for the nearest building to ride out the storm, feeling both snug and a little smug in my third-floor aerie. Then I settled in to writing up questions and thinking through my murder scenario in fuller detail. I'd already texted Peter my original questions, but I wanted to make good use of our next meeting on Monday to get as many points covered as I could. I was so absorbed in my task that I didn't hear the faint knock on my office door until Sam jumped down and headed in that direction. He is a most excellent watch cat.

I have two sets of stairs that lead to my place. The back stairs come up from the back entrance to the *Times* building. I use them most often because I usually park my car in the back parking lot. You can access the front stairs from a door on the street. It's meant to be a private entrance, but because of a quirk in the original building, inside the tiny entryway there's also a door on the east wall that opens into the reception area for the *Times*. The front stairs aren't for public use. However Courtnee, when she wants to annoy me, often sends visitors through that door in reception and up the stairs to my office, rather than calling me downstairs to meet them.

The knock on my office door was repeated, this time louder.

"Yes, can I help you?" I opened the door to a woman who matched Troy's description of my earlier visitor.

"Hello. I'm Marguerite Pierce. Hannah Vining's sister. I need to talk to you."

16

For a moment I was nonplussed. Hannah's sister had said in her email that she lived in Australia. I stared at her stupidly.

"I'm Marguerite," she repeated. "I emailed you about my sister."

"Yes, of course, yes. I'm just really surprised to see you. I thought you lived in Australia."

"I do," she said. Droplets of water were falling from her hair and onto her face. She shook her head impatiently, sending sprinkles flying everywhere, including on me.

"Oh, I'm so sorry," she said. "And I apologize even more for showing up on your doorstep like this. I know it's a big intrusion. But I have a big problem. When I got your second email, I booked my flight immediately. I knew that I couldn't convince you to help unless I made the case face to face. So I've just traveled ten thousand miles in twenty-five hours in the hope that you'll give me just a few minutes of your time. Please."

How could I turn her away?

"Yes, sure. Come in. Let me get you a towel to dry off."

"Thank you so much."

As she towel-dried her hair in the bathroom, I hung her dripping coat over the shower rod.

"Come into the living room, won't you?"

As we entered I pointed her to the sofa.

"Please, sit down. Would you like something to drink?"

"A cup of tea if you have any would be wonderful," she said.

As I boiled the water, Sam introduced himself to Marguerite. I'm not one of those people who have a cupboard or fridge filled with healthy snacks to offer. And unless my mother has stopped by recently I don't have any baked goods on hand, either. There was a bag of Cool Ranch Doritos in a drawer, but they'd been there a while. Even to my casual hostessing ways, that didn't seem appropriate for the occasion. I gave up the quest and took the tea to Marguerite. I settled on the rocking chair opposite her.

"Thank you so much," she said, raising the cup to her lips.

"You're welcome. After the trip you just made, a cup of tea and a hearing is the least I can do. But Marguerite, it's only fair to say that the least I can do is also the most I can do. The reasons I gave for turning you down in my email are still there. I'm finishing one book, planning another, and in the final months of a major shift at the newspaper I co-own. I can't add anything extra to my plate right now."

"And you also think that my sister killed her lover," she said.

"I'm afraid I do."

"Well, you've got it wrong. The jury got it wrong, everyone got it wrong. Hannah loved Matthew. She always has. Ever since they met in high school when we lived in Galen. She could never kill him."

"Well, someone did, Marguerite. And the case the police and prosecutor built points pretty damningly at your sister."

"I know it does. But she's not the only one who has a reason to want Matthew dead. But once the police found out she had a relationship with Matthew, that was it. They decided she was the one who killed him."

"From what I've read, there was a little more to it than that. Hannah is an experienced herbalist, she had her own shop, she kept aconite there. She knew that Matthew drank a special wellness tea every day—one that she compounded especially for him. She had easy access to his cabin. It would be very simple for her to go there, put aconite in the tea, and wait, knowing that Matthew would drink it and die. She knew enough about the properties of aconite to know that once ingested, it can mimic the symptoms of a heart attack. It's also something that isn't routinely screened for during an autopsy. It was a very well-planned murder."

"But not by Hannah. She didn't do it. I know she didn't. And I will never stop feeling guilty that because of my pregnancy, I couldn't be here to help her. Hannah went through everything alone." Marguerite paused as she blinked away tears.

"How is your baby doing? She's home, right?"

"Yes, she is. She's doing well now, but she's still so tiny. This trip is the first time I haven't been with her every day since the beginning. My husband is a pediatrician, and I know he can take as good care of her—probably better—than I can. But it was so hard to leave her. I'm going back home tomorrow. I can't bear to be away longer. But I had to come. I had to make you understand."

"What? You traveled twenty-five hours straight just to come and see me for an hour?"

"You, and Hannah. I saw her this morning. Now I'm here to beg you to reconsider and help my sister. I'm even more worried about her now than I was before I visited her in prison."

She wasn't able to hold back the tears this time. I got up to get her some tissues, feeling like the worst person in the world as she sobbed her heart out.

I gave her time to get the tears out, wipe her eyes, and blow her nose. Then I said gently, "Marguerite, there are private investigators who could help."

She answered in a voice flattened by despair.

"I called two of them. The first one said he didn't have time. The other one said proving Hannah was innocent would be like skating uphill, and he wasn't interested."

She reached inside her purse, pulled out her phone, and tapped on an app. When she passed the phone to me, it was open to a collection of photographs.

"You've probably only seen the awful photos of Hannah the media kept running—looking so grim-faced, her hair all pulled back tight, her mouth in a straight line. But my sister is a vibrant, kind, beautiful woman. Look at these photos. Tell me this little girl, this teenager, this woman isn't worth helping."

In the first picture, a little girl with fiery red hair was dressed in a frilly green satin dress with a matching bonnet and on her feet were tap shoes—she was obviously ready for a dance recital. Her arm was draped protectively across the shoulder of a smaller girl in a pink dress, who looked up at her with an expression of pure adoration. Marguerite. It reminded me of the way Lacey used to look at me when she was small.

Another photo showed a teenage Hannah at Lake Michigan, her face alight with laughter as she and her little sister built a sandcastle on the shore. The next photo was Hannah as an adult. Her exuberant red curls had been tamed into a soft knot at the nape of her neck, with a few tendrils escaping. She wore an ivory wedding dress and held the hand of a little girl wearing a pretty blue dress. The smile on the little girl's face was wide and infectious, and her large brown eyes shone with happiness.

"That's Hannah and her daughter Olivia at the wedding. Hannah adopted her right after she and Joel married. When she told me that they were engaged, she said it was the best two for one deal she could imagine—a husband and a daughter at the same time."

"How is Olivia doing with the situation?"

"I don't know. We used to FaceTime and text fairly often, but after Hannah was arrested, Joel, Hannah's husband, said he didn't want me contacting Olivia, that it would be too upsetting. I didn't want to put Olivia in the middle, so I honored his decision. I called him when I got here, but he said I couldn't see Olivia. He's very angry and very bitter."

"Does he let Olivia see Hannah?"

"Hannah doesn't want her to come to the prison. She writes to Olivia, but she never gets an answer. That's crushed her. I think Joel might have the housekeeper intercept Hannah's letters. He's away a lot during the week for work. It's so cruel of him, to cut her off from her mother. Olivia was only six when her birth mother died. Now she's lost Hannah, and in a way she's lost Joel, too. He's too angry to be the kind of parent she needs right now."

Marguerite was hitting all my buttons. When my sister Annie died in a fire, I thought it was my fault. I was Annie's older sister. I should have saved her. My mother tried to convince me that wasn't true, but it's how I felt. When my father left, I was sure he blamed me for Annie's death too, and that was why he went away. It took some serious therapy as an adult to help me see that I had abandonment issues that had affected my decisions my whole life. To be honest, they still do. You can know something with the logical part of your brain, but still not be able to overcome a deep-rooted emotional response.

"Marguerite, I empathize with you more than you know. But I still don't think I can—"

"No. Don't say it. Don't say you won't help. Leah, I'm speaking as a psychologist, not as a sister when I say this. Hannah is losing the will to live. She's in prison serving life for a murder she didn't commit. If she doesn't get some hope injected into her life, she's going to give up, and my sister could literally die."

That seemed a little melodramatic to me, and my skepticism must have shown on my face.

"When a person reaches the lowest ebb of despair, the body can follow suit. My sister isn't there yet, but she's on the path. Reading your book I felt such an intense connection to you. You moved heaven and earth to find out why your sister Lacey died."

"But I wasn't trying to prove that Lacey was guilty or innocent of anything when I started. I just had to know what had really happened."

"That's what I'm asking you to do for *my* sister. Just start from scratch without any assumptions. If you do, I know you'll find the true answers. You won't settle for the convenient ones like the police did."

She stopped then. I could see that she was literally holding her breath waiting for me to respond. Her love and her loyalty were palpable in the room. The weight of my own guilt and regrets over failing my sisters pressed down on me as well.

"All right. I'll do it. But you have to understand that this might not turn out the way you want it to."

I had barely finished speaking when she leaped from the sofa and hugged me, crying a little again. Thinking of my own sisters, I may have shed a few tears of my own.

17

Marguerite returned to see me the next afternoon. She'd visited Hannah's attorney and had her draw up a waiver of attorney-client privilege for Hannah to sign. She'd then faxed the form to the prison for Hannah's signature and made the arrangements for me to see Hannah on Friday.

"Marguerite, how did you get that much done in less than twenty-four hours?"

"I had to. I've got a flight out tonight. I'm on my way to the airport now. And I feel so much better than I did when I arrived two days ago."

She grabbed my hand.

"What you're doing, Leah, it means everything to me. I told my husband Thomas when I called him last night that if we hadn't already named Alice for his mother, we'd call our baby Leah. Actually, maybe I'll call her that anyway," she said and smiled.

Her mood was ten times lighter than it had been the day before. The Eeyore in me felt the need to ground her a bit more in what the reality was likely to be.

"Marguerite, remember what I said yesterday. This may not have a happily ever after ending. When I've given it my best shot, we may be exactly where we are right now. I don't want to give you false hope."

"You're not. What you're giving me is a possibility, when before there was none. I understand that nothing is guaranteed. But please, let me feel just a little joy in the moment, knowing that you're going to try. Okay?"

"Okay."

She hugged me hard, and then she was gone, as suddenly as she had arrived on my doorstep.

The next morning I made the two-hour drive to the women's correctional facility in Fond du Lac. The visiting room was clean and bright with large windows that let in natural light and there were murals on the walls of peaceful nature scenes. I'd been expecting something grimmer, but then I noticed the chairs and tables were bolted to the floor, security cameras were trained on the visitors and inmates, and we were all under the watchful eyes of stern-faced guards.

As the inmates filed in, visitors were allowed a brief moment of physical contact with their friend or family member before they took seats across the table from each other.

Hannah was the last person to enter. I stood up from the table I'd claimed on the far side of the room and raised my hand to get her attention. She walked toward me slowly. Her red curls were limp and dull. There were dark hollows under her eyes, and she was so thin her jail uniform hung off her frame.

I offered her my hand to shake. She seemed surprised, and her grip was listless, but she took my hand in hers briefly.

"Hannah, hi, I'm Leah Nash. Thanks for seeing me."

I paused to give her a chance to comment, but she just looked at me with eyes that held no spark.

"I've read the news accounts of your case, and of course talked to your sister, but I'd like to go over some things with you," I said.

I waited for her to nod or tell me that she was fine with that. She said nothing, so I just started in at the beginning.

"I know that you and Matthew were together in high school. I understand that you broke up with him when your family moved away from Galen. And—"

"No."

"You weren't a couple? Or you didn't break up?"

"I wasn't the one who broke things off. Matthew was. We got in a fight because he said if I loved him, I would refuse to move. That I could stay at the farm with his family. He wouldn't listen when I told him I couldn't do that, my parents wouldn't allow it. But I'd come back to visit in the summer. He got angry. Then so did I. We both said some harsh things and he said it was over. Later, after we were settled in Atlanta, I wrote to him. He didn't answer. I heard from friends that he was with Ellen. I never heard from Matthew again."

Her voice was emotionless. I tried to shake her up a little by jumping right into the affair as the motive for murder to see if I could get a reaction out of her.

"Actually you did hear from him again, right? After you moved back to Galen to take care of your mother, you started an affair with him. One that he ended. So basically, he rejected you twice. Is that right?"

"No! That's not what happened."

This time there was a little life in her answer, so I kept prodding.

"The prosecution argued, and the jury accepted that you were furious at being rejected when Matthew decided to stay with his wife. Are you saying that Matthew didn't choose to go back to his wife?"

"What I'm saying is that we both decided to end our affair. Matt didn't reject me. We rejected each other if you want to put it that way."

"Why?"

"I told the police all that. It didn't matter."

"Tell me, please. I promised Marguerite I'd do my best to help you. I can't do that if you won't talk to me."

"Marguerite needs to focus on her baby and her life with Thomas. I don't want her worrying about me. It's too late for that."

"This poor me attitude isn't helping you, Hannah. Marguerite reached out to me, a total stranger for help. And when I turned her down—twice—she traveled thousands of miles to convince me that I had to try. This isn't just about you. It's about Marguerite, too. She is doing everything she can to get you out of here. And she will never forgive herself if she fails. If you can't muster enough interest in your case for your own sake, you could at least try for your sister's sake—and your daughter's."

I surprised myself with the vehemence of my words. Obviously I identified with Marguerite more than I did with Hannah. I think I surprised Hannah, also.

"I am thinking about Marguerite. It's the only reason I agreed to see you when I know it won't do any good," she said, sounding slightly chastened. "And you have no idea how much time I've spent worrying about Olivia. But I'm never getting out of here. I have to face that fact, and so does Marguerite."

"It's not a fact. It's your belief. And maybe you're right. But if you care about the two of them, then let's get on with it and see what happens. I don't have Marguerite's unwavering faith in you, but I'm willing to be convinced. If you want my help, you have it, as long as you tell me the truth. Do you want my help?"

She looked at me silently for a long minute. Then she nodded her head.

18

"Talk to me about you and Matthew. Start with when you first came back to Galen."

"My mother's health was declining, even before Dad died. After he passed, Marguerite and I realized one of us needed to be closer to our mother to watch out for her. But my sister has a husband and a career in Australia. It wasn't practical for her to move back to Wisconsin. My husband—ex-husband—Joel and I were able to make it work. He's a salesman for a paper company. As long as he was reasonably close to an airport, it didn't matter too much where he lived. I'd been working at an herbal apothecary and thinking about opening my own store. I could do that in Galen. So, we moved."

"How did your daughter feel about the move?"

"Olivia had spent part of her summers with my parents from the time Joel and I married. She already had friends here, so the transition wasn't that hard."

"Did you know that Matthew still lived in Galen when you made the decision?"

"Yes. But not because we were in touch. I lurk on the Galen High School alumni page, just to see what people are doing these days. Ellen, his wife, posts on it sometimes. That's how I knew."

"Were you looking forward to renewing your friendship when you came back?"

"No, I didn't feel any need to."

"Because you were still angry at him over your breakup?"

"Of course not. That was more than twenty years ago. He was married, I was married. We hadn't spoken in years. We didn't seek each other out."

"So then how did you reconnect?"

"About a year after opening Moonrise Apothecary, things were going fine. Then Mom had a stroke, a really bad one. She died within a week. It was a shock, because she'd been doing pretty well."

"And Matthew came to the funeral?"

"No. After the funeral, Marguerite went back to Australia. Joel went back on the road, and Olivia was busy with school and her friends. That's when I realized I'd been so focused on Mom and the store that I hadn't developed any close friendships. I felt very alone. It was a real low point for me."

"And that's when you met up with Matthew again?"

"Yes, but totally by accident. One day, he just walked into Moonrise. A friend of his had recommended a tea I make for stress relief and insomnia to him. I was at the register when he came in. We recognized each other immediately. We started talking and the years just fell away."

"And it was after that you started seeing each other?"

"Yes, but just as friends. Joel and I invited Ellen and Matt to dinner. The two guys got along well. Matt invited Joel to go fishing at his cabin, and then Joel started playing cards with Matt's poker group when he was in town."

"How about you and Ellen?"

"Ellen and I knew each other in high school, but we weren't close friends. It was the same when we saw each other again. We just didn't have much in common. We joined the same yoga class, and sometimes we'd go out for wine after. And occasionally she'd come to the store to pick up Matthew's tea, but that was about it."

"So when did your friendship with Matthew morph into a romantic relationship?"

"April of last year. Joel was traveling. Olivia was on a school trip. I was at a restaurant eating alone when Matt walked in. He was on his own because Ellen was at her sister's. I invited him to join me. We talked and laughed about the old days. He reminded me about the time a bunch of us were at his family's cabin for a beer party and got caught."

She paused then and smiled. It was the first time I'd seen her do that outside of the photos Marguerite had shown me.

"I reminded him that we never got to drink a single beer because his dad caught us before we could. But we both got grounded. Matt said he had a fridge full of Spotted Cow at the cabin." She paused.

"So the two of you went to the cabin?"

She nodded. "I knew it wasn't a good idea. I couldn't stop myself."

"And that's when the affair started?"

"Yes. Being with Matt, just the two of us, it made me feel like I was sixteen again. I knew what was going to happen that night, but I went anyway. I'm not proud of that."

"When did things end?"

"Last September, about a month before he died."

"Why did it end?"

"We woke up."

"What does that mean?"

"Ellen had a cancer scare. She'd been in remission and was doing well. But when she went for her annual checkup last year, the initial tests showed it had come back. She fell apart. I guess most people would. It turned out to be a false positive, but it changed things all the same."

"Why?"

"Matt and I had to face reality. We'd been acting like we were both teenagers again with no one to think about but ourselves. Then suddenly, Ellen needed Matt. And we had to talk about where we were going with things and what was possible and what wasn't."

She stopped talking. I waited and when she didn't go on, I prompted her.

"And you decided that it wasn't possible for you to be together?"

She sighed.

"Yes. This might be hard to understand, given what we did, but I loved Joel and Matt loved Ellen. What we felt for each other was the difference between loving and being 'in love.' But we'd been acting like we were the only two people in the world. Ellen's cancer scare brought us back to reality."

"How so?"

"We had to think not just about each other, but about each of us in relation to the other people in our lives. For me, it wasn't only about betraying Joel. There was Olivia, too. I love her so much. Leaving Joel would mean leaving her—I knew he'd be so hurt and angry he'd try to keep her from me. And I didn't want her caught in the middle of that. For Matt, well he had Ellen and almost twenty-five years of marriage to consider, as well as their son, and there was always the risk that her cancer would return. He and I both had choices to make, and we chose our families. I never saw Matthew alone again after the night we made our decision."

"What about the text you sent Matthew after you split up? The account of your trial in the paper said it was threatening."

"I didn't mean for it to be. It was just a week or two after we ended things. I was alone that night, depressed, and I'd had a little too much wine. I regretted sending it as soon as it was gone."

"What did it say? Do you remember?"

"Oh, yes. The police asked me about it enough times. *I saw you laughing with Ellen today. I hate that you're not suffering like I am. I think now I hate you, too.* They thought it meant that I wanted to kill Matt because he left me."

"Well, I can see how they'd interpret it that way."

"I can, too. But I told you I was a little drunk, and I was very depressed. And I guess I wanted Matt, who seemed to be so happy, to know that I was feeling miserable."

"Did you tell your husband about the affair?"

"No. Matt and I had been very careful, no one but us knew about it. I didn't see the point of hurting Joel. Matthew had said he wasn't going to tell Ellen either, for the same reason. But she testified at my trial that he had."

"Why do you think he did that?"

"Maybe he couldn't carry the guilt. Or maybe Ellen suspected something and asked him, and he didn't want to lie to her. I really don't know."

"Ellen's testimony was a little different from your story. She said that when Matthew confessed the affair, he told her you were very angry and upset that he'd left you."

"I was sad and hurting, but I wasn't angry. Why would I be? It was a mutual decision."

"Then was Ellen lying?"

"I don't know. I suppose Matt could have told her that to reassure her. Maybe he told her that I fought the breakup, but he chose her."

"Hannah, are you sure that no one else knew about the affair?"

"Yes. Absolutely," she said quickly. Perhaps too quickly?

"Is it possible that Joel had discovered your relationship with Matthew?"

"I don't see how. We were never together when Joel was in town. You're not thinking of blaming Joel for Matthew's death, are you?"

"I'm not blaming anyone at this point. But if you didn't kill Matthew, then someone else did. Any ideas?"

"None. Everyone liked Matt."

"Everyone? That's pretty unusual."

"Well, there was a woman who was pretty angry at him, but she had it all wrong. But that was all over months before he was killed."

"Hannah, I don't have many leads at the moment. I'll take anything. Who was the woman and why was she mad?"

"Her name is Kathy Boyle. She ran against Matt for the Board of Supervisors last year. Then the paper ran a story about her past as an adult film actor. Even though that was a long time before she came to Galen, it was a pretty big scandal. She withdrew from the race, but she accused Matthew of leaking the story to the paper."

"Did he?"

"No! Matt wouldn't do anything like that. I don't really think she was angry enough to kill him. Besides that situation was all over months before he died."

A voice over the loudspeaker warned us that visitation was over. Everyone began standing. We did, too.

"Hannah, I have to go, but I'll stay in touch."

"Okay," she said, turning to leave. She'd fallen back into the colorless tone of voice she'd used when we'd started the conversation. Then she turned back.

"Leah, I write to Olivia, but she's never answered. I know it's because she's still so hurt and so angry. And she has a right to be. But if you see her, will you tell her I love her more than anything, and I'm so, so sorry for the pain I've caused her? Tell her this is all my own fault. My fault," she repeated, before adding, "Say that I'm fine and that I—I—" she faltered for a minute. "Just tell her that, please."

19

I stopped by the sheriff's office to see Coop when I got back to town. When I'd told him about my plan to see Hannah, I could tell he wasn't in favor of me taking on Marguerite's request, though he hadn't come right out and said so. My report on the trip didn't change his mind.

"I know that Hannah's sister hit you where it hurts—the way you feel about losing your own sisters. But I think this is a lot to take on."

"It is. But Coop, Marguerite traveled thousands of miles to ask for my help, after I'd already turned her down twice. It's hard to say no in the face of that much determination. And after talking to Hannah myself, I see things a little differently now. I liked her, Coop. And it didn't feel like she was lying to me."

"I've met a few likable killers, Leah. That's how they almost got away with murder. You know, I ran into Kelsey Shepherd, the Trenton County sheriff yesterday. I've worked alongside her a few times, and I think she's pretty good at her job. I asked her about the case. She's confident that her detectives got it right, and so did the jury."

"I'm not saying they didn't. But the fact that she's standing up for them isn't necessarily a winning argument. I mean you didn't really expect her to say, 'You know what, I think we arrested the wrong person,' did you?"

"I expected her to give me a straight-on assessment and she did."

"Okay, but her detectives are human, right? They can make mistakes, be careless, even biased. What is it going to hurt to look at the case against Hannah with a fresh set of eyes?"

"You. I think it might hurt you. You're already under a lot of pressure—your writing, the *Times* transition, and now Marilyn trying to pull a fast one with Spencer. Do you really need to add a time-consuming and probably futile investigation to your list?"

"I can handle it. I'm just going to talk to a few people, ask a few questions, and see what I find. Maybe you're right, and there's nothing there. But maybe you're not."

"It's your call. I'm not trying to tell you what to do."

"That's good to know, because it kind of sounds like you are."

He sighed.

"No. I was just trying to help you think instead of feel your way to a decision on this. But I should know by now that you're going to do what you want to do."

"That's not fair. I don't *want* to do this. I know that logically I should just back away. And I tried to, you know that I did. But something is telling me that I need to at least take a closer look at it."

"Okay. Let's leave it alone for now. I have to get back to work."

"Yes. Let's. I do, too. I'll see you later."

It wasn't exactly a fight, but at the end of the conversation, neither one of us was very happy with the other.

It was after five o'clock when I opened the door to my place. Sam was waiting for me.

"Hi, honey, I'm home," I said, and scooped him up for a quick snuggle. "Are you hungry?"

I filled his food dish and grabbed a bottle of water. I took it, along with my trusty legal pad and a number two pencil, over to the window seat to write up my notes from my visit with Hannah. When I finished writing, I began tapping the edge of my paper, thinking about next steps.

Because the case was closed, I should be able to request the case file and get it from the sheriff's office without too many problems. Unless the custodian of records for the sheriff's office wanted to give me a hard time. Sometimes they do, but I'd cross that bridge when I came to it.

I put talking to Ellen Ferguson next on my list. She'd be in the best position to know of anyone besides Hannah who might have wanted to kill her husband. And, of course, there was also the fact that the number one killer-most-likely of a married person is the spouse. So Ellen herself was also on the suspect list.

Matthew Ferguson's political rival Kathy Boyle was my only real lead at the moment. I did some hunting in the *Galen Record* online archives and found the story that Hannah had referenced. It was pretty much as she'd outlined for me—Kathy Boyle had appeared in adult films thirty years ago. The local paper got hold of the story, and her budding political career died before it really got started. Was missing out on a seat on a county board really motive enough to kill someone? It seemed like weak sauce to me. The byline on the original story was Riley Dorner. I added her to the list of people to talk to.

Just then there was a light tap on my door, the knob turned, and Miguel poked his head in.

"Hey, Miguel. Come in and have a seat. What's going on?"

"I was on my way home, but I saw your car in the parking lot. You told me last night that you would let me know what happened with Hannah Vining. Why didn't you stop in the office when you got back? Did it go okay?"

"Yes, but it was a pretty long day. I'd just finished going over my notes when you knocked. Also, I had a bit of a tiff with Coop when I got back. He thinks it's not a good idea that I agreed to Marguerite's request."

"Oh, you know that I hate it when Mom and Dad argue. Do you want to go to Bonucci's for dinner and a consultation with Dr. Love?"

"Thanks, but I don't think we need therapy yet. Coop and I just don't see this the same way. Bonucci's sounds great, but I don't have the energy to drag myself out. Not even for a pepperoni pizza. I'll just grab a bowl of Honey Nut Cheerios."

"No! I will go and get the pizza and bring it back and we can talk. I want to help you!"

"I'd love your help, but I can't ask you to go out and get a pizza just because I'm too lazy to move. You were on your way home."

"I don't have anything to do tonight. It will be much more fun to be with you."

"I find it hard to believe that you have nothing to do on a Friday night. And I'm not feeling especially 'fun' right now. Still, the combination of you, Bonucci's pizza, and me not having to leave my place to enjoy both is irresistible. You talked me into it. Thanks."

As Miguel left, my phone rang.

"Leah, it's Peter Sullivan. Is this a bad time?"

"No, it's fine. What can I do for you?"

"I'm wondering if we can make our Monday morning meeting to talk about all things *naegleria fowleri* early. Very early, I'm afraid. I know it's dreadful to ask, but I forgot that Adele is having some dental work done and I need to take her to Madison for it. Is it possible to meet at 7:30 a.m.? We can do it at the coffee shop across the street from you, so you won't have far to go."

"Sure. I like getting an early start on the day."

"Marvelous. Thank you so much. I'll see you then."

20

"Mmm. Miguel, this looks and smells so good! It beats the heck out of cereal. Thank you for going to get it," I said as I opened the pizza box while Miguel got down plates and napkins.

"You are very welcome. Now, we will eat, and you will tell me everything."

We sat at the kitchen bar and, between mouthfuls of pizza, I filled Miguel in on my visit with Hannah. I finished up with Coop's less than enthusiastic take on my latest investigation. As expected, Dr Love zeroed in on that first.

"This is very easy. Coop, he's thinking that you already do not have much time to spend with him, and now you are taking on something else. He is just feeling a little sad that he will not be able to see you so much."

"If he is, he should look at his own schedule. He spends so much time working on his house he could have built the Taj Mahal by now."

"Is that really fair *chica*? There is only Coop and Dan working on it, and not full time. And this is only temporary. When his house is done, you will move in with him and I will move in here. Then we will all have all the time we need to spend where we want to."

"You never stop swinging, do you Miguel? I am not moving in with Coop, and you are not moving in here."

"Oh, I think you're wrong about that. One of my podcast listeners sent me a link to a YouTube video about the Law of Attraction. Do you know what that is?"

"Am I Carol Nash's daughter, and is she a charter member of the Oprah fan club? Yes, I know what the Law of Attraction is."

"Then I should tell you that every day I have been manifesting the thing that I want in my life by visualizing it. Watch me."

He sat up straight on his bar stool, breathed in deeply, let the breath out slowly and closed his eyes.

"Mig—"

He held up his hand to silence me, so I waited a minute until he opened his eyes.

"There. I visualized that you are visiting me here in my apartment. I am doing this three times a day. It is happening. Your resistance is futile in the face of my visualization powers. It is inevitable that this will soon be mine."

He made a sweeping gesture around the room with a satisfied smile on his face that made me laugh.

"All right, Oprah junior, we'll see how that works out for you."

"Ah, mock if you must. But soon I will invite you over to see what I have done with your office space," he said, unfazed by my teasing. "But now, I want to talk more about Hannah and her case. What are you going to do first, and how can I help?"

"I would love to have your help, if you have time."

"I will always have time for you. The investigative team of Nash and Santos will find out if Hannah is innocent or not. What are we going to do first?"

"I made a list while you went for pizza. Tomorrow we hit Galen—the Trenton County sheriff's office, the victim's wife Ellen Ferguson, Kathy Boyle who thinks Matthew ruined her election chances, and Riley Dorner the reporter who broke the Kathy Boyle story. Maybe see Joel Vining, too."

"Oh, but I can't go with you tomorrow. I am on call this weekend, I have to stay in the county. But let me take Riley Dorner. I know her a little. I can call her and see what she will tell me about how she got the story."

"Okay, but be careful, I don't want her writing a story about us looking at the Ferguson murder. The sheriff probably won't be happy about it as it is. If it's in the media, she may go out of her way to be uncooperative."

"I will be very discreet. But I think you should wait to talk to Sheriff Shepherd until I can go with you. She was on my podcast last spring talking about law enforcement careers and being the first woman sheriff in her county. I think she likes me."

"Everybody likes you. But I'd really like to get my hands on the case file asap."

"I know, but Sheriff Shepherd, she can be a little touchy."

"Touchy how?"

"I think she won't be very happy that you are redoing her sheriff's office investigation."

"I'm not redoing their investigation. I'm just looking at it to see if I can find something that might have been overlooked. Or maybe something a witness forgot or didn't think was important. Coop is a friend of hers. If I drop his name, she'll at least give me a listen. And if she gives me a listen, I can turn on the charm and win her over."

He didn't comment, but his raised eyebrow spoke for him.

"Hey, I have lots of charm."

"Of course you do. But sometimes when you are looking for answers, your charm is not so easy for other people to see. I am just thinking things might go faster if I can help you with the sheriff."

"Miguel, I'll concede that you have more charisma reserves than I do. But that file is going to answer a lot of questions I have. I want to get it as soon as I can."

"Okay," he said, but in a voice that conveyed he doubted the wisdom of my plan. But because he is Miguel and not me, he let it go and moved on. "Still, I am very sad that we cannot do a road trip together tomorrow."

"I do love a nice road trip with you, but this wouldn't be much of one. It's only twenty miles or so to Galen. But we'll compare notes later and see where to go from there."

An unexpected and big yawn escaped me just then. Miguel laughed.

"I think it is time for you to go to bed. You have a busy day tomorrow. Don't forget to call me when you get back and tell me what happened."

21

When Miguel left, I took a shower, put on my PJs and went to bed. Apparently my brain took that as the signal to get back into the game. After half an hour or so of lying there with my eyes closed and my mind racing, I gave up. I went back into the living room to see if I could find an old movie to take my mind off Hannah and her case.

I was happy to see that *Leave Her to Heaven*, a 1940s film that's a cross between psychological thriller and melodrama, had just started. I've seen it at least three or four times, but I'm always up for a rewatch when it pops up. But this time it didn't suck me in like it usually does. My mind kept returning to Matthew Ferguson's murder. Finally I turned it off and, much to Sam's disgust—he was sleeping on my lap—I got up to fetch my laptop, my legal pad, and my pencil. Sam retreated to the window seat.

When I settled back down on the couch, I started researching aconite poisoning. Coop hadn't been kidding when he'd told Miguel that aconite had been used to kill someone we knew when I was a kid. A neighbor of ours had colluded with a girlfriend to kill his wife using aconite from his girlfriend's garden. My reporting on the story had really boosted the circulation of my neighborhood newsletter *Life on the Street*. Now I wanted to see how easy it would be for someone who didn't have it growing in their back yard, or wasn't an herbalist like Hannah, to get hold of aconite to use to poison someone.

I found an Etsy seller offering raw aconite online, and there were two herbal pharmacies in Milwaukee that carried it. I also discovered that aconite grows wild in Wisconsin. So basically, it was possible for pretty much anyone to obtain aconite if they wanted to. A few more clicks on the keyboard also provided me with information on how to handle and prepare it for use in herbal medicine. Presumably the killer would have done a deeper dive than I had, but it was enough to confirm that it didn't take a degree in herbal medicine (which I discovered was a thing at several accredited colleges) to get the knowledge needed to kill a victim with it.

The access question resolved, I reviewed my list of the people I wanted to talk to either as suspects or witnesses, or both. I added Joel Vining to the list and the Vinings' daughter, Olivia. I wanted to pass along Hannah's message and find out if Marguerite was right in thinking that Joel was keeping Hannah's letters from their daughter.

Next I opened my laptop and skimmed coverage of the murder to get a fix on its location. According to the news articles, the cabin where Matthew was killed was on Clearwater Creek off Burdock Road. I didn't know Trenton County that well, so I opened a county map online, but it wasn't much help. I found Clearwater Creek, and Burdock Road, but no road leading to a cabin. I tried a county plat map next, and I figured out why. Instead of a county road, there was a private two-track off Burdock Road, about a mile before the road dead-ended at the county park. The two-track led to a footbridge that crossed the creek. From there it wasn't far to the parcel of land marked Ferguson. That's where the cabin must be.

So, to get to there by car you'd have to turn at the two-track, park next to the bridge and walk over it to the cabin. Or you could ride the county bike trail that ran from the park, past the back end of the Ferguson lot, and then continued to Nell Lake, a few miles north.

I wished that I had the Ferguson murder file with me right then. I'd love to know who the cops had talked to and what they'd said. Sam head-butted my leg to get my attention. I reached over and scratched him behind the ears. He purred contentedly for a minute and then yawned. A second later, I did the same thing.

"You did that on purpose, didn't you, because you want us to go to bed? Okay, you win. I think I'm just about ready."

I was heading out the door the next morning when Coop called.

"Hey, want to go to breakfast? Or are you still mad?" he asked.

"I wasn't mad, really. Just tired and easily irritated, I guess. But I feel better now."

"So how about breakfast then?"

"Sorry. I already ate. I'm on my way to Galen to talk to a few people and to see if I can get the case file for Matthew Ferguson's murder. I want to put in my request at the sheriff's office in person."

"Well, you might run into a problem there. Kelsey isn't going to be crazy about you poking around in a closed case. And she's the records custodian."

In Wisconsin, the Open Records Act allows pretty broad access to public records, of which a closed police file is considered one. However, the records custodians are the first people in line who can refuse the request. They're supposed to use the balancing test, which says that the public's right to know has to be balanced against other public interests. Basically that means weighing whether or not disclosing the information requested would result in more harm to other public interests—like the individual's right to privacy or the impact on other investigations—than it would benefit the person asking for the information. The records custodians have a lot of discretion. If they refuse to release the records, or slow-walk them, or provide heavily redacted versions, that can be the start of a very long journey through a series of gatekeepers to appeal the decision.

"I was planning to drop your name so she'll know I'm one of the good guys. Miguel said she can be a little touchy."

"Really? She's always been nice to me."

"That's because you're both on Team Law Enforcement. I'll have to win her over. Wish me luck."

"I always do. Call me later."

22

The Trenton County Sheriff's Office is an imposing two-story sandstone building across from the courthouse in Galen. But after I climbed the wide stone steps and walked through the door into the reception area, things were definitely less impressive. The wood flooring was clean but pretty beaten up. The plaster walls were a noncommittal beige, and the furniture looked like it hadn't been updated in a very long time.

A heavy-set man wearing the brown sheriff's office uniform sat at a large wooden desk, glaring at his computer screen and forcefully hitting keys on his keyboard. A slight sheen of sweat glistened on his forehead. It could have been due to frustration with his computer, or to the fact that there was no AC in the building, and it was an unseasonably warm autumn morning. Behind him on the wall was a bulletin board displaying various notices, wanted posters, and community announcements. He hadn't looked up when I came in.

"Hi," I said brightly, beginning my charm offensive. "I'm hoping to talk to the sheriff. Is she in?"

He looked away from his screen then and seemed to transfer his ire at his machine to me.

"You got an appointment?"

"I don't. But—"

"What's this about?"

Out of the corner of my eye, I noticed a door to the right marked Sheriff's Office. Next to it was a photo of the current sheriff—a woman with short dark hair and straight dark eyebrows over deep-set eyes. She was striking rather than pretty.

"My name is Leah Nash. I'd like to get a copy of the Matthew Ferguson case file. I understand that Sheriff Shepherd is the custodian of records. I filled out the request form online. I have it right here," I said, reaching into my purse and pulling it out. I smiled as I showed him.

"You can put it in there," he said, pointing to a filing basket on the corner of the desk. "Somebody will get back to you."

"The thing is, I'd really appreciate the chance to talk to the sheriff about it."

"Yeah? And I'd really appreciate it if my computer didn't freeze up every time I try to print something. I gotta get somebody in to fix it," he said, turning away and picking up his desk phone. "Just leave the form there. The sheriff will take a look at it when she has time." He punched in a number, turned his back, and began talking.

Just then the door marked Sheriff opened and a tall woman who matched the photo on the wall stepped out. Her eyes were focused on the man at the desk, who was now talking just one level short of a shout. She didn't notice me. I rectified that quickly.

"Sheriff Shepherd? Hi, I'm Leah Nash," I said, holding out my hand.

She looked surprised but took my hand with a firm grip.

"Hello. How can I help you?"

"I'd just like a few minutes of your time. You know Sheriff Cooper over in Grantland County, don't you?"

"Did Coop send you to see me?" Her voice was puzzled, and she looked over at my friend at the desk, possibly to foist me off on him. But he was too engrossed in his call to notice.

"I was talking to Coop yesterday about the Matthew Ferguson case and, well, if we could just step into your office I can explain and I promise it won't take long."

Again she glanced over at the guardian of the gate who was supposed to keep random citizens from barging in and bothering her. She made a quick decision there was no help from that quarter.

"All right. Come with me to my office."

I followed her through the door and down a short hallway. She took her place in the executive chair behind her desk and pointed me to one of the visitor chairs facing it. Her tidy desk held only a laptop computer, a phone with a pad of paper beside it, and a pen. She folded her hands on top of the desk and leaned forward slightly.

"Now, what's this about the Ferguson case, Leah? I just made the connection that you're the journalist who writes true crime books. Are you writing a book about Matthew Ferguson's murder? Is that why Coop referred you to me?"

"No, I'm not writing a book. And I didn't say that Coop had referred me to you. I just said that I'd been talking to him. We're in a relationship," I added by way of full disclosure.

An expression that looked a little like disappointment flitted across her face when I said the word relationship and her voice was slightly cooler when she spoke.

"I'm confused. If you're not writing a book, what's your interest in a closed case?"

I explained.

"That's why I need a copy of the case file. I want to be sure that I touch all the bases."

"Because my office didn't?"

"No, because a woman is in prison for life for a crime she swears she didn't commit."

"Our investigation and the prosecutor's conviction say that she did. I'm surprised that an experienced journalist like you wouldn't realize that everyone in prison swears they didn't do it. You can rest assured that the case was disposed of correctly."

"Sheriff, sometimes things can get overlooked, even by very competent investigators. Or sometimes people don't cooperate fully with the police, and they don't come forward with all the information they have. Information that might change the direction of a case. I'm not trying to second guess your work."

"From where I sit, that's exactly what you're doing."

I had set my request for the file on her desk. She picked it up now, skimmed it, put it back down and looked at me, her eyes narrowed with irritation.

"Your request is very broad. And we're short staffed right now. One of my detectives is out on maternity leave and another one just had emergency surgery and won't be back for weeks."

I knew what was coming.

"There is no specific time requirement for responding to an Open Records Act request. The rules are that it be in a reasonable timeframe. For my office that is typically ten days. In this case, I'm afraid it may take considerably longer. I'll want to make sure that there isn't any risk to confidential sources, or that the information in the file doesn't impact ongoing cases. I also have to weigh the public interest versus any harm that could occur as a result of disclosure."

So much for my charm offensive.

"So how long are we talking, Sheriff, twenty-six o'clock on the Twelfth of Never? Look, I didn't come in here thinking that your office had done a bad job investigating. But maybe that's where I should start."

I knew it wasn't the smart thing to say, but my frustration at the fact that she had the upper hand and knew it led me to say it anyway.

Her mouth compressed into a thin line before she spoke. When she did, her voice was icy.

"Ms. Nash, I'm done with this conversation. I will conduct a thorough review of your request and of the case file in a reasonable time frame. However, given the personnel constraints my office is operating under, it's impossible for me to give you a specific timeline. You've taken enough of my time. You can see yourself out."

She turned away from me and picked up the handset on her phone. I wouldn't have been surprised if she was ordering up a minion to throw me out.

I stood.

"I'm sure that at the end of your infinite timeline, I can expect to receive a refusal of my request, or at best a file so heavily redacted that it's useless.

I'm sorry you turned this into a showdown, Sheriff. At the moment you hold all the cards, but I'll be back."

She gave me a thin-lipped smile.

"I can't wait."

"Hey, why didn't you tell me that Kelsey Shepherd was such an asshat?"

I had called Coop as soon as I got out of the building.

"Because I don't think she is. Why, what happened?"

I explained.

"I'm sorry, Coop, if having me for a girlfriend damages your standing with your law enforcement buddies in the area. I doubt Sheriff Shepherd is going to speak very highly of me to any of your colleagues."

"I'm not worried. You didn't do anything you haven't done before, and I'm still standing. But maybe you could have been a little more careful in the way you approached it. I told you no police officer likes someone combing through their case files looking for errors."

"They'd rather let an innocent person spend the rest of her life in prison than admit to a mistake?"

"Come on, you know that's not what I meant."

"Wisconsin has one of the strongest Open Records policies in the country. That's because, supposedly, we value transparency and know that transparency builds trust. If your Sheriff Shepherd is so sure she got it right, why was she so unwilling to share it with me?"

"She's not *my* Sheriff Shepherd. Do you think maybe you put her back up a little with the way you asked for it?"

"I suppose one or two things I said could be construed that way."

"Listen, what Kelsey told you about being short-staffed is true. She was pretty stressed about it when I talked to her last. And if you were after a different case file, things might've gone differently. But the quick arrest and conviction in the Ferguson murder got her a lot of kudos. It's still not that easy for a woman sheriff around here. She probably feels a little protective about the case."

"Okay, I guess I can see that. But shouldn't a good sheriff want the outcome of an investigation to be the truth?"

"Kelsey's a good sheriff. She came up through the ranks. She has high standards for herself and her team. But she's still human. Look, from what you said, it doesn't sound like she presented her best self to you. I'm sorry things went off the rails at your first interview of the day. Where are you headed now?"

"To see Ellen Ferguson. Hey, maybe you should re-try that wishing me luck thing, and specify this time that you're wishing me *good* luck."

23

Ellen Ferguson was in her front yard trimming rose bushes when I arrived. She looked up as I pulled into the driveway. Her expression told me she was trying to place who I was. But she smiled and waved as she walked toward me. She wore khaki pants, a big broad-brimmed hat, and a long-sleeved blue work shirt. As she got closer I noticed how fair her skin was and saw tendrils of strawberry blonde hair peeping out from under her hat.

"Ellen Ferguson?" I asked, though I knew from a photo online that it was her.

"Yes, and you are?"

"My name is Leah Nash. I'm a writer and—"

"Are you kidding me? You're Leah Nash? My sister just gave me one of your books to read! What are you doing here? Wait, that sounds rude, doesn't it?" she asked, laughing at herself a little.

"Not at all. Every author likes talking about her books. Which one is it?"

"*Bury Your Dead*. I love true crime, and the description makes it sound very exciting. But my sister Lindsey said that you've started writing fiction, too."

"Yes, my first one came out a few months ago, and I've got two more in the works. One is in the editing stage, the other I'm just planning."

"This is so exciting! I've never met an author before. Would you like some iced tea? I've got some brownies, too."

I hadn't been sure what to expect from Ellen, though I was prepared for a cool, if not outright hostile greeting. Sadly, her warm reception would probably change when I explained why I was there.

Ellen directed me to her back patio while she went inside. I jumped up to help when she came out balancing two glasses of iced tea and a plate of brownies. When we were both seated at a table under the shade of a giant maple tree, I reopened the conversation with a few softball comments to put her at ease.

"You obviously have a green thumb," I said. "Your front yard is gorgeous, and your backyard is too. You must spend a lot of time taking care of it," I said.

"It's my passion. I love it. I was certified as a master gardener last year."

"Well, you've certainly put your knowledge to good use."

"Thank you. But I have to tell you, Leah, that in my mind, being a master gardener doesn't compare to being a published writer. I'm thrilled to meet you. But if you're selling your books door-to-door, I have to ask. Isn't online and in bookstores a better marketing strategy?" She smiled, teasing me a little.

I liked her a lot in that moment, and I wished that I didn't have to take us to a darker place.

"Ellen, I'll get right to the point. I was contacted by Marguerite Pierce, Hannah Vining's sister. She's asked me to look into your husband's murder. She's convinced that Hannah didn't kill him. I know it's asking a lot after all that you've been through, but I'm hoping you'll tell me a little about Matthew and his death."

The smile had left her face as soon as I mentioned Hannah's name. She sat up straighter, as though to put some distance between us.

"Matthew had an affair with Hannah. He ended it, and she killed him because she couldn't let him go. It's been a year, and still sometimes when I come home and the house is dark, I wonder why Matthew didn't leave a light on for me. And then I remember Matthew isn't here to do that anymore. Or anything else. So I go inside and put all the lights on and turn the television up loud to pretend I'm not alone. But I am. Matthew is gone and that's because Hannah killed him. Is that what you want to know?"

She didn't sound angry. Instead she sounded profoundly sad.

"I'm so sorry, Ellen."

"Are you? Then why are you helping the woman who murdered my husband?"

"Because her sister believes Hannah is innocent, as strongly as you believe that she killed your husband."

"I know Marguerite. When Hannah and Matthew and I were in high school, she was in middle school. She worshipped Hannah. I understand why she can't believe what her sister did. But why would you help her? Is she a friend of yours? Was Hannah?"

"No. I hadn't met either of them until a few days ago. But I do know that sometimes things go wrong in a murder investigation and innocent people are convicted. I agreed to see if I could find anything that might indicate a mistake was made in Hannah's case."

"I'm afraid you're the one making a mistake, Leah. Hannah not only seduced my husband, but she also almost destroyed our marriage. When Matthew told me about their affair, and begged my forgiveness, I wasn't sure I could give it."

"But you did."

"Yes. I've loved Matthew since we were in high school. He's the only boyfriend I ever had. The only man I've ever been with. And I doubt that I'll ever be with anyone else."

"You're awfully young to say that."

She shrugged. "I believe that some people have just one true love. Mine was Matthew. We married right after graduation. And we went through a lot in our twenty-five years together. When I was diagnosed with Stage III cervical cancer, Matthew got me through the chemo, the radiation, the hair loss, the nausea, the times I was so weak I couldn't get out of bed. The times when I felt I just couldn't fight any more. But I did, because he did."

She paused for a minute.

"He showed me that he loved me in so many ways. So when I weighed all of that against one affair that he regretted, yes, I forgave him."

Ellen's story was different from Hannah's. Was that because Hannah had lied to me about the mutual decision she and Matthew had made to sacrifice their happiness in order to be there for their families? Or had Matthew lied to Hannah and to Ellen?

"Did you ever question why Matthew confessed his affair? I mean if you were unaware, wouldn't it have been easier for him just to stop seeing Hannah and go on with his life with you?"

"He told me he felt too guilty to go on deceiving me. Sometimes I wish he had. But because he confessed when he didn't have to, I believed him. Hannah was a mistake. He found that out, and he came back to me. He chose me and that's why he died. Hannah hated him for not loving her. And she killed him. It all came out at the trial. There was no mistake. The text proved that."

"Hannah says that was misinterpreted. That she was a little drunk and feeling sorry for herself. Seeing you and Matthew together hurt and she wanted him to know. She regretted it after she sent it."

"Three weeks after she sent that text, Matthew was dead. You'll never convince me that the text wasn't a threat," Ellen said.

Understandably, Ellen wasn't interested in trying to parse out the meaning of a message from the woman her husband had an affair with. I moved to slightly less emotionally fraught territory.

"When you asked the medical examiner to do a second test to screen for toxins, was it because you suspected that Hannah had poisoned him?"

"No, not then. I asked for the second screening because I just couldn't accept that someone as young and healthy as Matthew could die from nothing. And that's basically what the medical examiner was ready to say the cause of death was. He called it a "negative autopsy." Apparently that's when they can't find a specific cause of death even after an autopsy. He said that five to ten percent of cases of sudden death are unexplained. As though that made everything all right. I couldn't let Matthew go without knowing why he died."

"And it was the presence of aconite that led the police to focus on Hannah?"

"Yes. As soon as the second screening result came in, they opened a murder investigation. They found the throw-away phone in Matthew's jacket at the cabin. I didn't even know he had a second phone. He'd never deleted any of the texts between them. Things went on from there."

"Ellen, I'm not saying that Hannah didn't kill your husband. But if she wasn't in the picture, is there anyone else you can think of who had a reason to want him dead?"

"No. I can't think of anything he could have done that would make someone angry enough to kill him. Except for Hannah."

"What about Joel Vining, Hannah's husband? It seems like he might have been pretty angry at Matthew."

"I know he was when he found out. But he didn't know about the affair. Hannah wasn't as honest with him as Matthew was with me. By the time he found out, Matthew was already dead, so he had no motive to kill him."

Unless Joel lied about when he discovered Hannah had been unfaithful, I thought, but didn't say out loud.

"There's really no one else you can think of? People can get surprisingly upset about things that look like no big deal to someone on the outside. Did Matthew get a promotion another employee thought should be his? Was he involved in a business deal that went bad? A property dispute with a neighbor that escalated, anything like that?"

"Well, there is a man who has a cabin next door to Matthew's. His name is Walt Sanders. He took Matthew to court because he said Matthew's storage shed was partly on his property line. It wasn't, and he lost. Several times. Walt was really angry about it, got into a shouting match with Matthew one day."

"Did this Walt threaten Matthew?"

"Nothing we took seriously. He drinks too much, and he's one of those people who doesn't get happy when they drink. Walt gets mean."

"Mean enough to kill Matthew over a property line?"

"No. I didn't mean that. Especially not the way Matthew was killed. Walt couldn't have planned something like that. Besides, he's the one who found Matthew and called 911. He wouldn't have done that if he had killed him."

I was thinking something quite different. Walt Sanders had extremely easy access to the cabin. His own was right next door. It wouldn't be the first time that a dispute over property lines ended in murder. And then there was the nasty drunk aspect. And it's a fact that the person who "finds" the body is always looked at as a suspect, at least initially.

"Okay. And there's no one else who had a similar kind of grudge against Matthew? Something Matthew had done maybe without realizing how upsetting it would be to a friend or an acquaintance?"

I wanted to know if Ellen would come up with the same name Hannah had given me, without feeding it to her.

"Well, there is someone who ran against him for the Board of Supervisors. She was really angry with Matthew for a while. But I don't believe that she would have killed him over it."

"Who is it?"

"Her name is Kathy Boyle."

Bingo.

24

"What happened?"

Sometimes you ask questions you know the answer to, just to keep things rolling.

"It got to be a really intense race. Kathy's very passionate about the environment. Matthew cared about clean air and water, too. But he was raised on a farm, he worked in agricultural sales, he knew it was more complicated than Kathy was making it sound—that you couldn't just hamstring farmers with a lot of regulations. They wouldn't be able to make a living. Kathy said he was a greedy corporatist—whatever that is, and that he answered to the farm lobby, not to voters. People who knew Matthew knew that wasn't true, but a lot of others were listening to Kathy. It was a tight race until all Kathy's past came out in the paper."

Ellen recounted the story of Kathy Boyle's adult film star career, and that she believed Matthew was responsible for the story getting out.

"Did Matthew leak the story?"

"No! We both knew about her past before it came out, but neither one of us said anything to anyone."

"How did you and Matthew find out?"

"When the election was heating up, Matthew went to a bachelor party the first weekend in January. A friend of his from high school, Kenny

Marston, was there. Kenny had just cleaned out his dad's house and found a porn video with his things. It was the same video he and Matthew found hidden in the Marston garage when they were kids in high school. Kenny thought it would be funny to show it at the party. He's one of those men who never grew up."

"And the video featured Kathy Boyle?" I asked.

"Yes. Matthew said as soon as 'Angel Starr'—that was Kathy's stage name—came on, he recognized her, even though she looked so different. All the time I've known her she's had short brown hair, glasses, and she's on the heavier side. In the movie she had long blonde hair, lots of eye makeup, the whole glam thing, I guess."

"If she looks so different, how could Matthew be sure it was her?"

"Her voice. It's very distinctive, kind of low, and smoky. It doesn't really go with the way she looks now. And when he saw the tattoo on the inside of the actress's wrist there wasn't any doubt. Kathy still has it, but she covers it up with a watch or bracelet most of the time."

"What's the tattoo?"

"An angel holding a star. To go along with her Angel Starr name, I guess."

"So when Matthew came home from the bachelor party he told you about it?"

"Yes. We laughed about it a little. I know that wasn't very nice. It was just that the Kathy we knew was so strait-laced. But we agreed that it was nobody's business but hers, and it was a long time ago. We were as shocked as anybody when it came out in the paper."

"If Matthew didn't leak the information, who do you think did?"

"We both thought it must be Kenny. Matthew blurted out Kathy's name when he realized who it was in the video. Kenny couldn't stop laughing, Matthew said. He had a grudge against her because she fired him for padding his hours when he worked for her. Which, knowing Kenny, he probably did. Matthew told him to just let the video story go. But Kenny's always liked to stir things up."

"Did Matthew ever ask Kenny if he was the one who gave the story to the paper?"

"He tried to reach him when it came out. Kenny lives in some little town in Michigan. Breckville or Ridgeville or something like that. But when Matthew called, his number wasn't in service. Kenny's always changing his phone number to keep ahead of bill collectors. Usually he'd let Matthew know how to reach him, but he didn't that time. I didn't even hear from him after Matthew died."

"What happened when the story came out?"

I already knew from what Hannah had said. I wanted to hear what Ellen had to say about it.

"It was bad. Kathy's life turned upside down. Her husband left her, her son was humiliated, her business went under, people said vicious things about her, or they laughed at her. And she was certain Matthew had done it to win the race."

"Did Matthew try to convince her otherwise?"

"Yes. Matthew ran into her at the bank. He tried to tell her how sorry he was about what had happened. Kathy just lost it. She started screaming at him and told him payback was a bitch, and he'd get his one day. Then she stormed out."

"It sounds like Kathy had plenty of reason to want to punish whoever leaked the video. She believed it was Matthew. Why do you dismiss the idea of her being Matthew's killer so easily?"

"Because she said those things in the heat of the moment. Matthew wasn't killed until months later. And she had reached out to me before that. I had a scary test result at my annual exam, it turned out all right though. Kathy sent me a very nice note. Then after Matthew was killed, she sent me a card saying she was sorry things had gone so wrong between us and that she was praying for me. I don't think she would have done that if she had murdered my husband."

"So you and Kathy are friends again?"

"Well, no. Too many things were said for that to happen. But I'm not angry with her, and she was never angry with me. It was Matthew she was mad at. I suppose you could call us neutral acquaintances. The police did interview Kathy, you know. But there was no evidence against her, and so much against Hannah. I think the police usually know what they're doing, don't you?"

"Yes, I do, for the most part. My significant other is a cop— he's the sheriff in Grantland County. I know how hard he works, how fair he is, how seriously he takes his job. I think most police do the same. But even good cops can get things wrong if they get a favorite theory in their heads and start trying to make the facts fit the theory instead of the theory fitting the facts."

"I suppose that does happen sometimes. But I can't believe that Hannah is an innocent victim."

I could tell she was ready to wrap things up. Ellen had been far nicer than the circumstances required. Best to leave while we were still on polite terms.

"Thank you, Ellen, for the tea, for the time, and for your amazing brownies. I'm so very sorry about Matthew's death."

"Thank you. I can't say that I enjoyed our conversation, but it was still a little exciting to meet you. And I do look forward to reading your book," she said as I turned to leave.

Now that's Wisconsin nice for you.

Despite Ellen's firm belief that Hannah had killed Matthew, what she'd said about Kathy Boyle made me even more interested in her as a possible suspect. The view as I followed the road around Nell Lake to her home was really lovely. Sun-dappled blue water contrasted with trees beginning to show their orange, red, and gold fall colors. An osprey zoomed down and snagged a fish as I was watching. A young man stood in the driveway of the Boyle home, fiddling with the controls for a drone which hovered overhead as I parked my car. He was nice looking, with dark blond hair and a gold stud in one ear. He wore jeans and a Foo Fighters T-shirt.

"Excuse me, is this 1012 Lakeside Drive?"

He looked up then.

"It's not officially listed yet."

Confused, I said, "Listed for what?"

He brought his drone down then and gave me his full attention.

"You're not here to look at the house?"

"No. Kathy's selling?" I asked. I deliberately used her first name to imply that I was at least acquainted with her.

"Finally. I've been trying to get Mom to put the house on the market for almost a year. I shot some really good footage last fall and I'm going to get some more today. I'm Patrick Boyle, her son, by the way. And you are?"

"Leah Nash. I was hoping to catch up with your mother. Is she around?"

He looked down toward the lake and pointed out a woman in a bright yellow kayak paddling toward shore.

"That's her, coming into the dock."

"Great! I'll just run down and see her for a minute, and let you get back to your filming. Thanks," I said.

I gave a friendly wave as I hurried toward the steps leading down to the water before he asked me anything else.

25

Kathy Boyle was just getting out of the kayak as I reached the dock.

"Hi, Kathy. I'm Leah Nash. Can I give you a hand?"

She looked up, startled. Kathy was basically as Ellen had described her—on the sturdy side, with a no-nonsense short haircut, and the weathered skin of someone who spends a lot of time outdoors. She wore denim capris, water shoes, and a plaid short-sleeved shirt. When she spoke it was in the husky low voice Ellen had described, completely at odds with her matronly appearance.

"Are you from the realtor's? I didn't expect you today."

"No, I'm a journalist. I own the *Himmel Times* in Grantland County. Hannah Vining's sister asked me to look into Matthew Ferguson's death."

She had finished securing the kayak. I reached out and she took my hand as she stepped onto the dock.

"What's there to look into? She's in prison for killing him."

"Do you think she did it?"

"The jury thought so. I wasn't at the trial. Why are you asking me?"

I could tell by her tone of voice that she was on the verge of telling me to leave.

"I'm looking for other people besides Hannah who had reasons to want Matthew dead. Could we talk for just a few minutes?"

"Because you think I'm one of them? I suppose you're here because of that damn video. The bastard destroyed my life just to win an election. Am I sorry he's dead? No. Did I kill him? Also no."

Her tone of voice was more matter of fact than angry.

"I heard that you had a heated confrontation with him at the bank. Is that true?"

"I was angry. Very angry. He was trying to say he didn't leak the video to the paper. I said a few things I probably shouldn't have, but it felt good at the time. That's all that happened. But people like to talk."

"I see. Do you mind telling me where you were the night Matthew died?"

"Nope. Like I told the police, I was here all night. My son Patrick was here, too."

"Were you together the whole night?"

"Yes. Patrick came by to convince me to sell, and to test out a new drone he had by shooting video we could use to market the property. I wasn't ready to sell then. I'm really not ready now, but I don't have any choice."

"He must have been outside for a while if he was shooting video."

"He went out around quarter after six to get some footage. He liked the light just then. He came in maybe a half hour or so later. We ate, did a puzzle, and we both went to bed around 9:30."

"Kathy, Ellen Ferguson thinks it could have been someone named Kenny Marston who gave the film to the *Galen Record*. She said he used to work for you."

"He did. But there's no way that moron could have pulled off leaking the story to the paper without leaving a trail that led straight to him. In fact, he wouldn't want to be anonymous, because he'd want everyone to know what a great 'joke' he'd played. No. Matthew did it. I know that for a fact. I lost everything because of him."

"I'm sorry that happened to you, Kathy."

"You know, I'm not *proud* of being in adult films, but I don't think I deserve to be persecuted for it. I aged out of foster care—which was no picnic —and I had nothing. I was young, stupid, and I needed rent money. I got out of the business as soon as I could. Then I met Dave, we got married, I moved here with him. We made a good life. It's all gone, except for Patrick.

I didn't kill Matthew. But Hannah Vining did me and the world a favor when she did."

"Hannah says she didn't kill him."

"What else would she say?"

"What if she's telling the truth, Kathy? What if she's in prison for the rest of her life for something she didn't do?"

"If that's the case, I'm sorry. Look, if you're trying to find people who had it in for Matthew, you should try his sister Rory."

"I didn't know Matthew had a sister. Is she a friend of yours?"

"No, I never met her. I knew that she was an actor and lived in New York, but I hadn't heard anything about her in years. She called me one night, though."

"If you didn't know her, why did she call you?"

"To sympathize, I guess. I can't remember the exact date, but it was around the time when Matthew got himself murdered. By then everything had fallen apart for me—Dave was gone, my business was gone, most of my 'friends' were gone. She must have thought I'd listen to her sad story because I had one of my own. But she wasn't very coherent. She sounded drunk. She said she knew how it felt to be screwed over by Matthew. That he cheated her out of her inheritance like he cheated me out of my election. I thought maybe she had some evidence that Matthew had leaked the video, but I couldn't get her to focus enough to answer. Finally I hung up because she was just rambling."

"Does Rory live in Galen?"

"I don't know."

I made a mental note to follow up on Rory Ferguson.

"Did you know Hannah Vining well?"

She shook her head. "I took a class she offered last year. But we never socialized."

"What was the class?"

She hesitated for a second, then said, "It was called *Beautiful but Deadly*. It was about dangerous plants."

"I see. Was aconite one of the plants?"

"It was. But don't think this is a gotcha moment. It was about a lot of different plants and how to recognize and handle them. It wasn't about how to turn them into murder weapons."

Kathy had been mellowing a little, but I could see that my questions about plants had irritated her. I switched gears.

"You said earlier that you know 'for a fact' that Matthew leaked your story to the *Galen Record,* but you can't prove it. Why not if it's a fact?"

"I know because he as good as admitted it to me, only no one else was there to hear him."

"He confessed?"

"In *my* mind he did. Just before the video hit, Matthew and I were both going to a candidate forum. It was raining hard. My glasses were covered with raindrops, and I could hardly see when I reached the building. I pulled on the door instead of pushing. Matthew was right behind me. He leaned in and pushed it open. And he said, "Take off your glasses, Katie. You'll be surprised what you see." That was the exact line another actor says to me in the film. Matthew said it to taunt me, to let me know that he knew, and pretty soon everyone else would too."

"What did you do?"

"Nothing right then. I was in shock. That line took me right back to a movie I hadn't thought about for decades. But Matthew had obviously seen it. I was worried sick about what he might do. Then a few days later, the story came out in the paper, and I knew. When my husband Dave found out, he was crushed. And then he was furious with me. And then he left me. The funny thing is, I didn't tell him because I was afraid he'd leave me if I told him the truth. But he said the reason he was leaving was because I hadn't trusted him enough to be honest. So the joke was on me, right? And now I'm the one who's leaving."

She attempted a wry smile, but her eyes were bright with tears.

"Kathy, are you sure you heard Matthew right? He couldn't have said something like 'Take off your glasses, Kathy, so you can see?' You know, just normal kidding?"

"You sound like my son. He thinks I need hearing aids. And even if I did, which I don't, Matthew was so close to my ear that I heard every word he said, perfectly."

That little scene didn't fit with anything I'd heard about Matthew to date. I didn't press her, though, because she so clearly had determined that's what Matthew had said, and she wasn't going to change her mind.

I changed the subject instead.

"Your son said that you're moving. Where?"

"Patrick and his partner Mark live in Sun Prairie. Patrick does video for a real estate company there, and he found a condo that I can afford. I'm busted, so I have to sell this place. I hate to. I love it here."

"Well, it's a gorgeous spot. I'm sure you won't have any trouble selling it."

"I remember the day Dave and I bought the place. Patrick was just a little guy. The house needed a lot of work. That first summer we were both dead tired every night. But then after Patrick was asleep, we'd come down here and sit on the dock. I'd have a glass of wine and Dave would drink a beer, and we'd watch the moon rise and talk about the future. We both agreed that we'd stay here until we died. Now Dave's married to someone else, and I'm moving alone to a one-bedroom condo in the middle of a town where I don't know anybody. Things don't always work out the way we plan, do they?"

She stopped.

When she spoke again, it was in a much less emotional tone.

"Listen, I have a lot to do. I've got to get going."

It sounded as though she was reminding herself that she had to leave not just the dock we were sitting on, but the life she didn't want to let go of.

"When are you moving?" I asked.

"The end of next week. So there's not much time. I've got to take photos of the furniture I'm selling—the condo is a lot smaller than this place—and get them up on social media. And I promised Patrick I'd look at the video of the house and the property that he took last fall. But I have to find it first. When he shot it, I still thought I'd be able to figure out a way to keep the place. Denial is a powerful emotion, right? I don't even know where I put that thumb drive he gave me."

"I'll get out of your way now. Thanks for your time. If you think of anything that would help, give me a call," I said, handing her a business card.

"I've told you everything I know, which, like I said when you started, isn't much." Still, she took the card.

Patrick Boyle was still in the driveway as I left. An idea hit me suddenly and I stopped to talk to him.

"Patrick, do you ever freelance and shoot video with your drone as a side hustle?"

"I do. Are you interested?"

"I might be. A friend of mine inherited some property with a pond and lots of woods. I'm thinking drone footage showing an aerial view of the place might be kind of a cool present for him."

We exchanged business cards, and I was on my way.

26

I went to a drive-through and picked up some lunch, then I found a little park with some nice shade trees and a small play area. A few kids rode up on their bikes as I settled in at a picnic table to eat my lunch. The autumn sun was warm on my back and the air was crisp and clear. As I ate and jotted down notes from the morning's interviews, shouts of laughter from kids playing made a pleasant backdrop.

As I reviewed what I'd written, the thing that struck me most was that Ellen had never mentioned Matthew's sister Rory. But Rory's drunk dialing call to Kathy indicated there were some serious issues between the siblings. Why hadn't Ellen mentioned that when I asked her who besides Hannah might have had it in for Matthew?

I tapped my pencil on my notepad while I thought about next steps.

Sheriff Kelsey Shepherd had successfully slowed my roll when it came to getting the Ferguson file. I probably should have waited until Miguel could come with me to work his magic on her. I could go back on Monday, apologize and try to reset the conversation. However I was pretty sure the ill-advised Twelfth of Never remark I'd made had closed down the apology route back into her good graces.

My phone dinged with a text just then. Marguerite. Holy cow, it was 1:30 in the afternoon here. That meant it was 4:30 a.m., in Sydney.

Did you talk to Hannah? How did it go? Have you talked to anyone else yet?

Yes, I talked to her. It went okay. I'm out doing some interviews in Galen today. What are you doing texting at 4:30 a.m.?

The baby's fussy. Been up all night. She just went down for the third time. Hope it's the charm. Did you talk to Hannah's lawyer yet?

Reading that, I literally slapped my forehead.

How could I have forgotten about the letter Hannah had signed giving her attorney permission to discuss the case with me? I didn't need Kelsey Shepherd! The attorney's file would have all the disclosure material the prosecution had turned over—crime scene photos, autopsy results, witness statements, and more.

Just finished a round of interviews. Will be talking to Macy Belding soon. Get some sleep. I'll be in touch.

I called Hannah's attorney, expecting to get voicemail. It was a Saturday afternoon, after all. Instead a live person answered.

"Macy Belding Law Office."

"Hi, is Ms. Belding in? This is Leah Nash calling."

"You're talking to her. Please, Leah, call me Macy. I've been expecting to hear from you."

"I'd like to set up a meeting with you to talk about Hannah's case."

"I'm in court three days next week, and I'm out of town for the other two. But if you can come to the office, I'll be here all afternoon catching up on things."

"I'm in Galen. How does now work for you?"

"Fine. My office is 716 Third Avenue. It's in an old two-story stone house with a big porch. My secretary isn't here today, so just come in, go through reception, and my office is way to the back. I'll see you in a few minutes."

"Great, thank you!"

Macy Belding was a middle-aged woman with dark blonde hair cut in a chin-length curly bob. Her smile was so wide when she greeted me that her eyes almost disappeared in her heart-shaped face. She stood and came around her desk to shake my hand.

"Leah, good to meet you. I had my secretary make a copy of Hannah's files for you as soon as Marguerite faxed me Hannah's consent. Here you go," she said, handing me a thumb drive that I dropped into my purse.

"Thanks, Macy. I really appreciate it. If you have time, I'd like to ask you some questions about the case."

"Sure. Have a seat." She pointed to a visitor chair in front of her desk and then she pulled up the one next to it and turned it to face me.

"Okay, shoot," she said once she was seated.

"Why didn't you put Hannah on the stand to testify?"

"Because I knew she'd be a terrible witness. Frankly, she was a terrible client."

"In what way?"

"She didn't seem to want to participate in her own defense. The prosecutor had a strong case against her. In addition to her motive, she was an expert on herbs, and she had access to Matthew's cabin. On our side, I had Hannah swearing she didn't kill Matthew, and not much else."

"So what did you come up with?"

"I planned to try and build reasonable doubt by using an alternate suspect theory, but Hannah refused to let me."

"Who was the alternate?"

"Her husband, Joel. He said he didn't know about the affair until after Matthew was killed, but we only had his word for that. Hannah put the kibosh on that."

"Why?"

"She said she didn't believe Joel had killed Matthew, and he'd been through enough. I explained that an alternate theory is to help the jury see that there are other ways a crime could have happened besides the case the prosecution makes against a defendant. That I was going for reasonable doubt, not trying to convict Joel. She said she didn't want me to use a smoke and mirrors trick to get her off the hook at Joel's expense."

"But did *you* think it was smoke and mirrors?"

"In my mind, Joel was and still is someone who would make a very strong alternate suspect. The motive was very clear. Matthew stole his woman."

"But if he didn't know about the affair until after Matthew was dead…" I said, playing devil's advocate.

"Hannah says she didn't tell him, but that doesn't mean Joel didn't find out on his own. Hannah was obsessive about deleting texts between her and Matthew after she read them. But he could've seen one that came up on her screen when she was in the shower, say. Or, he could have overheard a conversation or spotted them together. But Hannah was adamant that he didn't know, and that she wouldn't have him offered up as a suspect. My hands were tied."

"What about Ellen Ferguson? The spouse is always the first suspect."

"Watch a lot of true crime, do you?"

"Actually, I've lived a lot of true crime. I was a reporter and then a true crime writer for a while. I just started writing fiction. A mystery series."

"Yeah? I'll have to check it out. I like a good whodunnit. Though I don't get much time for reading. A solo law practice can get pretty hectic. On the other hand, better to be in a constant state of too-much-to-do than to be in a constant state of panic because I can't pay the bills."

"How long have you been in practice?"

"Seven years total, just two years on my own."

She saw the surprise on my face.

"Yeah, I know that I look a little 'mature' to only have seven years in as a lawyer. I am. I made a career switch from teaching to law after I got divorced. The first five years out of law school I worked in a corporate firm in Milwaukee. It wasn't for me. I came back home and started up my own office. I like the variety in general practice. And the autonomy of being my own boss. I've been told I don't always play well with others," she said with a wry smile and a shrug.

"I've heard that a time or two myself. But back to Ellen. Did you consider using her for an alternate suspect defense?"

"Briefly, but when I got the whole history on her, I knew it could backfire big time."

"How's that?"

"The jury would've been more likely to sympathize with Ellen—nice person, widow, battling cancer—than they would have been to buy her as a suspect. Also there was the inconvenient fact that Ellen insisted on the second tox screening. Up to that point Matthew's death would have been written off as a result of unknown causes. If Ellen had killed him, she'd have been thrilled with the original autopsy findings and skated away scot-free."

"Right. Why do you think Hannah was so reluctant during the trial, and still when I talked to her, to do anything to help herself?"

"I think it's because deep down Hannah believes she deserves to suffer."

"Because she did it, you mean?"

"No, because she feels tremendous guilt about the impact her affair had on her family, as well as deep depression. She just didn't have the will to take part in her own defense. I couldn't put her on the stand because the prosecutor would've decimated her on cross."

"Do you believe Hannah is innocent?"

"They teach us in law school that the bedrock principle of our legal system is that a person is innocent until proven guilty in a court of law. It's not a lawyer's job to judge a client, it's the jury's. The prosecution's job is to prove guilt beyond a reasonable doubt. Mine is to provide a strong defense. Hannah tied my hands, so I wasn't able to do that effectively. But yes, for the record, I do believe her. Do you?"

"I liked her, and for her daughter and her sister's sake I hope she didn't kill Matthew. But for me it's too early to come down on one side or the other. Though I have turned up a couple of interesting bits of information. Does the name Walt Sanders sound familiar?"

Macy's phone rang before she could answer my question.

27

"Excuse me," she said, going back around her desk to grab her office line.

"Macy Belding Law Office."

After that her conversation was punctuated with several "I sees" and some long pauses as she listened. Then, "It's not ideal." More pausing. She ended the call by saying, "No. You did the right thing calling me. Yes, I'll get there as soon as I can. Don't talk any more until I get there."

She hung up and said, "I'm sorry, I can only give you a few more minutes. A client got himself into a situation with a cop who pulled him over. He's at the jail now. I need to get there and see what I can do before he digs himself in deeper."

"Oh, sure, I understand. I'll make it quick. We were talking about Walt Sanders."

"Right. He's the next-door neighbor who found Matthew's body at the cabin. Why?"

"Did you interview him?"

"I didn't, because his statement was pretty cut and dried. He heard Matthew's truck pull into the parking area they have to use next to the foot bridge. You know that there isn't a direct road to Matthew's cabin, right?"

I nodded. "Yes, you have to go down Burdock and turn off at the footbridge, or else walk or ride a bike down the trail that starts at the county park and goes behind Matthew's property."

"You'll see Walt's statement in the file, but basically, he heard Matthew drive in that night around seven. In the morning he saw that Matthew's truck had blocked him in and he went to ask Matthew to move it. He found Matthew dead and called 911. Do you know something more than that?"

I told her about the property dispute.

"Oh, damn! I should've dug deeper. I just don't have the investigative resources for a case like this. Hannah didn't have the money either. Otherwise she could've hired a better lawyer than me. Now I wonder what else did I miss?"

She was so angry at herself, I felt bad for her. I thought fleetingly of mentioning D&D Investigations and potentially throwing some future business Darmody's way. But I liked Macy, so I didn't.

"Hey, the police and the prosecution didn't spend any time on Walt either, don't beat yourself up. He doesn't seem like a very likely suspect to me, either."

"Maybe not, but he might have made a pretty good alternate suspect. Losing a case is always hard, but losing one that sends your client to prison for life? That's what keeps you awake nights."

"Macy, it sounds like you did what you could with what you had. I've got what I need here," I said, holding up the thumb drive. "I'll let you know how things go. It was really nice meeting you."

"Same here. Call me anytime. If there's anything I can do to help, I will."

I was just pulling away from the curb when Macy came running out of her office building.

"Leah! Wait a sec!"

I pulled back into my space and lowered the passenger side window.

Leaning in, Macy said, "I just thought of something that isn't in the case file. You should talk to Olivia, Hannah's daughter. She came to see me shortly before the trial started."

"She had information for you?"

"No, more like she wanted information *from* me. I explained I couldn't discuss the case with her and why. She started to cry, said she was so scared her mom might go to prison, no one would tell her anything. Her dad wouldn't answer any of her questions, wouldn't let her visit her mom."

"That must have been a hard conversation."

"The worst. All I could give her were some reassurances she didn't believe—turns out she was right not to. But the whole time she was there, it felt like she wanted to tell me something, but just couldn't get it out. I tried pressing her a little, but that was a mistake. She jumped up like a skittish cat, said she was fine, and then she couldn't get out of there fast enough."

"Did you follow up with her?"

"I told Hannah about the visit. She asked me not to talk with Olivia again. She felt that her daughter was too young and too highly strung to be part of things."

"Do you have any thoughts on what Olivia might have wanted to say to you?"

"I wish I did. And I could be reading things into the conversation that weren't there. Maybe Olivia was just feeling down and scared that day. I'm sorry, that's all I got, but I thought you should know."

"Thanks, Macy. I'm going to take a run at Joel, and maybe I can get Olivia aside when I do."

It was almost three o'clock as I drove toward the Vining home, and I was having second thoughts about the interview. I felt like I'd put in a pretty good day's work, and I was really anxious to get home and plug in the thumb drive that Macy had given me. I could always come back on Sunday. On the other hand, with Joel Vining's work/travel schedule, there was a chance he could head out and be gone for a week if I didn't catch him today. I talked myself back into attempting the interview, even though it was almost a given that he wouldn't talk to me.

The Vining home was a one-story, prairie-style house built of natural stone with wide overhanging eaves, windows grouped in horizontal bands, and a wide front porch. I tried the doorbell, but it made no sound, so I knocked vigorously. After a few seconds I tried again. Still nothing. Then I heard the noise of a leaf blower starting up. I followed the sound around the house to the back yard. A tall man with a set of headphones on his ears had his back to me as he used the leaf blower strapped to his back.

When he shut it off, I walked toward him.

"Hi. I'm looking for Joel Vining. Is that you?"

His back was still toward me, and he didn't answer. It clicked in then that he still had headphones on. I walked up and tapped him on the arm. Startled, he jumped a little then turned around. He had a long narrow face with a strong nose and deep-set eyes. He pulled his headphones off, and I started again.

"Hi. I'm looking for Joel Vining. Is that you?"

"Yes, I'm Joel Vining. And you are?"

Directness was really my only option here. Either Joel was going to talk to me or throw me off his property. There wasn't any point in trying to ingratiate myself. I got right to the point.

"Joel—may I call you Joel?"

I didn't wait for an answer.

"I'm Leah Nash. Your sister-in-law Marguerite asked me to look into your wife's case. She's convinced that Hannah didn't kill Matthew Ferguson."

"You're late to the party, aren't you? And it's ex-wife. Hannah is in prison for the rest of her life. We're divorced, so she's out of mine. I don't see any point in speaking with you. If you'll excuse me."

He turned away and reached for the starter cord on his leaf blower.

"Wait! You have a daughter together. That means you'll always be connected to some degree."

"Olivia is *my* daughter. My flesh and blood. And I have sole custody. Hannah will never see her again."

"Is that what your daughter wants? I understand how you feel about your wi—your ex-wife. But Hannah is Olivia's mother—surely your daughter has the right to decide whether or not she wants to see her."

"You understand how I feel? No, you can't possibly understand what Olivia and I have been through and are still going through."

"I'm sorry. You're right. I don't know how you feel. I should have said that I understand how being betrayed feels. Because I do. When my dad abandoned us, my mother refused to let me talk about how I felt. If I brought it up, she'd say we just had to move on. It wasn't until years later that I found out the truth and what she'd been hiding from me. It nearly broke our relationship."

"Not that it's any of your business, but I'm not hiding anything from Olivia. She's a very bright kid. She knows what Hannah did. If she wanted to talk about it to me, she would. But she doesn't. She wants to forget her. It's what she needs to do. What we both need, and we're doing it. I'd like you to leave now."

His voice was tight with anger, and I noticed he was clenching his fists at his side to keep his temper in check. Or maybe to keep himself from punching me.

Still, I had to take one more go at it.

"Joel, you loved Hannah once. You, and Olivia, and Hannah were a family. Do you really believe that Hannah is the kind of person who could be so consumed with jealousy and revenge that she would not only kill her lover but destroy her own family?"

"You're wrong. I didn't love Hannah."

"You married her. You built a life with her, but you didn't love her?"

"No. I loved the person she pretended to be—warm, kind, a loving wife and mother. But the real Hannah turned out to be a liar, a cheat, a hypocrite. A person so wrapped up in herself that she didn't care how she hurt me or Olivia. And yes, I believe that person, the real Hannah, killed her lover and didn't give a damn about him in the end either—she only cared that she didn't get what she wanted. Hannah didn't just betray me. She betrayed our family. She deserves what she got."

"I'm sorry I've upset you. You've made your feelings clear, but if you don't mind, I'd like to speak to Olivia while I'm here."

"I do mind. I don't want you talking to my daughter. Ever. Now I'd like you to leave. Or do I need to report you for trespassing to make that happen?"

Time to exit, stage right.

28

Although the encounter had been a bust as far as getting any factual information, I got a sense of Joel Vining. The words that came to mind were bitter, angry, and deeply wounded. It happens when someone you love betrays you. Some people work through the painful emotions and move on. Others nurture them until they blossom into a twisted garden of hate and grievance. Joel seemed a good fit for the role of gardener.

I was a block away from the Vining's house when I glanced in my rearview mirror and saw a girl on an e-bike waving frantically for me to stop. I turned at the next side street, parked and walked around to the passenger side to wait for her. She pulled up on the sidewalk and put her feet down to steady the bike, but she didn't get off it.

"Have you talked to my mother? Have you seen her? How is she? Is she all right? Did she say anything about me?"

Her eyes were the same as those in the photo Marguerite had shown me of an eight-year-old Olivia holding onto Hannah's hand. Only now her big, brown eyes weren't shining with happiness. They were filled with anxiety.

"Olivia, hi. I'm Leah Nash. You must have overheard me talking to your dad."

"Yes. I was in the kitchen, and I heard you in the backyard with him.

Why did Aunt Marguerite ask you to help her? Are you going to get Mom out of prison?"

"I'm a journalist. Your aunt read a true crime book I wrote. She asked me to look into your mother's case and see if I could do anything."

"Can you get her out of prison?" she repeated.

"I don't know. It depends what I find out. Right now I'm talking to people who know your mom, and who knew Matthew Ferguson. I'm on the hunt for any leads that the police didn't find, or didn't think were important. Can you think of any—"

"No. I don't know anything," she said, before I could even finish. "I just know that my mother didn't kill him. She would never kill anyone. She just wouldn't. Only she doesn't know that's what I think," she said. As she said the last part, she looked down and I saw how tightly she was squeezing the grips on her handlebars. The kid was really nervous.

"I'm sure she knows you believe in her," I said.

"No! She doesn't! When I found out about the affair, I told her that I hated her. I said she was a selfish, horrible person, and I wished she'd never married my dad. That she ruined everything, and she wasn't my real mother anyway so why didn't she just get out of our lives. I didn't mean it!" she said, looking up at me as tears filled her eyes and spilled onto her cheeks.

"Hey, I'm sure she knows you didn't."

"Then why won't she write to me?"

"Have you written to her?"

"I tried but Dad caught me, and he was really upset. He said she threw away our family and she has to pay the price for what she did. He asked me to promise I wouldn't write to her, and I did. But not because I think she killed Mr. Ferguson. I know she didn't. She couldn't. I promised not to write to her because it upset my dad so much. I love him, too."

I was rapidly losing the little sympathy I'd felt for Joel. Yes, he'd suffered a terrible shock and loss, but he was making a hard situation even worse for his daughter by dragging her into his wounded feelings. "You know that because of facts you have, or you know it because you know your mother, and you're sure her character wouldn't let her kill anyone?"

"I don't know 'facts' or anything. But I know my mother is a good person. I know that she had an affair and broke up our family, and I really, really wish that she hadn't. But I don't hate her. I think my dad does though. He's just mad and sad all the time now. He cried so hard when the police arrested her. It really freaked me out. He said we were never a family. It was all fake. It isn't though. I know she loved us. She did!"

Clearly Joel's own pain and anger over Hannah's affair had made him oblivious to what he was doing to his daughter.

"Olivia, when I saw your mother, she wanted me to make sure that you know that you mean everything to her, that she loves you more than anything."

"She really said that? You're not just saying that to make me feel better?"

"She really did."

"They why doesn't she write to me?"

I didn't tell her that Hannah *had* written. I suspected now that Marguerite had been correct in thinking that Joel had intercepted—or had the housekeeper intercept—Hannah's letters before Olivia got them. The poor kid was caught between the two people she loved the most.

"Maybe she thinks it's easier for you if she doesn't."

"It isn't. It's worse. Way worse."

I switched topics then because I wanted Olivia's take on something else and she was poised like a butterfly ready to take flight at any moment.

"Olivia, if your mother didn't kill Matthew, can you think of anyone else who—"

She didn't give me a chance to finish before she jumped in.

"No. I don't know anything about Mr. Ferguson, so how could I? I just know it wasn't my mother."

"Okay, but Macy Belding, your mother's attorney, said you stopped by to see her during the trial. She got the impression that you wanted to tell her something, but—"

"No. I didn't. I only wanted to know what was happening. I have to go. Dad will wonder where I am. Just, when you see my mom, tell her I don't hate her like I said that time. Tell her I love her, and I miss her so much!"

She took off before I could say anything else.

29

I thought about Olivia as I headed back to Himmel. She was definitely wound pretty tight—though who wouldn't be in her situation? The mother she loved was locked away beyond her reach. And the father she also loved had locked himself into the prison of his own anger and hurt. The way she shot off on her bike as soon as I brought up her visit to Macy Belding made me believe Macy was right. Olivia was hiding something.

My phone rang when I was almost home. Miguel.

"Are you done in Galen? How did it go?"

"I'm done for the day, as far as interviews go anyway. It went good and bad."

I hit the highlights of my meetings with the sheriff, Ellen, Kathy, Olivia, and Joel.

"Ah, the sheriff. I'm sorry, but I told you that you should wait for me."

"Nobody likes an I-told-you-so, Miguel. But yes, I did burn a bridge or two that might still be standing if you'd been with me. But Ellen and I got along all right, and so did Kathy and I. Though I have to admit Joel wasn't very enamored of me. Still, I got the digital file I need from Macy, Hannah's attorney, so I feel pretty good about the day. I'm going home now to review it. How about you? Were you able to get in touch with Riley Dorner at the *Galen Record*?"

"I was, but she doesn't know who her source was."

"What? How can she not know?"

"She never talked to them. Riley said she got a letter in the mail, addressed to her at the *Galen Record*. Inside was a photo of the front and back cover of an adult video called *Overdue Love*. A sticky note with block printing said, 'Angel Starr is Kathy Boyle.'"

"There was just a sticky note, nothing else? What about a return address on the envelope? A postmark?"

"No return address, and the postmark was from the processing center in Milwaukee. So Riley, she started digging. She found the video online and ordered a copy, and then she got the name of the production company, Euphoria Studios. It was based in Los Angeles. From there, she went to the online archives for the *LA Times*. The owners of Euphoria Studios were convicted in a big drug and sex trafficking bust in the early 1990s. One of the witnesses was identified as an actor in some of the films. Her name was Kathleen Albaugh."

"So she searched for a marriage certificate for Kathleen Albaugh and David Boyle?" I asked.

"Yes! How did you know?"

"That's what I would've done. You know, if we ever get this nonprofit news organization off the ground, maybe we could lure Riley Dorner away from the *Galen Record*. It sounds like she's got a lot of smarts and follow through."

"She does. But I'm sorry I could not find out if Kathy Boyle is right, and Matthew was Riley's anonymous source."

"Do you have time to check out Matthew's friend Kenny Marston? Ellen said he's the one who brought Kathy's video to the bachelor party where Matthew saw it. He lives in Michigan now."

"Yes! I can do that. Do you know what town?"

"I'll check my notes when I get home."

"What else can I do?"

"After I get a chance to go through the case file I got from Hannah's lawyer, you can come over and help me think. I—oh wait!"

"Wait why, what?"

"Matthew's sister. Rory. She called Kathy after Matthew was killed and gave her an earful about Matthew, I guess. Kathy said she was very drunk and very angry at Matthew. Can you reach out to her? Find out what her relationship with her brother was like?"

"Rory Ferguson? She owns DanceFusion studio on Fourth Street here in Himmel. I am taking ballroom dance classes from her starting on Monday."

"Has she ever talked about her brother?"

"I only met her once, just to sign up. Your mother knows her though. She's the one who told me about the ballroom dancing. You should come with me to the class, it would be very fun!"

"Hmm. I need to think about that. Okay, I thought about it. No."

"I know you would like it if you just try it."

"Miguel, you know how I am. I got the music in me, but sadly it did not come with the voice of a singer or the feet of a dancer. Maybe Troy would like to go with you."

"He already took the class. Maybe I will ask Carol."

"There you go, Mom would love it. Plus, she, unlike me, will be good at it. Okay, well, I'm almost home. Sweet! There's a parking spot right out front," I said as I maneuvered my car into it. "I'm going to dive into the murder file and that'll keep me busy for a while. Are you off Monday?"

"I have the morning off, but I have to cover the D&D Investigations open house in the afternoon," Miguel said.

"Can we meet for coffee at Woke on Monday at 8:30? I'll fill you in on what I find in the files, and you can help me strategize next moves."

"I will be there."

Usually I park in the back lot of my building, mostly because with the Woke coffee shop across the street, there's rarely an empty parking spot out front. But I'd snagged one the day before, and it was open again when I reached my place. I rummaged in my purse for my front door key, but when I tried it in the lock, I didn't need it. Ope! I'd forgotten to lock it when I left, a bad habit of mine.

As I climbed the steps to my apartment, I called my mother.

"Hey, Mom. What can you tell me about Rory Ferguson?"

"She owns DanceFusion. She's in her late 30s, I'd say. She choreographed all the dance numbers for *Anything Goes* last spring and did a wonderful job. Oh, and she lives in Galen with an aunt. Why are you asking?"

I realized then that I hadn't told her that I'd changed my mind and agreed to Marguerite's request to help her sister Hannah. I gave her a quick overview.

"So now I want to talk to Rory. Any backstory you can fill me in on?"

"Not much. I gather she went to New York to become a star, but she found talent isn't enough. You need luck too, and she didn't have much of that. She mentioned once that her aunt had been a lifesaver. I know Rory had some serious addiction issues, but I don't know the details. She seems to be on track now, though. Leah, be careful with Rory, will you? She's got kind of a tough facade, but underneath I think she's pretty fragile."

"I'm not going to waterboard her, Mom. I just want to find out about her relationship with her brother."

"Because you think she could have had something to do with his murder?"

"No. Maybe. I don't know, Mom. I'm just at the gathering stage."

"Well, just remember that she's been through a lot."

"I will. I'll talk to you later."

30

When I reached the third-floor landing, a fall flower arrangement of dahlias, chrysanthemums, and roses blocked my entrance. It was gorgeous. But why was it there? It wasn't my birthday or any special occasion. I moved it and unlocked the door that opens directly to my apartment. I'm pretty good at remembering to keep that one locked.

I carried the flowers to the living room, where I spied Sam sitting on the kitchen bar precisely where he's not supposed to be.

"Caught you! Get down please, I need to set this exactly where you're lounging."

Sam stared at me long enough to make it clear that he was jumping down because he felt like it, not because I was the boss of him.

I looked for and found a small white envelope tucked in the middle of the flowers. I pulled out the card.

From an ardent admirer

No signature. Now that was weird. I'm not the sort of person who gathers a lot of anonymous admirers as I walk through life. On the off chance that Coop had taken an unexpected turn down Romance Lane, I called him.

"Hey, you," he said. "I was just thinking about you."

"Really? Were you wondering if I found the flowers you left on my doorstep?"

"What flowers?"

"So you're not the one who left me a lovely flower arrangement with a card that reads 'From an ardent admirer'?"

"I am not. But I'd like to know who besides me has ardent feelings for you. No name on the card?"

"Not even an initial."

"How about an old boyfriend, someone from your past who wants to be in your present?"

"No one I can think of. Anyway, at present my dance card is full. I can't think who—" I paused as an idea that popped into my head gave the lie to the statement I'd been about to make.

"Hello? Are you still there?"

"Sorry, yes. But I just thought of someone it could be."

"Okay, I'll get my dueling pistols and come by for the name and address."

"I've got a first name and an email address, but I have no idea if she's local or not."

I explained about the email I'd received from my reader Sharla, who had described herself as an ardent admirer.

"Hmm. You know, you might have picked up not just a fan, but a stalker."

"Oh, come on. That sounds like the plot of a mystery I haven't written yet."

"I'm not saying it's a strong possibility, but you shouldn't dismiss it, either. Keep the email and the card for now . . . wait a second. You said the flowers were outside your door? That has to be the door at the top of the front stairs that opens into your office, right? Because you need a key code to get in the back."

"It was. I forgot to lock the street level door. But the landing door to my office was locked up tight. So, no harm. Plus don't forget I have Sam, my watch cat, patrolling the premises. Coop, you know I do get gifts from readers sometimes. Don't be so suspicious."

"It goes with the job. Were the gifts you received in the past left on your doorstep? Were they anonymous?"

"Well, no. I got some cookies from a lady at a book signing once, and somebody gave me a framed photo of DeMoss Academy after they read my first book, but that happened at the library."

"Okay, so these flowers were delivered by someone who knows where you live and knows how to get into the building. I don't think we should ignore that."

"You're starting to freak me out a little."

"No need to freak out. See if this Sharla reaches out again. Don't email her but hold on to anything she sends."

"Why shouldn't I email her? She sent me a nice note. It's rude not to write back. And we don't know that she's the flower giver."

"You don't email her because a stalker will consider that encouragement—like you welcome more attention from her. Ignore her and she may go away. I'd like to take a look at the email from Sharla, and the card that came with the flowers. I'll stop by later, okay?"

"Sure. Will you bring food?"

"What would you like?"

"General Tso's Chicken and an egg roll."

"You got it. I need to finish up out here at the property. I'll be there around 7:00."

It wasn't until after I hung up with Coop that I realized I had an easy way to find out who had dropped the flowers off. I called Tony Crosby, the security manager at Caldwell Properties who takes care of my building.

"Hey, Leah, what can I do for you?"

I explained the situation briefly.

"Yeah, sure. Let me call up that camera feed and see what we've got. Okay, I've got it here now. Hang on while I take a look." He was quiet for a few minutes and then said, "Sorry, Leah, all it shows is you leaving this morning, then you coming in and picking up the flowers."

"How can that be?"

"I'd say we need to take a look at repositioning the camera we've got in there or maybe add another. Or both. I'll put in a work order for it, and we'll get that taken care of for you."

"Okay, thanks, Tony."

"No problem. Sorry I couldn't get you a shot of your secret admirer."

I set the flowers on the bar between the kitchen and the living room. They added a nice touch. If I had a stalker at least she had good taste. Maybe it was a sign that I was making it in the fiction world. I wondered if Nora Fielding had a stalker. I'd have to ask the next time I saw her.

Before I did anything else, I sent a quick email to Marguerite. I wasn't on Hannah's approved email list at the prison, so I couldn't communicate with her directly, but I knew Marguerite would pass Olivia's message on. I hoped it would make Hannah feel a little better.

Then I grabbed my laptop and the thumb drive from Macy Belding and took them over to the window seat. I fluffed my pillows until I had just the right back support, then tucked one leg under myself and settled into the corner with my computer balanced on my lap. I plugged in the thumb drive and started looking at the files.

They were arranged in chronological order, beginning with the call to 911 that had sent the Galen County Sheriff's Office to Matthew Ferguson's cabin. Because Matthew's death was of unknown cause, they had taken photos and secured the scene to await autopsy results.

The cabin photos showed a combined kitchen and living room with a wood stove, a couple of mismatched armchairs and a well-worn green sofa. A navy jacket hung on the back of the front door. On the round kitchen table was a flat, open box holding a pizza with two slices gone—apparently Matthew's last meal. An empty coffee cup was in the sink. A cell phone was on the kitchen counter. On the floor between the table and the sofa lay Matthew's body.

I moved on to the autopsy report. The warmth of the room—the wood stove had been fully loaded and had burned all night—had made it harder to estimate the time of death. The receipt on the pizza box had helped. It had been picked up at 6:50 p.m., and given the distance between Cheesehead Pizza and the cabin, that supported the statement from Walt Sanders that he'd heard a truck arrive a little after 7:00 p.m.

The autopsy had identified the presence of pizza, partially digested, in his stomach. Based on that and other factors, the medical examiner had estimated Matthew's death between 9:00 p.m. and 1:00 a.m.

The report detailed that there was no significant narrowing of any arteries which could have caused a heart attack, and no heart damage. Also, no sign of stroke or aneurysm. No blunt force trauma or other injury. The initial toxicology report showed no drugs present. The medical examiner had been ready to write Matthew's death off as the result of "unspecified natural causes."

But Ellen, as she had told me, had refused to accept the "unspecified" result. Following a second toxicology screening, the aconite was discovered. The death investigation turned into a murder investigation. That's when things really began to move.

The coffee cup in the sink had shown traces of aconite. Police had used password information Ellen supplied to open Matthew's cell phone, which had been found on the counter at the cabin. There was nothing useful on it. But then they'd found Matthew's second phone in his jacket pocket. The texts had made it clear Matthew and Hannah were having an affair. That's when the focus shifted to Hannah.

She had the easiest access to aconite, she knew how to handle it safely, and Matthew had made a lot of passionate promises to Hannah in the texts that were found. Promises that Matthew broke when he chose to stay with Ellen. And there was that last text from Hannah that could be interpreted to mean—as the police, the prosecutor, and Ellen believed—that Hannah's love had turned to hate. A very strong motive for murder.

The investigation had been handled by Detective Sgt. Dana Cutter. She hadn't ignored other possibilities. In addition to Hannah, she'd interviewed Ellen, Joel Vining, Kathy and Dave Boyle, and Walt Sanders. I noted that Rory Ferguson, Matthew's sister, wasn't on the list. The only one with a solid alibi was Dave Boyle. He had been in Fond du Lac, at his wedding rehearsal and the dinner that followed until 10:00 p.m. He'd taken a transfer to Fond du Lac County after he and Kathy split up and hadn't been living in the area when Matthew was killed. The fact that he was remarried made it seem unlikely that he was angry enough over the demise of his marriage to Kathy to kill Matthew. He was definitely one to put on the back burner.

The fact that none of the remaining possible suspects had great alibis wasn't as important as it sometimes is, because the poison could have been left anytime to await Matthew's use. The killer didn't need to be present to administer it. Reading through the statements it was easy to see why Hannah had emerged as the suspect most likely.

Even though Marguerite was desperate for me to find something that would help her sister, so far things weren't looking great. But something was nagging at me. When that happens, rather than try to pull it out from the dark corners of my mind, I usually stop and stare into space for a few minutes to see if something pops up. This was one of the times when something did. I went back to the crime scene photos and enlarged one of them. Next I checked the autopsy report again. Then I called Ellen Ferguson.

31

Ellen answered on the first ring.

"I've told you that I'm not interested in a time share. Please stop calling me or—"

"Ellen, wait, please. This is Leah Nash."

"Oh, Leah! I'm sorry. I thought you were this woman who keeps calling trying to sell me a time share in Florida."

"I just have a quick question for you. Did Matthew like mushrooms?"

"No, he hated mushrooms. Why are you asking me that?"

"Was he allergic to them?"

"No, he just thought they were disgusting—the taste, the texture, the mouth feel. Does it matter?"

"It might."

"I don't understand. What do mushrooms have to do with anything?"

"I'm looking at the crime scene photos from Matthew's murder. I noticed there was a pepperoni pizza with mushrooms on one half sitting on the table. Two slices were gone. The autopsy found pepperoni in Matthew's stomach contents, which is logical. But there weren't any mushrooms."

"Well no, there wouldn't be. I told you, Matthew hated mushrooms. I'm sorry, Leah. I guess I'm a little slow. I still don't understand why mushrooms matter. I don't care for them either. Lots of people don't."

"Matthew got a pizza for his dinner that night, right?"

"Yes, but—"

"Ellen, why would he order half with mushrooms if he was going to be eating it alone?"

"Ohhh," she said, as comprehension dawned. "One of the two missing pieces came from the mushroom side?"

"It did. So I think it's possible—no make that likely—that Matthew had invited someone to meet him at the cabin."

"Who? Are you saying that Hannah was there? That can't be. He wouldn't see her again, not after everything. I know he wouldn't."

"No, I'm not saying that. At this point, the big takeaway is that Matthew wasn't alone the night he was killed. And that does shift things a bit."

"What things?"

"Alibis, mostly. Originally the police believed—I did, too— that because the aconite-laced tea could have been left at the cabin anytime, the killer didn't have to be there to kill Matthew. But the pizza indicates someone else *was* there. That could mean that the killer took the risk of being there because they wanted to witness Matthew's death, wanted to see him suffer."

"That's a terrible thought!"

"Yes. But it's also a strong possibility. Several people besides Hannah have revenge motives and weak alibis—Kathy Boyle, Hannah's husband Joel, and what about Matthew's sister Rory? You didn't mention her when we talked."

"Rory? How does she come into this?"

"I thought maybe you could tell me. Apparently she called Kathy Boyle to commiserate with her after Kathy dropped out of the election. According to Kathy, Rory was pretty drunk, and she had some harsh things to say about her brother. Why didn't you mention that Matthew had a sister, and there was bad blood between them?"

"I suppose because Rory hadn't been a part of our lives for years. When Robert, their father died, he left the farm to both of them. Rory, who was in college then, wanted the money so she could go to New York and become a famous actor. She was very immature. Matthew and his dad spoiled her after Marjorie—Matthew and Rory's mother—died. No one ever told her no. We tried to talk her out of her plan, but she was insistent. So we borrowed money from the bank and bought her out. She took the money and left. She never looked back."

"But Rory is in Galen now, right?"

"Yes. She never made it as an actor, but she did develop an addiction to drugs. About two years ago she overdosed. Matthew went with Aunt Jean—she was their dad's sister and close to Rory—to bring her back to Wisconsin. They got her into a good rehab program, and I thought maybe it would stick this time."

"It didn't?"

"No. She fell off the wagon not long before Matthew was killed. Aunt Jean got her back into rehab. I washed my hands of her after she attacked Matthew and me when we didn't have the money to lend her for the dance studio she wanted to buy."

"When Rory called Kathy Boyle, she said that Matthew had cheated her out of her inheritance money. What's that about?"

"Nothing but Rory's sense of entitlement."

"How's that?"

"About six months after we took out a mortgage to buy Rory's share of the farm, a developer offered us triple the price that farm acreage was going for. It was too good an offer to refuse. Because it was such a short time after we'd bought Rory's share, Matthew felt that we should share the windfall with her. I didn't agree. I knew Rory would just run through the money like she was already doing with what she'd gotten for her share of the farm. We compromised. We set up an account separate from our regular savings. The money in it was to go to Rory when she grew up and got her life together. We didn't tell her about it, though."

"Okay, that seems fair enough. Why did Rory tell Kathy Boyle that she'd been cheated?"

"Rory never reached the point where she could handle the money. Then she overdosed. A long stay in a rehab facility is very expensive. We used the money we'd set aside for Rory to pay for it."

"But if Rory didn't know that the money even existed, why would she have said that her brother cheated her?"

"Rory did well after rehab. She got a job at the dance studio in Himmel. She really seemed to like it. We'd started inviting her for dinner now and then and we both could see the change for the better in her. Not long before Matthew died, Rory had the chance to buy the studio. The bank wouldn't lend her the money, though, because her credit was so bad. Aunt Jean told her about the funds we'd set aside for Rory. She didn't know we'd used it to pay for Rory's rehab. Rory came and asked for it, and it wasn't there."

"What happened then?"

"A terrible scene. She accused Matthew of stealing, said their parents would be ashamed of him. Matthew finally got angry and told her that she'd taken advantage of everyone who ever loved her. He told her to leave, and she did."

"Did they ever speak again?"

"No. Matthew hated the way things had ended. He called her to see if they could get together to talk. She said no, she had no interest in seeing him ever again. She was drunk, Matthew said. I heard from Aunt Jean that she went back into rehab right after Matthew was killed. Aunt Jean paid for it this time. And I'm sure Aunt Jean gave her the money to buy the dance studio, too."

"Ellen, did you tell the police about Rory? She's not mentioned in any of the coverage of the trial. Hannah didn't bring her up either."

"If Matthew had been shot, or stabbed, or pushed down the stairs I might have wondered about Rory. But she would never have been able to carry out a murder that involved the planning and patience that poisoning someone with aconite would take. And I always believed that Hannah had killed Matthew. Rory wasn't even in the mix for me."

"And do you still believe that?"

"I don't know," she said, hesitantly. "It seemed so obvious that it must be Hannah. Everything about the police investigation pointed that way."

"It did. But the pizza for two at the cabin opens up a line of investigation that the police didn't follow. So does the information about Rory."

"So you're going to follow it?"

She sounded both tired and resigned which wasn't surprising. She'd gone through a lot of big things in a pretty short time. First the trauma of Matthew's betrayal, then the determination to rebuild their marriage, then the shock of his murder. And just when her emotions were beginning to heal, I showed up to rip the scab off, bringing the pain of uncertainty back into her life.

"Ellen, I know this must be really hard for you. But if there's a chance that Hannah didn't kill Matthew, you don't want her in prison for the rest of her life do you? And you don't want Matthew's killer to go free, do you?"

She didn't answer for a minute. Then she said, "No. I don't want that. I didn't want any of this, but we don't get to choose, do we? Are you going to tell the police what you've found?"

"Eventually. Right now the pizza isn't enough to make the prosecutor decide to reopen an investigation that was a big win for his office. Neither is the information about Rory. But I'm going to see what else I can turn up."

"Leah, can I ask you a favor? Would you keep me in the loop? The police really didn't. Matthew was my husband, after all."

"Yes, sure I can do that, Ellen, if that's what you want. But I might learn some things that you find hard to handle."

"When you go through what I did to beat cancer, you learn that you can handle anything. You don't have to baby me. I just want to know what really happened to my husband. Can you understand that?"

"A hundred percent I can."

32

After I hung up with Ellen, I went back to the case file and started looking at the alibis.

Ellen's story was that she'd been home alone. She worked on a quilt she was making, watched an episode of *Midsomer Murders*, and went to bed at 9:00 p.m. She took a Benadryl because her allergies were bothering her. That knocked her out until 6:00 a.m.

Joel Vining told Detective Cutter that he'd been at a conference and originally planned to stay over but decided to drive home instead. He got home around 11:00 p.m.

Hannah's story was that with Joel out of town and Olivia spending the night at a friend's, she went to the Apothecary to catch up on some paperwork. Joel was home when she got there around 11:30.

Kathy had given the police the same alibi she gave me—that she and her son Patrick had spent the day and evening together and gone to bed early.

Walt Sanders, Matthew's neighbor had no alibi. He was home alone listening to the high school football game.

None of the potential suspects interviewed had great alibis, but that wasn't that odd. In fact, it's pretty common because people who aren't planning to kill someone often don't have proof of where they were at the time of the crime. I'd have to see what Walt Sanders had to say and take another run at Joel Vining and Kathy Boyle. I added Olivia Vining to my list of must-talk-to-again as well. Olivia wasn't a suspect, but I'd observed the same thing Macy had—she was struggling with something. Most likely it had something to do with the murder. I looked at my watch and saw that it was almost 7:30. I hoped Coop would show up soon because my stomach had begun to growl.

Then in an example of perfect timing, the door opened, and he walked in, bringing with him the delicious aroma of General Tso's Chicken.

He put our dinner on the kitchen bar, and I handed him my laptop with Sharla's email pulled up. He read it over while I got out plates for our dinner.

"Well, she's sure a fan," he said. "Do you get a lot of email that's this flattering?"

"I get a lot of nice emails, but most aren't quite as fulsome as Sharla's. In fact the one I read just before I opened hers was pretty harsh. My non-fan FisherKing97 suggested I do something more in line with my writing skills —like find a job where I wouldn't have to use writing at all."

"Ouch!"

"Yeah. You think you're in danger as a cop. I take hits too, you know."

"Well, the flowers are really nice—and expensive, I bet. Your ardent admirer seems to really like you."

"Well, I've been told I'm very likable," I said, batting my eyelashes at him. "Are you sure you don't want to claim credit for sending them? It would get you an excessive amount of romantic gesture points."

"I thought your favorite romantic gesture was a surprise chocolate-covered-strawberry concrete mixer from Culver's. Am I wrong?"

"You are one hundred percent right. Although this General Tso's chicken order also gets you some points," I said, handing a plateful to him. I filled my own plate and sat down beside him at the bar.

"Oh, this is so good," I said, around a mouthful of sweet and savory chicken with just the right amount of spicy heat. "So, what do you think?

Should I report the flowers and the email? It seems kind of premature. Nothing's happened, no threats, no harassment. The only vague link to Sharla is that she used the phrase ardent admirer and that's how the card was signed. Oh, and I checked with Tony to see if the security camera in the stairway caught anyone dropping off flowers. It didn't. He said it needs to be moved because there's a blind spot. So I don't think Owen is going to be very impressed with what I have so far."

"That's probably true. But don't get rid of the email or the card. Hold on to them in case anything else happens. Just because nothing jumped out at me when I looked at the email header doesn't mean there's nothing there. I'm no cyber security expert."

"So I know you said don't communicate with Sharla, but I'm going to."

"This is my surprised expression," he said, staring at me with a blank look on his face.

"No, listen, I'm not ignoring you, I just have another idea. I'm going to thank Sharla for her nice email, like I always do when a reader writes to me. I want them to know I appreciate them. But when I write to Sharla, I'll just ask her if she sent the flowers and see how she responds."

"I see a flaw in that plan. If she says no, how will you know she's telling the truth?"

"I guess I won't, unless I don't hear from her again, which could mean that I scared her off. And if she's a stalker, that's the end result I'm looking for, right?"

"It doesn't usually work like that. I told you, stalkers believe that their attentions are welcome. If you bring up the flowers she may escalate."

"I suppose. But I feel like I still need to answer Sharla's email. If she's not stalking me, I don't want her to think I'm just ignoring her. Remember, maybe I don't have a stalker at all. The flowers could be from someone out there who is mad with desire for me. Who knows what will come next—first class tickets to New York, a penthouse overlooking Central Park, a lifetime supply of Culver's concrete mixers? You may need to up your game. Especially because I have so much free time on my hands with you always working on your property."

"Oh, really? Maybe I'd better start now."

He stood and then took my hand and pulled me off my stool. He leaned down and kissed me. Then he said, "Am I still in the game, coach?"

"Well, I'll give you a chance, but you're going to have to show me that you can score," I said.

He kissed me again.

Later, just as we were falling asleep, I turned my head over on my pillow so I could see him.

"Touchdown," I said.

33

"So, how is your plotting coming?"

Peter Sullivan was waiting for me by the barista station and handed me a chai as I walked through the door on Monday morning. He was looking very dapper for that early hour, dressed in a gray suit complete with tie and pocket square. In marked contrast to me, in jeans, tennis shoes, and a long-sleeved shirt. Though I will give myself fashion points because it was not a Badgers t-shirt, and my tennis shoes were new.

"Thank you! How did you know chai latte is my favorite?"

"I asked the barista, and he told me. I thought since you were good enough to meet me at such an early hour, the least I could do is buy you your favorite beverage," he said, as we found a table and sat down.

Peter's use of language was a little old-fashioned and formal, but I decided that I liked it. His manner of speaking went well with his distinguished appearance.

"Oh, you didn't have to do that. You're doing *me* a favor but thank you. I appreciate it! To be honest, my plotting is not coming at all. A lot's happened since I talked to you last week. I've gotten involved with another project that's taking up most of my time."

"Another book? Just how many manuscripts do you work on at once? You've got one with your editor that you still have to do revisions on, and you're plotting your *naegleria fowleri* story, right? Now you've got another story in the works? You amaze me," he said with a smile.

"Don't get too dazzled. It's not another book. I'm looking into a closed murder case in Trenton County."

"Really? I knew you wrote about crimes. I didn't know you still investigated them as well."

"I don't, usually. But sometimes people ask me to help, and what can I say? I love a mystery," I said. I quickly summarized Hannah Vining's situation for him.

"Oh, yes. I remember something about the case. But if she's already in prison how can you help?"

"I don't know that I can, but I promised her sister I'd try. I'll just keep chasing down leads, most of which won't go anywhere, until I either find the answers or have to admit defeat—which I hate to do. I think that might be one of the things I like about fiction. I can make up all the facts, and I can change them if I don't like the picture they're forming. Plus, I never have to worry about finding the answer, because whatever I write *is* the answer," I said.

He laughed. "Well, I hope you like the answers I've got to the questions you sent me."

He pulled a folded sheet of paper from his suit coat pocket and handed it to me. "I'll email this to you, but I thought it would be good to do a face-to-face so I could answer any follow-up questions you might have."

I glanced through the responses he had typed out.

"This is great, Peter. And I'm so glad you wrote the answers out in plain English and not scientific gobbledygook. No offense," I said.

"None taken. Scientific terminology and acronyms can be confusing, I know. What's shorthand for us can be a little overwhelming to a non-scientist. I think that your murder-by-neti-pot, with the killer being a lab assistant, should work very well. You'll see I detailed the lab protocols that would be followed and how your killer could overcome them to obtain the *naegleria*, and also how he could manipulate the records to cover up the fact that he removed some from the lab. And I hope I was detailed enough in answer to your other questions," he said.

"Yes, this is all good stuff! Thank you for spending so much time on this."

"My pleasure. I hope you'll continue to ask me any questions that come up. This was a very enjoyable exercise for me."

"Oh, believe me I will. You know, once I get the investigation I'm working on cleared up, I'm thinking of making a field trip to your old stomping grounds."

"Buckner College?"

"Yes. I did a little online research, and it seems a lot like the small, imaginary college I have in mind for my killer to work at. And as a bonus, I discovered there was a meningitis outbreak there in 1987, which is also a good fit with my plot. Were you there then?"

"Yes. I was at Buckner in 1987. I remember the meningitis outbreak very well. My first wife died in it."

For a second I was shocked into silence, then I began stumbling out an apology.

"Oh, Peter, I'm so sorry. Why didn't you say anything before? There I am blithely babbling about what a great cover meningitis will be for my murder and, for you, it was a tragedy. I feel terrible."

"No, no. It's all right. I didn't mention it initially for the very reason that I didn't want to make you uncomfortable. Elizabeth died almost forty years ago. It was very difficult at the time, but it's no longer painful. I've been very lucky in love, first with Elizabeth and then with Adele. There's no need for you to apologize. Really."

"That makes me feel a little better. Do you really not mind talking about it?"

"I really don't. Now tell me about your plan to visit Buckner. What are you hoping to learn? As a researcher myself, I'm curious about your process."

"I want to get a feel for the place, maybe talk to some people who were around during the meningitis outbreak, see how it would have been handled by the health department there, how the college would have reacted, what resources the community had to combat it."

"Are you going to set your story in the actual town of Buckner?"

"No, my college town will be fictional, but it helps to have something to base it on."

"Well, my memories of the community and the college at the time of the outbreak are still quite vivid. I'm happy to answer any questions about the community that I can help with—and that might save you a trip."

"I would love to get your recollections, especially on the small details like where students hung out, where faculty lived, how the Buckner community looked and felt. But I think I'll still take a trip down there myself. It's always good to see a setting firsthand if you can."

"Of course. But please do call on me for help if you'd like to. I feel very honored that you trusted me with your plot. I'll enjoy telling my friends that I played a small part in the writing of your latest mystery. At this point, am I still bound to secrecy as far as your plot? But I would never share any spoilers," he hastened to add.

"Absolutely you are. I haven't even told my agent the storyline yet."

"Understood. I won't exercise bragging rights that I helped a famous author with her book until after it's published. Well, I'm afraid I have to leave you now. As I told you, Adele has a dental procedure this morning. I'm hoping it won't be as bad as she anticipates, and that she'll be able to come with me to the open house for D&D investigations this afternoon."

"Oh, I'm going to that, too. How do you know the Darmodys?"

I hoped I didn't sound as surprised as I felt. It was hard to imagine how Darmody's world had intersected with the Sullivans.

"Angela Darmody cleans for us. When Angela gave us notice because of opening the business with her husband, Adele begged her to keep on with us. It took quite a while to find someone particular enough to suit Adele. Angela agreed and she invited us to the grand opening of D&D Investigations, so we really have no choice but to go."

"Maybe I'll see you there. Thank you, Peter, for the chai and the information. This was very helpful. I'll be in touch."

"I look forward to it," he said.

34

A minute or two after Peter left, Miguel walked in. I waved from the back booth where I was sitting as he stopped to order his current favorite coffee drink, Badger Bliss—espresso, milk, maple and butter pecan syrup, and whipped cream, topped with candied pecans.

"Geez, Miguel, that's a big sugar rush so early in the morning," I said as he slid into the booth across from me.

"I know, but it is so good! Try some," he said, handing the cup to me.

I did and shuddered a little as I handed it back to him.

"That's a little too sweet, even for me. I'll let you enjoy it while I fill you in on where I am now."

I went over what I'd found in the murder file from Hannah's attorney, finishing with a flourish on the half mushroom pepperoni pizza with two missing slices, found at the murder scene.

"Oh, that is a very good catch! So someone who likes mushrooms was there with Matthew. It makes the alibis—and the no alibis— matter more."

"It definitely does. Are you up for a visit to Rory Ferguson today? And then I'd like to go and see Matthew's cabin and talk to the neighbor who found his body."

"Yes, if I am back by one o'clock. I have to take photos at the grand opening of D&D Investigations."

"Yes, I have to hit that too. It runs from one to five, right?"

"Yes, but I will be there all afternoon, because I am doing some side work for Darmody."

"Really? What kind of work? Am I going to have to compete with Darmody for your investigative skills?"

"No. I do not want to do divorce work and missing pets. They need a brochure for their business. I'm going to put it together for them, so I want to get some extra photos and some quotes from people at the open house."

"We should get going then to be sure we get you back from Galen in time. Oh, I almost forgot. I need to call Ellen Ferguson and ask if I can borrow the key to the cabin."

"She will be okay with that?"

"I think so. Hang on and we'll find out."

Ellen answered on the first ring, and I explained why I was calling.

"I don't know what you'd find there that the police didn't. But yes, you have my permission. There's a spare key stored on the back of a wooden welcome sign that says Gone Fishin'. Would you drop it off to me when you're done? I've been meaning to go out and get it—it's probably not a good idea to have the cabin empty and the key in such an easy place to find. I just haven't been able to make myself go get it."

"Sure, I'll come by when I'm done. Thanks, Ellen," I said as I hung up.

"Okay, we're set, Miguel, let's hit the road. First stop DanceFusion, then on to Galen."

Rory Ferguson was standing at the reception desk when we walked in. She looked up from the paperwork she was reviewing and smiled. Her dark hair was in a bun on top of her head and the leotard she wore showed that she had the lithe body of a dancer.

"Well good morning, Miguel. I love an eager student, but the ballroom dancing class doesn't start until tonight," she said.

"I know. I'm very excited. I'm taking it with Carol Nash. This is her daughter, Leah."

"Hello, Leah," Rory said, shaking my hand with a firm grip. "Are you interested in dance lessons, too?"

"No. I'm afraid I have an incurable case of two left feet. I was hoping to talk to you about your brother Matthew."

A series of expressions passed fleetingly across her face—surprise, confusion, concern—she settled on confusion when she spoke.

"I'm sorry, I don't understand why my brother's death is your concern," she said.

I explained what I was doing and why.

"I've known Hannah since I was a kid. She and my brother dated all through high school—until Hannah moved. I was shocked when she was found guilty of killing him. But I don't see how I can help. Matthew and I weren't close for years before he died."

"Yes, I heard that from your sister-in-law, Ellen."

"Oh. I'm sure she made me the villain in that story," Rory said, in a less friendly tone.

"No, she didn't actually. She just said that you'd had some issues with addiction over the years and that eventually drove a wedge between you and Matthew."

"Well, that's true. I'm not proud of it, but you can't change the past, right? I'm firmly focused on the future—not the Broadway star future I thought I'd have, but I'm determined to run the best dance studio in Grantland County."

"Your studio looks great. And my mother says you're a wonderful choreographer and teacher."

Her previous frown was replaced by a smile. "That's nice to hear. Carol's been very kind to me."

Okay, that was as good an opening as I was going to have to get to the heart of why I was there. Riding on the wave of her good feelings about my mother I said, "She mentioned that your chance to buy the studio almost fell through. Was it Matthew who helped you get the financing in the end?"

I knew of course that it wasn't, but I wanted Rory to give me the story from her perspective.

"If you've talked to Ellen, I'm sure you know that he didn't. And that I didn't react very well when he turned me down."

She was sharper than I'd expected.

"She did mention it. I'm interested in hearing about it from you."

"Because you think I killed Matt after he turned me down? I didn't. Though I was pretty rotten to him. It was a huge shock finding out the money Aunt Jean told me was there for me, wasn't. But I got over it. I apologized to Matt, and we had a good talk and were able to sort out some things before he died."

She fidgeted as she spoke, and her eyes didn't meet mine.

"That must have been a comfort to you."

If that had ever happened, I thought. Surely Ellen would have said something about that when I asked her about Rory. It was possible that Matthew hadn't mentioned that he'd reconciled with his sister, but that didn't seem likely.

"Yes, it was. You know, I'm teaching a senior tap class at 10:00 that I have to get ready for, so—"

"Oh, sure. I just have one other question. Where were you the night your brother was killed?"

Sometimes a shocker will prompt a surprising answer. Not this time though.

"I was home, alone. I live with my Aunt Jean in Galen. And as I said, I didn't kill my brother. I like Hannah, I always have. I'm sorry she's in prison, but I don't know anything that could help you. So, if you'll excuse me," she said, walking to the door and holding it open for us, "I really do need to get ready for my class."

"That did not go so well," Miguel said as we settled into my car and headed toward Galen.

"It went well enough that I got what I wanted," I said.

"What is that?"

"Confirmation that she and Matthew fought over money, and that she has no one to corroborate that she was home. The only thing I forgot to ask was if she prefers mushrooms on her pizza. You can do that later, though. She still likes you."

"But Matthew is her brother! I could never kill my brother," Miguel said.

He doesn't actually have any siblings, a fact which he makes up for by being very close to his many cousins.

"You could never kill anyone, Miguel. But sadly there's a lot of sibling-on-sibling homicide happening in this wicked world. Especially when money is involved."

"But I do not think that Rory would kill anyone."

"People will do a lot of unexpected things when they're under the influence of drugs or alcohol. Rory went in for a second round of rehab right after Matthew was killed. That raises the possibility that she might have been under the influence the night he died. And that she may have killed him. And that she went into rehab as much to get away from the investigation as to get herself back under control."

"I think you are wrong this time."

"That could certainly be true. We'll see how things play out. Which reminds me, were you able to find out anything about Matthew's friend Kenny Marston?"

"I was."

"Is he the one who tipped the paper off about Kathy Boyle?"

"No, he can't be."

"Why? Spill, please."

"I searched for Kenny online. I found him in a town called Breckenridge in Michigan. But the phone number listed wasn't his. So then I used an app to find the names of the neighbors on his street and started calling them. It's a very, very small town. A village, really. Finally one picked up my call. He told me Kenny Marston used to live there, but after he got out of jail he moved."

"He was in jail? When? What for?"

"A second offense arrest for drunk driving with a high limit. That happened the day after he was with Matthew at the bachelor party. He drove home through the Upper Peninsula and he was arrested and jailed there, too. He would not have time to send the anonymous letter to the paper before he was in jail. And he was there for a year."

"Are you sure?"

"I am. I checked an online database the Michigan State Police run. The public can use it to look up criminal offenses. I think that Ellen is wrong, and Kenny Marston can't be the one who tipped off Riley Dorner at the *Galen Record*."

"Good work, Miguel!"

"Not *so* good. We still don't know who sent the information about Kathy to the paper."

"No, but we know who didn't, and that helps, too."

35

We could have parked at the Trenton County Park and walked the short distance on the bike trail to Matthew's cottage. But because Miguel was on a tight timeline, we took Burdock Road, parked, and walked across the footbridge that spanned Clearwater Creek.

Matthew's cabin was actually that—a rustic structure made from logs, no more than 800 square feet in size, nestled into a stand of pine trees. I could see a small storage shed behind it, as well as glimpses through the trees of the bike trail.

I found the key behind the Gone Fishin' sign and unlocked the door. When we stepped inside, it was obvious that someone had cleaned up after the police had finished with the crime scene. The counter and kitchen table were cleared, the chairs were neatly pulled into the table, and the living room furniture was all in place. But it was also evident that no one had been in the place for quite a while. There was a thick coat of dust on everything. I opened the cupboards to peek inside and sent dust flying through air which, in turn, got us both sneezing.

"What are we looking for?"

"I don't really know. I thought being at the crime scene might shoot a lightning bolt of insight into my head, but so far, no. Come on, let's check out the rest of the place."

The rest turned out to be a small bedroom that contained a queen size bed that took up almost all the floor space and a small closet with empty hangers on a rod and empty shelves above. A plaid curtain served as the closet door. The bathroom was very small as well, with a toilet set so close to the sink that there would be a knee issue for anyone over five who used it.

"Miguel, I think we found the answer to your housing dilemma. You should check with Ellen and see if she's interested in renting. It's got all the basics—kitchen, living room, bedroom, bathroom. There's even a wood burning stove in the living room. And the view—once the windows are clean—of Clearwater Creek running by your front door is very nice."

"It is pretty, but I can't live outside the county. Too far to drive when things are happening. I need to be closer to the action."

"True. But it's a very private, quiet place. Very relaxing."

Just then the sound of a chainsaw starting up rent the air and gave the lie to my words.

"Sounds like Walt Sanders is home. Let's go see if he's in a chatty mood."

We followed the sound of the saw—not hard to do—across Matthew's lot and around the back of the cabin next door. It was similar in size to Matthew's, though not as well kept. One of the windows on the side was cracked and the roof looked seriously in need of repair. We spotted a slight man with wild white hair using a chainsaw. He wore no safety glasses and no headphones against the deafening noise. We walked over and stood in front of him, because there was no way he'd be able to hear us over the roar of his wood cutting. It took a second for him to see us and turn off the motor. He set the saw down on a tree stump.

"Walt Sanders?"

"That's me. Who're you?" His voice was high-pitched and querulous.

"I'm Leah Nash. I'm a journalist and this is my colleague Miguel Santos. We'd like to speak to you for just a few minutes about Matthew Ferguson."

He pulled an old-fashioned blue bandana out of the jeans that hung loosely on his skinny frame and wiped his forehead before he answered.

"He's dead. What's there to talk about, and what's it to you?"

I explained what I was doing and why.

"I know that you're the person who found Matthew's body. I wonder if you could tell me about that?"

It felt a little awkward to conduct the conversation standing in the sawdust and wood chips as squirrels chattered over our head. But needs must, and it was clear Walt wasn't going to ask us in for a nice cup of tea.

"Not much to tell. I seen his truck was blockin' my way out. He pulled in all kinda crooked, and I couldn't get out without him movin' his truck. So I went to his place, knocked on the door. He didn't answer, so I poked my head in and called out. That's when I seen him lyin' there on the floor. I could tell he was dead from where I was standin'. His eyes was open but just starin'. I called 911 and that was that."

"Did you see any evidence of anyone else having been there? Two bottles of beer, or two coffee cups on the table, anything like that?"

"Girly, I wasn't doin' a house tour. Once I saw Matthew's body, I shut that door and got my phone. I wasn't gonna stick around with a dead man's eyes starin' at me. I waited at my place for the cops and everybody to get here. Then I went out and told the cops what I seen and answered their questions and went back to my place. End of story."

"Were you and Matthew friends?" Miguel asked, though we both already knew the answer.

"Not hardly. He screwed me outta part of my property. Court didn't see it that way, but I measured it all out myself and had my property deed and I don't care what that fancy surveyor Matthew hired said. I know what land my granddad bought. Matthew had no right to put that shed where he did. He took a good foot of my property to do it. Court didn't see it that way. The whole thing was rigged for the rich guy. Nobody cared about my rights. And it cost me a lotta money before I figured that one out."

"That must have made you pretty angry."

"Course it did. I'll admit I had some words with Matthew, some pretty loud words, but that's all. Him and me, we just stayed away from each other. That suited me. We wasn't friends before the lawsuit and we sure as hell wasn't after it. I liked his wife though. She wasn't out here much, but she was always nice. Felt kinda bad for her when I seen Matthew had a girlfriend. She was a looker, I'll say that. I always had a thing for redheads."

"You knew Matthew was meeting Hannah Vining here?"

"Kinda hard to miss her car sittin' there next to the bridge. And I seen her leavin' sometimes."

"Did you ever say anything to anyone about seeing Hannah here? Did you mention it to the police after Matthew died?"

"Nope. None of my business. I keep myself to myself. It's why I kept the property all these years. I like to be alone. Now that nobody uses Matthew's cabin, it's real nice and quiet out here. Except for the damn hikers and bike riders on the trail back there. I wish the county never put it in. I didn't vote for it. Nothin' but a waste of money and a disturber of my peace."

"The trail, it is a little far back from your cabin for the noise to bother you, isn't it?" Miguel asked.

"Some of them bike riders don't stay on the trail. This here is private property. I got it posted. But they come in here anyway and go traipsin' down to the creek like they own the place. I come out with my shotgun now and then, and that scatters 'em pretty good. They usually don't come back, cause they think I'm a crazy old man that might shoot them. And they ain't wrong," he said and then began a cackling laugh that ended in a cough and sent the aroma of Jim Beam wafting our way.

When his cough didn't stop, Miguel stepped forward and patted him on the back and offered him a drink from the bottle of water he had with him. Which I thought was above and beyond if he was planning on drinking it again himself. Walt took it gratefully and downed it all in one long drink. Lucky Miguel.

"Are you okay, Walt?" Miguel asked.

"I am, thanks," Walt croaked out.

"So did you notice anyone ever trying to get into the cabin?" I asked.

"No, I woulda called the cops for that. There was this one young girl kept comin' back maybe three or four times. I chased her off. She was ridin' one of them e-bikes. Those puppies can really move."

The words young girl and e-bikes stirred something in my brain.

"How young was the girl? A kid like 9 or 10, or older, like a teenager?"

"She was young, but she wasn't a little kid. I guess maybe she was a teenager."

"What did she look like? What color was her hair?"

"How the hell do I know? She was wearin' a helmet. I didn't even see her hair."

"What color was the helmet? Did you notice anything else about her? You said you saw her more than once."

"Her helmet was blue. I noticed because that was my wife Billie Jo's favorite color. Her bike was the same color."

"And it was an e-bike?"

"I already said it was. Why you askin' me all this?"

I ignored him. "When was the last time?"

"Long time ago. Last year probably."

"Think hard, please. Was it before or after Matthew died?"

He squinted as though that helped his thinking process, and it must have because he came up with the answer I hoped he would.

"Before. I know it was before because after Matthew died, for a week or two there was a whole passel of people, not just kids, rubberneckin' out here, peekin' in the windows and what not. I got my shotgun out, and for a coupla days I sat out here in the afternoons and that put a stop to it pretty quick."

"Was the girl with the blue helmet one of the people 'rubbernecking'?"

"No, that's what I'm sayin'. She wasn't in that crowd, and I never seen her come back."

Miguel was eyeing me, wondering, I knew, what my fixation on trespassing teens was all about.

"Okay. Well, thanks for your time, Walt. We appreciate it."

36

"Why did you keep asking Walt about the bike riders who have been bothering him?" Miguel asked as we walked across the bridge to my car.

"Because I think the kid he chased away was Olivia. I told you she followed me on her e-bike after her dad told me to leave. Her bike was blue, she was wearing a blue helmet—not definitive, I know. But Olivia is hiding something. Hannah's attorney Macy saw that and so did I. I assumed that Olivia had learned about her mother's affair during the investigation into Matthew's death. But what if she knew before?"

"How could she?"

"She might have seen or heard something that made her suspicious. And she might have come out here to see if her suspicions were real. And if she found out they were, maybe she did something about it."

He'd been about to get into the passenger seat, but he stopped and stared at me across the roof of the car.

"You think Olivia killed Matthew?" he asked, his voice combining disbelief and horror.

"No. Maybe. I don't know. But she would've had access to aconite—she worked at Hannah's store. You saw how easy it was to get into the cabin. She could have put the poison tea there."

"But how does that fit with the half mushroom pizza?"

"Maybe she called Matthew and asked if he'd meet her here to talk. I think he would have agreed to see what she had to say about him and Hannah, and maybe to persuade her that she had jumped to the wrong conclusion. That could explain the missing slice of mushroom pizza."

"I can believe that she would want to ask Matthew to stay away from her mother. But why would she want to kill him?"

"Because, Miguel, she viewed him as a threat to her family, to her happiness. She was afraid that her mother might leave Joel. The family that she had been so happy in would be destroyed. What would she do to stop that from happening?"

"But she was only fourteen!"

"Emotions run very high at that age, and impulse control and judgement can run dangerously low. She might have decided that killing Matthew was a kind of self-defense to keep him from killing her family."

"Maybe," Miguel said, but his voice made clear his reluctance to go along with my new hypothesis.

"I'm not saying that I believe Olivia killed Matthew. But we can't take the possibility off the table. Also, think about this—maybe the reason Hannah has been so bad at defending herself, and so seemingly resigned to life in prison is that she either knows or is afraid that Olivia is the one who killed Matthew. Mothers will do just about anything for their children."

He shook his head. "I hope that is the wrong answer."

"Me too, Miguel, me too."

We rode in silence the rest of the way to Ellen's house to return the cabin key.

It wasn't Ellen who opened the door to her house when Miguel and I rang the bell. Instead it was an attractive woman with striking blue-green eyes, blonde hair cut in a layered bob, and a nice smile.

"Hello. You must be Leah," she said. "I'm Ellen's sister, Lindsey Franks. She said you'd be stopping by."

"Yes I am, and this is my colleague Miguel Santos. Ellen asked me to drop off the key to the cabin. Is she in, or can I leave it with you?"

"She isn't, but she should be shortly. She had a doctor's appointment in Madison. It ran late, but she's on her way home now. I know she'd like to see you."

I glanced at my watch.

"I'd like to see her, too, but Miguel has to be back in Himmel by one o'clock and it's almost 12:15. So maybe—"

"No, that's all right," Miguel said. "It's only a twenty-minute drive, we can wait at least a little while for Ellen."

Miguel never likes to pass up the opportunity to meet someone new—and I did want him to get a sense of her.

"All right, we'll wait."

"I don't know if Ellen mentioned it," Lindsey said as the three of us sat down in the living room to wait for Ellen's arrival. "But I've read your true crime books, Leah, and I'm just starting the fictional mystery that came out this summer. I really enjoy your writing."

"Thanks Lindsey, that's very nice of you to say."

"But I just wonder—you're not going to use Ellen and the whole story of Matthew's murder in a new true crime book are you?"

"No, I don't plan on writing a book about it. Right now I'm committed to learning how to write good fiction. I don't see myself going back to true crime, at least not for a while."

"Oh, I'm glad. Matthew's death was so devastating to Ellen. I can't imagine what it would do to her if a book came out and raked it all up in public again. To be honest, I wish you weren't even looking into it now. I know that Hannah's sister wants to help her, but this isn't easy for Ellen. She's just started putting it behind her."

"I understand. Still, as a sister yourself, wouldn't you want to do the same thing for Ellen that Marguerite asked me to do for Hannah?"

"Yes, I suppose I would. But it's hard for me to forget how awful it all was. Ellen is a very strong person. But the way she responded was really scary to me."

"How do you mean?" I asked.

"Well, Matthew was her everything. I thought she'd be hysterical, or that she'd collapse with grief."

"But she did not?" Miguel prompted when Lindsey paused.

"No, just the opposite. I came as soon as I got the call, but I live almost two hours away. I ran in the house, but I couldn't find her, and she didn't answer me. Then I caught sight of her through the kitchen window, in her garden. She was kneeling in front of some flowers with a trowel in her hand, but she was just staring into space. I hurried out, but when I spoke to her, she didn't seem to understand what I was saying. I got her up and into the house. She still hadn't said anything. I sat her down on the sofa and I went to get a shot of whiskey for her."

"How long before she came out of it?" I asked.

"When I came back into the living room, I noticed that her right hand and part of her arm were covered with a bumpy rash that looked painful. She has very sensitive skin and she usually wears gloves when she gardens. I put my hand on her cheek and turned her head so that she had to look directly at me. Ellen, I said, what happened? Why were you in the garden? Do you understand that Matthew is dead? She looked at me like she was really seeing me for the first time. Then her eyes filled with tears, and she broke down. I hugged her and we sat there for a long time while she sobbed so hard she couldn't catch her breath. It was just awful."

"That must have been frightening," I said.

"It was! Ellen has always been so . . . I don't know the right word, not reserved exactly. Composed I guess. She's always the clear thinking one. Even when she got the cancer diagnosis and we were all falling apart, she was so steady, so practical. Seeing her like that after Matthew was killed . . . I just felt so helpless. When she finally stopped crying, I got some calamine lotion for her rash and asked her again what she was doing in the garden."

"What did she say?"

"That after the deputy left, she couldn't think straight. She'd been in the garden when he arrived, pulling out some stinging nettle. When he left, she'd gone back out there, but couldn't remember anything else. She didn't even realize she'd been out there for at least two hours by the time I arrived. I called her doctor and got a prescription for something to calm her down a little. I knew when Colin got here—that's her son, she adores him—that would help. I can't believe what my sister's had to go through. First cancer, then Matthew has an affair, then he dies, and then we find out it was murder!"

"Lindsey, did Ellen tell you about the affair when Matthew confessed it to her?"

"No. She never said a word to me about it. When it came out after he died, she said it was between her and Matthew. She said he'd asked her to forgive him, and she had, and she didn't want to hear me say anything bad about him. I was pretty angry at him but if she could forgive him, I figured I could. I'd always liked Matthew. He was an absolute rock during all her cancer treatment. She's cancer-free now, has been for four years. Her appointment today was the big one, the five-year anniversary of her going into remission. I wanted to go with her, but she said no, that she needed to prove to herself that she can take care of herself."

"It looks to me like she's doing a pretty good job," I said.

"She is," Lindsey said, the pride obvious in her voice. "His affair really hurt her, but she focuses on all the good things about Matthew. And there were a lot. I guess that's why she forgave him. I don't have it in me to be that good."

"At least by confessing to her, he was able to tell Ellen how sorry he was, and she knew that he'd chosen to come back to her, not go with Hannah."

"That's true. I hadn't thought of it like that before," she said.

"Did you know Hannah?" Miguel asked.

"A little. She was in Ellen's grade at school. I'm Marguerite's age. Hannah was in Ellen's group of friends, but they weren't besties or anything. She was always nice to me, but I don't have very warm feelings for her after she went after my sister's husband. But if she really didn't kill Matthew, I don't want her to be in prison for something she didn't do."

A ring tone that belonged to neither me nor Miguel trilled out and Lindsey reached in her pocket for her phone.

"Ellen, hi. Where are you? . . . Oh, no. Okay, sure, I'll let her know. See you when you get here."

She turned to us after clicking off the call.

"That was Ellen. She's just five miles away, but there was an accident on the highway and traffic is backed up quite a distance. She's not sure when she'll be able to get here."

I looked at my watch. It was 12:30.

"I'm afraid we can't wait. I've got to get Miguel back to Himmel. It was nice meeting you, Lindsey. Please tell Ellen I'll call her later."

"I will. She'll be sorry she missed you, too. Ellen is lonely these days, with Matthew gone, and Colin working in Ashland. They were her whole world. I'm trying to get her to move to Platteville where I live. Well, I'd better let you go, or you'll be late."

37

"Okay, Miguel. I got you back with twelve minutes to spare. Are you going inside?" I asked as we pulled into the parking lot behind the *Times*.

"No, my camera is in my car."

I pulled up beside his yellow Mini Cooper.

"Here you go. I'll talk to you later. Thanks for going with me today."

"Don't forget about Darmody's grand opening. He will be sad if you do not come."

"I'll be there."

As he got out of the car, my phone rang. Kathy Boyle. I gave Miguel a quick wave and proceeded to my parking space as I answered.

"Hi Kathy, how are you?"

"You asked me to call if I thought of anything else." She paused.

"And you have?" I asked.

"Well, it might be nothing. But you need to see it to decide for yourself."

A loud horn went off in the background.

"Damn. I hate the traffic in Madison! That guy just about sideswipes me, and he honks the horn like it's *my* fault!" Kathy said.

"You okay?"

"I probably shouldn't be talking in this heavy traffic, I need to focus. But it just popped back into my head. I called now because I knew I'd forget again if I didn't. I'm so busy with this move I can hardly think straight. Can you stop by tomorrow afternoon?"

"I could come by this evening if that works," I said.

"No, I've got too much to do tonight. Tomorrow's better."

"What time?"

"Around four would be good. I have to be in Sun Prairie to sign some paperwork in the morning and then I'm going to lunch with my son."

"You don't want to give me a hint about the thing I should see?"

"No, it'll be better if you look for yourself, I—" There was another loud blare from a horn.

"I've got to go. I'll see you tomorrow."

"Hello, Sam. Did you miss me?" I asked as I walked into my apartment and he curled around my ankles purring. I picked him up and carried him over to the window seat with me, stopping on my way to get my legal pad and a pencil off the kitchen counter.

Sam gave me an aren't-you-forgetting-something look. I went back into the kitchen and put some food in his dish. I wasn't hungry at the moment myself.

The window seat cushions were warmed by the sun streaming through the windows and it was very pleasant to lean against them in my favorite corner. I began jotting down notes from the morning, starting with Rory at DanceFusion and on through Walt and Lindsey. When I was done, I tapped my pencil on the edge of the legal pad and stared aimlessly into space, processing what I'd written.

After a while, I made a list of things I needed to follow up on. Right at the top was Olivia. If my idea was right and she had known about her mother's affair before Matthew was killed, that could change everything. But Miguel's question nagged at me. Did I really think that Olivia could kill someone? It's one thing to be furious and frightened and want to kill someone. It's quite another to do it. Bottom line, I had to talk to Olivia again, this time armed with what Walt had told me about her frequent jaunts to the cabin. And I needed to try another run at her dad Joel as well.

Then there was Rory. She'd offered a reasonable version of her disagreement over money with her brother. But the reconciliation story she told seemed unlikely to me. And her nervousness while telling it also made me think that she was making it up on the fly. I needed to do some serious digging into her story.

And I still hadn't answered the question of who had leaked Kathy's past to the *Galen Record*. If it wasn't Kenny Marston, then Matthew did seem a likely candidate, despite Ellen's protests. Was Matthew a caring brother and supportive husband who had a brief fling that he regretted? Or was he an asshat who deliberately ruined Kathy Boyle's life to ensure that he got elected? Kathy's story about Matthew taunting her with a line from her adult film, if she'd heard him right, was certainly at odds with Ellen's view of him as the good guy everybody loved.

"But maybe he was both, " I said out loud. "Oy, this is a twisty mess right now, Sam!"

Sam twitched his tail but otherwise gave no sign that he'd heard, or cared, about my angst over the investigation.

My phone rang then. Ellen.

"Hi, Ellen. I'm sorry we missed you today."

"It wasn't your fault. I'm the one who's sorry. I was sure I'd be home from the doctor's before you got there. But you know what doctors' offices are like. You wait for half an hour in the waiting room, then they take you to the examining room and you sit half-naked another half-hour, wondering if anyone remembers that you're there."

"How did your checkup go?"

"Fine. Some poking and prodding and a few tests. Now it's just waiting for the results to come in."

"Does that make you nervous?"

"Oh, a little maybe, but it's pretty routine. This year it will be five years in remission. That's a big landmark. My sister Lindsey and I are going to take a cruise to celebrate."

Personally, being on a cruise ship in the middle of the ocean with no escape doesn't appeal to me. And don't even get me started on the prospect of the ship going down. Okay, so I know it's not a *likely* prospect, but I was emotionally scarred by *The Poseidon Adventure* and *The Perfect Storm*.

"You deserve whatever kind of celebration you'd like," I said.

"Thank you, and thanks for asking. But I called to say that you forgot to leave the key to the cabin."

"What?" I felt around in the pocket of my jeans. "Oh shoot, I did! We left so fast in order to get Miguel back to Himmel on time that I forgot the whole reason we stopped at your house in the first place. I'm sorry."

"No, no, it's not a big thing. I thought that since you have to come back with it, maybe you'd like to stay for dinner tomorrow. Just pizza and a glass of wine, nothing big. No problem if you're too busy for that. And you probably are," she said, finishing on a wistful note.

Although we hadn't made plans, I was hoping to spend Tuesday evening with Coop. However, I remembered what her sister Lindsey had said about Ellen's loneliness. I made some rapid internal calculations about the timing of the things I needed to do the next day.

"Sure, that sounds good. I'll be in Galen tomorrow afternoon anyway."

"Oh, good! Have you ever had pizza from Cheesehead Pizza? Matthew and I always ordered from there even though they don't deliver. It's the best pizza ever."

"I haven't tried it. I think Cheesehead is a Galen thing. And I believe that as a loyal Himmelite, I'm required to claim best pizza for our very own Bonnuci's pizza. And it really is the best."

She laughed.

"Well, maybe we'll do a pizza tasting contest one day. What time tomorrow works for you?"

"I'm meeting with Kathy Boyle at 4:00, so how about after that, say around 5:30?"

"Sure. But I thought you already talked to Kathy. Are you following a new lead?"

"I don't know yet. She called to say she had something she thought I should see, but she didn't elaborate. She was in heavy traffic in Madison at the time so she couldn't stay on the phone long."

"That's interesting. Do you think she remembered something she didn't tell the police? Or that she figured something out?"

"She said it was something I should 'see' so it sounds like something physical more than just something she recalled or an idea that came to her. But I honestly don't know."

"Well, maybe whatever Kathy wants to tell or show you will be something that makes a difference."

"Let's hope so. Hey, I just thought of something. I'll be driving right by Cheesehead Pizza when I leave Kathy's. Why don't I pick up the pizza and save you the trouble?"

"Oh, I couldn't ask you to do that. I'm the one who invited you to dinner. You shouldn't have to bring the dinner with you."

"I don't mind at all. Are you okay with a plain pepperoni and cheese pizza? It'll put Cheesehead to the test—if they can make a basic like that taste fantastic, which by the way, Bonnuci's does, then I'll add them to my pizzeria hall of fame."

"Yes, I like pepperoni, and trust me, Cheesehead won't let you down. I'll let you pick up the pizza. But you are definitely not paying for it. You can text me as you're leaving Kathy's. I'll put the order in, and the timing should be just about right for it to be ready when you get there."

"All right. Sounds good. See you tomorrow."

38

All that talk of food with Ellen had awakened my appetite. I made a peanut butter sandwich, then remembered I didn't have any Diet Coke, my preferred beverage with peanut butter. I made the trek to the pop machine in the break room and poked my head in my mother's office before I went back upstairs. I'd talked and texted with her over the weekend, but hadn't actually seen her since she dropped the bombshell that she and Paul were on a break.

"Hey, Mom, how's it going?"

"Leah? Is that you? It's been so long since I've seen you. Come closer and let me make sure."

"You're hilarious, Mom. Also, we just talked on Saturday."

"Today is Monday, so that was last week. Also, it was only on the phone. I have to assume that you have been very, very, busy to neglect your aging mother."

"Yeah, I have been. But I'm never too busy to bring a little sunshine into your golden years. In fact, I made a special trip downstairs in the middle of what I'm working on, just to—"

"Get a soda from the machine?" she asked, looking pointedly at the Diet Coke can in my hand. "I know that's why you really came down. But now that you're here, what have you been up to? Have you talked to Rory Ferguson yet?"

"I have."

"Did she tell you anything useful?"

"She did."

"Am I going to have to drag it out of you?"

"Maybe."

"Do you want me to use persuasion or force?"

"Depends. What have you got for persuasion?"

"I'm making your favorite mac and cheese this week. There's a bowl with your name on it if that's persuasive enough for you. For force, you don't even want to know what I have in store."

"Okay, I'll take the mac and cheese. Rory admitted that she and Matthew had a rocky relationship, and that she was furious with him for not helping her buy her dance studio. But she said they reconciled before he died, and things were fine between them. Also, for the record, no waterboarding was used to secure those answers."

"Well, there, I told you she didn't have anything to do with Matthew's death. Now you can cross her off your list."

"I can, if I believe her."

"You don't? Why not?"

"I didn't say that. I just don't know enough yet to take her at her word."

"I think I'm a pretty good judge of people, and Rory doesn't strike me as a liar—let alone as someone who could kill her own brother. She was really shaken when he died. I think she really loved him. She fell off the wagon right around then, and I thought at the time it was the grief and stress that caused it. Did she tell you that?"

"She didn't, but someone else I interviewed told me that she spoke to Rory not long before Matthew died, and she was drunk or high. So maybe she was already relapsing and maybe she did something while drinking that she wouldn't have done sober."

"Maybe she started drinking again when she was so disappointed that Matthew didn't give her the money for the studio. But it doesn't mean that she went on a bender and killed him. Whether it was before he died or after, she went right into rehab and didn't let herself fall all the way back to where she was. That doesn't sound like a killer to me. It sounds like someone who took a brief wrong turn, then got herself back on track," my mother said.

"Or like someone who wanted to get out of the way of an investigation into her brother's death. It took a couple of weeks for the second round of toxicology reports to reveal that Matthew had been poisoned. Once the police found the texts between Hannah and Matthew, the focus was on Hannah. Rory was pretty much in the clear, or at least she definitely was out of the cross hairs as a suspect."

"Are you suggesting that Rory faked a relapse to avoid becoming a suspect?"

"No. I'm suggesting that I have to look at everyone who might have a reason to kill Matthew, and Rory had a pretty good motive, from her perspective anyway. She thought he cheated her out of her fair share of the money from the sale of the farm she and Matthew inherited when their father died."

"Is that your theory?"

"No. I don't have one yet. Right now I'm just wondering—not theorizing, not deciding—just what if-ing, if you will. I get that Rory's your friend and you don't want to go there. And I also respect your judgement, so I'm not married to Rory as the murderer. But I still have to take the *X-Files* approach on this and trust no one. Not even Hannah or Marguerite. Because everybody lies."

"That's a very cynical outlook."

"Agreed. But it's a realistic one—that I know from years as a reporter. The saving grace is that while everyone lies sometimes, very few people lie all the time. The hard thing is figuring out when it's happening. At this point I don't know who's lying to me. But somebody is."

"Okay. I see your point. I just hope after all your investigating is done, Rory comes out all right. Oh, speaking of investigating, I almost forgot. Dale Darmody stopped by to remind me that he and Angie are having a grand opening for D&D investigations. He asked if you're going. Are you?"

"Yes. Do you want to go over together later?" I asked.

"I would, but I don't want to run into Paul, and I don't know when he's planning on going. I told Dale I wasn't able to come today but I'd stop by later in the week to see their new office."

"So you and Paul are still on that break that Paul doesn't want to take?"

She nodded.

"Mom, you and Paul have always been so good together. I really don't understand why you think you need to take a step away."

"I know you don't. I'm not entirely clear on it myself. I know that I need some space to think. Maybe turning sixty started it—realizing that I have a dwindling number of years left and thinking about how I'm spending them. Paul is a fine man. I'm comfortable with him, we have fun together, and I know that I can rely on him. But I'm not sure that comfortable is what I want at this stage of my life. I'm feeling like I need to take a few chances, see what I can do with whatever time I have left."

"Mom, you're sixty, not a hundred and sixty. You have lots of years left. Stop talking like you're going to drop dead tomorrow."

I kept my tone light, but her words had sent an icy shard of fear through me. I'd never heard my mother talk seriously about aging before. She's always seemed ageless. The thought of her not being there was something I didn't want to even consider.

"I'm not planning on keeling over anytime soon. I'm just aware that it can happen. And there are some things I'd like to do before it does."

"Like what?"

"Reconnect with old friends I've lost touch with. Learn how to swim. Go to Nova Scotia. Finish reading Moby Dick. All kinds of things."

"You can do those things and still be with Paul, can't you? He's going to retire from his dental practice next year, right?"

"Yes, but Paul sees a different future than I do. Coffee with friends in the morning, puttering around the house, playing golf, having dinner at the Country Club every Friday night, winters in Florida, volunteering at Pioneer Days..."

Miguel's comment when I told him about the taking-a-break thing echoed in my mind. Maybe he was right.

"Those are all good things to do," I said.

"They are. And Paul should do them if that's what he'd like. But I want to live whatever life I have left a little more adventurously. A friend from high school got in touch with me about a month ago, just out of the blue. We caught up on life and laughed about things we'd done back in the day and the plans we'd had. It was really fun. But after I hung up, I started thinking about how differently my life turned out than I thought it would back then."

"How so?"

"I was going to travel in Europe for a few months after college for one thing. Then I was going to law school. I wanted to be a public defender. Instead, I married Tommy the day after college graduation. I got pregnant with you, then Annie. I thought I could manage law school when you girls were both in school. But then Lacey came along. And there were all the issues with your dad. Then Annie died, your dad left, and there was no time left over for dreams. I had a family to support."

"Mom, I never knew you wanted to be a lawyer."

"I never told you because I didn't want you to think I wasn't happy with the life I had. I'd made my choices, and I had to play the hand I was dealt. I don't mean to make it sound like it was a bad hand. I've had a lot of good things in my life. But after talking with my friend, I realized that I'm holding different cards now, and I still have a hand to play. I can make some different choices. That's all."

"That's a lot, I'd say."

"Yes, well, that's why I need some time away from Paul to figure out what I really want."

"Okay, I can understand that I guess. But Paul's a good man, Mom. Try not to leave him hanging for too long. He deserves better than that. If you don't want him, there are lots of other women who would."

My mother stared at me for a minute, then she shook her head.

"What?"

Before she could answer, a voice called from the reception area.

"Hello? Hey, where is everybody? I could use a little help out here."

"Damn, where is Courtnee?" My mother jumped up from her desk and hurried toward the door. As she left she said, "Glass houses and stones, Leah. Maybe you should take your own advice."

39

I went back upstairs and worked until quarter to three, then left for Darmody's grand opening. On my way over, I called Coop to see if he wanted to meet me there. When he didn't pick up his cell phone, I called his office number. Jennifer answered.

"Hey, Jen. I take it Coop's not in?"

"He is, but he's in a budget meeting. It started at 2:30, but he's got it blocked off on his calendar until 4:30. Do you want to leave a message?"

"No. Wait, yes I do. I'm on my way to Darmody's grand opening. If the meeting wraps up early, tell him to meet me there."

"Oh, he already went. He buzzed over right after lunch."

"Did you already go, too?"

"No, Charlie and I plan to stop by around 4:30. Will you still be there?"

"Lord, I hope not. I'm going right now, just to say hey and congrats. I won't be there long. But you and I should get together soon. There's lots to catch up on."

I had heeded Coop's recommendation that I stay away from Jennifer's romance with Ross, but it had been bothering me. I didn't want to see Ross hurt, and I couldn't shake the feeling that Jennifer didn't realize how serious his feelings were. I know, I know, it wasn't my business, but in a way it was because I cared about them both.

"How about next Friday night?"

"That sounds good, Jen. I'll let you know later in the week for sure. Okay, I'm here at D&D Investigations, and someone is just pulling out of a parking space right in front. Got to go. Talk to you later."

When I walked through the door I found a pretty big crowd milling about and the conversational buzz was quite loud. I was glad Darmody and Angela had a good turnout. I remained skeptical, however, that there was enough work in the county for two private investigation agencies, one of which was long established. And even if the work was there, it seemed unlikely to me that Darmody would be able to instill enough confidence in people that they'd actually hire him.

I headed for the refreshment table and grabbed a cookie. I hadn't taken my first bite before Darmody appeared at my elbow.

"Leah! Glad you made it. It's a real good crowd, isn't it?" His round face was beaming as he looked around at all the people.

"It is. The office looks really nice, Darmody," I said.

"Yeah, well that's Angie, she did all the setting things up. And we got our first client!"

"That's wonderful," I said concentrating on keeping the surprise out of my voice.

"I can't tell you who it is, though. Client confidentiality is one of our core values, Angie says."

"I'm sure she's right. I—"

"But I can tell you this, it's a lady who wants to know if her husband is cheating on her. He's done it before and so she knows the signs. This time she wants proof because if she's right, she's gonna divorce him. So I'll be doing surveillance, getting photos, documenting everything, all that stuff. She seems like a real nice lady. And she didn't blink an eye when I told her our rates. They live over—"

In an attempt to save Darmody from himself I interrupted before he gave me her name and Social Security number.

"Sounds like you're off to a good start. I won't ask you any questions because I know that as a professional investigator, you wouldn't give me any details about her anyway. Discreet, Dependable, Darmody. That's your motto, right?"

"Hey, yeah," he said, beaming again. "You remembered. I told Ange it was a catchy saying. So, how's your investigatin' goin'? I heard you were up in Trenton County trying to get the married lady that killed her boyfriend out of prison."

"I'm looking into the Matthew Ferguson case, yes. It's going fine."

"Don't be embarrassed if you need a little help. You're a real good investigator for an amateur. But there's nothing like having a real professional, with real police experience to kind of guide you along if you're stuck. You can call on D&D Investigations anytime. We'll give you the Friends and Family discount. It'd be great to work together on a case, wouldn't it?"

I took a large bite of my cookie to give myself time to come up with a truthful but not brutally honest answer. Just as I'd thought of something, I felt a tap on my right shoulder. When I turned, it was to face someone I was completely unprepared to see. Spencer Karr.

"Hey, Spencer. Got yourself all cleaned up at that rehab place, I guess. You sure look better than the last time I saw you," Darmody said.

I was glad he'd jumped in, because it gave me a minute to recover from the shock. It had been over a year since Spencer got a pass from drug dealing charges by flipping and giving the police everything they needed to put the boss of the operation away. When Spencer had entered the very fancy but highly regarded rehab facility outside of Chicago, he'd been skinny, bleary-eyed, and barely able to hold himself together. Darmody was right, he did look a lot better.

He was now slender, but not skinny. His eyes were clear, his hands were steady, and he'd even ditched his usual, pretentiously fashion-forward glasses for a pair of basic black frames that suited him.

"Hello, Darmody. Congratulations on your retirement, and on your second career. You've got a nice office here."

It was more than Spencer's appearance that was different. He'd actually said something nice instead of snarky to Darmody.

"Thanks. Lemme give you one of my cards. You never know when you might need a good private investigator."

"That's true," Spencer said, taking the card Darmody held out. "Could I ask you a favor though? I'd like to talk to Leah for a minute."

"Sure, you go ahead and talk," Darmody said, remaining where he stood, looking as though he had every intention of participating in whatever Spencer had to say.

"Actually I was hoping to have a few minutes just with Leah. I have something that's a little personal to talk to her about."

"Ohhh. Oh, yeah. Sure. You guys just go ahead and talk. I'll see you later."

As Darmody lumbered away, Spencer said, "It's been a long time, Leah."

"Really? The time has just flown by for me."

"You're looking well," he said.

Okay, I'd been puzzled by the unexpected politeness—dare I say kindness?—that Spencer had shown Darmody. Now that he was extending his good manners to me, that seriously put my antennae up. Spencer had never said a single nice thing to me in all the time I'd known him, and that stretched back to grade school.

"What's up, Spence? Is this the beginning of your campaign for the director job at the *Times*?"

He hates to be called Spence.

"I'm not campaigning for anything, Leah. I'm just hoping we can re-set our relationship. As for me, I'm fresh out of rehab and you might call this my atonement tour. I'd like to start with you."

I stared at him for at least ten seconds before I answered.

"All right, who are you and what have you done with Spencer Karr? You look like him, but you definitely don't sound like him."

Instead of coming back at me with a sarcastic remark, he smiled.

"It's me. A better version I hope. But from the expression on your face I can tell that you don't believe a word I'm saying. That's okay. I'll have to earn your trust. I understand that. Maybe we can start with a cup of coffee at the Elite sometime this week."

"Okay, now you're making me feel like I'm Alice and you're the Mad Hatter. For real, what's going on with you?"

"It's pretty simple. I've been in rehab before, but this time I took it seriously. I've gone through a year that sometimes felt like hell—detoxing, counseling, confronting what I've done, and figuring out why. It wasn't easy but it got me to here."

"And where is here?"

"The place where I finally know the kind of person I want to be, and I'm willing to do the work to get there."

"That would be nice if it were true, but I don't think it is."

"Maybe if we talk, I can change your mind."

"I doubt it. Look, Spencer, you almost got me killed the last time I saw you. I don't want to be friends with you. There's no need to put on an act. I already know who you are."

He shook his head. "You're not going to make this easy on me, are you?"

"If by that you mean am I going to make you a friendship bracelet and tell you all is forgiven, then no, I'm not. I don't know what your game is—yet. But I'll find out and I'm pretty sure I'm not going to like it. Feel free to circulate and share the new Spencer. There are lots of people you may be able to fool. But I'm not one of them. Now if you'll excuse me, I see someone I'd actually enjoy talking to."

"This isn't the place, but I've got something to tell you that you really need to hear. Please, Leah. Just half an hour of your time. You set the place and the day."

I wanted to say no, but I really did want to know what he was up to. In fact, I needed to know in order to combat it.

"Okay, fine. Wednesday afternoon, two o'clock. My place," I said over my shoulder as I walked away.

40

I'd spotted Father Lindstrom out of the corner of my eye as I was talking to Spencer, and I made a beeline over to him. Father Gregory Lindstrom is the parish priest at St. Stephen's Catholic church, and one of my favorite people—even though I haven't been an active Catholic since I was twelve. I quit because it didn't make sense to me. I couldn't believe in a God who could help good people but didn't, and who could stop bad people but didn't do that either. So what the heck was He doing?

However, I do respect (and maybe envy a little) people who have unwavering faith. People like Father Lindstrom. If anyone were able to convince me that organized religion is a force for good and I should get with the program, it would be him. Not because of any persuasive argument he might present, but because of the way he lives his own life, with kindness, acceptance, and grace—in every sense of that word.

"Hey Father," I said leaning in and giving him a hug. "I haven't seen you in weeks!"

"Leah! What a delightful surprise. I almost didn't come today because the weather turned so rainy and cold, and I was reading a very good book. But I didn't want to disappoint Dale and Angela. Seeing you is my reward for braving the elements," he said. His light blue eyes behind his wire-framed glasses twinkled and he smiled. "Tell me what you've been up to these last weeks."

I gave him a very short version of the Hannah Ferguson case and touched lightly on where things stood with my current book and the one to come.

"It sounds like you've been very busy. How are things going with the newspaper? Have you found someone for the director position yet?"

"No. We haven't even started interviews, but Marilyn is pitching for Spencer. Which would be a disaster."

He looked surprised. "Spencer has applied for the job?"

"Not formally yet, at least as far as I know. But Marilyn has big plans for him."

"I don't think I understand."

I explained.

"Leah, are you certain that Spencer is interested in the position?"

"Well, it's a chance to wreak havoc. That's one of Spencer's favorite things."

"I know that you've had some very unhappy—even dangerous—dealings with him. I understand your wariness. But perhaps you're fearing the worst needlessly."

"Where Spencer is concerned, fearing the worst is the only sensible approach to take. He's got some kind of game he's playing. I just don't know what it is."

"Sometimes, Leah, bad experiences in the past make us suspicious and fearful in the present when there isn't any need. Spencer's been away for a long time. He went through a very in-depth residential rehabilitation treatment program. Without ignoring the fact that in the past he's acted in ways that were destructive to himself and to others, it's still possible to consider that he has changed. That he's not the same man he was."

Father Lindstrom is such a good person, and he was trying so hard to help me find my way to being a little more tolerant, that I couldn't give him the flip answer that was on the tip of my tongue. But I couldn't agree with him, either—not after twenty-plus years of knowing Spencer.

"Let me ask you something, Father."

"Of course."

"Do you really think that people change? More than just around the edges, I mean. Do you believe a person can truly transform from evil to good?"

"Well, with the caveat that I've run across very few people who I would call evil, yes, Leah. I believe that a determined person can fundamentally change for good. I'm in the wrong line of work if I don't," he said with a bemused smile.

"I don't know, Father. I think it's pretty unlikely that Spencer's gone through some kind of moral metamorphosis. But I'll concede that you may be a better judge of that than I am. So, I'll try to listen to him with an open mind, but it won't be easy."

"If you're willing to try, Leah, you're halfway there. Now tell me, what else has been happening in your life. How is Coop?"

"He's good. I feel like I don't see that much of him right now, though. He's really working hard at his property. He and his dad are getting the outside of his house done so they can work on the inside during the winter. Have you ever been out there? It's a pretty spot."

"Yes, I have. It's a very nice property. Speaking of nice places, I was talking to Miguel a few minutes ago. He was telling me that he's going to have to move soon."

"Uh-oh. Don't tell me that he's been enlisting you to plead his case that I should give up my apartment so he can rent it."

"Not directly, no. He did tell me that he thinks that would be an excellent solution."

"For him, yes. For me, not so much. I don't want to give up my place and move in with Coop. My own space, my independence really, is important to me. You know that. We've talked about it enough."

Darmody's wife Angela came bustling up just then. She's a small but forceful woman who had recently let her hair go from an improbably dark and dull black to a surprisingly pretty silver. I was about to compliment her on it, but she was on a mission and didn't give me a chance.

"Sorry, Leah, I need the Father."

Her commanding voice is at odds with her short stature, and she uses it very effectively to ride herd on Darmody like a drill sergeant. Actually, it works pretty well on the rest of us as well. She turned to Father Lindstrom and barked in her strong northern Wisconsin accent, "So Father, are yous set to go with the office blessin' or what?"

Like most of us when addressed by Angela, Father Lindstrom snapped to attention.

"Oh, is it time, Angela? Certainly I'm ready. Leah," he added, "I'm sorry to end our conversation so abruptly."

"Yous can finish your talkin' after the blessin'," Angela said as she grabbed Father Lindstrom by the elbow and began steering him away.

I hadn't anticipated a grand opening that would also include a religious ceremony, but Angela does like to cover her bases. And for D&D Investigations to succeed, a little divine intervention would probably come in handy. I, however, did not feel the need to stay.

"Oh, gosh, Angela. I'm sorry. I won't be able to stick around for the blessing. But congratulations on the new business. Father, I'll be in touch."

"Come for the cookies, leave for the blessin' eh, Leah? Okay there. Thanks for comin'. No time to talk, I got a schedule to stick to."

"Oh, sure. See you both later."

41

When I got to my car, I found a happy surprise. A chai latte, in the cupholder with a one-word note. *Enjoy!* Coop must have gotten back from his meeting early.

I called and he answered on the first ring.

"Hey you, what's going on?" he asked.

"I just called to thank you for my surprise. I'm drinking it right now."

"You know what happened to Snow White don't you?"

"Yes, she ate the poisoned apple without checking the source. But I think I'm pretty safe with a chai latte surprise from you."

"You would be. But I didn't leave it."

"But who else would? Miguel is still at the grand opening, and he's been there since one o'clock. I know that my mother didn't leave it, she's at the office and not planning to come to the open house. Jennifer is at work and, sadly, that's about the extent of people in my circle of friends who might make this thoughtful gesture. You're not teasing me are you?"

"I'm not."

"Who else knows about my deep-rooted chai addiction?"

"What about your ardent admirer, the one who sent you the flowers?"

"Sharla? How would she know where I was going to be? Or that I like chai? Or what my car even looks like?"

"All good questions. But three things have happened: a very over-the-top email about how wonderful you are, then the flowers, now the chai. Taken separately, they might not be enough to warrant action. Taken together though, I think you need to call Owen Fike. It bears looking into."

Owen used to work in the sheriff's office. Now he's a captain with the Himmel Police Department. He and Coop have always gotten along. Owen and me, not so much.

"No, I don't want to do that until something more, I don't know, something more *real* happens. If anything does. I don't want to go to Owen and have him think I'm a weirdo who freaks out over some flowers and a chai latte."

"Since when do you care what Owen thinks? Also you're not freaking out. It's just common sense to let the police know that you've had a couple of incidents."

"You don't think it's possible that some normal not-stalker person left the chai just to be nice? You know, one of those pay-it-forward things. And sent the flowers, too. Though I can't think of who that would be."

"You said you were going to send a thank you email to Sharla for the flowers and then see how she responded. Did you?"

"I didn't. But full disclosure, it wasn't because I followed your advice. I just forgot because I've been so busy."

"That's good. Don't do it. Call Owen and let him do his job."

"Coop, you don't truly think this is anything serious, do you?"

"I don't know."

"That's not very comforting."

"I'm not trying to comfort you. I'm trying to make you aware that you should be a little more careful until we know what's going on. Even though it may turn out that none of this is anything to worry about."

"Okay. But what if I just send her a thank you note and mention that fall is pumpkin flavor season at Culver's and I'm very fond of their pumpkin milkshakes? Just in case, you know, she wants to really touch my heart."

"You're not taking this seriously at all, are you?"

"Ummm, a little bit I am, but a lot I'm not."

Though I couldn't see his face, I could easily imagine his exasperated expression.

"Oh come on, I will be watchful, I'll triple check that I locked all my doors, including my car door, and I won't let strangers in. And I'll think very hard about calling Owen, all right? On condition that you say nothing to my mother about this. She listens to way too many true crime podcasts. I don't want her freaking about nothing."

"I won't say anything to Carol. It's up to you to decide what to tell her."

"Good to know there's something that's up to me."

"I just want you to be safe. I'm not deciding things for you. But I want to be sure you're aware that this could be serious."

"Hey, I get it. I promise that I'll be careful, and if anything else happens, I'll call Owen. Now, how about coming for dinner tonight? I have some startling news to share."

"Sorry, I can't. Dad and I have some work to finish at the property. He's going back up north tomorrow and it's a two-person job. We're going to be working pretty late. Tell me the news now."

"No, I want to see your face when I tell you. You'll just have to wait. You know, I feel like I hardly see you anymore. You're either working at your day job, or working on your auditions reel for a new HGTV show, *Building with Coop*. I figure that must be what you're doing or why else are you spending so much time at your property? This whole build a house thing is taking way more time than I thought it would."

"Tell me about it. I'm sorry. I know I've been really busy. But I just have to get some things done now to stay on track so I can move into the place in the spring."

"Well, if you'd just stay put in town you'd have more time to be at my beck and call, and isn't that what I hired you for?"

"And if you would just move in with me, we could be together all the time."

"*Touché*. Okay, I won't complain about the amount of time you're working on your new place, and you won't bring up me leaving my current place. Deal?"

"Deal."

"Why don't you come by for breakfast in the morning? We can catch up a little then."

"I'll be there. 7:00 okay? I've got a lot going on tomorrow, so I need an early start."

"Sure. I'll have to get up a little early to pull breakfast together. But for you, I'll do it."

"What's it going to be, Honey Nut Cheerios or regular Cheerios?"

"That would be funny if it wasn't so accurate. I'll surprise you."

"You often do."

When I got back to my place, I saw Charlotte Caldwell's car in the parking lot. I found her in the newsroom. She looked, as she always does, very pulled together. Her black leggings and boots emphasized her long legs. The red tunic top she wore skimmed lightly over her slender body.

"Leah! I was just looking for you."

"Hey, Charlotte. I want to talk to you, too. I thought I'd see you at Darmody's grand opening. Did you go early, or are you on your way now? If I were you, I'd wait a few minutes before you go, just to be sure the blessing of the office is done."

"I'm sorry, the blessing of the office? What's that?"

"Apparently it's a thing you can have a priest do. I imagine it's to bring all good things to your new business, but I left before it started so I don't really know what it entails. But before I left, I had an unsettling encounter that you're going to want to hear about."

"Really? Who with?"

"Spencer Karr."

"He's back in town? I didn't realize that. Did you get in a fight with him?"

"I did not. In fact it was probably about an eight-point-five on the Leah-Spencer civility scale. According to Spencer, he's seen the error of his ways, and he's determined to become a better man. He pretty much glossed over every rotten thing he's done in the last twenty years by saying it's all behind him now. I don't believe that for a minute, but I'm quite intrigued by his sudden alleged transformation. The open house wasn't really the place to dig into the details though. So when he practically begged me to meet with him later, I told him to come to my place on Wednesday afternoon."

"Do you need a referee?"

"No, I can handle Spencer. Especially on my own turf. But has his resume turned up in the email inbox we set up for applicants? I'd like to see how he's going to present himself for the job."

"Nothing has come in from him yet. That's what I came to tell you. The deadline is tomorrow at midnight. If he's going to apply, he's leaving it to the last minute. So, I'm thinking that he won't be submitting an application."

"Those are sweet, sweet words to hear, Charlotte. You've given me enough hope that I'm going upstairs to make an appropriate sacrifice to the gods to increase the odds that you're right. And if we don't see his resume by tomorrow at midnight, I may cancel my Wednesday meeting with him. If he's not a threat, I'm a lot less interested in what he has to say."

"Don't do that. Aren't you curious about why he wants to talk to you?"

"Well, yes. I admit to being extremely curious. And I guess I can always throw him out if he annoys me too much."

"I can't wait to hear the replay of your conversation. Now, news business aside. How are you doing with your next book? Got a plot yet?"

"I do. In fact Peter Sullivan is helping me with it. I mentioned that I needed to run some things by a microbiologist, and he volunteered. Turns out he taught microbiology at one time, before he went to Kelmar Pharmaceuticals. He's been great but I've been too busy to do much with my plot."

"How's that?"

"I've gotten caught up in a closed murder case."

"What murder? And if it's closed, why are you caught up in it?"

I explained.

"I think Darmody should have offered you a partnership in D&D Investigations. Clearly that's where your heart lies, not in all this book writing stuff," she said with a smile.

"You're joking, but in a way, you're not wrong. I really do like following the threads and untangling them to get to the heart of things. This time, though, it's a very tangled knot. But I have a few ideas."

"I'm sure you do."

42

When I got back upstairs and opened my laptop to do some more work on my case notes, I found an email from my reader Sharla.

I haven't heard from you. I hope that doesn't mean you didn't get the flowers. Maybe I should have signed them Sharla, instead of an ardent admirer, but I thought you would get the joke and connect it with my email. In case you didn't, it was moi! The chai was just supposed to be a fun little surprise. You did get it, didn't you? I hope I didn't put it in the wrong car! 😊

Love,
Sharla, your favorite fan

That answered the who-sent-the-flowers question. I made a call to Owen Fike.

"So in the past couple of weeks you've received an email from a fan, you got flowers that you now know came from that fan, and you found a chai in your car. Any threats? Any indication the person is watching or following you?" Owen asked, after I gave him a brief overview of my situation. His voice wasn't exactly friendly, but it was professional. Which I counted as progress because our last interaction had been fairly hostile on his part. And, okay, maybe a little on my part, too.

"No, nothing like that," I said. "So far, it's just a very excited fan who has done several nice things for me—sent me two very flattering emails, gave me flowers, and left me a chai. Am I making too much of it?"

"Not when you consider that this Sharla knows where you live, apparently knows what your car looks like, knew where you would be this afternoon, and even knows that chai latte is a favorite of yours. You're right to be concerned."

I'd been hoping that he'd tell me I was watching too many true crime shows and I should relax.

"But nothing criminal has happened, right? She hasn't threatened me or anything. In fact all she's really done is give me presents."

"In Wisconsin it's a criminal act to get into an unlocked car you don't own or have permission to enter, whether or not you take or damage anything. Also, Sharla—if that's her real name—has invaded your privacy. And she might have done more than that."

"What do you mean?"

"I mean she might have left you a hidden present. A GPS tracker so she knows where you are."

"Whoa! Way to escalate me from slightly concerned to almost alarmed. You think she's tracking me?"

"I don't know. I'm assigning your case to Jane Williams. She's got a background in stalking investigations. She'll do a sweep and make sure there isn't a tracker on your car. She'll also want a copy of all the emails from this Sharla. Though if she's using a VPN to hide her real location that will make things harder. Still, we can try a few things to unmask it. I don't suppose you kept the cup of chai?"

"No. I drank it and threw away the cup. I've got the card that came with the flowers, though."

"That probably won't be much use. You said both you and Coop handled it. If she left any prints, they'll probably be too smudged to be useful. But put the card in an envelope and give it to Jane, just in case we can pull something from it. Jane will call you and arrange an interview. She'll take it from there."

"Thanks, Owen. You've been really nice. I appreciate it."

"You did the right thing reporting it. Stalking is nothing to fool around with. Now try to keep on doing the right thing. And by that I mean let Jane do her job and don't get in her way. She's the investigator, not you. That's a concept I know you have a hard time with."

"You know what? I'll stick with thank you for listening and responding to my report, but I take back the thank you for being really nice."

I hung up and vented my irritation to Sam as he came into my office.

"Once a jerk, always a jerk, Sam," I said. "But I'd appreciate it if you'd up your watchcat game in case we do have an unwanted visitor one of these days."

The knock on my office door that immediately followed could not have been better timed if it were scripted.

I looked through the peephole and considered just walking away. But curiosity got the better of me, so I opened the door.

"Well, now, Leah, how you doin'?"

Cole Granger is the head of a loosely organized clan of small-time drug dealers, petty thieves, conmen and a few random members who go in for serious crime. He likes to think of himself as the Tony Soprano of Grantland County, though he is less ruthless. Still, he's smart enough to rarely get caught, and when he does, pragmatic enough to throw his nearest and dearest under the bus to keep himself out of trouble.

"I was doing just fine, Cole. Until I opened the door. What do you want?"

"When you gonna stop playin' this game, darlin'? I know you got a strong attraction to me and this here hostile attitude is your way of tryin' to fight it off."

Even though it's been a long time since Cole moved with his family from Kentucky to Himmel, he still has a very strong Appalachian drawl. Personally I think he cultivates it to make people think his mind is as slow as his speech. It isn't. I'm not afraid of Cole, but I'm always a bit wary.

"Cole, I'm busy. And I don't enjoy drop-in visits from people I don't like. So again, what do you want?"

"Now that's real hurtful, even though I know you don't mean it. I come here because I heard you're re-investigatin' that murder up in Galen County last year. The one where the woman kilt her boyfriend and got sent to prison."

"Do you know something about it?"

"Well, I just might. I got word that you been lookin' at a acquaintance of mine and where she was the night the deed was done."

That caught my attention.

"Who are you talking about?"

"Name's Rory Ferguson."

"What about her?"

"Well now, hold on. This information ain't free. I need a little quid pro quo like they call it. You help me, I help you."

"And how is it that I could help you?"

"You could invite me to that fancy cocktail party I hear you're throwin' for all them sponsors and donors and whatnot for your newspaper business."

Charlotte was organizing a drinks party to introduce our board members, some donors, and sponsors to community leaders in the county, to gather more support for our new venture. No Grangers were on the guest list, nor could I imagine why Cole would want to be included.

"Why would you want to go to a party like that?"

"I got some business interests in the community as you know. And my Ride EZ car service is preparin' to expand. We're gonna have a special deluxe shuttle service from the Milwaukee and Madison airports. We can transport people in one of our luxury cars with free bottled water and wi-fi with headsets. It's gonna be real classy. I'd like to schmooze a little and drum up some business. Also, now don't get mad when I tell you this, I got my eye on Charlotte Caldwell. I'd like to give her a chance to get to know me better."

I couldn't stop a snort of laughter from escaping.

"You? And Charlotte Caldwell? I guess we all have our dreams Cole, but

I'm telling you that one is unattainable for you. She is way out of your league."

"No need to be jealous, Leah. I'll always have a special feelin' for you. But I can't wait forever for you to make up your mind between me and the sheriff. I got to move on. I think me and Charlotte would make a real nice couple."

I paused a moment. There was definitely a risk of Cole doing something wholly inappropriate at the cocktail party. Yet, on occasion, I have seen him pass as a nearly normal person. It might be entertaining to watch him try his charms on Charlotte. It would be even more entertaining to see him interact with Marilyn Karr. And I was very interested by his claim that he knew something about Rory Ferguson that I could use.

"First you have to give me what you know about Rory and the night Matthew died. If it's something useful, then we'll talk about the cocktail party. Otherwise, goodbye," I began to close the door.

"Hold on, now. In light of our long friendship and the bond of trust we have, I'm willing to tell you what I got. But I ain't gonna do it standin' out here on your doorstep. Invite me in and we'll have a chat."

43

I handed Cole a bottle of water as he took a seat on the sofa. I pulled up the rocking chair and sat across from him.

"Okay, so, what do you know and how is it of any use to me?"

"Well, now, I'm not sayin' we got somethin' serious goin', but me and Rory did have this one night together that I think you're gonna find interestin'. I was drinkin' at the Night Owl Tavern in Galen one night last fall. To be real specific it was Friday, October 7, around 7:00 p.m."

He paused to make sure I had caught the significance of the date. I had.

"The night Matthew Ferguson was killed?"

"That's right. So I'd already had a few brews when this woman comes in and sits down on the stool next to me. She wasn't bad looking, a little older'n me maybe, but I don't mind that. Them ones can be a little more grateful for the attention, if you know what I mean. She already had a buzz on, I could tell. I bought her a beer and we got to talkin' and drinkin' like you do. She told me her name was Rory Ferguson. We did some more drinkin', a little dancin', and some more talkin'."

"Okay, and so?"

"So this Rory, she goes through a lotta moods while we're talkin'. First she's all flirty, then she gets real affectionate, then she wants to dance, then she's laughin' and then she gets mad."

"What did you do to her?"

"I didn't do nothin' but be a good listener and a true gentleman like my mama taught me. She wasn't mad at me. She was mad at her brother. She starts tellin' me how he screwed her outta money she shoulda got. He sold their farm or somethin'. I never did get it straight, but she was real pissed about it. I just let her talk and she settled down a mite and then it got be about 11:00 or so. I offered her a ride. I figured she was in the right frame of mind to thank me for all the attention I give her, once we got to her place. If you catch my drift."

"Sadly, I do."

"Anyways after we get in the car she gives me the address, and we drive over to this real nice neighborhood, and she tells me to pull into the driveway of one of them McMansions they got there. I turn off the car and start to get out, and she says no, wait a minute, I'll be right back. So then I'm thinkin' what the hell? Is this a situation that comes with a husband? Cause I don't want no part of that. But when I ask her, she says no. This is her brother's house. She wants to go in and tell him off, then we'll go. I decide to wait and see what happens. I already had a lot invested in the evenin'."

He paused to take a swig of water, though it seemed to me that it was more for dramatic effect than to quench a thirst.

"So far this is a pretty boring story, Cole. It's not going to get you invited to our cocktail party."

"Now hold on. I'm comin' to the best part. So, Rory goes up to the door and starts poundin'. There ain't no lights on in the house, mind you, but she's ringin' the bell, beatin' on the door. She comes back to the car, and she says no one's home, but she knows where he'll be. Then she tells me to take her to his cabin five miles out of town. Well now I got to decide to fish or cut bait. What kinda payout am I gonna get for goin' even more miles outta my way? I already put a lot into the evenin,' and I do like a gal with some fire in her blood. Rory's got that all right. I figure she gets herself all riled up with her brother, then I take her home and help her put some of that firecracker energy to good use. I drive her to the cabin."

Cole had my full attention now.

"You can't drive your car right up to the door. You gotta take a little two-track off the road and then park and cross a footbridge. I wait in the car while she goes to see her brother. She's only gone a minute when she comes runnin' back cryin'. I can't hardly understand a word she's sayin', except 'he's dead.' I go back in with her to take a look. She's right. There's a dead guy layin' on the floor. She says it's her brother Matthew. No blood or nothin' and I didn't hear no gunshot, but I am not about to get mixed up in this. I say sorry for your loss and double time it back to my car and I leave."

"You just left her there? She just found her brother dead, she's half-drunk at least, and you leave her in the middle of nowhere? You're a regular knight in shining armor, aren't you?"

I was unable to keep the incredulity out of my voice at what was, even for Cole, an unbelievably jackass move.

"Hey, not my circus, not my monkey. Due to several false and unfair run-ins with the cops in my life, I can't afford to be caught in any sketchy situation that ain't got nothin' to do with me. When I found out later the guy was murdered, I knew I made the right call."

"How did Rory get home?"

"I got no idea."

"You're unbelievable."

"Hey, now, what was I gonna do? I never come out on top in a run-in with cops. I barely knowed the woman. A course I skedaddled out of there."

"Is this story, every part of it, true? Because if it is, and Rory was with you from seven o'clock on, and you both found the body together, she has a solid alibi for the murder night."

"It's true all right, but don't be thinkin' you're gonna drag me into the middle of things. I'm just givin' you somethin' so you'll give me somethin'—my invite to your fancy party."

I was shaking my head, still thinking about how he left a scared, drunk, distraught Rory in the middle of the country with no ride home.

"You abandoned Rory, and now you're telling me that you're not willing to give her an alibi?"

He shrugged.

"I got my family businesses to protect and my reputation. Anyway, it all come out fine, didn't it? Rory didn't get arrested, and I give you some inside information so's you won't waste time investigatin' her. You don't have to thank me. Ever since I nearly got kilt savin' your life not that long ago, I feel I kinda got a vested interest, as they say, in your career."

"You don't. And you didn't rescue me. In fact, you wouldn't have come anywhere near where I was if Miguel hadn't forced you to."

Now it was his turn to shake his head.

"It's true, what Shakespeare says ain't it? Words is sharper than a serpent's tooth. You wound me, Leah. You truly do. But I forgive you because I know you always hurt the one you love, right? Now, let's talk about that little soiree you're gonna be havin'. What time should I be there, and is it fancy dress?"

I toyed with the idea of giving him the wrong time, but a deal is a deal. And now I could move Rory to the bottom of my list of suspects, if not quite all the way off yet. She was the only one with an actual verifiable alibi so far.

"It runs from 5:00-7:00 at the paper. It's a mix and mingle thing, so people will be coming and going. No need for you to be there for more than fifteen or twenty minutes."

"Why, I'll barely be started circulatin' by then. No worries. I'll be there the whole time."

"Great."

44

"So, do you think I'm way off base to wonder if what Olivia Vining is hiding is her own involvement in Matthew Ferguson's murder? I kind of want you to say yes, because I don't like thinking where that leads."

Coop was sitting at the bar in my kitchen eating breakfast as I gave him the rundown on my most recent interviews.

"It's not off base to consider all the possibilities, though I'm not sure that's the strongest one. It's pretty rare for a kid that age to commit murder. But you have to ask the questions. Now that you know Matthew's neighbor saw someone who sounds a lot like Olivia multiple times in the area of Matthew's cabin, you might shake her up if you press on that. But what really catches my attention is the call you got from Kathy Boyle."

"Yeah, mine, too. If she'd said she had something to *tell* me, I'd be interested for sure. But something to *show* me? That seems like she might be holding a tangible piece of evidence. And I could definitely use that. Oh, I forgot to tell you Cole came by with some really interesting information."

I told him the story that Cole had given me.

"So you believe him?" Coop asked.

"Unless Rory tells me something totally different. Picking up a drunk woman at the bar hoping to get lucky is totally on brand for him. As is leaving her stranded and alone in the middle of the night with her dead brother's body. Cole gave Rory a pretty solid alibi. I want to ask her why she lied and said she was home all night."

"Think about it. She had a big blow up with her brother, then she's the one who finds him dead, plus she's drunk or nearly so? I wouldn't want that to be my story to the cops."

"I guess that's true enough."

"Have you considered that Rory could have planted the aconite at the cabin earlier and faked her drunk act so Cole could be her alibi?"

"Oh, you're really going to make me work for this aren't you?"

"All theories should be tested."

"Okay, if Rory left the aconite tea at the cabin for Matthew to take, she couldn't know when he'd drink it. So she couldn't know when she'd need an alibi. Also, she couldn't be sure she'd meet someone at the bar to give her one. It's not like she knew Cole and arranged to hook up with him. It was totally random. Rory as the killer doesn't work for me."

"It doesn't really for me either. I'm just helping you kick the tires a little. So, if not Rory, who's left?"

"Someone I haven't spent near enough time with, Joel Vining, Hannah's former husband. When I tried to talk to him last Saturday, he threw me off his property."

"Have you got any reason to suspect him besides the fact that it's usually the spouse?"

"Nothing concrete, but I'm wondering if he knew about the affair all along. I'm already considering the possibility that Olivia knew about it. What if she did and told her dad, and *he* killed Matthew? Joel could have carried it off pretty easily. He was a casual friend of Matthew's, he'd been out to the cabin to fish and to play cards. He had easy access to aconite through Hannah's store. All he'd have to do is call Matthew and arrange to meet on that Friday night."

"Why would Matthew agree to meet with his lover's husband?"

"He might have felt guilty enough to think he owed Joel a chance to talk it out. Or, maybe Joel said the meeting was about something else—say a business problem he wanted advice on. I don't know. I'm just riffing on some ideas. But I do know I have to talk to Joel again. And that's going to be tricky because he's pretty unhappy that I'm investigating. I have to be in

Galen to talk to Kathy today and then I'm having pizza with Ellen Ferguson. I checked online and Olivia's school has a half-day today. Her dad works out of town during the week, so I'm going to try and see her. Joel won't be pleased. He ordered me not to talk to her, but that—"

"I know, that just makes you want to do it more," Coop said.

"No. Well, okay, maybe. But I'm not doing it to defy Joel. I'm doing it because Olivia has something that's bothering her. Maybe it's about Joel."

"I wouldn't throw Kathy Boyle out as a suspect, if I were you. She doesn't have much of an alibi. And she does have very easy access to Matthew's cabin. Maybe what she has to show you is something calculated to point you away from her."

"I haven't thrown her out, but she's not at the top of the list. And before you say it, I haven't eliminated Hannah either."

"Good to know. After all she's the one who was actually arrested, tried, and found guilty. I know her sister Marguerite made a big impression on you—and I know why. But if you look at it objectively, at this point it seems like maybe the police got it right."

I sighed.

"I realize that. But I promised Marguerite I'd give it my best shot. I have to eliminate everyone else before I come to that conclusion. And I can't do that yet. So, what are you up to today?"

"I've got to do performance evaluations. Not my favorite. If I can wrap them up early this afternoon, I'll go out to the property to do some work."

"So, do you want to come over tonight? I should be back from Galen by 8:30 or so."

"I'd like to, but Dad left me a list of things he wants me to get done before he gets back at the end of the week. He's a pretty tough taskmaster. Let's try for tomorrow, okay?"

"All right."

"Thanks for breakfast. I really like what you did with the Cheerios today. Cutting up that banana really took them to the next level."

"You're welcome."

He stood up to take his bowl to the dishwasher when I suddenly remembered my biggest piece of news.

"Wait, I can't believe I forgot to tell you. I saw Spencer at the open house yesterday."

"And how did that go?"

"It was weird. He was actually very nice, which was a little unsettling. He said the open house wasn't the place to talk. Charlotte told me afterward that Spencer hasn't applied for the job yet. The deadline is midnight tonight. After that we're home free. He's coming over tomorrow to talk to me."

"Huh."

"Exactly. I don't believe him, but I want to hear what he has to say."

"Whatever it is, proceed with caution."

"Oh, I will. And speaking of caution, I called Owen about my possible stalker."

"How'd that go?"

"He was a little better than usual, until the end. He said he'd have Jane Williams handle the investigation. She's supposed to call me this morning. Do you know her?"

"I don't, but I'm glad she'll be looking into it."

"Also, I should tell you that the reason I called Owen when I did is that I heard from Sharla again. She confirmed that she sent the flowers and she was disappointed that she didn't hear from me. Also she left the chai in my car. That's why I called Owen."

"That was a sensible move. You know, Leah, maybe Sharla is just a lonely person who doesn't have good boundaries. But equally possible, she may have some mental health issues that could lead in an ugly direction. Whichever it is, we need to find out who she really is."

"Agreed."

"Okay, I have to go. I'll talk to you later," he said, and kissed me goodbye.

"I think that's about it, Leah," said Detective Jane Williams as she put her notebook away. She was a tall woman in her late thirties or early forties. The all-black outfit she wore—black blazer, shirt, pants, and ankle boots, made her look even taller. Her light brown hair was chin length and tucked behind her ears. She had a wedding ring on one hand, but no other jewelry. Her eyes were an unusual shade of brown, almost golden under arched brows that made her look like she was always on the verge of asking a question.

"Thank you, Jane. It was nice of you to come here instead of having me go into the police station."

"You're welcome, but it wasn't about being nice. I needed to check out your place, look for points of entry an intruder could use, see what kind of security you have. I like the security cameras in the back. But given that your building security manager told you no one showed up on the tape from the camera in the front stairway means it needs to be repositioned. Sharla was obviously able to evade it when she dropped off the flowers."

"Right. I forgot to say that Tony—he's the security manager—is going to have that done and maybe add another camera."

"Good. Make sure they get that done as soon as possible. And be careful about locking your front and back doors, as well as that door that opens from the *Times* reception area into your front hall."

"You're making me a little nervous."

"It's good to be a little nervous in a situation like this. It keeps you on your toes."

"What's next?"

"Forward me copies of Sharla's emails to you. I've got the card from the flowers, but I'm not very hopeful that we'll find any useful prints. I swept your car with a GPS tracker detection device. It's not standard department practice, but I've found it very helpful in the past to do it before there's a serious incident, not after. I didn't find anything so we're good there—for now."

"What do you mean for now?"

"I mean that stalking often escalates. Sharla hasn't put a tracker on your car at this point. But you park your car overnight in an open parking lot. She has easy access if she wants to do that. And she might. Sometimes cutting off contact with a stalker shuts them down and they move on to another victim. Sometimes it makes them angry, and they double down.

Until the case is either resolved or designated a cold case, I'll be doing periodic checks on your vehicle. And checking in with you."

"Okay. That makes me feel both good and worried. Good that you're on it, worried that you need to be."

"At this point, I don't think you should be overly anxious. Like I said, cutting off contact with Sharla in combination with increased security measures may discourage her enough to move on. Meanwhile, just be cautious and careful and you should be all right."

"Well, cautious and careful aren't words usually used to describe me, but I'll definitely try to make them part of my persona for now anyway."

"Do that," she said. "I'll be in touch."

45

After Jane Williams left I made a quick call to Charlotte, who happens to be my landlord as well as my business partner and friend, and explained my situation.

"Oh, Leah, that's kind of scary. I'll talk to Tony and make sure that work order for the camera goes to the top of the list. Have you thought about staying at Coop's until the situation is resolved?"

"No, I don't want to let a stalker chase me out of my own home. Besides, Coop is gone so much between sheriffing and working on his new house he's hardly there. I think I'm safer in a building on Main Street, right across from a busy coffee shop, than I would be at his out-of-the-way place."

"I suppose," she said a little doubtfully.

"Seriously, I'll be fine, Charlotte. I've got to get going, I'm behind on my rounds for the day. I'll talk to you later."

It was almost 10:30 when I arrived at DanceFusion to talk to Rory. A sign on the door said the studio was closed until 6:00 p.m. I'd have to try her at her aunt's house. I Googled the address and set out for Galen. I had no trouble finding the house. It was on a quiet street of mostly two-story older homes. A few people were in their yards raking leaves, but otherwise the neighborhood looked deserted. When I rang the doorbell, a short, round woman with beautiful white hair opened the door.

"Jean Ferguson?" I asked.

"Yes," she said. "And you are?"

"I'm Leah Nash. I was hoping to talk to Rory."

"Rory just came back from a run. She's in the shower now but she should be done in a few minutes. Would you like to come in and wait for her?"

"Yes, thank you."

She led me to a living room with floor to ceiling bookshelves on every wall. They were filled with an eclectic collection of current bestsellers, classic fiction, nonfiction, and there was one set of shelves totally devoted to mysteries. I spotted several by Nora Fielding and used that as a way to connect with Rory's aunt.

"Oh, I see you like Nora Fielding. I do, too. Did you know she recently moved to the area?"

"She's one of my favorite mystery writers! Do you know her?"

"I do. I'm a writer myself. I used to write nonfiction, but I've just started writing a fiction mystery series. I've been lucky enough to get to know Nora a little."

"What did you say your name was again? I'm afraid I don't hear as well as I should, but I hate wearing hearing aids. Since I'm mostly by myself at home, I don't always put them in when I'm here."

"My name is Leah Nash," I said raising my voice a little.

"Oh, of course. I read one of your true crime books. It was very good, but I'm afraid I haven't read any others. So many books, so little time—especially at my age," she said with a sweet smile. "What do you want with Rory? Oh, wait. Is it about Matthew? You're not going to write a book about it are you? It was all so upsetting for all of us. I wouldn't want to relive it."

I'd hoped to sort of skate over the reason for my visit, in case it upset Rory's aunt, and she threw me out. But when she asked flat out, I had to answer.

I explained Marguerite's request. After I finished she didn't say anything for a minute. Finally I asked, "Are you upset?"

"No, my dear. I was just thinking. I wish you didn't have to dig things up all over again, but I understand why you must. How terrible for Hannah's sister to be so far away, unable to be there for her. Of course she wants everything possible done to prove her innocence. But it seems a fruitless exercise. Who else could have killed Matthew?"

"Well, there are some others who had motives and pretty vague alibis."

"She means me, Aunt Jean."

We both turned and saw Rory, dressed in jeans and a T-shirt, her dark hair still damp from the shower.

"I was on my way downstairs. When I heard your voice, I stopped to listen."

She addressed herself to her aunt again.

"Leah thinks I might have killed Matthew because of the money. Would you mind if I spoke to her alone, Aunt Jean?"

Her aunt's face had taken on a concerned expression at Rory's words.

"Oh, I think that I should stay, dear."

Rory smiled, then walked over and gave her aunt a swift hug.

"Thank you, but I'll be fine. I think I can help Leah clear a few things up."

"Well, all right if you're sure. But I'll just be in the kitchen if you need me, Rory," she said, patting her niece's hand as she stood to leave. "It was nice to meet you, Leah."

"Same here."

As she left I turned to Rory.

"I talked to—"

"I know what you came to ask," she said interrupting me before I could finish.

"Oh?"

"Cole Granger called me. I guess he felt a little guilty after he talked to you."

"Really? Guilt isn't an emotion I usually associate with Cole."

"He said he wanted to give me a heads up. That he'd told you what happened that night—that I was drunk, picked him up in a bar, had him drive me out to the cabin, and we found Matthew dead. He said that I might as well come clean with you because you won't leave me alone until I do. What Cole said is true. And I'm telling you the truth now. I didn't kill Matthew. Do you believe me?"

"I'm inclined to, Rory. But why did you go out to the cabin in the first place? What did you think you'd gain?"

She shook her head.

"I don't know. I wasn't really thinking at all that night. Aunt Jean was out of town and had her car. Mine was at the garage again. I walked down to the bar to drink my troubles away. Cole hit on me, and I took all the beers he pushed my way. I told him my sad story. After a while, it seemed like a good idea to find Matthew and tell him off again. Cole said he'd drive me to see my brother. We went to the house first. No one was there, so I had Cole take me to the cabin. Matt was there all right. Dead. I freaked out and Cole took off."

"You didn't call the police. Why?"

"I'd had a huge fight with Matt. I started drinking again. I reeked of booze and cigarette smoke, but I was sober enough to know that I shouldn't be the one to call the cops."

"You and Matthew weren't close. When he brought you home from New York, you chose to stay with your Aunt Jean, not with him and Ellen. Why did you think that he'd finance your purchase of the dance studio?"

"Because Aunt Jean told me they'd set aside some of the money they got from selling the farm for me to have when I got my life together. I was clean and sober at last, and I felt like that was the universe giving me a fresh start. When I found out there wasn't any money, it was like I'd missed the brass ring again—the one that Matt always seemed to catch."

"But according to Ellen, they spent the money on your rehab."

"I know, and now I realize that it was a good thing they did, and I was lucky the money was there for that. But at the time all I could feel was my disappointment, my anger that I wouldn't be able to buy the studio. It wasn't really Matt that I was so angry at, it was myself. But I couldn't accept that I was paying the price for a lifetime of bad choices. So I projected all my anger and blame onto Matt."

"How did you get back to town after Cole took off?"

"Matt kept a mountain bike in the shed. I rode it home. It's still here in the back of Aunt Jean's garage. The next morning I checked into rehab again. Aunt Jean helped me out. I'd been there a couple of weeks before they figured out that Matt had been poisoned. A cop came to interview me.

By then I was able to tell a coherent story. I lied and said that I'd been home all night. And that Matt and I had reconciled so that I'd make a less likely suspect. And then they found Matthew's burner phone with the texts from Hannah, so they didn't bother with me. They focused on her."

"Do you think Hannah did it?"

"I told you before, I was shocked when she was found guilty. She was crazy about him in high school. It's hard to believe that she could ever kill him.. But people change, and that was a long time ago."

"Okay what about anyone else? Was there anyone in Matt's life you can think of who might have been angry enough to kill him?"

"Look, Matt wasn't the monster I made him out to be, but he wasn't perfect either. He was funny, but he could push a joke too far and not realize the other person was really hurting or had had enough. So, maybe. I don't know that much about his life after I left Galen. But there is a woman, Kathy Boyle. She had some porn star past and when she ran for office against Matt, somebody leaked that to the paper. She thinks it was Matt. I called her when I was losing it and was pretty drunk one night. I don't remember exactly what we said, but I know she agreed with me that my brother was a total ass. And I suppose that Hannah's husband probably wasn't crazy about Matt. And of course there's Ellen."

"You think Matt's wife could have killed him?"

She shrugged.

"Ellen got Matt on the rebound. I don't think he would've married her if she wasn't pregnant. That had to bother her. It must have devastated her when she found Matt and Hannah had gotten back together again. I don't know if she killed Matt or not, but bad things can happen when people lose their illusions."

Ellen hadn't had any kind words when she'd spoken about Rory. It appeared the feeling was mutual.

46

It was 12:30 when I left Rory. Next up was another fraught family relationship—Olivia, her father, and her mother.

I knew Joel wouldn't be there because he worked out of town. But I expected the Vinings' housekeeper to answer the door, and I was prepared to have to talk my way in. But it wasn't a middle-aged woman who opened the door. Nor was it Olivia. Instead, a petite, pink-haired teenage girl wearing aqua and yellow braces and sporting a wide smile greeted me. I offered her a modified version of my please-let-me-in pitch.

"Hi, my name is Leah Nash. I'm looking for Olivia. Is she home?"

"Sure. She's in the kitchen. Come on in."

As she chatted me into the kitchen, I realized she shared Miguel's love of talking to everybody.

"I'm Maya Gordon. I'm Olivia's bestie. We don't have school this afternoon. That's why we're here now. Mr. Vining is at work and Mrs. Nichols the housekeeper is shopping. So Olivia and I are on our own. We're making grilled cheese sandwiches. Well, she is really. I'm not that good at cooking. Actually, I'm terrible," she said and laughed. "I'll be doing the clean-up."

"Olivia, the door was for you," she announced as we walked in. "It's your friend Leah."

I hadn't given myself the title of friend, but I was pretty sure that Maya used that description for everyone she met.

At the mention of my name, Olivia turned away from the sandwiches she was tending on the stove. She did not look happy to see me.

"My dad doesn't want me talking to you."

"I won't stay long. I just have a few questions to ask that might help your mother."

"Did you tell her what I said? Is she okay? Did she send you here to talk to me?"

"I'm not on her approved contact list, but I sent an email to your Aunt Marguerite, who is. I know she'll pass it on to her. I'm sure that she'll be very happy to get the message. But I'm afraid she might be very worried if I tell her something I found out yesterday."

"Something about Olivia?" Maya asked, unable to contain her curiosity. I liked the kid, but she didn't need to be here for this.

"Maya, would you mind if I talked to Olivia alone for a few minutes? I won't be long."

"Oh. Oh, sure, yeah. I'll just go in the other room."

"No. Maya. I want you to stay," Olivia said.

"Um, well—" Maya hesitated, torn between the adult figure who wanted her to leave, and her best friend who wanted her to stay.

I wanted to be gone before the housekeeper got back, so I capitulated quickly.

"All right, that's fine if you'd rather she stays. But Olivia, could you turn off the stove and sit at the table with me? I need your full attention."

She complied and both of the girls sat down across from me at the kitchen table.

"Olivia, I know you were in the habit of riding your bike out to Matthew Ferguson's cabin before he died. Why was that?"

"I never rode out there. Who told you that?"

"You were seen on multiple occasions. One of them was just a week or so before Matthew was killed. What were you doing out there?"

"I told you," she said, her voice sullen and her eyes downcast. "I never rode my bike out there."

Meanwhile, Maya was looking at her friend with wide, astonished eyes that told me Olivia was lying.

"If you want me to be able to help your mother, you have to tell me the truth. Matthew's neighbor at the cabin, Walt Sanders, said he saw a girl matching your description with a blue e-bike, like the one you have, wearing a blue helmet, also like the one you have, near the cabin several times. One of those times he spoke to you and told you to stay away from his property."

"I don't know any Walt Sanders. I have a blue e-bike. So what? Lots of people do. And lots of kids ride the trail out there. Maybe I've been out there once or twice. I really don't remember. But I never went to Mr. Ferguson's cabin, and I never talked to some crazy old man. And I'm not going to talk to you, either."

"Olivia, what were you doing the night Matthew Ferguson was killed?"

"I started to go to the game with Maya, but I got sick and came home. I told the police that."

"You knew about your mom's affair before Matthew Ferguson was killed, didn't you?"

Although she tried to hide it, I saw the shock on her face and the fear in her eyes.

"You can't come in my house and call me a liar. I don't know what you're talking about, but I'm done talking to you. Please leave. Now!"

Maya was staring at her like she'd never seen Olivia before. And maybe she hadn't. Not this Olivia, anyway.

"Olivia, I'm not going to stop asking questions. And I *will* find the answers. I don't know why you're lying, but I'm sure that you are. Please, let me help you. Let me help your mother. Whatever you're hiding is going to come out. And it will be so much better for you if you bring it out first."

Her voice was cold, and her eyes were hard as she said, "If you don't leave, I'm going to call my dad. Please go."

"*Chica*, what are you doing? And where are you doing it?"

"Miguel, hi. I'm in Galen. I'm pulling into a park to sit in my car so I can write up the notes. I talked to Rory Ferguson this morning, which went pretty well. I just talked to Olivia Vining and that did not go well at all."

I gave him the gist of it.

"Oh, yes, she is not telling the truth for sure. What's your plan now?"

"I don't know. I thought confronting her directly about being at Matthew's cabin would shake her up enough for her to tell me the truth. That didn't work. I have to talk to her dad, but Joel Vining is not going to want to talk to me. I'm going to have to think on that, too."

Suddenly I noticed a black SUV speeding much too fast on the path that circled the park. As it neared me, the driver made a sharp turn, pulled up next to me, and a man jumped out. Joel Vining.

"I've got to go Miguel. I'll call you later."

47

Without waiting for me to even acknowledge him, Joel yanked the door of my car open and plunked himself down in the passenger seat.

"What do you want?" I asked, though I had a pretty good idea.

"I told you to stay away from my home and from my daughter. Instead you sneaked over when you thought I wouldn't be there. I saw your car pulling out. Olivia came running out of the house crying so hard she could barely speak. She's a minor. You have no right to interrogate her without her parent present."

In the close confines of my car, his raised voice was loud enough to be a little scary. Still, what was he going to do to me in a public park in the middle of the afternoon?

"Joel, it's not illegal for me to talk to your daughter, even if you're not there. I rang the bell, I was invited in, and I talked with Olivia about Matthew Ferguson."

I wanted to say calm down, but I know that's a phrase almost guaranteed to send an upset person into a full-on rage.

"Olivia is a child. You took advantage of that, and you badgered her with ridiculous accusations and now she's home crying like she'll never stop. I hope you're proud of yourself."

"I'm sorry that Olivia is upset. I really am. But my questions weren't ridiculous. And your daughter isn't a ten-year-old child. She's a bright, fifteen-year-old adolescent, who was seen multiple times in the vicinity of Matthew Ferguson's cabin in the weeks before he was killed. At least one of those times she was walking around his property. I asked her about it, and she got angry and defensive. Do you know why that would be?"

"Olivia was at Matthew Ferguson's property?"

His voice had switched from anger to shock. "Why would she be there?"

"I thought you might know," I said.

Surprise and concern showed on his face. Did his concern stem from the fear that what Olivia was hiding had to do with her involvement in Matthew's death—or his own?

"I-I, uh I don't know."

His voice had lost some of its righteous fury. "She never said anything to me about being at Matthew's cabin. Are you certain it was her? Who told you she was there?"

I didn't want Walt to become the target of Joel's obviously quick temper.

"I'm certain. But I'm not going to turn your anger loose on my source."

Oddly, instead of making him madder at me, my refusal calmed him down a bit. Enough so that I took the plunge and asked him the key question.

"Joel, where were you the night Matthew Ferguson died?"

I braced myself for a fresh round of anger. It didn't come.

"I was in Milwaukee. At a conference. I planned to stay over and go home in the morning. But after I was in my room for a while, I decided I'd rather drive home and sleep in my own bed. So I did. I got to Galen around 11:00 p.m. I told that to the police and they moved on. You should do the same."

"Was Olivia home when you got there?"

"Yes," he said firmly. "She'd planned to spend the night with a friend, but she didn't feel well and came home instead."

"And your wife?"

"My ex-wife. She arrived shortly after I did. She *said* that she'd been working at her store. But the jury didn't believe her. I didn't either."

"You were a friend of Matthew's at one time. You were pretty familiar with his cabin, right?"

"I know where this is going. Yes, I'd been to his cabin. But not nearly as often it turned out as Hannah had been. I did not drive to Matthew's cabin to kill him. I drove home. My daughter is struggling to come to terms with the fact that her mother is a murderer who betrayed both of us. As a concerned father I am asking you not to speak to Olivia again."

He didn't wait for my answer before he opened the car door and got out. A good thing because I wouldn't have been able to agree to that.

After Joel left, I wrote down some notes from that conversation, as well as from my earlier talk with Olivia. I remained convinced that Olivia was lying, and I had a strong feeling that Joel might be as well. I still needed to figure out a way to get Olivia to talk to me . . . Or maybe not. Maybe that was a job for Miguel. Olivia viewed me as the enemy. Miguel strikes very few people that way.

I started to call him with my idea but noticed when I did that it was time for me to get to Kathy Boyle's.

When I made the turn onto Lakeside Drive, I saw a couple of cars parked along the side of the road in the general vicinity of Kathy's house. As I got closer I saw that one of the vehicles was an unmarked patrol car. Beside it stood a deputy wearing the uniform of the Galen Sheriff's office. He was talking to a woman holding the long, narrow, spiral-bound notebook that marked her as a reporter.

I drove past them and parked behind her car. Had there been a break-in at Kathy's? If so, I hoped they hadn't gotten away with whatever it was she wanted to show me. I grabbed my purse and opened my car door as the deputy was getting into his car. But my purse strap got caught on the gear shift (purses with long straps are the bane of my existence). By the time I disentangled it and got out, the deputy was driving away and the woman I'd pegged as a journalist was walking toward me.

"You're Leah Nash, aren't you? I'm Riley Dorner, with the *Galen Record*," she said.

"I thought you might be."

I like a firm handshake, and Riley had one. She also had a narrow face with green eyes that looked like they didn't miss much, and a generous mouth that softened her sharp features.

"What's going on?" I asked.

"Don't you know? I thought that's why you were here. Kathy Boyle is dead."

48

"Kathy's dead? I just talked to her yesterday. I was supposed to meet her here today at four o'clock," I said, a little stupidly, the way you do when your brain finds it hard to catch up with an unexpected reality. "What happened?"

"Hey, I haven't even filed my story yet. I can't give a rival paper the details."

"The *Times* isn't a rival paper. Trenton County isn't in our coverage area, you know that. I didn't ask because I'm trying to scoop you."

She looked unconvinced—which I understood. Reporters can be friends, can even share information, but when there's competition for the same story, friends turn into frenemies pretty fast.

"Look, you already talked to Miguel. You know that I'm looking into Matthew Ferguson's murder. It's not for the paper and it's not for a book. It's a favor for Marguerite, Hannah Vining's sister."

"Yes, that's what Miguel said. But he asked me a lot of questions about the story we ran on Kathy's porn star past. And now Kathy is dead, and you're here, and I can't help wondering what's really going on."

"Just what he said. Kathy was part of my attempt to figure out who else could have killed Matthew."

"She was a suspect?" she asked quickly.

"Okay, wait a sec. I'm willing to have an off-the-record conversation with you. But I really don't want to see what I'm telling you on the front page of the *Galen Record*. Not yet anyway. Not until I get the answers I need to either identify an alternate killer or satisfy myself that Hannah is where she belongs. After that, you're free to use what I give you now any way you like. If you can agree to that, I'll answer your questions, as long as you answer mine."

She scanned my face, weighing her desire for what I could tell her against her suspicion that I might be trying to do an end run around her.

Finally she said, "Okay. Here's what I know. I got it off-the-record from the deputy I was talking to when you got here. He's an ex-boyfriend of mine."

"Oh?"

"If I can't keep them as a boyfriend, I try to keep them as a source," she said with a grin.

"So what did he say?"

"That Kathy's son called the sheriff's office and asked for a wellness check on his mother. She didn't answer her phone when he called last night around 10:00. He assumed she was in bed and that she'd call him back in the morning. He was so busy this morning that he didn't realize she hadn't called him back until 11:00. He texted to remind her they were meeting for lunch at 11:30 in Sun Prairie after she finished a walk-through of her new condo with the manager. He finished up what he was doing and went to the restaurant. When she didn't show, he called her and got no answer. He was worried then. He called the manager of her condo, found out she didn't show for the meeting. That's when he called for the wellness check."

"When did the sheriff's office get here?"

"About 2:30. They found Kathy lying on the floor in a room she used as an office. It looks like she was using a ladder to get something out of the attic and fell. Access to the attic is just one of those push up panel kind of things in the ceiling. The ladder was still standing, poking up through the attic opening. Kathy wasn't breathing when the deputy checked, and she had no pulse. He called it in. The medical examiner came out, declared her dead at the scene and they took the body away about five minutes before you got here."

"Did your ex tell you if they have an estimated time of death?"

"He did. But it's pretty broad at this point. Rigor mortis was fully present and hadn't begun to recede, so Kathy was probably killed between 8:00 p.m. and midnight. But that's really rough," she cautioned.

"Understood. How did you find out about Kathy? Did you hear the call over the scanner?"

"Nope. The sheriff's office started encrypting radio communications about six months ago. So now I spend more time than I'd like on Trenton County in the Know—it's a Facebook page where people post whatever they know, or think they know, about local happenings. There were a couple of posts asking what the police cars and the medical examiner were doing on Lakeside Drive. I came out to see for myself."

"When do you expect the sheriff's office to release the information?"

"They'll probably put out a press release in an hour or two. But it'll just say that Kathy's body was found, that preliminary investigation suggests an accidental fall is the cause and that's it, pending the autopsy results. You know the drill."

I nodded.

"Okay, Leah. I showed you mine, now you show me yours. Why were you coming to see Kathy today? You didn't answer me when I asked you if she was a suspect."

"She was a cross between a source and a suspect to me. I'd already spoken with her. She gave me her perspective on Matthew Ferguson, told me she didn't kill him—well, what else would she say, right? And I was inclined to believe her. But I still had her as a possible. She called me yesterday and said she had found something she thought I should see."

"What?"

"I don't know. She wouldn't tell me on the phone. She insisted that I needed to see it myself to decide if it meant anything."

"And you don't have any idea what that could be?"

"Not really. Though, I think it might be some physical thing that could tie someone besides Hannah to the crime."

"Like what?"

"I have no idea. Except that I'm sure that it had to point away from her as a suspect, or Kathy wouldn't have been so eager to share. Now it seems pretty unlikely that I'll be finding out what it was."

49

After reassuring each other that our shared information would stay between the two of us until further developments dictated otherwise, Riley and I parted ways.

As I went back to my car, I saw Patrick Boyle coming up toward the house from the dock. When he reached the driveway, I walked over to him.

"Patrick, hi. I'm so sorry about your mom."

He looked at me with no recognition in his sad eyes.

"I'm Leah Nash. We talked the other day when I was here. I'm not sure if your mother told you, but I'm looking into the death of Matthew Ferguson. When I was here last week, it was to ask her about him. She called me yesterday and said she had something to show me, but she didn't want to tell me about it on the phone. She asked me to come out today to see it for myself. Do you have any idea what it is?"

"No," he said, surprised. "There's not much left here. Just a few odds and ends she was trying to sell online, some furniture, her old laptop. I bought her a new one for her birthday. I just got it set up for her a couple of days ago. She never even got the chance to use it . . . "

His voice trailed off and he blinked back tears.

"What was she even doing on the ladder? There was nothing left in the attic. I cleaned it out myself. I don't understand."

"She was probably just taking one last look around," I said.

"One last look. She said that all the time. Whenever we left the house for a vacation or a visit to my dad's family, she'd always say, 'Let's just take one last look to make sure we got everything.' And now that stupid last look in the attic killed her. It's just so wrong! She was only fifty-five. She should still be here. I'm twenty-six years old and I just want to cry like a baby. I still need her. I still need her," he repeated, this time letting the tears fall.

He was so distraught it was obviously time for me to go. I don't usually hug relative strangers, but I couldn't just thank him for his time and leave. I stepped forward and gave him a solid hug. That seemed to unloose something in him and a ragged sob escaped. After a few seconds, he regained control of himself and stepped away.

"I'm so sorry, Patrick," I said again.

He nodded, and I nodded, and then I walked away. There wasn't anything more to say.

On the way to pick up the pizza, I had a lot of thoughts swirling around in my head. I felt very bad for Patrick, no question. I knew that I hadn't provided him with any real comfort. The thing is, you can be there for someone in their sorrow, but you can't take the journey with them. That's a road that everyone who loses someone they love has to travel alone.

But I had to be honest with myself, I felt frustrated as well as saddened by Kathy's unexpected death. What had she wanted to show me? I hadn't realized until that moment how much I had been banking on Kathy providing a clue that would give me the right direction to move in.

"What kind of clue, Leah?" I asked myself out loud, as I am wont to do when no one else is around to be a sounding board. "Think!" I admonished myself. After a minute, an idea started forming in my head.

Kathy had a new laptop. She was going to sell her old one. And what do you do before you sell a computer or a phone? You clean it off. Maybe she had found something there—something she'd forgotten she had, something that didn't seem important until she was deciding what to delete. It could be a document, a photo, an email maybe?

In the parking lot at Cheesehead Pizza I called Patrick using the number on the business card he'd given me the first time I met him. He didn't pick up, but I left a voicemail. First I apologized for bothering him again at a time like this, then I plunged in with my request.

"Patrick, you said that your mom was planning to sell her old laptop. Could I possibly get a look at it before you clean it off? I'm wondering if what she wanted to show me might be something on there. I'd be happy to meet you anywhere and anytime that would work for you. Please give me a call when you can."

I know lots of people don't bother to listen to voicemail, especially from a number they don't recognize. But Patrick had a side business, so he'd have to respond to potential clients. I didn't expect to hear from him for a few days. But the laptop seemed to be the best chance of discovering what Kathy had wanted me to see. If I was smart enough to recognize it when I saw it, that is.

Cheesehead Pizza was jumping when I parked my car and went inside. There was a long counter at the back with one side for ordering and paying, and one side for picking up. Several benches and a few chairs provided seating for those waiting for orders. Of which there were at least half a dozen. But the pick-up line moved quickly and within a few minutes it was my turn.

"Pizza for Ferguson," I said, expecting to see the counterman, who was wearing a name tag identifying him as Cheesehead Roy, turn and pull our pizza from a waiting stack. Instead he got a pained look on his face.

"Yeah, sorry it's gonna be a minute. We got slammed right before the order came in and I'm down two crew members. Your pie's in the oven, but it'll be a few minutes."

As I turned away, I saw Olivia's friend Maya walk up to the counter. She didn't notice me, but I waited while Cheesehead Roy gave her the same information he'd given me—she'd have to wait. I hurried up to her as she turned to look for a seat.

"Maya, hi! Why don't you wait for your order with me?"

She looked surprised. She also looked uncomfortable, like not only had she not expected to see me, she also really wished that I wasn't there. But she walked with me to an empty bench, and we sat down together.

"I'm having pizza with a friend in Galen," I said. "She told me that Cheesehead is the best place around. Is she right?" I asked, thinking a little small talk might make her feel more relaxed.

"It's good."

"What's your favorite pizza?"

"Super deluxe."

"Do you get pizza here often?"

"I guess."

Her two-word answers—in contrast to her chattiness earlier in the day at Olivia's—and the way she kept twirling the ring on her finger and avoiding eye contact, made it clear she was nervous.

"Maya—" I began at the same moment she said, "Leah, I—" we both paused and laughed a little awkwardly.

"You go ahead. What were you going to say?"

She took a deep breath as though she were an inexperienced diver about to make her first jump off the high board. When she let it out, she plunged right into her story.

"Olivia lied to you today."

"What did she lie about?" I asked, careful to keep my voice neutral.

"I feel bad ratting her out, but what she said today about not ever going out to Mr. Ferguson's cabin and not knowing that her mom was having an affair, that's not true. She found out about it before Mr. Ferguson was killed. She told me and made me swear I wouldn't say anything. Her mom promised her that it was over, but Olivia didn't trust her. She used to ride out there all the time, checking to see if her mom's car was there. And that night when Mr. Ferguson was killed, it didn't happen like Olivia said."

My heart had begun to speed up and I hoped that my pizza—and Maya's—would take a while longer.

"How *did* it happen?"

"Olivia was supposed to stay overnight with me. We were going to the football game and then to the dance after. My dad let me have the car to drive without him for the first time. The game started at 7:00, and I promised that I would be home no later than 11:30. Olivia and I were listening to music and singing and feeling really happy. Then a black SUV going in the opposite direction passed us. I said, 'Hey, look it's your dad! I thought you said he was in Milwaukee.' Right away she said it wasn't him. But I saw Mr. Vining when he drove past us. And when I looked in the rearview mirror I saw the OBX on the back of his car."

"OBX?"

"Outer Banks in North Carolina. It's how they call it. I went there with the Vinings once. Me and Olivia put the bumper sticker on his car. So I knew for sure it was him. But Olivia kept saying it wasn't, and then she said she didn't feel good, and she wanted me to drop her off. I didn't believe her. All I did was say I saw her dad and she got all salty with me."

"Did you have a fight?"

"No. I just dropped her off. I went to the end of the street, that was the shortest way to the high school, but it was blocked off. I had to turn around and go back the way I came. When I did, I saw Olivia. She was on her e-bike, coming out of her driveway."

"Do you know where she was going?"

"I asked her afterward. She said I was wrong, that it wasn't her. It must have been someone else. But she was lying to me then, just like she lied to you today when she said she never went to Mr. Ferguson's cabin. I saw her myself turn on the corner that leads to where the cabin is."

"Why are you telling me this now, Maya?"

"Because Olivia is falling apart, and I don't know how to help her. She dropped out of choir. She doesn't come to art club anymore. When I ask her to go with me, she just says she doesn't feel like it. I'm about the only friend she has. Ever since all that stuff with her mom, Olivia's been moody and none of her moods are happy. She's either mad, or sad, or she doesn't care about anything. But I don't want her to not have anybody. I'm afraid she might, like, do something to herself."

"Do something? You mean she might try to harm herself?"

"Maybe. I don't know. She's cutting though. She always wears a long-sleeved shirt, but I've seen the scars on her arms. I don't know what to do. I don't know if her dad would listen to me, and maybe he'd just get mad, or Olivia would get mad at me for talking to him. I don't know how to like, get to her. The real her, I mean. She's not the same Olivia. I guess how could you be, though, if your mom was in prison for killing somebody? Especially if you maybe thought your dad did it."

She clapped her hand over her mouth as though she were trying to stuff her last words back in.

"Olivia thinks her dad killed Matthew Ferguson?"

"No! I mean, she never said that. And I don't think Mr. Vining would ever do that, he's always been really nice to me. But why else would Olivia be lying so much? She's really mixed up and so am I and—"

"Order up for Gordon!"

Maya jumped up. "Oh! I have to go. My dad hates it if I let the pizza get cold. Don't tell Olivia I said anything to you, please! I'm just worried about her, that's all."

"Maya, wait I—"

But she was already at the counter grabbing her pizza. I slid off the bench and tried to reach her, but a wave of customers swarmed through the front door just then. When I managed to squeeze around them, another patron whose order had been called stepped in front of me and inadvertently blocked my path to Maya. She was out the door before I could catch her.

50

"I can't believe Kathy Boyle is dead! How did it happen?"

Ellen asked the question as she walked me to the kitchen. I'd told her about Kathy as soon as she opened the door.

"Off-the-record—the police haven't released the details yet—but it looks like she fell off a ladder. When I got there today, the police were just leaving. Her son Patrick was there, and I talked to him."

"Oh, poor Patrick. I should call Colin and let him know. Did I tell you that the two of them were friends in school?"

"Yes. I think it would be nice if your son reached out. Patrick seemed pretty lost when I left."

"I will definitely call Colin," she said.

We sat down at the table where Ellen already had plates and napkins laid out. As she handed me a slice of pizza, I noticed for the first time her sapphire and diamond wedding ring set.

"That's gorgeous. The stone's a sapphire, isn't it?"

"It is," she said, holding her hand out so I could see it better. "It's my birthstone. I got so thin during cancer treatment that my original engagement ring fell off and I lost it. I was so upset. When I completed treatment, Matthew gave me a whole new set. This is much fancier than what he could afford when we were eighteen. It meant so much to me that he understood how I felt about losing my engagement ring. I only take the set off when I'm digging in the garden or cleaning. It's a little fancier than I'd have chosen, but it means the world to me. Besides, some days I like to feel fancy," she said and laughed.

Then she stopped abruptly.

"What's the matter?"

"I just realized that laughing and talking about my fancy ring when we were just talking about Kathy Boyle's death is a little inappropriate."

"Well, you weren't close. I think it's okay in this rough old world to grab a laugh when you can."

"I know, but thinking about her son and what he's going through right now that seems a little cold."

"Well, if you're cold, then I'm frigid. I do feel bad for Patrick, but I'd be lying if I said I didn't also feel bad that I'm not going to get the lead I was hoping for."

"Maybe Patrick knows what his mother was going to tell you. Did you ask him?"

"I'm a little ashamed to say I did. But it was while I was explaining that his mother had asked me to come to the house. He didn't have any idea what she might have meant."

"I'm sorry, Leah. I can imagine how disappointing that is."

"Yeah well, it happens. Nothing much is breaking my way right now."

"Tell me about that. Where is your investigation? Are you finding *anything* that says Hannah didn't kill Matthew?"

I shook my head.

"The opposite, really. The list of people with motive and opportunity keeps shrinking. Rory seemed like a good prospect, but she's got a pretty strong alibi and someone to confirm it. I thought about Kathy originally. I suppose there's still a chance she could have done it. You could argue that she lost the most, and she put the blame for that on Matthew. But I don't see her having the patience for poison. Did I tell you this already—the reason that Kathy was so sure Matthew had given her story to the paper?"

"No, you didn't. What was it?"

I relayed what Kathy had told me about Matthew allegedly tormenting her with the line from her adult film that later convinced her Matthew was the leaker.

"Does that seem like something Matthew would have done—stick the knife in her like that, just before all hell was going to break loose with the newspaper story coming out?"

Ellen was shaking her head no before I even finished.

"She had to have misheard him. She's needed hearing aids for years, but she won't wear them. She told me once that she doesn't want to look old. I guess I can understand that, but it doesn't make you look young to ask, "What did you say?" every time someone makes a comment."

"So you think that she just misheard what Matthew said?"

"It has to be that. Matthew liked to tease but he would never have done that to Kathy. Remember, I told you that we'd both agreed not to mention the video to anyone. He wouldn't have brought it up to her."

Ellen spoke firmly, but Rory's comment that Matthew could push things too far sometimes when he was trying to be funny was still in the back of my mind.

"So what's next?" she asked.

It was too soon to say anything about Olivia Vining or her dad—those leads could fizzle too. And for sure I didn't want Olivia's name to start circulating as a possible witness—or a potential killer. I still had a lot of thinking to do about that.

"I'm not sure."

"But you still think Hannah is the wrong person?"

"I don't think I ever said she was the wrong person. I'm trying to find a reasonable alternative, but so far I haven't found much to quibble with in the sheriff's investigation."

"I want you to find the truth, and I believe it's that Hannah killed my husband. But ever since you showed up, this little voice in my head has been whispering, but what if it's not? What if I'm wrong? I don't care so much about Hannah—she did have an affair with my husband after all. But I'm a mother too, and thinking about Hannah's daughter, I really do feel for her. How long do you think it will be before you know one way or another for sure?"

"I don't know that I'll ever know 'for sure' unless the killer confesses.

I'm shooting for knowing that I turned over every stone I could find and there is no one else with motive, means, and opportunity that is stronger than Hannah's."

"Let's not talk about Hannah or Matthew or murder anymore. Tell me about pizza. How does Cheesehead stack up against your beloved Bonucci's?"

We had pretty much demolished the pizza by then.

"Cheesehead is very good, probably the best pizza I've had—that isn't Bonnuci's. Sorry, Ellen. You'll have to come to Himmel one day and I'll treat you to one of their pizzas so that you don't have to take my word for it."

"Well, don't delay too long on the invitation. I'm leaving town for a while, maybe a long while."

"Oh? Where are you going?"

"To Platteville—that's where my sister Lindsey lives. I'm going to look around for an apartment there. If I find something, I'll rent for a while and see if I like it there.

"Wow, that's a big change."

"Lindsey's been after me to move. At first I couldn't think about leaving this house, and my garden, and the memories. But with Matthew gone, and Colin on his own, it feels like I need to start a new chapter. The two of them were the center of my life for so long, that now I feel a little hollow inside. I need to find a way to live that makes me feel whole again."

"Well, you and Matthew were together for a long time. Eighteen is very young to make a huge commitment like marriage."

"It is, but there was never anyone for me but Matthew. How about you, Leah? Have you ever been married? Are you in a relationship?"

"Yes, and yes," I said. "I was married for a short time in my twenties. It ended badly. I'm with a man now that I've known since I was twelve years old. We were very good friends before we started a romantic relationship, and we still are."

"Do you think you'll marry him?"

"For sure I'm not ready for that now. I don't know if I ever will be."

I didn't really want to talk about my relationship with Coop. Ellen seemed to sense my reluctance and changed the subject.

"Hey, I've been meaning to tell you. I finished your book, *Bury Your Dead*. I loved it! I have a couple of questions though."

"Ask away. Every author enjoys talking about her work."

We spent the rest of our evening talking about books we enjoyed—not just mine. I was surprised when I heard the grandfather clock in Ellen's hallway chime 8:00 p.m.

"Well I'd better hit the road, Ellen. I didn't mean to stay so long. Thanks so much for the pizza and the conversation," I said, getting up to leave.

"This was really nice, Leah. Thanks for coming. Let's do it again before I leave.

"Absolutely, Ellen. And thank you for the introduction to the very good, but not superior to Bonucci's, Cheesehead pizza."

On the way home I remembered that we were out of cat treats, a situation I try to avoid because Sam has a more guilt-inducing stare than my mother. I stopped at the grocery store to pick up a couple of boxes and ran into Peter Sullivan in the pet food aisle.

"Hello, Leah, you're shopping late," he said.

"Cat necessities, or I dare not go home," I said, shaking a box at him. "You, too?"

"A dog, in my case. Adele's baby—our Corgi," he said. "I'm glad I ran into you tonight. I have an idea for your mystery plot, a twist that I think would surprise your readers, but be entirely believable."

"Really? I'm—"

My phone buzzed with a text. The preview made me open it immediately.

51

Leah, this is Sharla. I just listened to an episode of a podcast where you were interviewed. I just had to tell you that you sound EXACTLY like I thought you would! You have a beautiful voice. That's all I wanted to say. Oh, you can text me anytime at this number. Your number 1 fan.

"Oh hell," I said as I finished reading it.

"Bad news?" Peter asked.

"I seem to have attracted the attention of a very devoted fan. She's sent me flowers, dropped off a chai latte for me, and has emailed me several times. Now she's got my phone number so she can text me. Yay," I said.

"That sounds like a stalker, not a fan, Leah. Have you contacted the police? This isn't anything to take lightly."

I was touched by the concerned expression on his face.

"I've been resisting the idea, but it does kind of look that way, I guess. Yes, I've talked to the Himmel Police Department, and I'll let them know about this, too. The detective who's investigating it seems like she's on top of things, and, in a way, I suppose you could say it's been a positive experience so far—free flowers, free chai, and loads of positive feedback," I said.

He shook his head. "I don't think this is something to joke about. Stalkers can be very dangerous."

"I know. You're right. But the Nash family go-to response in times of stress, or too much emotional honesty, is to deflect with a joke or a smart remark. But other than follow police advice there's not a whole lot I can do. So I think I'll fall back on another Nash family staple—a problem ignored is a problem solved. It's engraved on our family crest," I said.

It was a joke of course, but if we actually did have a family crest, that would be an excellent description of how we face life's challenges.

He smiled a little reluctantly and said, "I'm glad to know you're working with the police on this. But do be careful."

"I will. Thanks, Peter. Now if I don't get these treats home to Sam, I'll be in *real* danger. I'll talk to you soon."

It wasn't until I was in the car and driving away from the store that I realized the interruption of the text had kept Peter from giving me the plot twist he had for my next mystery.

Coop and Sam were on the couch reading in front of the fireplace when I walked into my apartment.

"Coop! I thought you weren't coming over because you wanted to do some more work at your property," I said. I shook the box of cat treats at Sam and he ran over to me.

"I finished earlier than I thought with the sanding, and I was just too tired to start painting. I decided to give it up for the night and spend some quality time with Sam, waiting for you to get back from Ellen's. How was dinner?"

"It was fine, but I have lots of breaking news for you from my day."

"You found something to exonerate Hannah?"

"No. I didn't say it was good news, just breaking news. Let me get Sam his treats and me a Jameson and then I'll join you. Do you want another beer?"

"No, I'm good."

When I had taken care of Sam and poured my Jameson, I got myself into position in the corner of the couch opposite Coop.

"Are you finally settled down?" he asked. "You make a bigger production of getting comfortable than Sam does, and his settling in involves making biscuits."

"Hey, I thought you were here to offer me support and comfort after a very taxing day. I needed to scooch in just right, so I don't spill my Jameson."

"Are you fully scooched?"

"I am," I said and took a sip of my drink. "And now I am also in full story-telling mode. A lot has happened since I sent you off to work with a good breakfast this morning."

I went in chronological order, beginning with Jane Williams and the stalker report all the way through Rory and Jean Ferguson, Olivia and Maya, Joel's surprise visit to me at the park, and then the news of Kathy's death.

"You weren't kidding. That's a lot. Kathy's death means you'll probably never find out what she wanted to show you."

"I know. And I have a gut feeling it was something important."

"Gut feelings are usually based on something you observed that your conscious mind ignored because you were thinking about something else. That's when your unconscious pops up and tries to let you know that you're missing something. Have you tried going back over your conversation with Kathy? Or her son? Maybe that would bring something to the surface."

"Listen to you, Sigmund Freud. I get what you're saying, and I believe that, too. But I already tried that, and I got nothing."

"What about the timing of Kathy's death? Does it strike you as a little too convenient?"

"You mean because it happened so soon after she told me she had something for me? It would maybe, but she wasn't murdered. She fell off a ladder."

"Is that the official autopsy finding?"

"No, that won't be ready for a couple of days. Wait, are you thinking someone pushed Kathy off a ladder because she was going to give me incriminating evidence? How would they know?"

"Kathy told you about it. She could have told others as well."

"She wasn't stupid, Coop. She wouldn't go to someone she thought was the killer and say, 'Hey, by the way I have a piece of evidence that points right at you for Matthew Ferguson's murder.'"

"No, but you said she wasn't sure that what she had would interest you. She was offering you the chance to assess it. Maybe she shared it with someone else, too. Someone she trusted and didn't connect with Matthew's murder. And that person was the real killer."

"Like who?"

He shrugged. "I don't know. It's your case, not mine. I'm just trying to remind you that you have to take a 360-degree view in a murder investigation. You can't let a favorite theory narrow your vision too soon."

"I don't have a favorite theory. I have lots of disjointed ideas and bits of information that refuse to come together in any coherent way. One minute I think it's Olivia, the next I think it's Joel, and up until a few hours ago I still had Kathy as a possibility."

"What about the sister, Rory? Her story checked out with Cole's but remember the killer didn't have to be there when Matthew died."

"No, they didn't. Except what about the pizza? Matthew hated mushrooms, two pieces of the pizza were gone, one with mushrooms, one without. Who ate the mushroom piece? Someone else was there, and it couldn't have been Rory."

"You're probably right on that."

"Thank you. I was beginning to think you'd lost all faith in me," I said.

"Never. I'm just trying to help you shake up your thinking. Take those bits of information and disjointed ideas you just told me you have and throw them up in the air and see where they land. It's possible to overthink a case, you know. Sometimes you have to stop trying so hard."

"I guess you're right. I'm tired of talking about Matthew Ferguson's murder. I'm tired of thinking about it. In fact, I'm just tired. So tired, in fact, that I forgot to tell you that I heard from Sharla again. This time via text."

I showed him the message I'd received.

"But she hasn't threatened me in any way. In fact, quite the opposite. She's over the top praising me."

"She's got your phone number now, Leah. She's watching you, too. She had to be in order to know you were at Darmody's open house. Your fan Sharla is officially your stalker Sharla. You didn't answer her text did you?"

"No, but would it really be so bad to just respond and firmly but nicely tell her she needs to stop? I could just say that I'm glad she enjoys my work, but I try to draw a line between my personal life and my professional life. I'd like her to stop communicating directly with me."

"That could turn Sharla's ardent admiration into nasty anger at your rejection. And she could turn up in person on your doorstep. If you don't respond, she may move on."

"I don't think that's going to work. I didn't answer the email she sent about the flowers, and so now she's texting me. But Jane told me the same thing you did. Don't communicate with her."

"And?"

"And I'll let Jane know about the text. There's not much else I can do. Oh, wait, I could hire Darmody to be my bodyguard. No, that won't work. He's got his big surveillance job, so he won't have time for me."

He shook his head.

"I guess I should be glad you're not panicking. Look, just remember to lock your doors whenever you leave, and be aware of your surroundings. And keep Jane Williams in the loop."

"If I do all those things, will that satisfy you?"

"Yes. I will be satisfied that you're acting like a responsible adult."

"Don't I always?"

He shook his head, but he smiled.

"I love you," I said.

He stood up then. "I love you, too and that's why I'm not going to stay over."

"You're not?"

"No. I've got to get a couple of things done before Dad gets back on Friday. So I'm going to pay the price for quitting early today and coming to see you. I have to get up early, *very* early, and get out to the property to do that painting I left behind so I could see you tonight. Which was well worth it, by the way. And then I'm going in to the office. I don't want to wake you up at 4:30 in the morning when I roll out of bed."

"Okay. I don't want that either. You know, I hate to see you move out of town, but I'll be glad when you finish working out there so we can spend more time together on a regular basis."

"I'll be glad, too," he said.

52

As it turned out, Coop's chivalry regarding my beauty sleep was for naught. My phone rang at five o'clock the next morning. When I saw that the call was from my mother I came instantly awake.

"Mom? What's wrong?"

"Leah, I'm sorry to call so early, but I'm on my way to the airport to catch a flight to Portland that leaves at 7:30."

"Portland? What are you going to Oregon for?"

"Not Oregon. Portland Maine. I'm going to see my college roommate Judy. Her sister called me last night. Judy's in hospice. I feel terrible. I knew she had cervical cancer, but she was always so positive on the phone and in her emails. I thought she was still in remission."

"Oh my God, Judy Dawson? Mom, I'm so sorry. I know you guys have been friends forever."

"Since freshman year in college. I might be too late, but I have to try to get there before she passes."

"Oh, sure. Absolutely. Do you need me to do anything, check on the house or whatever?"

"No, Mrs. Nowicki from next door will do that. I just wanted you to know I'm leaving town. I'll be gone a few days, a week at the most. Oh, God. I was going to call her this week to chat. Why didn't I call her earlier? I can't believe pretty, lively, funny Judy is dying, and I didn't even know it. What kind of friend am I?"

"Mom, this is hard enough on you. Don't make it worse by guilting yourself," I said.

"I can't help it, Leah. You know what Judy did when she was first diagnosed? She called me right away, not for sympathy but to make sure that I knew cervical cancer is caused by a sexually transmitted virus. She wanted to tell me to get checked annually, because she hadn't been doing that. I think her asshat husband Doug gave it to her. One of the reasons I didn't go out to visit her so often after Ben died and she married Doug is that I can't stand him. He came on to me once when I was there, and Judy was right in the next room! I should have told her. Maybe she'd have kicked him to the curb, and she wouldn't be dying now."

A sob escaped and I knew Mom's anger was a cover for her grief.

"Mom, no. I'm no expert but I think the HP virus that causes cancer can live in your body for a long time. Years even. Judy could have picked it up before she even met Doug. She's not dying because you didn't warn her about Doug."

"Did I ever sing *The Traveling Typist* to you?"

I was surprised by the random question, but I let Mom steer the conversation where she needed it to go.

"That's one I haven't heard of. What is it?"

"It's a silly song about someone who travels from place to place doing typing jobs. Our parents were always asking us what we were going to do with an English degree if we didn't teach. Judy told them we were going to be traveling typists. One night after some Boone's Farm in the dorm, Judy and I made the song up. She worked out the tune on her guitar, and we both made up the words.

"One verse is "Just me and my Underwood we travel along. Between typing jobs I stop for a song. And when my traveling days are over, there's a fisherman waiting in Nova Scotia." We thought it was really funny. And we sounded pretty good too. I think I'm going to sing it for her, even though she's in a coma. I've heard that hearing is the last thing to go, so maybe she'll know I'm there . . . Oh, Leah, I'm going to miss her so much!'

She started crying in earnest then.

"Mom, you're driving. It's dark. There are deer. Stop crying, just breathe, and focus on the road. There'll be plenty of time for crying later. Where are you right now?"

She drew a shuddery breath as she brought her emotions under control.

"About five miles from the exit for the airport."

"Okay, good. I love you, text me when you land. Call me anytime day or night, whenever you need to. I'm here."

"I know you are. Thank you, hon. I'll be in touch. I love you, too."

It was only 5:15, but there was no way I'd be able to go back to sleep. It hit me then that the midnight deadline to apply for the director position at the *Times* had passed. I got up and checked the email account we'd set up to receive applications. Nothing from Spencer. Yes! I did a brief happy dance and thanked whatever God or gods there are for the narrow escape. Then I showered and put thoughts of stalkers, sad mothers, and Spencer on ice. I sat in the window seat to figure out where to go next with my investigation.

Then I got up, grabbed my notes and a handful of highlighters and sat at the kitchen bar, so I had room to spread out. I needed to organize my information so I could organize my thinking. I read through everything, highlighting passages, circling key points and sometimes drawing arrows to link them with other significant bits of information. When I finished, I sat for a few minutes letting the parts and pieces sort themselves out in my mind.

Then I went through my original list of potential suspects and began winnowing it down. First to go was Walt Sanders, Matthew's neighbor at the cabin. He just wasn't smart enough or together enough to carry off a crime like poisoning that required a little finesse. If Walt were to kill someone, he'd do it by using his shotgun, probably after a few too many shots of Jim Beam.

Ellen was easy to cross off the list. She was definitely smart enough to do it and get away with it. But she was the one who had insisted on the second toxicology report that proved Matthew was murdered. If not for that, his death would have been declared death from undetermined causes.

I felt pretty safe eliminating Rory. Her night of golden memories with

Cole let her off the hook for the night of the murder. Any chance that she could plan a murder by poison and plant the aconite at the cabin ahead of time—during a period when she was sinking back into addiction—was too slim for serious consideration.

Kathy Boyle wasn't a strong candidate either, even without the phone call she'd made to tell me she'd found something. She lived very close to Matthew's cabin, so access would have been easy. But I couldn't see Kathy joining the mushroom-hating Matthew for a slice of pizza the night he died. Plus the only time she and her son weren't together was when he was shooting video with his new drone. Though I did make a note to check the story with Patrick to make sure his recollection matched hers.

I couldn't take Olivia off the list until I knew for sure where she had gone and what she had done after Maya had dropped her off at home that night. But I felt strongly that her obvious stress and anxiety wasn't because she had killed Matthew, but because she was afraid that she knew who had.

Then there was Hannah. It seemed quite likely to me that she had nixed all of her lawyer's efforts to help her because she was afraid that Olivia might be the killer. God, I hoped Patrick would get my voicemail and let me look at Kathy's laptop. And if he did, please don't let Kathy's new evidence be a photo of Hannah or Olivia walking into Matthew's cabin with a cup of aconite tea.

That brought me to Joel. Maya had let slip that she believed Olivia thought her dad had killed Matthew. He'd told the police that he had no idea about the affair until they told him about the texts found on Matthew's burner phone. That could easily be a lie. If Joel knew and wanted revenge, how would he do it? Just then my intercom erupted with a loud, insistent bid for attention. I literally jumped off my stool.

53

"*Chica*, why is the door to your front stairs locked? I tried to come up that way because look what I brought you from Woke," he said, holding out a large and steaming *chai*.

"Hey, thank you, Miguel. I've been up since five. I can really use that. Sit down," I said. "The door is locked because I promised Coop I'd be more careful."

"That is always a good idea, but why are you changing your ways now?" he asked, dropping down on the stool next to me.

I realized then that I hadn't kept him in the loop about Sharla. I filled him in.

"A stalker? Oh, that is not good. You have to take this seriously," he said when I finished.

"I am. I'm doing what Jane Williams said I should do. Beyond that, I just have to live my life. Don't look so worried. It's possible that Sharla will lose interest if I don't engage."

"And if she doesn't?"

"If she doesn't then I'm sure Jane will catch her. Now, why are you here so early, besides bringing me a chai?"

"I have the morning off, and you did not call me back yesterday. So I'm here to see where you are—on the Hannah investigation, I mean."

"I'm sorry, I forgot. A lot of things have happened since the last time I saw you. For one thing, Kathy Boyle is dead. Do you want some cereal?"

"No! I want to hear what happened. And I want to help you."

"Perfect, I can definitely use your help."

I brought him up to speed on everything to date.

"Okay, so you're all caught up. Now, I'll run down my thinking on my current list of suspects and then you can react to it."

I did, without indicating who I had eliminated and who I favored.

"Okay, now that you know what I know, who do you favor as the top suspect?"

"Joel," he said without hesitation.

"Ah. Two great minds with but a single thought. Why is Joel your favorite?"

"I don't believe his story he told the police. That he didn't know about the affair. I think he is lying."

"I do, too, and not just about that. He says he didn't get home until 11:00 p.m. on the murder night. But Maya and Olivia saw him in town at 6:30. So where was he for over four hours?"

"I can tell you have an idea. What is it?"

"I think he found out about the affair, and he was enraged at both of them, Hannah and Matthew. Hannah was his wife and Matthew was his friend, and they betrayed him. He wanted, no, he needed, to make them both pay. So he came up with a plan that would get revenge on them both. He would kill Matthew using aconite, and that would point the finger at Hannah. Matthew would be dead, and Hannah would have a kind of living death, locked away forever from the daughter she loved."

"That is very clever. Very evil, but very clever. But how did he make it work?"

"He used his friendship with Matthew for Matthew's undoing. It would have been easy for Joel to call Matthew and suggest they get together on that Friday night at the cabin, have a pizza, just hang out, talk about fishing, guy stuff, whatever. That would have been super awkward for Matthew, but if Joel was insistent it would be hard to refuse."

I could see the light of understanding in Miguel's eyes. He knew where I was going.

"So Joel picked up the pizza, half mushroom for him, the other just pepperoni for Matthew. Wait— do we know if Joel likes mushrooms?" he asked.

"We do not, but that won't be hard to find out. My guess is yes. I mean, not that many people hate mushrooms, right? But the murder couldn't have been simpler. Joel arrives. The pizza is a little cold. Joel says let's put it in the oven. And he makes up some excuse for not having a beer—like maybe he says he's on antibiotics and he can't drink. Then he says he's got a new tea Hannah created that's supposed to be better than a beer to relax you. Matthew puts the pizza in the oven to reheat. Joel makes the aconite-laced tea for Matthew, and a poison free one for himself. Then he waits for the sweet revenge of watching it take hold. As Matthew gets very ill, he asks Joel to drive him to the ER. Joel says no and possibly proceeds to tell him that he is going to die, and why."

Miguel shuddered. "*Chica,* that is so cold!"

"It is. It's also a very good plan. The only flaw in Joel's blueprint for murder was something he couldn't help. The random chance that he'd be seen by Olivia and Maya on his way to the meeting with Matthew. I think that when Olivia saw her father's SUV, she went where she feared he was going—to Matthew's cabin."

"But she couldn't see the murder, she wasn't inside."

"Right, but she could have seen her father's car there, and that would be enough to worry her. Not that her dad was murdering Matthew, but that they were having a confrontation that was going to lead to what she dreaded, her mother and father splitting up. But then the next morning she learned that Matthew had died of an apparent heart attack. That would have relieved her because the threat to her family was gone," I said.

"Until a few weeks later when the second tox screening showed that Matthew had been murdered!"

"Yes. She couldn't *know* that her father had poisoned Matthew, but she's too bright not to realize that was the most likely scenario. But then the police came, and they arrested her mother! That poor kid had the ultimate dilemma. If she told the police about Joel's car being there, then he'd be arrested. If she didn't tell, then her mother would be tried for murder. She loved them both. There wasn't a clear-cut answer for her, and she was tortured with trying to know what to do."

"Oh, poor Olivia. So much worry, so much sadness."

"Yes. I think she was paralyzed by the version of Sophie's choice she was facing. She loves her mother, and she loves her father. In the end she said nothing, and it's eating away at her."

"So if it is Joel, how do we prove it?"

"That's the question I don't have an answer to . . . Maybe if I ask nicely, he'll confess?"

"No matter how you ask, I don't think that will happen."

"Unless . . ."

"Unless what?"

"Unless Joel recognizes how much his daughter is suffering. I believe he loves her, but he's so consumed with his own rage and pain that he can't see how what he did is affecting Olivia."

"So what do we do?" Miguel asked, his voice conveying his discouragement.

My phone rang then, and we got the answer.

"Leah, this is Olivia Vining. I need to talk to you."

Her voice was high and tight, and she rushed through her words, maybe to get them out before she lost her courage. I put her on speaker so Miguel could hear.

"Of course, Olivia. Tell me what's on your mind."

"No. It's too much for on the phone. Can you come to Galen this morning? Like right now? Not to my house, our housekeeper Mrs. Nichols is there, and my dad is in town today. I pretended to be Mrs. Nichols and called myself in sick from school this morning. I'm at Maya's. Her parents are both at work. Could you come here? It's really important."

"Yes, sure. Do you mind if I bring someone with me—"

"You mean like the police? No! I don't want to talk to them. I want to talk to you."

"No, not the police. A friend of mine who's helping me investigate your mother's case. He's a reporter and—"

"No! Not a reporter. I don't want this in the paper. I can't talk to you if—"

"Hey, hey, it's okay. This is not going in the paper. Miguel isn't doing this for a story. He's helping me because I'm trying to help your mother. I promise you."

"Miguel? Like the *Ask Miguel* podcast Miguel? OMG, he's fire!"

For the first time since I'd met her she sounded like a normal kid.

"That's the one," I said.

"Well . . . ," she said, still hesitant.

Miguel spoke up then.

"Olivia, this is Miguel. I think you are very brave to reach out to Leah. She has promised you, and I do too, that we will not use anything you want to share for a story or for a podcast, unless you want us to. I want to help. If you give me the honor of your trust, I will not let you down."

I'd rarely heard Miguel speak quite so seriously. We both waited for Olivia's response. The silence stretched on for what seemed like minutes but probably was just seconds. Finally she answered.

"Okay. You can both come. But you better come fast because I'm not sure I can do this."

We were already up and moving toward the door as she gave me Maya's address.

54

"Come in, please. Olivia's in the living room. It's this way," Maya said when she opened the door. As we followed her down a hallway she turned her head to ask, "Would you like coffee, or water or something? Oh, I can take your jackets and hang them up."

It was odd to have little pink-haired Maya in her ripped skinny jeans, vintage t-shirt, and black combat boots assume the manner of a hostess welcoming us to an afternoon bridge game.

"Nothing for me, thank you," I said, and Miguel responded the same way.

Olivia was perched on the edge of a wing back chair, biting her lip. Her upper body rocked lightly back and forth as though to soothe herself.

"Hello, Olivia. This is Miguel Santos. Miguel, this is Olivia Vining and her friend Maya Gordon."

"I'm very happy to meet you both," Miguel said with a warm smile. He seemed to surprise both girls when he shook each of their hands.

"I love your podcast. My mom does, too," Maya said.

"Yeah, I love it, too," Olivia said.

"Thank you. I love doing it."

An uncomfortable silence fell as we seated ourselves on the sofa across from Olivia. Maya dropped down on an ottoman next to her.

"I don't know how to do this," Olivia said.

"Just start wherever you need to, and we'll follow along. Whenever you're ready," I said.

She looked at Maya, who reached out and patted her arm. That seemed to be what Olivia needed to start talking. And when she did a virtual tidal wave of words poured out.

"Okay. Well, first I'm sorry for lying to you when you asked if I was ever at Mr. Ferguson's cabin. I was. Lots of times. You were right before. I knew about my mom and Mr. Ferguson."

She stopped then and Miguel prompted her.

"How did you know?"

"I used to work at Moonrise in the afternoons after school. One day I wasn't scheduled, but we got out early because the power went out. I stopped at the store before I went home to see if Mom needed me. I heard voices and I thought she was talking to a delivery person. I went to her office and that's when I saw them. Mom and Mr. Ferguson. They were kissing. I shouted, 'Mom! What are you doing?'

"They both jumped, and I ran out the back of the store. Mom came after me. She told me to get in the car. She could explain. On the way to our house she tried to make me think that it wasn't anything. That she and Mr. Ferguson were just friends. But I wouldn't listen. I told her I knew what I saw, and to stop lying to me."

Again Olivia paused, clearly struggling with her story. Then she went on.

"I said if she ever wanted me to speak to her again, she had to tell me the truth. So she said that she and Mr. Ferguson had a 'relationship,' but it was over. That what I'd seen was her and Mr. Ferguson saying goodbye. She begged me not to tell Dad about it. She said it would hurt him so much."

"Did you believe her?"

"I wanted to. But I was so angry at her for what she'd done. I told her that if I found that she was lying to me, that I'd tell Dad everything. She said that she wasn't. That she chose me and Dad, not him. I tried to believe her, but it was hard. That's why I started going out to the cabin. When she'd say she was going shopping in Madison, or she was going to an herb class in Milwaukee or anything that could be a made-up story, I went out to check and be sure she wasn't there."

"And did you ever see her there?"

"No. I didn't like spying on her but I just—I had to know."

"Did you ever tell your dad about your mother and Matthew?"

"No. I was scared that if Dad knew about it, he'd divorce her. I was really angry at her, but I wanted her to stay with us. I was always afraid that she wouldn't. And I was always afraid Dad would find out about the affair."

"That's a lot of worry to carry, *chiquita*."

She looked at Miguel teary-eyed, but didn't respond.

"How long did you keep riding your bike out to Matthew's cabin?" I asked.

"I don't know, a few weeks maybe? And then I got caught by the old man that lives next door. I lied to you about that, too. He said he was going to come after me with his shotgun if he saw me again, and he'd call the sheriff, too. That kind of scared me. If he called the police on me then they'd call my parents, and everything would come out. I didn't want that. I thought if Dad didn't know about the affair, and Mom was keeping her promise, maybe things would be okay. So I made myself stop going to check."

"I can see why you didn't tell me the truth before, Olivia. But I think you asked me to come today because you're ready to tell me something about the night Matthew Ferguson was killed. Is that right?"

She nodded.

"Maya came to my house last night. She said she told you about us seeing my dad that night. She said if I didn't stop lying, then she couldn't be my friend anymore. I couldn't stand that. Maya's the only one who still hangs with me. Plus, I'm just so tired of feeling worried all the time. Going out to the cabin wasn't the only thing I lied about—to her and to you. I want to tell the truth now."

She paused and Maya put her hand on Olivia's arm again and that seemed to give Olivia the boost she needed to go on with a story she didn't want to tell.

"The night Mr. Ferguson got killed started out as the most fun I'd let myself have in a long time. Maya had just got her regular license so she could drive us around. We were singing and laughing on our way to the game. Then she saw Dad's SUV. I saw it too, but I told her she was wrong, that it wasn't him. But I knew it was. I wasn't lying when I said that I felt sick, and I had to go home."

"Why was that so upsetting to you?' I asked.

"Because Dad told us that he had a meeting in Milwaukee, and he wasn't going to come home until Saturday morning. When I saw his car, it wasn't driving toward our house. It was heading out on the road you take to get to Mr. Ferguson's cabin. I had this horrible feeling that Dad knew about Mom and Mr. Ferguson, and he was going out there to catch them. I knew I had to get out there before anything bad happened."

"What did you think might happen?" Miguel asked.

"Like my dad would be so mad he'd tell Mom he wanted a divorce, or Mom would tell him, and everything would be over."

"But what did you think you could do if that happened?"

"I wasn't thinking anything. I just knew I had to be there. I didn't have a plan. I just got my bike, and I rode out there. I didn't go to the county park and down the trail. I rode right down Burdock Road because it's shorter and there wasn't any point in trying to hide. I wanted to get there fast."

"And you saw your dad's car there?" I asked.

Miguel and I exchanged glances. This fit our theory of the crime. Joel wasn't on the road from Milwaukee while Matthew was getting killed. He was right here in Galen. We waited for Olivia to confirm it.

"No, it wasn't."

"It wasn't?" I asked unable to keep the surprise out of my voice.

"No, and I felt so relieved. When I saw that he wasn't at the cabin, I realized I was just being crazy. Dad was driving in the direction of the cabin when we saw him, but that was also the way to the good luck store."

"What is a good luck store?" Miguel asked.

"That's what Dad calls the Mini Mart. He won $5000 on a lottery ticket there one Friday. He buys one every Friday when he's in town, he says to see if lightning will strike twice. I turned around and headed home. I knew he'd be there before I was, but I thought I'd just put my bike behind the garage, come around the house and go in through the front door. Then I'd say I came home early because I didn't feel good.

But he wasn't there. And it got later and later, and he still didn't come home."

She stopped then and said, "Maya do you have any Tylenol? I've got a really bad headache."

Maya jumped up. "There's some in the kitchen. Come on I'll get it for you," she said, and the two of them left the room.

"So what do you think? Where was Joel when Olivia was at the cabin?" Miguel asked.

"Maybe he was picking up the pizza? So he arrived after Olivia had left. And he stayed there until Matthew was dead. That's why he got home so late. Joel needed not only to kill Matthew, he needed to watch him suffer. I think Olivia's come to that conclusion too. But it might take a gentle push to get her to say out loud what she's been tamping down for so long."

When the girls came back into the room I addressed Olivia.

"When your dad got home at 11:00, did you ask where he'd been? Did you tell him you saw him in town at 6:30?"

"No. When he didn't come home until hours later, I knew he couldn't have been at the convenience store. The only other thing I could think of was that maybe he knew Mom and Mr. Ferguson were meeting somewhere else, not at the cabin, and that's where he'd gone. But Mom came in right after Dad. I was too mixed up to ask anybody anything. So we all just went to bed. And by the time I got up the next day, Mr. Ferguson was dead from a heart attack, they said. I thought everything would get better. But it didn't. It all got worse. Mr. Ferguson was murdered, Mom got arrested, and our family fell apart just like I was afraid it would."

"Olivia, you called me because you wanted to tell me something important. Something you didn't want to hide anymore. Tell us, where do you think your father was?"

In a very small voice filled with heartache she said, "I think he was killing Mr. Ferguson."

Suddenly there was a loud pounding on the front door. Maya got up to answer it but before she could, Joel Vining burst into the room.

55

"What the hell is going on here?" Joel Ferguson's face was red, and his voice was furious as he loomed over me. I stood up to be on equal footing with him.

"What's going on here is that Olivia has finally told us the truth about the night Matthew Ferguson died," I said.

"I know what you did, Dad. I'm so sorry but I can't, I just can't keep it secret anymore." Her face crumpled and she dropped her head into her hands and began to sob.

"What? What are you talking about? What lies has this woman told you?"

He rushed over to Olivia and wrapped his arms around her. She responded like the hurt and weary child she was and leaned into him. As he stroked her hair the anger drained from his body, and he repeated over and over the timeless nonsense words of comfort that all parents use.

"There, there, sweetheart. It's going to be all right. Hush, now."

His daughter cried with abandon, free at last to give in to her feelings.

Maya, Miguel, and I looked on in silence as Olivia's sobs slowly diminished.

Joel turned to me with a look of pure loathing on his face. If I was a sensitive soul, I might have felt quite shattered. Fortunately, I'm not.

"This is all on you," he said. "What kind of person are you to put ideas like this in my daughter's head? You destroyed her belief in me to the degree that she thinks that her own father is a killer. You disgust me."

"You're wrong, Joel. I didn't—"

Olivia interrupted, pulling all the way away from her father and sitting up straight.

"No, Dad. It's not like that. Leah didn't make me think that. I already knew."

"Livy, no, whatever you think you know, you don't. I didn't kill Matthew."

"Dad, stop. When I found out about Mom and Mr. Ferguson, I felt like I hated her, too. What she did was really, really bad. But I don't hate her. I love her still. She saved us, Dad. She made us a family again. And I love you, too. But you killed Mr. Ferguson, and you let her take the blame. That's what happened isn't it?"

I've heard the expression shell-shocked many times. But I never really knew what it meant until I saw the mix of panic, horror, and stunned disbelief on Joel's face as his daughter's words hung in the air.

"No, no, honey. That's not true. That's not what happened at all. I'm so sorry that you believe that. I knew you were struggling. I thought it was all about your mother. I was struggling too. I still am. I thought the best thing was for us to not talk about it, just move forward, the two of us. I'm so sorry that I handled everything so badly. But please, sweetheart, those ideas she put in your head—" He paused to glare at me. "Whatever she told you it's not true. Just listen and I'll tell you everything."

Olivia was done crying. She gave him a stare so cold it sent shivers down *my* spine. I could only imagine how it made Joel feel.

"Tell me, then. Tell me everything about you and Mom and Mr. Ferguson and what you did."

Joel began to tell his story. I sat back down to listen.

"A couple of months before Matthew died. I started to feel that Hannah was distracted. Distant, even. When I asked her about it she said she was just really busy at work. But then I noticed that when I called or texted her, sometimes she didn't answer for hours—or at all. She always had an excuse. She'd forgotten her phone, or the battery was dead, or she forgot to take it off airplane mode. It bothered me, but I didn't want to seem over possessive or jealous. Hannah is a very independent person. And I always knew that I loved her more than she loved me. I used to kid her that she fell in love with Olivia, not me. But it was true.

"One morning when she was in the shower and her phone was on the dresser, it pinged with a text. I couldn't help seeing it. I was standing right there. I read the preview that popped up on her screen. It just said '7 p.m.' But there was a heart after it. I asked her who it was from. She said it was from her friend Cynthia. They were meeting up for drinks, and that Cynthia always put a heart at the end of her texts. I knew she was lying, but I didn't confront her. The next day I stopped by Moonrise."

He quit talking to gauge how Olivia was taking this. Her face remained stony.

"What happened?" Miguel prompted.

"Matthew and Hannah were both there, back by the register. They were so deep in conversation they didn't even hear me come in. The way they were standing, just a little too close, the way she touched his arm and looked up at him. I knew he was the one. I was so hurt, and I felt so betrayed. I walked away. They didn't even know that I'd been there. The next day I left for a business trip. The time I was away was two weeks of torture, imagining the two of them together, and then telling myself I was wrong. That my jealousy made me imagine that they were having an affair. Then the next minute I was sure that I was right."

He paused and shook his head.

"When I got home, I stayed in town for a week and I watched every move Hannah made, trying to find confirmation that my worst fear was true. I came close to confronting her multiple times, but I backed away. I was afraid if I brought things in the open, Hannah would leave. Or that if I was wrong, she'd leave because I had accused her of something she hadn't done. When I couldn't take it anymore, I set a trap for her."

"A trap? What kind of trap?" Olivia asked.

Joel looked away from her, as though he was too embarrassed to face her as he answered.

"I had a conference in Milwaukee the next week. It ended on Friday, but I said I was going to stay overnight and drive home early Saturday to avoid traffic. I knew that Olivia was spending the night at Maya's, and Hannah had said that with neither of us home, she planned to catch up on paperwork at the store. But I didn't stay. I left Milwaukee right after the conference and drove to Galen. I got here around 6:30 and drove to Matthew's cabin."

So far, he was basically lining up with the scenario I'd suggested to Miguel.

"I didn't want the headlights or the sound of my car to alert them that I was there. So instead of going down the road and parking by the footbridge, I parked my car at the county park and walked down the bike trail that runs from there past Matthew's cabin.

That explained why Olivia hadn't seen his car there and had ridden her bike happily back to town.

"There was a light on in the cabin. The curtains weren't completely shut. I could see Matthew. He was talking to someone. I couldn't see who, the opening in the curtain wasn't wide enough. But then a hand—a woman's hand—reached out and touched his arm. I couldn't see more than that, but it was enough. I knew Hannah was there."

Miguel looked at me, his eyes wide. I gave a slight nod. I was stunned, too, but I didn't want to stop Joel's story.

"I don't even remember getting back to my car. I was gutted. I got in and just started driving. I wound up outside the Tenney Road Tavern, way out near the county line. I went in and sat at the bar. I was consumed with hate and anger and fear. I hated Matthew. I was angry with Hannah, but I still loved her. And pathetic as it sounds, I didn't want her to leave me. Finally, I decided to go home. It was about 10:30 when I left."

"What happened when you got home?" Miguel asked.

"The lights were on. Olivia was there. She told me she didn't feel well so Maya had brought her home. A few minutes later, Hannah walked in. She was surprised to see us. I told them both that I'd decided to drive home because I wanted to sleep in my own bed. But that I took the wrong road after a construction detour and that's why I'd just gotten home. Olivia didn't say much but I thought that was because she didn't feel well. Hannah checked to make sure Olivia didn't have a fever. Then we all went to bed.

"The next day I heard that Matthew had a heart attack and had been found dead at his cabin. I was glad. With him gone, I thought that if I was patient, if I waited it out, Hannah would forget about him. That she'd stay with me. I didn't know until the police showed up at our door a few weeks later that Matthew had been poisoned. I was shocked. I knew that Hannah had been there the night he died. And then they told us about the texts they'd found on Matthew's phone. And that Matthew had confessed to Ellen and ended the affair a month ago."

"But you never told the police what you saw. You stuck with the story that you'd told Hannah and Olivia. Why didn't you tell them about seeing Hannah at the cabin?" I asked.

"Because I knew that would put me under suspicion. I couldn't prove what I saw. I was there, just an hour or two before Matthew died. I knew how that could look, what they would think. That I was a jealous husband who killed his wife's lover and tried to put the blame on her."

Since that was exactly the conclusion I'd come to, I couldn't say he was wrong.

"But Dad, you said you were at the Tenny Road Tavern. Couldn't the bartender or someone there be your witness?" Olivia asked.

"Yes, but honey that wouldn't prove anything. I could have left the poison in Matthew's tea anytime, and he could've drunk it when I wasn't there. Me being at the tavern didn't matter. Then when the detective told Hannah that Matthew had confessed the affair to his wife, and she had forgiven him, I knew why Hannah had killed him. She was the jealous one and she'd killed Matthew because he didn't want her."

56

It was a dreary drive home with rain falling and both our moods matching the gray skies above. We were silent for most of the way, but Miguel finally spoke as we neared Himmel.

"I think Joel was telling the truth," he said.

"Yeah. Me, too. But we should still confirm his story about being at the Tenny Road Tavern that night."

"Yes, I can do that. I will stop there tonight. But now do you think that Hannah is the killer after all?"

"I don't want to think that. I dread telling Marguerite. And I feel so bad for Olivia. But realistically, it looks that way. Ellen, Rory, Walt Sanders, Olivia, Kathy—they're all out of the picture. And now Joel turns out to have an explanation that rings true. And it involves seeing a woman at the cabin. Who else could it be but Hannah? The only faint hope I have that she isn't guilty lies with Patrick Boyle.

"You mean because you hope he has found the thing that Kathy wanted to show you on her laptop? But if there is anything on it, it could be something that proves that Hannah was there."

"Yeah. I know. I said it was a faint hope."

"So you do not want to say case closed until the last clue is found?"

"That's about it. When I talk to Marguerite I want to be able to tell her that I followed every possible lead."

When we got back to Himmel, Miguel went to the newsroom, and I went upstairs to regroup. It felt like that was all I'd been doing since I started investigating Hannah's case. I had just settled on the window seat with Sam to think when there was a knock on my front landing door.

"What fresh hell is this, Sam?" I asked as I grumbled my way to see who it was. I half-expected it to be Cole, checking on the invitation he'd extorted from me to Charlotte's soiree. It wasn't, though my visitor was equally unwelcome.

"Spencer?"

"You look surprised, Leah. We had an appointment today. Did you forget?"

"Actually, I did."

"I can come back tomorrow, if that's better for you."

I wavered internally for a second. I really wasn't in the mood for talking right then, especially not to Spencer. But I decided to just get it over with.

"No, that's all right, come in. I usually like people to come to the door in the back. This one is kind of for my personal use," I said.

"I'm sorry. I went to the front desk and the receptionist told me just to go up the front stairs."

"I'm sure she did. Never mind. Take a seat," I said, as I plunked down on the rocking chair across from the sofa. I didn't offer him any beverage. I didn't want him to stay that long, nor did I feel like being a good hostess to Spencer.

"I've never been here. It's a beautiful place. And I really like the bird's eye view from your window seat."

For some reason he was making an attempt to be pleasant, but I was in too bad a mood to care.

"Thanks. So what did you want to say to me?"

"Well, I was going to lead up to this because it's going to be a shock to you, I'm sure. But I can see you're not in the mood for a long story, so I'll skip the introduction and get right to the point."

"Good room read, Spence. What is it?"

I knew I was making it hard for him to say whatever nonsense he wanted to throw at me, but I didn't care.

"I'm not interested in the director position at the *Times,* despite what my mother may have said."

"Good thing, because the deadline has passed. But you wouldn't have gotten it anyway. I would do anything to prevent you from sabotaging the last hope we have of retaining community journalism in Grantland County."

"I was never interested in the job. That was my mother's idea. It was her last desperate attempt to keep me from the work I've chosen," he said with no trace of animosity or sarcasm in his voice. I can't say the same about mine when I responded.

"Well, I can't fault her for not being over the moon that her only son plans on running a drug cartel. I assume given your history that's where your career aspirations lie."

"Leah, please. Hear me out. I know after what I did that I deserve any sarcastic, cutting, mean-spirited remarks you'd like to make. But I'm asking for your indulgence. I'm here to apologize for the way I behaved after you saved my life. And if I'm honest, and I'm trying to be, that's not the only time I did something to you that I should apologize for. I don't think we have time for all those mea culpas," he said and smiled.

I was taken aback, both by what he said and the way he said it. He sounded like he meant it. And a sincere Spencer was not a version that I'd encountered before.

"I can see that you're surprised, Leah. But I really mean it. I know you don't believe me now, but over time, I hope you'll see that it's true."

"Surprised doesn't begin to cover it, Spencer."

"Well, if you think that's surprising, you'll be glad you're sitting down when I tell you what else I came to say. I wanted you to be one of the first people to know. I'm entering the seminary. I'm going to become a Catholic priest."

For once I couldn't think of a single thing to say.

"Yes, Charlotte. It's for real. I checked with Father Lindstrom. Spencer is going to be a priest! Apparently he's been in spiritual counseling—it's going to take a while for me to get used to using that phrase in conjunction with Spencer—with Father Lindstrom for the last six months. And that's where he's landed—in a seminary."

I'd called her with the astonishing news as soon as I verified it.

"Leah, what a great thing this is! Now you can stop worrying about what Marilyn, in conjunction with Spencer, could do to our nonprofit newspaper baby," she said.

"Maybe. I'm relieved for now, but I remain suspicious that Spencer's turnaround isn't for real. He could just be taking a break from evil for a while. And then he could come back even worse and do more damage because we've been lulled into complacency."

"Leah, you are the only person I know who can always see the dark cloud in the silver lining. What's making you so grumpy?"

"I'm sorry. Things aren't going well with my investigation into Hannah Vining's case. I've got one lead left out there, and if it doesn't pan out, and there's not a big chance that it will, I'm going to have some very bad news to deliver to Hannah's sister."

"Hey, good things come in threes, right? So now Spencer's taken care of, next up you'll prove that Hannah Vining didn't kill her lover, and the third thing will be that we find the perfect director of the nonprofit."

"Actually, I believe the saying is troubles, not good things, come in threes. I don't have that sunny outlook, but I appreciate yours. I hope you're right."

57

I couldn't settle down after Spencer's visit. I walked over to the sheriff's office to tell Coop the astonishing news about Spencer's new career path and to get his take on the latest developments with Hannah Vining. When I walked into the reception area, Jennifer wasn't at her desk and Coop's office was dark. I felt a sharp stab of disappointment. I knew he was busy and always had a lot on his plate. But it seemed like whenever I wanted to talk with him lately, he wasn't around.

I had turned to leave when I saw Ross coming down the hall.
"Hey, Nash. You lookin' for Jennifer or Coop?"
"Either would work. Do you know where they are?"
"Jennifer's off today, she's got an exam. Coop went to give a talk over to Omico High School. Career day or somethin'. He's not back yet."
"Do you know when he will be?"
"Nope."
"That figures. Absolutely nothing today has turned out the way I wanted it to. I should go home, climb back into bed and wait for tomorrow to come. It has to be better than today."
"Instead of that, c'mon back to the break room. I'll buy you a cup of coffee and you can tell me all about it."
I hadn't expected Ross to offer sympathy, but I was down enough to take

it and ask no questions. Half an hour later I had finished telling him the ups and downs of my Hannah investigation and also had managed to swallow the really bad cup of coffee he'd made for me.

"So you're outta suspects, are ya?"

"Pretty much."

"Nash, what do I always tell you?"

"Stay out of my investigation?"

"Well, yeah, that. But after you ignore me and get involved anyway, and then you get stuck, what do I tell you?"

"Umm, 'I told you, Nash, leave it to the professionals'?"

He shook his head. But I know he enjoys our back and forth. Although it started off with genuine hostility when we first met, over time it's evolved into kind of a bit that we do.

"Not that. That's a given. Look, work your case. You believe Hannah. If you're right and she didn't do it, you're missin' somethin'. Go back to your notes, go back to your suspect list, and try again. That's what you gotta do. Find what you overlooked, check for where you maybe took a wrong turn, or jumped when you shouldna—that's kinda your specialty. And if you don't find anything, then whether you like it or not, ya gotta accept that the answer you don't like is still the right one."

I was silent for a moment, then I said, "It pains me to say this, Ross. But you're right. Once more unto the breach. I have to give it one final try."

"Henry the V, ain't that?"

"It is, Ross. You never cease to amaze me."

It's true. Every now and then Ross comes up with something totally unexpected. Like knowing a line from Shakespeare.

"What? You think I don't know who Shakespeare was?"

"No, but I didn't think you'd know him well enough to recognize a quote."

"I got hidden depths, Nash. I told ya before. When you gonna get that?"

That made me laugh and I realized that I felt much better than I had when I came. I felt a surprisingly strong wave of affection for this stubborn, impatient, gruff, quick-tempered man. And that made me say something I probably shouldn't have.

"You know what, Ross? You're a pretty good guy. How are you and Jennifer doing?"

"Whaddya mean how are we doin'?"

"I mean you seem to be seeing quite a lot of each other. I was just wondering if, you know, it was getting serious. It's a normal question for a friend to ask."

"No. It's a normal question for *you* to ask, you mean. We're doin' fine. Tonight we're gonna make the boys Halloween costumes. Nathan's gonna be a velociraptor and Ethan's goin' as a T-Rex. Hey, I was gonna ask you. Allie's birthday is coming up. You heard her say anything she'd like? I wanta get her somethin' special. She's gonna be sixteen ya know. I can't hardly believe it."

I knew he was deflecting but I answered anyway.

"Allie hasn't mentioned anything, but I'll see what I can find out. If you don't want to talk about you and Jennifer, just tell me."

"I don't wanna talk about me and Jennifer."

"Okay, I'm just—"

"Listen, I know what you're thinkin'. That I'm outta my league. That Jennifer is twelve years younger than me. That she needs someone to lean on now and I'm just the guy who's around—"

"No, that's not true. I didn't mean—"

"Come on. I know that's what ya think. Hell, I think it too. But I'll say this, and I don't wanna talk about it again. And don't be runnin' and tellin' Jennifer what I'm sayin, okay?"

"Yes, okay."

"I know Jennifer's not in love with me. I know she maybe never will be. But I'm happy right now, Nash. Real happy. Maybe it won't last and then I'll be real sad. But I been sad before. I'm not gonna ruin the happy I feel now thinkin' about how it's gonna end. Cause maybe it won't. I figure I got my own sort of—what do they call it—charisma? Yeah, that's the word. My kind of a charisma, it takes a while to grow on people, right? But look at me and you now from where we started. So, we'll see."

"You're right again, Ross. Twice in one day. You do grow on people, and I hope Jennifer is one of them," I said, reaching out and covering his hand with mine.

He let it rest there a moment before he stood saying, "Hey, I got costumes to make. You got an investigation to sort out. Let's get at it."

"Ross, how is it that you can irritate me so much sometimes, but you're still one of my favorite friends?"

He shrugged.

"Charisma. You can't fight it."

When I got home, I followed the advice Ross had given me and once again sat down with all my notes and began reading through them. I hadn't gotten far when the door opened, and Coop walked in.

"Hey, you. I was just at your office a little while ago. Ross had to fill in for you in my hour of need. He said you were in Omico doing a talk at the high school. How'd that go? And how come you didn't mention it?"

"Talking police careers to a bunch of high school kids? That was a tough crowd. But it went okay. A couple of kids came up and asked me more questions after. I didn't realize I hadn't told you about it. But it seems like we haven't seen much of each other lately."

"Agreed, but who's the one whose every waking moment is spent building a palace? I assume that's what you're building anyway, because it takes up so much of your time."

I said it in a teasing way, but at the same time I did feel a little left behind.

"I know. I'm sorry. It's just that I need to get some things done before winter weather sets in. You're always welcome to come out and help. We could spend a lot of time together then."

"When you get to the painting part, I'll come. I like to paint. Inside. But outside, on ladders, freezing in the cold, hammering my thumb instead of a nail—sorry, not for me. Besides, I've got a few things on my own plate."

"I know you do," he said, sitting next to me. "Is that what all this is?" He gestured to the papers scattered across the counter.

"Yeah. They represent that hour of need I mentioned."

"I'm here, I'm listening, so tell me."

We moved to the sofa, I turned on the fireplace and I began talking.

Almost an hour later I had walked him through the crashing and burning of my Joel theory, Spencer's stunning news, and my intrusion into Ross's romantic life.

"Well, you've had a very busy day," he said. "Did you want my opinion on anything, or did you just need me to vent to?"

"Please, opine away. I could use your perspective on all three."

"I'll start in reverse. Charlie's romance? I already told you, don't go there. Charlie's a private guy. He told you a lot more than he's told me. But I wouldn't poke around there anymore. Respect his privacy. On Spencer? I don't know if he's for real or playing a game. But Father Lindstrom is no fool. He wouldn't support Spencer entering the seminary if he thought Spencer was scamming. So, all I have is wait and see for you there."

"Okay, I agree on both counts. But that's minor stuff. What about Hannah's case? Am I just being stubborn to keep pursuing it? Should I throw in the towel?"

"That's your call, you have to make it. But I think Charlie was right. Go back to your notes again. Make a list, connect the dots. You're good at seeing separate pieces and finding the pattern. You'd make a good police detective, except that you'd never follow department rules, you don't have much respect for authority, and you leap too quickly sometimes. But still, you usually find the answers."

"Wow. I don't know whether to thank you for saying I'm a great detective or punch you in the arm for saying I don't investigate, I just leap into space and hope for a soft landing."

"I said good detective, not great detective," Coop said with a grin. "Listen, it's never easy to reinvestigate a closed case. Time passes, memories fade, some doors are closed. But you're good at taking the road less traveled, and that's what you need to do. Take the turn that someone else missed. You'll find your way out of the maze."

"You get an A in advising," I said.

"Why? Because I told you what you were going to do anyway?"

"Yes. You know I always like affirmation. And you get an A+ in Leah-ing, because you know me so well."

"Put that on a card and I'll hang it on my fridge. Now, tell me, any more communication from your stalker?"

"Nothing since yesterday. I forwarded Sharla's last text to Jane, but I didn't get anything today. So, maybe she will go away after all."

"Let's hope so. But I'd feel better if you and Sam came to stay with me until this gets sorted. And before you say it, this is not a stealth attempt to trick you into moving in with me."

"I wasn't going to say that. Thanks for the chivalry, I appreciate it. But I feel pretty safe. I haven't changed the code on the back door lock, but I will tomorrow. I promise. The front door is locked—I did that after Cole dropped in—and so is the side door from my side. You could go right now and check."

"I trust you, but just stay on top of it. Locks only work if you use them. And it wouldn't hurt to remind Courtnee that the proper protocol is not to send people directly to your apartment. It's to call and let you know someone wants to see you."

"And it probably wouldn't help, either. You know Courtnee. But yes, I'll talk to her."

"Okay, good enough. Now I have a suggestion for the rest of the evening."

"What? You're not going back out to your property?"

"I am not. It's five thirty. Put your papers away for the evening and put Hannah and everything to do with her case out of your mind. We'll go across the street, get some soup and a sandwich for dinner, and then come back here and watch a couple of movies. You get one pick, and I get one. Then we'll get a good night's sleep, and you can start fresh tomorrow."

"That sounds perfect. As long as neither of the movies has anything to do with murder."

58

Coop had been right. When I got up in the morning, I felt ready to tackle my notes one last time.

"You're up and at 'em early," he said when he came into the kitchen to grab a cup of coffee to go.

"Yes. I'm pretending that someone else gave me these notes, that I don't have any feelings about the people I interviewed, and I'm just looking for any comments or bits of information that jump out at me as possibly relevant."

"Good. You sound better."

"I am. I always feel better when I have a plan."

"I'll be in court most of today on that meth lab we busted last month, so I'll be hard to reach. But if you leave a voicemail or text I'll get back to you as soon as I can," he said.

"Okay. I'll talk to you later."

I was highlighting with abandon when Patrick Boyle returned my call from Tuesday.

"Patrick, thanks for getting back to me. I'm so sorry to bother you but—"

"No, it's okay. I'm trying to stay busy. I can't arrange a memorial service until after the autopsy is done, so there really isn't that much to do. Anyway,

I called with some bad news. The laptop has already been wiped clean. I showed Mom how to use the secure erase option, and it looks like, for the first time ever, she remembered something technical I showed her how to do. Her computer is clean. There's nothing left."

The deep disappointment I felt at the news made me realize how much hope I'd been hanging on receiving a clue via Kathy from the Great Beyond.

"Would you consider letting me take it to a forensics expert to see if they can find anything?"

"I don't think that would help, Leah. I started out in computer security before I switched to film and video production in college. Secure erase is really effective at removing all data. You can have someone look at the laptop, but I don't think they'll find much."

"No, never mind. I don't even know what I'd be looking for. I appreciate you checking out the laptop when you've got so much on your mind. How are you holding up?"

"Oh, you know. It comes and goes. I really miss her," he said, and his voice broke on the last word. He paused and when he spoke again, his voice was steady.

"Like I said, I'm trying to stay busy. Trouble is, the only major thing to do now is editing the video I shot of the house and the area last fall. I want to get the house listed as soon as possible. I put the footage on a thumb drive for Mom a year ago. I have no idea what she did with it. I should probably forget hunting for it and just look for the original footage on my computer. That'll be a journey. My digital filing is pretty unorganized."

"I hear you on that. I'll let you get at it. Take care, Patrick."

When I hung up, I released the huge sigh that had wanted to escape when Patrick had said the words "secure erase option."

Then I got back to work myself.

I continued to plow through my notes, adding things to my list whenever I came across a detail I'd forgotten or something that hadn't registered with me initially. When I was finished, I read the list I'd compiled. Then I put it aside, sat on the window seat, and zoned out as I petted Sam. Sometimes if I stop trying to organize my thoughts they organize themselves and I find the links I'm looking for.

After a few minutes, a tiny little idea, more of a notion, really, that had been lodged in the deep recesses of my untidy mind floated to the surface. I considered it for a minute, then I made a phone call.

"Connie, if a body doesn't clear the HP virus, how long would it take before cancer showed up?"

"I'm fine, thank you, Leah. Yes, it's been a while. How are you doing?"

Connie Crowley is a retired physician, who is now the medical examiner for Grantland County. She's a friend of my mother's, and I've known her forever. She's also a very valuable source for me. When she's in the right mood. I moved quickly to get her there.

"Hey, I'm sorry I jumped in without a greeting. Yes, it has been a while. How are you? How are things going?"

"Too late. I'm already irritated. But I'm also curious. Are you worried? Get a pap smear and an HPV test. It's not something to fool around with."

"No, it's not about me. I just want to know how HPV works in the body, so I called the best doctor I know."

"Uh-huh," she said, her tone conveying she wasn't interested in my flattery. "Most times, the body gets rid of the virus on its own. If it doesn't, and HPV sticks around, the virus starts messing with normal cell reproduction. Then it causes precancerous changes in the cells it's infected. Over time those cells can get together and create a cluster of precancerous cells. Left untreated, those cells can eventually develop into cancer."

"Got it. But how long is eventually?"

"It varies. Usually it's pretty slow. Maybe five-ten years to get to precancerous cells and up to around twenty years for them to develop into invasive cancer."

"Okay, thanks. Talk to you later."

"Hey—is that all you wanted? I thought maybe you were calling to sweet talk me out of the inside dope on the autopsy consult I did yesterday. Not that you're ever very good at sweet talking."

Despite her gruff manner, I know that Connie gets lonely. She's been divorced for years, her daughter lives in Oregon and her son is in the Navy. She's been a workaholic her whole life and doesn't have a lot of friends. I usually chat with her for a while when I run into her or call her for information. But right then my mind was racing so fast, I just wanted to get off the phone so I could think. I tried to end the conversation without being rude.

"You're right. Sweet talking isn't my forte, for sure. Thanks for the help, Connie. I'll—"

"Yep. That was one for the books," she said, talking over me. "Hey, maybe for one of your books. It was a really interesting autopsy. Jim Mitchell over in Galen is a little gun-shy after he missed a murder by poisoning last year. That's why he called me in for a second opinion."

As soon as I heard the word Galen, I decided I had all the time in the world to talk to Connie.

"What autopsy do you mean?"

"This is off the record, okay? It's for Trenton County to put out the official information."

"Okay, no problem."

"When he called and asked me to take a look for him, I couldn't figure out why. The woman fell off a ladder, hit her head, and died. Sounded pretty routine. Turns out it wasn't."

"The woman, was it Kathy Boyle?"

"It was. How did you know?"

"I was at her house Tuesday when they removed the body. I was supposed to have a meeting with her. What wasn't routine about it?"

"She did have a head injury, but that isn't what killed her."

"Connie, come on. Don't mess with me. What did she die of?"

"Asphyxiation. Most likely from a plastic bag held over her face."

"She was suffocated? As in she was murdered?"

"Yep. It would be pretty easy to miss if you weren't really looking close. Which I was. I found facial congestion present, swollen tongue, and petechiae were present on the face as well. Those were pretty suggestive, but the capper was that I also found a tiny scrap of very thin plastic, like the kind used for those godawful plastic grocery bags, under her nails. My educated conclusion is that she fell or was pushed from the ladder, hit her head and got knocked out. The killer went after her with a plastic bag over her face and finished the job."

"Holy cow! Who knows about the autopsy results?"

"Not many. I gave Jim my findings yesterday, but he spent this morning crossing his T's and dotting his I's before he took it to the sheriff. He didn't want to get burned again. As far as I know, no press release has been issued. They've got to notify the family first. She's got a son, and he isn't local. Lives in—"

"Sun Prairie. I know. Thanks, Connie. I'll buy you lunch and fill you in soon. I have to go now."

After an hour of flipping through my notes, mumbling to myself, and making a quick call to Matthew's Aunt Jean, I stopped, looked at the list I'd made, and finally felt like I had a solid working theory. That's when my intercom buzzed.

"Can you come out and play?" Miguel said.

"No. But can you come up and work? You'll say yes if you want to hear who killed Matthew. And possibly Kathy Boyle."

"I am running all the way up the stairs to hear."

When he appeared panting at my door I said, "You weren't kidding, were you? Come on in and sit down before you have a heart attack."

I handed him a Diet Coke as he collapsed on one of the bar stools.

"*Gracias.* Now, tell me everything."

"I will. But first something entirely different. Did you know that Spencer Karr is going to become a priest—so he says, anyway?"

"Yes, yes, Courtnee told me. We can discuss later. Tell me who killed Matthew? And what is this about Kathy Boyle? I thought she fell off a ladder."

"Kathy was murdered. Connie Crowley told me off the record. She was called in by the Trenton County medical examiner to consult on the autopsy," I said starting with his last questions first.

"But who is the killer?"

"It's Ellen Ferguson."

59

The astonished expression on his face mirrored what my own must have looked like when I figured it out.

"No! How can that be? It does not make sense."

"Miguel, it does if you look at the whole picture. Which I didn't do because I liked Ellen. I felt sorry for her. And that made me ignore what was right in front of me."

"Stop, you are torturing me. Just tell me what you think and why you think it."

"It started to come to me after I read all my notes over again this morning. I took a step back to just think and I remembered something my mother told me."

"Wait—Carol is investigating?"

"No, no. Though she'd love to be invited to, I'm sure. But she's a big part of how I figured this out. Miguel, be just a tiny bit patient with me. Some of what I'm going to say, you already know, but I need to say it again because I'm walking through my whole theory for the first time out loud."

"I'm here for you. I will sit so quiet like a mouse. Patience is one of my top talents."

He sat up straight on his stool. Then he folded his hands in his lap, cast his eyes downward and assumed a serene expression.

"You look like Buddha's number one student. At ease, Miguel. I didn't mean you couldn't move or speak, I just wanted you to know it might take a while to go through this."

He relaxed immediately and leaned back, his elbows resting on the bar behind him.

"I'm going to start at the beginning, which is twenty-five years ago, when Matthew and Hannah are in high school. And they're in the throes of first love."

"I love a love story."

"I know you do, but this one doesn't end happily. Matthew was pretty crazy about Hannah. Hannah was in love with him, too. But they had a huge quarrel the night before she and her family moved away. Hannah reached out after they were settled in Atlanta. Matthew didn't respond. By then he was with Ellen."

"The rebound. It is real," he said.

"It is. But this rebound lasted. Ellen got pregnant and they got married when they graduated. Ellen has a different version of Matthew and Hannah as a couple. She says it was a casual thing, and once Hannah was gone, Matthew realized that it was Ellen he wanted. Ellen always knew Matthew was the one for her. He's the only man she's ever been with."

"Matthew was her OTP—her one true pairing," he added.

"Yes, that's what she says. But I think underneath, Ellen knew she was second choice. It had to bother her a little anyway, knowing that Matthew only turned to her because Hannah was gone. Then Hannah and her family moved back. Matthew walked into her store one day, and eventually the inevitable happened. They began an affair. And that set the stage for murder."

"Okay, but wait. Ellen said she didn't know about the affair until after Matthew and Hannah broke up and he confessed to her. Why would Ellen kill him if she already forgave him?"

"I don't think that ever happened."

"Ellen was lying?"

"Yes. I think she said it to help deflect suspicion after Matthew died. She wanted the police to believe that she didn't kill Matthew because she had no reason to. She'd already forgiven his sin."

"How did she find out about the affair?"

"Well, we know that Joel saw a text from Matthew to Hannah that tipped him off. I think it's safe to assume something similar happened for Ellen."

"Okay, so Ellen knows that Matthew is cheating on her, and she is devastated. But he is Ellen's OTP. I don't think she would kill him. Maybe she would kill Hannah, but not him. I think she would wait to see if the affair ended on its own. Like she did when Matthew and Hannah were a couple in high school."

"Hey, I said be patient. You're getting ahead of me. I told you this was twisty and there's more to come."

"Sorry, sorry. But hurry, hurry."

"I'll try. You're right, Ellen loves Matthew. They have a history together, a son, and Matthew took incredible care of her when she had cancer. That says to Ellen that he must truly love her. She thinks if she is patient, he will come back to her. And it turns out that's what happens. Hannah and Matthew break up. But by then it's too late. Because Ellen discovers something about Matthew that's even worse than having an affair with Hannah.

"What, what is it?"

"Matthew, the loving husband who was her superhero during her cancer treatment is the reason she got cancer."

"I am so not following you now."

"Sorry, you're the one who wanted it speedy. Let me throw in some context and go back to what Mom said that started me rethinking the murder motive. You know Mom went to Maine because her friend Judy is in hospice care right?

"Yes. That is very sad. I know she is one of Carol's best friends. But what does that have to do with Ellen and Matthew and murder?"

I gave him a short version of the conversation my mother and I had about Judy's illness. I followed that with what I'd learned from Connie Crowley about the origins of cervical cancer and the longevity of the HP Virus that causes it.

"Do you see how I got to Ellen as the killer now?"

"I think so. Ellen has never had sex with anyone but Matthew. Ninety-nine percent of cervical cancer is sexually transmitted. That means that Matthew gave the virus to Ellen. And years later, the cancer came."

"Exactly. Matthew cheating with Hannah was awful but forgivable. But I really don't know how you'd feel anything but murderous after learning that your husband gave you the cancer that almost killed you—and still could. The affair or the cancer are two reasons for murder. Put them together and they become a supernova of a motive."

"But wait. Wouldn't Ellen know way before the affair, when she first got cancer that Matthew had passed the virus to her? He was the only man in her life. Her doctor would tell her that HPV causes cervical cancer, wouldn't he?"

"Some doctors feel it's their right to decide what a patient needs to know. Maybe Ellen's doctor thought knowing that her husband gave it to her would be too much extra emotional trauma for Ellen to handle."

"But then how does Ellen find out about the HP virus and her cancer?"

"I'm not sure. Remember I just put the framework together this morning. I don't have all the pieces yet. She might have read an article online, or seen something on TV, or maybe someone mentioned it to her in conversation. For now let's go with the idea that she found out about the HPV and the affair around the same time. She is deeply hurt and even more furious. She wants revenge. On both of them. She plans to get it by killing Matthew using aconite, which will point to Hannah as the killer. They'll both pay for what they did to her," I said.

"Ohhh. And that is why Ellen says there must be a second tox screening when the medical examiner at first says the cause of death cannot be determined. It isn't enough that Matthew is dead. She needs the aconite to be found so that Hannah will be blamed. Hannah must suffer, too," Miguel said.

"Exactly. And by demanding the second test, she gets a side benefit. The police take her off the suspect list, because no killer would ask for a second test for a murder they already got away with."

"Ellen, she is very smart. But what about Kathy Boyle. Why did Ellen kill her? And how?"

Before I could answer my phone rang. I glanced at the caller ID.

"It's Patrick Boyle, I'm guessing the police have told him that his mother's death wasn't an accident."

60

I put the phone on speaker so Miguel could hear.

"Patrick, hi. I—"

"Leah, the police just left. They said my mother was murdered! That somebody suffocated her! Then they started asking me questions like did she and my dad get along, did they have any fights about the property settlement in the divorce. They even asked did Mom 'maintain contacts with the adult film industry.' I don't believe it! She's not going to get any peace about that even after she's dead, is she?"

"I'm sorry, Patrick. I found out about the autopsy results just a little while ago—probably around the same time you got the news. Listen, I think there's a connection between your mother's murder and Matthew Ferguson's. Someone knew what she was going to show me and wanted to make sure that never happened."

"But who could know that?"

I wasn't ready to share my Ellen theory with anyone but Miguel just yet, so I didn't answer him directly.

"I've got a possibility in mind, but I'm not sure enough to say. I really wish we knew what Kathy wanted to show me."

"I think I know. I found the drone footage. I was looking at it just before the police got here."

Miguel and I exchanged wide-eyed looks. Finally, maybe, we caught a break.

"Did you show it to them?"

"No, I didn't think it had anything to do with Mom's death. Should I have?"

"Not just yet. I'd like to get a look at it first. What is it, Patrick? What's on the video?"

"It's in my Dropbox file. I'm texting you the link right now. I want you to see it before I say anything."

It took only a minute to grab my laptop. I wanted a screen much bigger than my iPhone had to view the footage. Patrick stayed on the phone as I clicked on the link he'd sent.

"Okay, it's running, but all I'm seeing is the bike trail and it's just starting to get dark. But there's no one on it—oh! Wait, no that was just a deer running across. What am I looking for?"

"Fast forward to the 15-minute mark."

"Okay, but I still—"

And then I saw it. The footage had been taken as the drone moved north on the bike trail, away from the county park and toward Kathy's house. Someone riding an e-bike came into view. They were bundled up in a jacket and a hoodie with the hood pulled down low. It was hard to determine if they were male or female. As I watched, the figure on the bike approached the area of Matthew's cabin and turned onto his property. The drone moved on and the rest of the footage was random wild life.

"Patrick, is there any way you could use editing software to zoom in and get some detail on the rider's hands—that's about the only exposed part."

"Yeah, I should be able to, but what will the hands tell you?"

"For one thing if the person is a man or a woman. And if we get super lucky, there might be something distinguishing like a ring or a bracelet. Can you get that much detail?"

"Maybe. Give me a few minutes."

We both hung up and I turned to Miguel, who looked ready to burst.

"Is that Ellen in the video?"

"I'm pretty sure it is. Ellen has a flashy wedding ring set—sapphire and diamond. If that's on the hand, then we'll know it's Ellen. I'm hoping she wore Matthew's pledge of eternal love on the night she sent him to his eternal rest."

"I have another question, but this is about Kathy's murder. How could Ellen know that Kathy had something to show you that could be dangerous to her?"

"I'm afraid that's on me. And I don't look forward to answering that question when Patrick thinks to ask it."

"Why is it on you?"

"Kathy called me late on Monday to tell me she had something I should see. We arranged to meet Tuesday at her house. Shortly after that, Ellen called to invite me for pizza on Tuesday night. We chatted a little and when she asked me if I had any leads, I said that I might. I told her that Kathy Boyle had called to say she had something to show me, and that I was going to meet with her and then go to Ellen's for dinner. Kathy was killed later that night, sometime between 8:00 p.m. and midnight. It's not much of a stretch to think that Ellen needed to know whether what Kathy had was something she should worry about. She went to see her, and it was, and she killed her. If I hadn't said anything to Ellen, Kathy would still be alive."

"No. You just answered her question, and Ellen wasn't even on the suspect list. Kathy's death is not your fault. The killer murdered her, not you."

"Yeah. I'm telling myself that, but I'm not buying it."

We both jumped when my phone rang.

"Leah, I zoomed in as much as I could. I did a frame capture and saved it as a still photo," Patrick said without preamble. "I'm sending the link right now."

I turned to my laptop and clicked the link. A woman's hand appeared on the screen. On the third finger of her left hand was a sapphire and diamond wedding set.

"Well?" Patrick asked. "Do you recognize the ring? Do you know who the woman is?"

"I do."

"And?"

"And I can't tell you yet, Patrick. I need to do a little more work first."

"It's my mother, please. I want to know," he said.

"I know you do. And I understand. But please, just trust me with a little more time on this. I promise it won't be long now. And Patrick, please keep this to yourself. Don't talk about it to anyone. You've got a very valuable piece of evidence. I don't want you to be in danger because the killer finds out. Can you hang on for just a little longer?"

He didn't answer right away, but finally he said, "All right. But just a few days."

"Thank you."

61

"So what is the more work you have to do?" Miguel asked after Patrick hung up.

"I want to get myself organized to share this with Hannah's lawyer. I don't know what all is entailed in trying to prove that the wrong person is in prison, but I'm thinking there are a lot of steps. And Ellen, as you said, is a very clever woman. She's also a good actress. She fooled the police once already, she fooled me for a while, too. I don't want her to get away with this."

"But that is easy! First there is the half mushroom pizza at the cabin. That proves that someone else was there with Matthew."

"Yes, and I called Matthew's Aunt Jean this morning. She told me that Ellen loves mushrooms and Matthew hated them. That they always ordered pizza with mushrooms on only one half so they could both enjoy it. But when I asked Ellen about it earlier, she lied and told me that she hated mushrooms, too. She lied because she realized that by eating the mushroom side of the pizza Matthew brought to the cabin, she'd made a mistake," I said.

"And Rory and Cole can prove that Ellen wasn't home the night of the murder because they were at Ellen's house. And also, too, Joel saw a woman through the curtain when he was at the cabin on the murder night. Ellen had a rash on her arm the next morning—her sister saw it, too. You said contact with aconite can cause a bad rash," Miguel said.

"Don't forget the cancer," I added. "Matthew is the only man Ellen was ever with. He's the one who gave her the HP virus. And after I screwed up and told Ellen that Kathy had something to show me, Kathy was killed before she could give it to me."

"But now we have the video of the bike rider with Ellen's hand, wearing Ellen's rings. There is no way that Ellen can find a way out of this."

"I'd like to think so, Miguel. But with someone as smart as Ellen, there's always a way. She'll pull out all the stops. And the sheriff's office isn't going to be excited about admitting they were wrong and re-opening the case. It's not just that they arrested an innocent person, but the real murderer went on to kill again. I just want to take some time to think. I want to talk to Coop, too. I want to be sure I do this right for Hannah, for Olivia, for Marguerite, for Patrick, and most of all for Matthew and for Kathy. Do you understand?"

"I trust you, *chica*."

"Thanks, Miguel. I'm going to call Coop."

But before I could, my phone rang. It was Ellen. I held up the phone, pointed to the caller ID so Miguel could see, before I answered.

"Hello Ellen," I said trying to keep my voice sounding normal.

"Leah, I wonder if you could come over. I have something important to tell you."

"Now?" I asked.

"Within the hour, if you can."

"Is everything all right, Ellen? Can you give me an idea of what it is you want to talk about?"

"Yes, of course everything is all right. But I have some information that I think will help you. It's a lot to take in. You will come, won't you?"

"Yes. I'll leave right away."

"Don't bother to knock, just come in. The front door will be open."

Miguel, who is usually quite happy to go along with my plans, was not down with this one. As soon as I told him, he dug in his stylish boot-clad heels.

"No, no, no! You cannot go alone. If you don't let me ride with you, then I will follow you in my car. You cannot go to see a killer by yourself!"

"She may freak out if you're there. Ellen wants to talk to me, not an audience."

"One more person is not an audience. She has killed two people," he said, folding his arms and standing squarely between me and the door.

"Come on, it's eleven o'clock in the morning. Ellen lives in a neighborhood with lots of people around. She's not going to do anything. Remember, she has no idea that we've figured out who the killer is. And that means I may have a chance to trap her into saying something, or several somethings, that we can use against her. Will you feel better if I promise not to drink anything or climb any ladders while I'm there?"

"This is not funny, Leah. I know that you are smart and strong, but we know that Ellen is also smart. She has something planned. Why else would she want you to come right away? Go ahead, go without me. But I will be right behind you. Or we can go in my car, and you can tell Ellen I gave you a ride because your car wouldn't start. I am your friend. I love you. And I cannot let you go into her house without me. That is final."

As soon as he called me Leah, I knew the argument was over. Miguel almost always calls me *chica,* unless he is very serious.

"Okay, fine. Let's stop arguing and get over there. I'll just tell Ellen that you and I were already together coming home from a meeting, so I just changed course and brought you along. Satisfied?"

"Yes."

Ellen's street, which when I'd been there before always had people out walking or working in their yards, or kids playing and riding bikes, was eerily quiet.

Miguel looked at me and raised an eyebrow. He didn't say it, but I knew he was pointing out that the neighborhood that I'd described as a hub of activity teeming with people appeared to be the deserted set of a Twilight Zone episode. And though I wasn't frightened, I did feel just a teeny bit better paying a visit to Ellen with Miguel in tow. Though I would never admit that.

We hurried up the walk and though Ellen had said I didn't need to knock, I tapped on the door before opening it and stepping inside.

"Ellen?" I called. "Where are you, living room or kitchen?"

She didn't answer so I tried the living room first. It was empty.

"She must be in the kitchen. It's in the back of the house," I said to Miguel. "She must not have heard us come in."

I started in that direction, but Miguel grabbed my arm.

"Wait," he said.

"What for? She said to go in. She's expecting us—me, anyway."

"No, listen," he said, standing very still.

"To what? I don't hear anything."

"That is what I mean. It is too quiet. Something is wrong. It feels like no one is home."

"That's ridiculous. She called and begged me to come over. She wouldn't just leave," I said, striding in the direction of the kitchen and calling her name.

"Ellen? Hello? Ellen?"

There was no one in the kitchen.

"Let's try upstairs. Maybe she's ill, or listening to music with the headphones on, or something," I said, though by then I knew that Miguel was right. Something was wrong.

When we reached the top of the stairs, I saw a door slightly ajar. I hurried down the hallway and pushed it open all the way. Ellen was there, lying on the bed. Dead.

62

We rushed into the room. I checked Ellen's pulse and couldn't find one. As I called 911, Miguel spotted an envelope on the dresser with my name on it. He handed it to me as I hung up. Inside were several pages written in a clear, confident hand. I began to read it out loud.

Dear Leah,

You've worked so hard to prove that Hannah Vining didn't kill Matthew, that I felt I owed my final farewell and explanation to you. I've mailed separate letters to my son and my sister Lindsey.

About a month or so before I killed Matthew, I discovered his affair with Hannah. I was in his office, looking for our passports. The desk where we kept them was locked, which was strange, but I found the key in his filing cabinet. I opened his desk and found a cell phone in the main drawer. I opened it using the password Matthew always used, our son's birthdate.

The texts on it between Matthew and Hannah stunned me. I was hurt and furious. Matthew was out of town for a few days, so I had time to decide what to do. Part of me wanted to confront him. Part of me was afraid that if I forced him to make a choice, he'd choose Hannah. I'd worked very hard for 25 years to make him love me. And I know that he did. But not the way he loved Hannah.

In the end I decided to wait to see if the affair burned itself out. But a few days later, I got a letter that changed everything. It was from an old neighbor of ours, Terry Danton. We were friendly with her and her husband, but not close at all. They divorced two years after we moved here. I hadn't heard from or seen Terry in almost 20 years. I didn't even say goodbye to her, because I'd taken my son to visit my mother in Texas the week she moved. I was very surprised to get a letter from her. I was incredibly shocked when I read it.

Terry wrote that after leaving Galen she took a job at a Catholic hospital in Massachusetts where her sister lived. While working there, she found her vocation and became a Catholic nun. Sister Teresa. She was diagnosed with cervical cancer several years ago, but she wasn't as lucky as me. She was writing to me from a hospice center. Unlike my doctor, hers had explained that virtually all cervical cancer is caused by the HP virus, which is sexually transmitted. She was shocked, because she hadn't had sex since her divorce. Her doctor explained that the virus can stay in a woman's body for decades before it causes cancer. She realized that she could have gotten it from her husband, or from an old boyfriend—or from my husband.

Apparently Terry and Matthew had a short fling while I was in Texas. The usual story—she was lonely and depressed about the divorce, Matthew was at loose ends, wine was involved, they both regretted it. She didn't know if she'd had the virus already, or if Matthew had given it to her. She was writing to me because either way, Matthew had had sex with both of us, so I was at risk. She gave me her phone number in case I wanted to talk to her. I called it. I didn't speak to her, because Terry had died three weeks earlier. Her sister had found the letter among Terry's things and mailed it to me.

That's when my love for Matthew turned to hate. And that's when I began to plan how to kill him. His selfish, reckless behavior had given me cancer and nearly killed me. And his affair with Hannah wasn't the only time he had betrayed me. How many others were there? I wanted him to suffer and to know that I caused it. Like he caused mine. That's when I got the idea to poison Matthew. He would die while I watched and told him why. And Hannah would be blamed. It was a simple plan, really, and very easy to carry out. I bought the aconite at an herbal store in Milwaukee, and I waited for the right time. It came when Matthew had business in Racine on a Friday and decided to spend the night at the cabin instead of driving home. I said that I'd meet him there and spend the night, and he could help me hang the new curtains I'd bought.

I drove to the parking lot at the start of the bike trail that runs behind the cabin. There was no one around. I took my bike out of the back, rode it up the trail to the cabin, and went inside to wait for Matthew. As I got the tea ready, I spilled some of the aconite leaves I was adding to the mix. That's when I got some on my arm. It caused a painful rash that my sister noticed, but I convinced her it was from stinging nettle in my garden. Matthew stopped at Cheesehead Pizza on his way to the cabin for our usual order, pepperoni and half-mushroom. That was really my only mistake. The two pieces missing, one from each side, was the clue you needed, wasn't it, Leah?

When Matthew got there, I already had two cups of tea made, though mine was different from his. I said he should put the pizza in the oven to warm up. We drank the tea. And then we each had a piece of pizza. Within 15 minutes or so Matthew started feeling sick. His symptoms quickly became worse—severe abdominal pain, nausea, his heart was racing. He asked me to call 911. I told him that wasn't going to happen. Then I explained why. All the while he was retching and moaning and begging me to help him. I felt nothing but vindication. He'd brought this on himself.

When he was dead, I put his second phone in his jacket pocket. I'd brought it with me in a plastic bag. I used the plastic to hold it as I put it in Matthew's dead hands, pressing his fingers onto it, in case the police looked for fingerprints. I didn't worry about leaving prints in the cabin. After all it was mine, too, and I had a right to be there. I washed and dried my teacup, but I left his in the sink and the aconite-laced tea in the cupboard. Then I turned out the lights, rode my bike to the parking lot, put it in the car and drove home.

It was the perfect crime. So perfect that the medical examiner was ready to rule it a heart attack from unknown causes. I couldn't have that. I wanted Matthew dead, but I wanted to punish Hannah, too, for what she had done to me. So I insisted on the second screening for toxins that turned up the aconite.

When you got involved because of Hannah's sister, it was actually a little fun —making you like me, throwing a little suspicion on Rory—she was terrible to me. But when you put together what the mushrooms on the pizza meant—that someone else had been with Matthew, that worried me. But I got lucky because you made a mistake, too. You told me that Kathy Boyle had something to show you. I didn't know if I'd have to kill Kathy or not, but I had to find out what she had. It was surprisingly easy.

After you left my house that night, I drove to Kathy's. We had a civil relationship because she didn't know that I'd tipped off the paper after Matthew told me about her adult film work. She thought it was him. The race was too close. I had hopes that Matthew's local political career would lead to something bigger. I didn't want him to lose. After the story hit, I persuaded Matthew that Kenny Marston must have done it.

When I showed up at her door she was surprised. I told her I was interested in the computer desk she was selling. She told me it was gone but invited me in for coffee. It went smoothly from there. I brought up your investigation, Leah. I said you'd mentioned that Kathy might have a lead for you. Kathy said maybe, she wasn't sure if it would help. She said she had it on a thumb drive she was going to give you. That it was a video. I asked if I could see it. We went upstairs and she played it, and there I was riding down the bike trail.

Kathy thought it might be Hannah. I noticed then that the ladder in her office was leaning into an attic opening in the ceiling. I knew how to kill her then. I said that a friend was looking for a place on the lake, but she needed a lot of storage space. I asked Kathy if I could look at the attic. If it was large enough, she might just make a sale herself and save the realtor fees.

Kathy climbed the ladder first. When she got to the top step, I shoved it, and she fell. She hit her head and was knocked out. But she was still breathing. I picked up a plastic shopping bag I saw on the floor and dumped the stuff out of it. I put the bag over her face. She started to come to and clawed at the bag. I held firm. It didn't take that long before she stopped breathing. I took the bag off, took the thumb drive out of the computer, went downstairs, washed and put my coffee cup away, and left. I drove over the thumb drive with my car, then I picked it up and threw the smashed pieces into the woods. Then I went home.

Are you wondering why I killed myself when I've covered my tracks so well, Leah? My doctor called this morning. He had the results from my five-year checkup. The one that was supposed to show me cancer free. It didn't. The cancer has spread to multiple locations. He started outlining the treatment plan—more chemo, more radiation. I let him talk, but I knew I wasn't going through that *again. Last year after my brother died, I took the fentanyl he had left, just in case. Well, this is that case.*

I don't regret what I did to Matthew and Hannah. I feel bad about Kathy. I wouldn't have killed her if I'd known that I was dying. I did like you, Leah. I knew you'd never figure out the truth, so this is my parting gift to you. Enjoy.

Ellen Ferguson

As the sirens came closer, I put the pages of the letter on the bedside table and photographed each, then put them back inside the envelope and put the envelope back on the dresser.

"Wait, don't you need that to prove Ellen did it?"

"It has to stay here. It's part of a crime scene. I took photos so I can get it to Hannah's lawyer so she can start working on Hannah's release right away. The ambulance is pulling in. Will you go down and direct them upstairs? I'll stay with Ellen."

63

"I'm proud of you, Leah," Coop said, as we sat on the sofa at my place. It was 5:00 p.m. Miguel and I had just gotten back from a lengthy interview with two detectives from the Galen Police Department.

"Really? Because I'm not feeling so proud at the moment. I'm feeling pretty awful about Kathy Boyle. If I hadn't opened my big mouth and told Ellen that Kathy had information to share, Kathy would still be alive."

"Don't go down that road. Ellen wasn't a suspect, she asked you a question, and she had a legitimate interest in her husband's murder."

"Well that's the thing, isn't it? Ellen *should* have been a suspect. I dismissed her way too early. She was friendly, and nice, and I felt sorry for her. I'm getting soft in my old age."

"You're not the only one she fooled. I'm guessing Sheriff Kelsey Shepherd isn't feeling her best tonight. The Trenton County prosecutor either. The thing is, you worked the case, and you figured it out. And this was a tough one. But man, that Ellen was a piece of work. It takes a cold heart to watch your husband die and then send his lover to prison for the crime."

"True. But—and I'm in no way saying that what Ellen did was justified —imagine how she felt. First she finds out Matthew cheated on her, and then she finds out he gave her cancer. I'm not sure what I'd do in those circumstances."

"Well, you'll never find out, because I would never do that."

"Good to know," I said.

"So, what's next?"

"Well, I already gave Ellen's letter—the photos of it I took, I mean—to Hannah's attorney before we left Galen. Miguel drove on the way home so I could focus on letting Marguerite know—she couldn't stop crying. And then I called Patrick Boyle, too. That was a tough one, but I couldn't just let him read about it online. So, aside from any additional information the police want from me, I'm pretty much done.

"Now, I'm going to focus strictly on fictional murder. I saw Peter Sullivan briefly at the grocery store on Tuesday night, and he said he had a great idea for a plot twist for me. I'm going to call him tomorrow and see if we can meet."

The next morning while we were eating breakfast, my phone pinged with a text coming in.

"Oh, for God's sake!" I said with a mixture of irritation and surprise.

Coop looked up from reading the news on his phone.

"Bad news?"

"It's from Sharla. I haven't heard anything since Tuesday, so I was hoping she gave up. But not responding to her apparently made her mad."

I read the text out loud to him.

I thought we were friends. That we had a special relationship. You can't just ghost me like that. You're going to be sorry for this.

"Leah, you need to call Jane Williams, tell her about this. That text is a serious escalation. Sharla is threatening you. I think the best thing for you to do now is move in with me temporarily."

"Coop, I appreciate your concern. I really do. But I'm not going to lock myself up until Sharla is caught. I've got all the safeguards Jane suggested in place. The front stairs security camera is repositioned now, I'm locking my doors, I'm paying attention to my surroundings. What else can I do?"

"Stay in closer touch with me, okay? Just a quick text will do when you're moving from place to place, all right?"

"You mean like, *10:15 I'm going downstairs to the newsroom.* And then later, *10:45, all's well. I'm on the window seat.* Then later, *Noon. I'm going down to the pop machine.* Is that it?"

"It's a good thing I love you, or I'd find you seriously annoying."

"But you do love me, and so you find me amusing and courageous as I laugh in the face of danger? Ha! Ha! Take that, Danger!"

He shook his head, kissed me goodbye and said, "Don't forget to call Jane, and do forget to be such a smart ass, okay?"

Actually, Sharla's latest text had made me a little more concerned than I'd let on to Coop. It's unnerving to know that someone is watching you and getting progressively more annoyed with you. I've seen enough stalker movies to imagine quite a few unpleasant scenarios. But I didn't want to give in to scaredy-cat fears. Sharla had sounded pretty irate, but she hadn't said she was going to kidnap me and hide me in her basement. I called Jane and made my report. She instructed me again not to engage with Sharla but admitted she had made no progress in unmasking Sharla's identity, hidden as it was by her use of a VPN.

When I hung up, I decided to push all stalker worries out of my mind and call Peter Sullivan.

"Leah, lovely to hear from you. I stopped by the newspaper yesterday, but you were out. I wondered how your real-life murder investigation was going, and if you're ready to talk about your fictional plot again."

"Yes, the investigation is pretty much over, for me, anyway. And yes, I'd love to hear your idea for a plot twist."

"Oh, good! I'm really enjoying the small part I'm playing in the construction of your new novel. Are you still planning to travel to Buckner College for some—what do they call it? Local color?"

"I am. It's been a tough couple of weeks. I'm ready to take a giant step away from real life murder and take a deep dive into fictional crime. I was wondering if you know anyone who's still there who was at the college when the meningitis outbreak happened? Or in the medical community?"

"Well, it was almost forty years ago, and I haven't kept in close touch with anyone. But Adele is quite active on social media, and she may be in contact with people back there still. I'll check with her and let you know tonight. Is 7:30 this evening at the library all right with you? I'd meet you for dinner, but I'm already committed."

"No, the library's fine. I can return my overdue books and throw myself on the mercy of the circulation desk. I'll see you tonight."

Then, despite Sam's attempts to get me to play fetch with him by dropping his red ball at my feet—yes, my cat sometimes thinks he's a dog—I settled in to do some work on the plotting. I wanted to use the opportunity with Peter not just to hear his plot twist ideas, but to run a few of my own by him. I stopped to give Sam his lunch and grabbed a peanut butter and jelly sandwich for my own, then went back at it. I'd be lying if I said I didn't occasionally stop and check my email to see if there were any more messages from Sharla.

Around three o'clock Father Lindstrom called and invited me to tea. He sold the offer with the promise of cookies from the Elite Café.

I happily accepted and texted my change in location to Coop, as promised.

64

On my way down the back stairs to the parking lot, my phone rang.

"Mom, how are things?"

"Judy died this morning, Leah. She never regained consciousness, but I was with her. I sat with her all night. I talked about all the things we laughed about, and worried about, and cried about over so many years of being friends. I reminded her about some of the crazy things we did in college, and the dreams we had, and the plans. And I did sing *The Traveling Typist* to her. And you know what? I swear this is true. She squeezed my hand when I was singing to her. The nurse who came in said it was just an involuntary reaction. But I know she heard me. I know she did. I'm sorry. I'm rambling, aren't I? It's just that I feel so . . ."

She paused for a minute as though searching for a way to describe the loss of a life-long friend.

"Unmoored, I guess. I really loved that woman," she said, her voice quavering a little.

"Mom, when are you coming home? I think you need a hug."

"Not until Sunday. Judy is being cremated, and there won't be a service. She didn't want one. But there's going to be a small family gathering tomorrow, and her daughter asked me to stay. And you're right, then I need to get back to Himmel and hug and be hugged by everybody I love."

She was quiet for a second, then said, "Okay. That's enough self-pity from me. How are you doing? What's happening with your investigation?"

I summarized recent events for her as I got into my car and began to drive to Father Lindstrom's.

"So, now it's up to her lawyer. With what she's got to work with, I hope Hannah won't be in prison much longer. In fact I think that will be the easy part. It's hard to imagine how she and Joel and Olivia can put their family back together."

"You'd be surprised what can be mended if people really want to do it."

"Maybe so. People can surprise you—a lot. Like Spencer finding his calling to be a priest."

I knew that tidbit would take her mind off her loss for a minute.

"What? Could you repeat that please?"

"Spencer's entering the seminary. He told me Wednesday. Though I remain very skeptical. I'm on my way to Father Lindstrom's for the real story. In fact, I'm pulling up in front of his place right now."

"All right, hon. I'll let you go. I'll see you Sunday. I love you."

"Love you too, Mom."

Before I went into Father Lindstrom's building, I texted the fact to Coop. I wondered who would get tired of this sooner, me or him? I was pretty sure it would be me.

After the St. Stephen's rectory burned in a fire, Father Lindstrom had moved into a small apartment near the church. It was eclectically furnished with donated furniture from his parishioners, so it had no identifiable style of decor, but Father's presence made it a warm and welcoming space. We made a little small talk, and then I brought up the topic of Spencer Karr.

"When I talked to you at Darmody's open house, you didn't tell me that Spencer was entering the seminary. Is it true? And that you're part of the reason?"

"It's true that Spencer believes he has a vocation, and that I've served as his spiritual advisor. And yes, he plans to enter the seminary. But the process of discernment or determining that you are truly called to the priesthood is a journey. Many men enter the seminary only to discover that they do not have a vocation."

"Do you think Spencer does?"

"I can't speak for him, Leah. And I'm not comfortable speaking about him on this subject. Have you asked Spencer your questions?"

"I was too stunned when he told me to question him, Father. And frankly, I'm not at all inclined to believe anything he says. And I sure as heck don't think he had a road to Damascus moment."

The little priest smiled. "Yes, well, few people who commit to God do so because of something as dramatic as the conversion experience that transformed Saul the persecutor into Paul, the apostle. But would you agree that we cannot see into another person's heart?"

"Well, yes, but we're talking Spencer here. I think there's scant evidence that he even has a heart."

"I can only say this, Leah. Spencer sought me out for spiritual advising. We had what I believe were very honest and sometimes painful discussions. Spencer's spiritual work continues. The vocation director at the seminary was satisfied that he met the requirements for admission—which are significant."

"Okay then. I guess we'll see. I hope that you're not disappointed, Father."

"My hope, Leah, is that you are."

"What do you mean?"

"I think if Spencer's transformation proves lasting and true—whether he becomes a priest or not—it might shake your cynicism enough to let the light of faith shine for you, too."

"Oh, Father. I don't see that in my future."

"Ah, but the future remains unknown to all of us. It contains all possibilities, that's what makes it so interesting. More tea?"

It was my turn to smile. "Okay, okay, I can tell we're done with Spencer for now. And yes, I'd like another cup."

"I hear that Miguel hasn't found a new place to live yet."

"No. But in case you're still lobbying for him, I have to tell you it's not happening."

"I see. I assume it's because you're still reluctant to fully commit to your relationship with Coop."

"Father, did Miguel also enlist you as a disciple of Dr. Love? You know how I feel about that. I've bent your ear enough times about it."

"I know what you've said—that you fear that marriage would change things between you and not for the better; that the marriage could fail as your first one did, that you need your independence for your sense of self."

"Yes, all those are true."

"I don't doubt that, but I wonder if they are cover for a deeper truth that is harder for you to admit."

"I'm not following."

"Is it possible that the real resistance you have is caused by the guilt you carry and have carried for so many years? You blame yourself for the loss of your two sisters. And as a penance you deny yourself a chance for a fully committed relationship with Coop because Annie and Lacey were denied their chances. You believe you failed them."

"I did fail them. I wasn't paying attention. I let Annie slip away and go back to the house to look for her cat. She died of smoke inhalation. Lacey died because I wasn't there when she needed me. She wouldn't have gotten into drugs and everything else if I'd been a better sister. Both my sisters lost their chance to grow up, to have a family, to grow old, to be happy. And it's my fault."

"When will you stop punishing yourself for things that you were not in charge of? Annie was eight, you were ten. You weren't an adult, you were a child yourself. Lacey's tragic path had nothing to do with you. You didn't cause her death. Denying yourself happiness as a sacrifice on the altar of your guilt will not bring them back."

"That's not what I'm doing," I said, in a testier tone than I usually use with Father Lindstrom. He didn't seem to notice.

"Isn't it? I can see that this conversation is distressing to you. I'll leave you with this thought. You did not fail your sisters in the past. But perhaps you are failing them now. You are still here. Shouldn't you live your life to the fullest not just for yourself but for them? Surely that is what they would want."

"Father, thank you. But I don't believe that I'm guilting myself out of happiness. And I do know that I failed my sisters despite your very kind attempt to dissuade me. Now, let's talk about something else. Tell me, how are plans for the Christmas Bazaar coming?"

65

When I got home, Charlotte called to talk about the reception she was planning. I broke the news to her that I'd extended an invitation to Cole in exchange for information I'd needed. She doesn't know Cole that well, so she wasn't aware of how wrong things could go. I didn't have the heart to detail the potential hazards. Internally I vowed to stick as close to Cole as I could to prevent any of them from happening. I'd enlist Coop to help, too.

After I hung up, I remembered that I hadn't texted Coop when I got back from Father Lindstrom's. I sent a short one saying that I was home.

By then it was time to feed Sam. Due to the late afternoon tea and cookies I'd had, I wasn't hungry. But I was in the mood to work on the plot for my third mystery novel. I opened my laptop and began developing my cast of suspects. By the time I stopped to stand and stretch, it was 7:15. Yikes, now I *was* hungry, but I didn't have time to eat and still make it to the library by 7:30.

Dutifully I sent a text to Coop that I was leaving to meet Peter. Then I grabbed my coat and purse and ran down the back stairs and out into the night. I hit the key fob to unlock my car and slid onto the driver's seat. As I was putting on my seatbelt, the passenger door opened. I jumped. Then I saw who it was.

"Peter! You gave me a scare. What are you doing here? Weren't we supposed to meet at the library?" I noted that he was dressed more casually than I'd ever seen him. Sweatpants and sweatshirt under a light gray jacket, running shoes on his feet. He slid onto the passenger seat without answering me.

"Are you okay? Has something happened?" I asked.

"May I borrow your phone?"

"Sure," I said, pulling it out of my coat pocket and handing it to him.

He unrolled the window and tossed the phone into the nearby dumpster.

"What are you doing?" I started to unfasten my seatbelt.

I felt cold metal against the side of my neck and turned to look at him. Peter was holding a gun and pointing it right at me.

"Peter, wha—"

"Don't make any sudden moves, and don't try to do anything clever. You're going to drive out of the parking lot, go north on Maple and then turn onto Pit Road."

"But I don't understand," I said, playing for time as I tried to figure out what the hell was happening.

"I said drive. Do it."

My mind raced. I had no idea why Peter was pointing a gun at me like some gangster in a movie. But there was no immediate escape. My best bet was to do as he said and keep my eyes open, and my brain fully engaged. I drew a tiny bit of solace from knowing that if Coop didn't get a text from me saying I'd arrived at the library he'd do some checking.

I shushed the little voice in my head that said *It won't matter. He won't know where you are because there's no way to track you without your phone.*

I drove in silence for a few moments. When we approached Pit Road Peter said, "Turn here."

"Could you at least tell me where we're going?"

He didn't answer. We had passed the outskirts of town. With no streetlights and no houses in view, it was extremely dark. Pit Road is a curvy gravel road through thick woods, with very little traffic.

"You do know this road doesn't lead anywhere, right? It dead ends at the abandoned gravel pit."

"Yes, I know," he said as I made the turn. "It's where we're going."

Okay, so the what's happening part of my original question was partly—and horrifyingly clear. Peter was taking me to the gravel pit. He had a gun. Was he going to kill me? But why?

In the rearview mirror I caught a glimpse of headlights and felt a flutter of hope. If I could distract him by getting him talking, maybe I could hit the emergency flashers. The flashers might make the other car notice us and maybe call for help.

"You're going to shoot me, aren't you?"

"Yes, I am."

"But why? I don't understand at all."

"The best possible motive. Self-preservation."

"What does that mean?"

"It means, Leah. That you don't know what you know right now, but if you make that trip to Buckner, it's very likely that you will become a major threat to me."

"A threat to you? How could I be that?"

Peter seemed oblivious to the car behind us. It was still fairly far away, but not too far to see the hazard lights flash. I tensed my right hand on the steering wheel, ready to snake out and hit the hazard switch. I glanced in the mirror and saw the car turn off onto another road. My heart sank. I was barely listening to Peter's answer until he said the words *naegleria fowleri*.

"What did you say?"

"You should be listening, not trying to attract the attention of that car that is no longer following us."

He'd been paying attention after all.

"Yes, I saw you look in the rearview mirror. So I looked in the side mirror. Just in time to see that car turn off on another road. I think we'll be fine now. And I think I'd like to answer your questions more fully. I've been quite clever about this, and you're the only person I can tell."

I didn't want to give him the satisfaction, but if I was going to die, I had to know why.

"All right. What is it I've done to you, Peter?"

"I know that it wasn't intentional. Bad luck for both of us, really. But your *naegleria fowleri* plot is exactly the way I killed my first wife forty years ago."

"You killed your wife?" I asked, not certain I'd heard him correctly.

"Yes. And I did it the same way you planned to have your fictional killer do away with his wife—with *naegleria fowleri* in her neti pot. When we met for coffee to discuss your plot in detail that first time, I realized your fictional murder was far too close to what I had done. My strength is planning. I had to prepare for what might come. That's when I brought in Sharla."

"Sharla? You know my stalker?"

"Leah," he said, his voice amused, "I *am* Sharla. I invented your stalker to take the blame after I kill you."

I was too shocked to ask a coherent question. I didn't need to. Peter was so enamored by his own cleverness that he didn't need any prompts to keep talking.

"It was a very good ploy, you must agree. And I thought of everything. I set up the emails and texts to send automatically, so that they'd go out when I was elsewhere. It was pure chance that I ran into you at the grocery store, but it was quite thrilling to be there when you got a text from Sharla. Then you told me that you'd notified the police, and I knew I'd succeeded in setting up a suspect for them to focus on after your disappearance. A stalker who didn't exist. I'll be shooting you once we get there and disposing of your body in the gravel pit. The water is over fifty feet deep you know."

"I still don't understand why you decided you had to kill me. I had no idea until right now that you killed your wife decades ago. The chance that I would find out just because my killer was using the same method was minimal."

"Possibly. But you're quite bright, Leah. Your plan to visit Buckner sealed your fate."

"How?"

"Buckner is a small community. Smaller than Himmel. People enjoy talking, especially about the past. And despite what I said to you, I do have a connection there. My first wife's brother still lives there. He was no fan of mine. He thought I'd married his sister for her money. Which I had. That's why I couldn't just divorce her. I wanted the money. But I wouldn't be able to spend it in prison, would I? So I had to wait for the right opportunity."

"And you found it when the meningitis outbreak happened?"

"Exactly. I was able to leverage my knowledge of *naegleria* and access to it with the meningitis outbreak and commit the perfect murder. Things unfolded just as you outlined in your plot summary to me. After using the naegleria-infused water in her neti pot, Barbara became ill, displaying all the symptoms of the meningitis that was ravishing the community. When she died, there was no autopsy, because it seemed clear that she had succumbed to what a dozen other people already had. Meningitis.

"But my brother-in-law was always suspicious. Especially when I married the department secretary Adele a year later. Luckily, no one paid much attention to him because he had a drinking problem and quite often wasn't all that lucid. But he's still alive and quite possibly he's attained sobriety. I knew that if you talked to him, you would start asking some very inconvenient questions. That could go very wrong for me. So, I have to kill you now, to keep that from happening. Well, here we are, Leah."

I had reached the end of the road, literally.

66

The abandoned pit loomed before us. A broken-down fence with no gate surrounded it. A lone security light flickered and buzzed on a pole next to a maintenance shed with a sagging roof and broken windows. The edge of the pit sloped steeply down to the watery dark abyss. I caught my breath.

"Your body won't be found for a very long time—if ever."

"What are you doing about my car? You can hardly drive it back into town."

"I appreciate your concern, Leah. I'm going to drive your car about three miles away from here, giving myself a nice five-mile walk back to town. When you're reported missing, and your car is discovered miles away from here, no one will think to check the gravel pit. They'll search the woods for your body. But long before that, I'll be back home. I'll take a shower and go to bed. Adele is attending a performance at Overture on Broadway in Madison. She won't return until tomorrow."

"I texted Coop that I was meeting you at the library. When he realizes I'm missing, you're the first person he'll question."

"And I'll simply tell him that I forgot about the appointment, and I never went to the library. I'll ask him if the stalker you told me about could possibly have something to do with your disappearance. I'll be very concerned as all your friends will be."

"You've got an answer for everything, don't you?"

"Yes, I do. Now, please move the car slowly and park it over there by the shed. I'll be using the wheelbarrow I left here yesterday to get you to your final destination. Unless of course you believe in an afterlife, which I do not. After you park, wait for me to get out of the car. Don't try anything foolish. I'm not a sadist, Leah. I won't make you suffer unless you make it necessary."

I'd been in some really tough spots before, but I'd always seen a way out. Sometimes on my own, sometimes with help. But there wasn't going to be any help this time. And there wasn't any way out. So, I might as well try something foolish.

I turned the car in the direction of the shed, but instead of moving slowly ahead as Peter had ordered, I hit the gas. Then I hit the brakes. We lurched forward. Hard. Peter lost his grip on the gun. I yanked my seatbelt off. As he fumbled to recover the gun, I opened the door and half-fell, half rolled out. I scrambled to my feet and started running. The headlights were still on. They provided visibility almost to the edge of the dark woods I was heading for. I needed the light to avoid the ruts and stones on the rough terrain waiting to trip me and make me a sitting duck for Peter. But the light also allowed Peter to see me clearly.

He shot, and a bullet whistled by my ear. My heart thumped so hard it felt like it was jumping out of my chest. I glanced back to see where he was. Bad move. I stumbled. Went down hard on one knee. I managed to stand but a jolt of pain shot through my knee.

I can't do it. I can't run. It hurts too much. Peter's footsteps pounded behind me. This was it. This was how I was going to die. Suddenly, I heard my sister Annie's voice, as clear as though she were standing right beside me. *Run, Leah! Run! Don't let him get us, come on!* She shouted it just the way she used to when we played a game of Bloody Murder in the backyard. *I can't, I can't!* And then it was my sister Lacey's voice in my ear, *Yes you can, Lee-lee. Yes you can!*

I hobbled forward toward the safety of the woods, trying to keep the weight off my knee. Each step set off a fresh burst of pain, but my sisters' voices kept urging me on. Another gunshot. Then shouting and another shot. I kept limping toward the safety of the dark forest. I didn't look back. Until a familiar voice called my name.

I turned. About twenty yards away Dale Darmody was standing with his gun pointed down toward Peter, who was on the ground holding his right arm. A dark stain was seeping through the sleeve of his jacket.

A siren wailed in the distance.

"Dale, what are you doing here? I'd hug you but I don't want you to stop aiming your gun at that asshat."

I was totally unprepared for his answer.

"I been followin' you since you left the parking lot."

"Following me? Thank God you were, but why?"

"Remember at the open house I told ya I had my first client, the one who wanted me to check up on her cheatin' husband?"

"Yes, but—"

"Peter here, he's the cheater. Only now I think he wasn't cheating. See, I been watchin' him every day for a while now, but I wasn't gettin' anything. I mean, I saw him meet with you a few times, but I knew you wouldn't be steppin' out on Coop. The rest of the time he was, you know, just doin' regular stuff. I figured if nothin' came of tonight, I'd have to tell Mrs. Sullivan she was wastin' her money."

"But there wasn't anyone following us out here. I would've seen you."

"I thought ya might've. Did ya notice a car behind ya that turned off on Jordan Road?"

"That was you?"

"Yep. When Peter left his house tonight, he was on foot. That made it kinda hard to tail him without bein' seen. He was goin' down Cedar toward town, though, so I cut over and took Norris. I waited at every corner until I saw him down on the Cedar corner. Then I'd go to the next block, wait again 'til I could see him crossin' up the block on Cedar. I lost him between Main Street and Felton. I cut over real quick to Main Street and caught sight of him in the parkin' lot behind your place. By the time I got there, he was gettin' into your car with you. I pulled over to the curb and waited. You guys drove out, and it looked to me like he was pointin' a gun at you. You can bet I kept on followin'."

"I didn't notice you."

"Hey, I'm a professional P.I. I got skills."

"I'll testify to that," I said.

"Anywho, I kept my distance, but then you got on Pit Road and there was nowhere to hide. That's when I called Coop, for back up. He was out to his property and said he'd cut across on Danley, while I turned off on Jordan and then on to Whitney, so I was runnin' parallel to Pit. That way I could come in from the west, park before I got too close and sneak up walkin, so's I could take Sullivan by surprise. So that's what I did. I saw Peter closin' in on you, so I had to take a shot. I missed the first time, but I got him in the end."

"You sure did. Darmody, you amaze me!"

The siren sound was close now and I could see flashing lights.

"I was just doin' my job."

"Hey, no false modesty here. You're my hero," I said.

As Darmody beamed happily, Coop's truck pulled up, followed by a police car, followed by an ambulance, followed by Miguel. Of course.

67

When they finally finished questioning me at the sheriff's office, and Miguel had his story for the paper, Coop and I went back to my place. He poured me a Jameson, but I literally fell asleep sitting upright on the couch with the glass in my hand. He nudged me awake and I managed to stumble into bed.

The next thing I knew, it was nine o'clock in the morning. Coop was gone, but he'd left a note saying he was stopping at the office and then going out to work on the property for a while. He also left me a chai. I reheated it in the microwave, then joined Sam on the window seat where he was sitting in a beam of autumn light streaming through the window.

He purred while I petted him and sipped my chai and thought about the night before. There's something very clarifying about the moment when you know you're going to die. Everything falls away except what really matters to you. And what really mattered to me was Coop, my mom, Miguel, Father Lindstrom, my other friends. When I was sure that Peter was going to kill me, it wasn't dying that terrified me. It was knowing that I'd never laugh, never argue, never talk, never just be with Coop again. I'd been given a reprieve, thanks to Dale Darmody, private eye. No, make that private eye extraordinaire.

I smiled at the image of him standing over Peter like a big game hunter who had just bagged a tiger. Which, in my mind, Peter Sullivan was—a tiger like Shere Khan in *The Jungle Book,* aggressive, arrogant, capable of the calculating charm of a narcissist. And then I finally thought about the thing I'd been avoiding. My sisters calling to me, urging me on, saving me, really, every bit as much as Darmody.

Had I actually heard them? No. That wasn't possible. Their voices were an auditory hallucination, brought on by my pain and fear.

"But what if they weren't, Sam? What if it really was Annie and Lacey reaching out to me? What if they were delivering the message that Father Lindstrom tried to get me to understand? That they want me to run toward a full and happy life, not feel like I don't deserve it. Do you think it could be that, Sam?"

He stared at me and then meowed.

"Is that a yes? Or are you telling me that I'm losing my mind? Maybe I am. I will never say this to another living soul, but I know they were there. I know that I heard them, both of them. And I know what I'm going to do now."

Coop's pickup was there when I got to his property. The outside of the house was looking good with windows, roof, and siding in place. I walked in.

"Coop? Where are you?"

My voice echoed in the empty house. I was surprised at how little had been done inside for the number of hours he'd been spending out here. In fact, it looked like almost no work had been done. But maybe it took all that time to do plumbing and wiring and things. Though, glancing around, I didn't see much of that either.

I left and went over to the barn. I heard movement overhead. I could see that he'd installed stairs since I'd been there last and when I ran up them I reached a landing with a door that was new as well. I opened it and stepped into—my apartment?

"Holy cow!"

My eyes took in a space that was almost a replica of my living room. Tall windows on the north side with a window seat running underneath them. A gleaming hardwood floor. Walls of reclaimed brick the same color as those in my place. The east wall had a fireplace with bookshelves on either side. The kitchen was much smaller than mine, but it had a sink, stove and refrigerator. And there was the same granite-topped bar separating it from the living room area.

A door on the opposite wall opened and Coop walked in.

"What in the actual what *is* this, Coop? This looks almost exactly like my apartment!"

"Leah, what are you doing here?"

"I came out to tell you something, but I'd like you to tell me something first. Am I in Wonderland? What's with my apartment on the top of your barn?"

He walked over to where I was standing.

"It was supposed to be a surprise."

"It's a surprise all right, but why? What's going on?"

"Okay. Well, I've been working on this for weeks. I know having your own space is really important to you. And I know how much you love your place. So I thought that if I could give you a space out here that was all your own, and it had the same things in it that you like so much about where you are now, that you'd see that moving out here with me doesn't mean you have to give up something you love. C'mere," he said, taking my hand and leading me over to the windows.

"See that over the trees? That's the clock tower on Himmel City Hall. You're really not that far from town. Woke isn't across the street, but look at the view," he said, his arm sweeping out as he pointed to the sight of trees in their full autumn colors—vivid red, gold, orange and yellow. "And there's an eagle's nest down by the creek. You can see it from here with binoculars. You won't find that in town."

I looked out the window and then back again around the room that Coop had so meticulously constructed to mirror my favorite space.

"You're not saying anything. Do you like it? Does it make you feel more like moving out here with me? It's okay if you don't. Miguel's been helping me with this and he's down to rent it if you don't want it. But I hope you do," he said, his voice uncharacteristically tentative.

"Coop, I love it. And I love you. This has got to be the most romantic gesture since that British king gave up his throne for his girlfriend. I can't believe you did all this for me. But before I answer you, I want to ask you a question. And it's not because you did this. I came out to ask you before I knew about it," I said.

"Okay, what is it?"

I'd made it through the set-up, but could I actually ask the question? Here goes, I thought.

"Coop, will you marry me?"

Before he could answer, Miguel burst out of the same door Coop had walked through minutes before.

"Oh, I am so happy! I knew you would love it. I did not know that you would propose, though! Well played, *chica!* And I have so many ideas for the wedding! Congratulations! When can I move into your apartment?"

Coop laughed and said, "Hey, wait a second. I haven't answered her yet. I need to think about this a minute, it's a big decision for a boy to make."

"This is a limited time offer," I said. "Going, going—"

"Yes. I will marry you," Coop said. "Anywhere, anytime. But let's make it soon before you change your mind. I love you, Leah."

And the Lake Will Take Them
Book #1 in the Sheriff Red Mysteries

Chilling cold cases resurface as Sheriff Red Hammergren hunts for a missing teen, exposing the dark underbelly of a storm-bound Minnesota town.

Amid a fierce snowstorm sweeping across rural Minnesota, near the icy shores of Hammer Lake, an isolated cabin goes up in flames, leaving a critically injured high school drug dealer and a missing girl in its wake. The disappearance propels Sheriff Red Hammergren into action to find the troubled young girl, Missy Klein, the daughter of Junior Klein—the victim of an unsolved cold case years prior.

As Red peels back the layers of Missy's vanishing, she uncovers a chilling nexus of drug trafficking pervading through her community with roots to the local high school. Unknown to Red, her investigations have roused a malevolent presence, a killer lurking within the storm...a killer that would do anything to stop the sheriff's probing.

Red soon reveals a terrifying link between Missy's peril and the unresolved cold cases she has tirelessly sought to solve. Engulfed in a battle against both the elements and time, Red must navigate her community's shadowy corners and frozen woods to rescue Missy and halt the advances of a killer—all before the storm engulfs the truth in its icy grasp.

Get your copy today at
severnriverbooks.com

ACKNOWLEDGMENTS

As a former journalist trained in checking facts, I spend what some might call an excessive amount of time researching details for each book I write. This one is no exception. While much of the research is done online, a sizeable portion of my quest to get it right involves talking to experts in their field. I may have one quick question to verify that a plot point could actually happen in real life. Or I may need a tutorial on a deadly biological hazard. The list of people who readily answer my queries is too large to acknowledge them individually here. But I'm thankful to each of them for being so generous with their time and expertise. I'm thankful to all my readers, too. Your engagement with Leah and the other characters in the world of Himmel make writing the series both fun and satisfying.

ABOUT THE AUTHOR

Susan Hunter is a charter member of Introverts International (which meets the 12th of Never at an undisclosed location). She has worked as a reporter and managing editor, during which time she received a first place UPI award for investigative reporting and a Michigan Press Association first place award for enterprise/feature reporting.

Susan has also taught composition at the college level, written advertising copy, newsletters, press releases, speeches, web copy, academic papers and memos. Lots and lots of memos. She lives in rural Michigan with her husband Gary, who is a man of action, not words.

During certain times of the day, she can also be found wandering the mean streets of small-town Himmel, Wisconsin, looking for clues, stopping for a meal at the Elite Cafe, dropping off a story lead at the *Himmel Times Weekly*, or meeting friends for a drink at McClain's Bar and Grill.

Sign up for Susan Hunter's reader list at
severnriverbooks.com

Printed in the United States
by Baker & Taylor Publisher Services